THE PROMISE OF A KISS . . .

Lindsay closed her eyes and drew a slow breath, her heart racing.

Sensation swept away all conscious thought. Feather-light and gentle, his kiss whispered promises of sweet, dark mysteries and low, wanton revelries. His tongue traced the path that his finger had blazed over her lip and she met it with her own, melting into him and sighing in welcome as he drew her closer and tasted her more deeply still.

She was molten and weak, soaring and stronger than she had ever been. Heady sensation and wonderment, the heat and potent tension of timeless instinct. . . . Then there was only the lingering shadow of what had been. And she hungered for more of what was gone.

Jackson, his breathing ragged, stepped back from her, back from the brink of too late. She was so damn easy to kiss, so damn delicious. He hadn't known just how intoxicating her lips were, how sweetly she could surrender. And as she looked up at him now, her lips still dewy from his kiss, her blue eyes softened by yearning . . .

Also by Leslie LaFoy

Leslie LaFoy

JACKSON'S WAY

Bantam Books

New York Toronto London Sydney Auckland

JACKSON'S WAY

A Bantam Book / October 2001

ISBN: 0-553-58313-1

Published simultaneously in the United States and Canada

Bantam Books are published by Bantam Books, a division of Ran-
dom House, Inc. Its trademark, consisting of the words "Bantam
Books" and the portrayal of a rooster, is Registered in U.S. Patent
and Trademark Office and in other countries. Marca Registrada.
Bantam Books, 1540 Broadway, New York, New York 10036.

PRINTED IN THE UNITED STATES OF AMERICA

OPM   10 9 8 7 6 5 4 3 2 1

For Phyllis

PROLOGUE

Republic of Texas
March, 1838

AND YEA, though I walk through the valley of the shadow of death, I shall fear no evil," the minister said solemnly, the pages of his Bible fluttering in the morning wind.

A bittersweet smile touched the corner of Jackson Stennett's mouth. He looked down at the simple pine box. No, Billy Weathers hadn't feared death. He hadn't feared anything. He'd charged through life with an unconquerable spirit and an unshakeable faith in his ability to make God do his bidding. Even now, Jackson half expected to hear Billy's fist slam against the wood and him cursing the ignoramus who'd had the gall to declare him dead.

But Billy was dead. And had been since the moment he'd clutched his chest and fallen from the saddle yesterday afternoon. No amount of hoping and waiting was going to change that fact. Jackson shifted his gaze to the rolling hills beyond the grave, beyond the small knot of cowhands and fellow ranchers assembled to witness the burial. The bluebonnets were beginning to fade and the Indian paintbrush was just coming on. The grass was green and growing. It would be a good year, if the rains came when they were supposed to, if the sun didn't bake the earth rock-hard in July and August. Just yesterday morning Billy had said it would be the best year they'd had in the last ten.

Jackson sighed. He looked back at the coffin and felt the pain of loss twist in his chest. It was a familiar sensation; he'd buried so many in the course of his thirty years. But losing Billy cut deep. It was Billy who'd taken in Jack when he was an angry thirteen-year-old boy, and whipped him into a man.

"Mr. Stennett?"

Jackson blinked in the direction of the voice, his gut hardening as he noted the minister's look of expectation.

"Would you like to offer a few words about the departed, Mr. Stennett? Share a few memories to lighten the hearts of those present and grieving?"

No, he didn't want to say a damn thing, but he'd do it just so this god-awful ordeal could end. Swallowing the lump in his throat, he lifted his chin and stared out over the hills. The wind ruffled his hair as he said evenly, firmly, "Billy Weathers was a damn fine poker player and an even better cattleman. He was the man you wanted at your back when you went into a fight. He was plainspoken and he was fair. He wouldn't ask anything of anyone that he didn't expect of himself. And if he's looking at us from up above, he's growling about the daylight we're wasting planting him. There's work to do, gentlemen. Let's be on with it." He slapped his hat back on his head, adding, "I'll see to the shoveling."

The minister's aghast expression didn't have the slightest effect on the mourners' responses. They nodded, put their hats back on their heads, and turned away. Jackson jerked the blade of the shovel from the mound of freshly dug earth.

Hastily, the minister reached down and grabbed a clod of dirt. "Ashes to ashes, dust to dust," he said, tossing it onto the lid of the box. It struck with a hard sound that rang in Jackson's ears and made him clench his teeth.

Billy had never been ash and he had certainly never been dirt. He had been a good man, made of stone and

steel. He had been a Texan to the marrow of his bones. At
the edge of his awareness, Jackson heard the cowboys and
other ranchers mounting and heading out, saw the minister
close his Bible and walk away shaking his head. Billy had
never had any use for religion, and, to Jackson's knowledge,
had never so much as darkened the door of any church.
That's why the minister's arrival at the ranch house that
morning had been such a shock. The fact that Billy hadn't
come vaulting out of the coffin in protest had been the final
sign that William Lindsay Weathers was indeed gone. The
numbness that had come in the wake of that realization had
been the only thing that had kept Jackson from sending the
black-robed vulture on his way.

"Jackson?"

He looked over his shoulder and found Elmer Smith
standing there, his hat still in his hand and his wire-rimmed
glasses sliding down his nose. "Don't tell me," Jackson said
dryly. "You want to talk about Billy's Will."

"I know you, Jackson," the lawyer replied, shifting inside his too-big Sunday go-to-meetin' suit. "If we don't talk
now, it'll be next year before I can slow you down long
enough to get said what needs to be said."

Jackson plunged the shovel blade into the mound of
earth and flung a load of dirt into the hole. To keep the
sound from his ears, the finality from sinking any deeper
into his soul, he said, "Unless Billy changed his mind and
left his half of the ranch to someone else, we don't have
anything to talk about, Elmer."

"There are other bequeaths you should know of,"
Elmer said over the sound of metal scraping dirt.

More dirt against wood, hollow and hard. "Such as?"
Jackson asked through clenched teeth.

"He left each of the hands a full month's salary."

"Doesn't surprise me." He imagined the light that had
been in Billy's eyes when he'd made that particular provi-
sion in his Will. "And it wouldn't surprise me to learn that
he'd stipulated that every penny of it be spent at Tia Rosa's
cantina. Did he leave Rosa something, too?" Another shovelful of dirt.

"A tidy little something." Elmer slowly cleared his throat, and Jackson glanced over his shoulder to see the lawyer push his glasses back to the bridge of his nose and square his stance.

Elmer took a quick, deep breath and continued, "And of course there's the matter of the debts that have to be settled before you can have clear title to Billy's half of the ranch. I figure I can delay posting the notices for maybe sixty to ninety days to give you some maneuvering room."

The weight that settled over Jackson's shoulders had nothing to do with the dirt on the shovel. "Twice that long won't be enough if the markets don't come up, Elmer. I can't get decent money for cattle and the creditors can't extend the loans they've made without courting their own bankruptcies. Can we hope that Judge Gilroy will give me some time to ride things out?"

"Billy thought of all that," the lawyer supplied. "In addition to his half of the ranch, he also left you some property he owned back East. It was his intention for you to sell it all and use the proceeds to pay the loans. He thought it would be sufficient to see you free and clear."

Jackson went on shoveling, his concern eased. Billy had seen to it that all their hard work wouldn't go to the bankers. That was Billy, always thinking two steps ahead. "I didn't know he had any other property. He never mentioned it." Which wasn't all that surprising. Billy had never spoken of the life he'd led before he'd followed Stephen Austin into Texas. Very few men did.

"I was surprised to hear of it myself, Jackson, but that doesn't change the fact that you've inherited it."

"Did he say what it was?"

"No, but he was clear about you owning everything—lock, stock, and barrel. He gave me the address of his attorney back East. Billy said you'd have to go see him in person to settle things up. He left a letter introducing you to the man." Elmer cleared his throat yet again. "He said for me to tell you he was sorry about leaving you with the mess to clear away; that he knew you'd do the right thing with it all."

The hair on the back of Jackson's neck prickled. He'd known Billy well enough to know that being in debt had been considered a minor nuisance and nothing more. Billy didn't ruffle easily. *Mess?* The last time he'd heard Billy use that term had been in a conversation about the slaughter at the Alamo. Jackson rammed the shovel blade in the dirt and leveraged the handle. "Who and where is this man?"

"His name's Vanderhagen and he's in New York."

New York? He was supposed to go to New York? Jackson laughed darkly. "I don't have time to traipse off East," he said firmly, tossing another load of dirt into the hole. "Write a letter, Elmer. Tell Vanderhagen that I don't want to own anything outside of Texas and that he's to sell it all off and then send what money there is."

"Billy knew you'd dig in your heels about leaving the ranch. He told me to tell you—and I'm quoting him—'You don't let another man do your business for you. Get your ass in the saddle and take care of it.' "

Yeah, that sounded just like Billy. *Square up to it, son. Be a man and get it done.* Jackson expelled a hard breath and heaved another shovelful of earth onto the coffin. The sound of it was growing duller, less hollow, more endurable. "Exactly when did you and Billy have this conversation?" he asked.

"Two weeks ago. Doc'd just told him his ticker was bad and he came straight from Doc to my office."

Jackson froze, the dirt-laden shovel suspended over the hole. Billy had been to see Doc Helstern? Had known he was likely to die? The pit of Jackson's stomach went hard and cold. "Goddamn you," he whispered, his gaze on the partially covered pine box. "You son of a bitch. Why didn't you tell *me*?" His throat closed tight. Anger heated his blood and clouded his vision. George Helstern had known. Elmer Smith had known. Both had had their chances to say thank you and good-bye. But Billy hadn't given *him* that chance.

As though from a great distance, he heard Elmer say, "There's more, but I'll let you read it for yourself. I'll leave a copy of the Will on the table in the house. You can look it all over when you're done here." There was a slight pause and then Elmer's hand briefly touched his shoulder. "I'm sorry," the lawyer said quietly, gently. "I know he was like a father to you."

Like a father. And a brother and a friend, a fellow soldier and a business partner. Billy Weathers had been a part of his every day for the last seventeen years. This was the first grave he'd ever dug that Billy hadn't helped him hack from the earth; the first hole in his life that Billy wasn't there to fill.

Blindly, Jackson turned the shovel and let the earth fall.

CHAPTER ONE

*S*HE STUDIED the big, shiny, block letters on the pebbled glass filling the top half of the massive office door. LINDSAY MACPHAULL. RICHARD PATTERSON. If the paint was gold, she could scrape away her name and sell it. Everyone knew it was her office. It didn't need to be so extravagantly labeled. Richard's name would stay, of course. Legally, he was the one in command.

"Today could be the day, Miss MacPhaull."

She turned to the young man who had spoken and found him standing behind his desk, his eyes bright and his upper lip faintly beaded with perspiration. Lindsay smiled and arched a brow. "Then what are you doing here, Jeb? Shouldn't you be home with your wife?"

"I have reports to—"

"The arrival of one's first child is more important than any report, Jeb," she asserted gently. "Close up your ledgers and go home. Lucy needs you more today than we do."

He fingered the corner of the leather-bound book. "Are you sure, Miss MacPhaull?"

"Absolutely," she said, taking the young man's hat

from the peg on the wall. Handing it to him, she smiled broadly and added, "Please give my best wishes to Lucy. And send word as soon as you have it. We'll be waiting anxiously."

He nodded, put the hat on his head, quickly closed the ledger, and stripped away his sleeve protectors. Lindsay watched as he walked sedately to the door of the MacPhaull Company offices, crossed the threshold to the busy sidewalk, and then broke into a dead run. With a quiet chuckle, Lindsay turned and resumed her regular morning course.

There might be as much as a half ounce of gold in her name, she decided as she entered the dark paneled office. Every bit would help.

"Good morning, Miss Lindsay." Benjamin Tipton, the head bookkeeper, stood across the desk from Richard Patterson in a manner approximating attention.

"Good morning, Ben," she answered, nodding to Richard. "Please don't let me interrupt your conversation."

He nodded crisply and turned back to the task. Ben was such an interesting blend of contrasts, she thought— not for the first time. He was a supremely efficient book-keeper, with a devotion to order and neatness that bordered on obsession, and yet there was something about him. . . .

Though he'd never said anything, Lindsay couldn't escape the sense that Ben magically transformed into a rakish ladies man when he left the offices each evening. His clothes were stylish and seemingly chosen to accentuate his blond hair and pale China-blue eyes. Lindsay knew that maintaining his wardrobe had to consume the vast majority of his wages. How he afforded to eat and entertain was beyond her.

Of course, she reminded herself as she stripped off her gloves, Ben could well have family resources from which to draw. He was at the age when most men could expect to receive an inheritance from their fathers. Somehow it didn't seem at all odd—or the least bit unseemly—that Ben would try to parlay a bit of inherited wealth into social connections that might lead to a wife with an inheritance of her own. It was, after all, the way the world worked, and Ben appeared appropriately discreet about it. She just hoped that it never occurred to him that she might be receptive to his advances. Ben was a pleasant, handsome, and intelligent-enough man, but he was simply too much of a dandy to appeal to any of her senses. He reminded her of a porcelain doll.

"The news is even worse than we expected, Lindsay," Richard said from his side of the huge mahogany desk, as Ben left carrying a stack of papers.

"You could have at least said 'good morning' and asked if I'd slept well," she countered, smiling at him and undoing her bonnet strings.

He rolled his wheeled chair from behind the desk, saying, "It isn't a good morning and you haven't had a good night's sleep in the last six months."

There was no denying the latter and there hadn't been a good morning in recent memory. She considered Richard, noting the creases in his brow and the tension in his powerful shoulders. "Are you all right?" she asked. "You look as though you didn't sleep well, either."

"The blasted headache won't go away," he said gruffly. "And no, I'm not having Dr. Bernard come by the office to check on me, so don't even suggest it again. It's the change of the season and nothing more."

With a silent sigh, Lindsay changed the subject. "Has Henry danced through the offices this morning?"

Richard's white brows knitted. "Are you expecting him?"

"He came by the house yesterday evening," Lindsay explained, removing her pelisse and taking it to the brass cloak tree in the corner. "Edith wants to buy a winter home in Charleston. My brother is of a mind to indulge his wife's latest whim and take advantage of the depressed situation in the South."

"Given the reports that came in this morning's mail, Henry would be hard-pressed to buy Edith a new privy."

Privy? The very circumspect Richard Patterson had actually uttered the word "privy"? Lindsay barely managed to keep her smile contained. "The news is *that* bad, Richard?"

He took a stack of paper from his desk and handed it to her, saying, "Read for yourself and see what you think.

I've sorted them, ranging from bad to worse. Would you care for your coffee now?"

Lindsay nodded absently, already reading as she moved to the leather divan. The first letter was from a bank in St. Louis reminding her that the loan payment on the warehouse was sixty days past due. Lindsay quickly moved on. The building had burnt to the ground three months ago. Given the current economic situation, there was no point in rebuilding it and no reason to pay for something that no longer existed. She and Richard had decided that the only reasonable course was to sell the land itself in an attempt to recoup the loss. If a buyer couldn't be found, they'd let the bank have it.

The second letter was from an architect who wanted payment for the design phase of a large renovation project being undertaken on the home of Mr. Henry MacPhaull. With clenched teeth, Lindsay moved it to the bottom of the stack. Richard wordlessly placed the cup and saucer on the wide arm of the divan.

The third piece of correspondence was from a man on Long Island who indicated that he would be most happy to sell Miss Agatha MacPhaull the land she wanted. He considered seventeen hundred dollars a very fair price and was instructing his attorney to draw up a bill of sale. Seventeen hundred dollars? Lindsay skimmed the letter again. For five acres? Perhaps in the center of the city, but certainly not for land on Long Island. In fifty years, seventeen hundred dollars might be a reasonable price, but not now. Besides, she didn't have the money. Lindsay expelled a long breath and took a careful sip of her coffee before going on to the rest of the news awaiting her.

The Emerson Bank of Ohio was demanding immediate and full payment from the investors in the Todasca Canal Company. The project had been abandoned and the managers had taken themselves to parts unknown. The bank showed the MacPhaull Company as having a fifteen percent interest in the concern and thus owing twenty thousand dollars of the outstanding debt.

Todasca had been Henry's idea. An old school chum had been the head of the firm and Henry had made an absolute pest of himself about it, eventually wearing down her patience. Against her better judgment she'd agreed to invest, just to get him out of the office.

Her blood pounding, Lindsay went to the last letter. Heavy spring rains had combined with a rapid thaw and led to widespread flooding in western Virginia. The MacPhaull Coal Company managers had been forced to suspend operations until the mines could be pumped out and the lost and damaged machinery replaced. They roughly estimated the temporary loss of revenues at forty thousand dollars, the cost of salvaging and rebuilding at another forty.

Her stomach leaden, she laid the stack of papers in her lap. She'd have to find the money to replace the machinery and get the mines operational again. There wasn't any other choice. The annual income from the mines last year had been close to a quarter of a million dollars, the revenues providing the fiscal foundation of the MacPhaull Company.

With cup and saucer in hand, she took a steadying breath and said, "What are we going to do, Richard? We don't have the cash reserves to meet these expenses."

"The first thing we're going to do," Richard answered briskly, "is put an end to Henry's renovations and Agatha's land acquisition."

"Agreed." Despite knowing the soundness of the course, she inwardly cringed. The scenes would be horrible. Henry and Agatha had never learned the difference between wanting and needing.

"Then there are a few properties we might consider selling," Richard continued, obviously having given the matter a great deal of thought before she'd arrived. "Henry's yacht, for instance. And Agatha's cottage at the shore. Neither produces revenue; they just consume it. Both are expenses the company can ill-afford given the present circumstances. Selling will not only give us needed cash but free up future money that can be used to keep the revenue-producing ventures in operation."

Having her sister out of the house for several months every year was a bit of heaven Lindsay was reluctant to surrender. But times were hard, she reminded herself sternly. Sacrifices were necessary. So was practicality. "Agatha leaves for the cottage in a couple of weeks and it's too late to change her plans. She won't cooperate in the selling, and being in residence will put her in a position to undermine the effort. I suggest we postpone putting the property up until after she returns to the city this fall."

Richard rubbed his forehead. "Is Henry's yacht fair game?" he asked, his hope wary.

Lindsay nodded. Everything was fair game. It was just a matter of timing. She'd been quietly selling off family heirlooms for the last three months to pay the household expenses. Last week had seen some of her mother's silver serving pieces, a Persian rug, and six oil paintings carted off to the auction house. "Henry won't be happy with the news. He'll resist until the bitter end and make it as unpleasant as possible."

"Henry is never happy anyway," Richard observed, backing his wheeled chair behind the desk. "Neither is Agatha. They were born wailing and they've never stopped."

"That's uncharitable," Lindsay observed quietly, "but largely true, I'm afraid." She laid the papers aside, rose, and reached for the silver pot on the corner of the desk. She felt Richard's scrutiny as she poured herself another cup of steaming coffee.

"The company holds title to all the family property, Lindsay," he said softly. "It's within my power of attorney to buy and sell as the needs of the company require. Your brother and sister have no legal say in regard to the actions I take."

"I don't either, for that matter," she pointed out.

"At least you have common sense and a head for business, girl. That can't be said for Henry and Agatha."

She returned to the divan and, slowly sinking down on the cool leather, confessed, "At the moment, my common sense is feeling absolutely overwhelmed by the circumstances."

"That's quite understandable. The situation's grave, Lindsay. We're teetering on the edge of bankruptcy."

How long would it be before they tumbled? she wondered. President Van Buren had assured the nation that the effects of the Panic would be short-lived, that business would rebound in a healthy and timely manner. In the year between then and now, matters had only become worse. There was no comfort in the knowledge that the MacPhaull Company wasn't the only business frantically bailing in a desperate attempt to stay afloat. Older and bigger companies than theirs hadn't been able to withstand the weight of the slowly collapsing economy. Factories and shops and businesses of every kind had ceased operations. Men all over the country were unable to find even the most menial of jobs. Faced with the loss of their homes and no food, they were, by the thousands, taking their families West. The land was free for the taking out there, and eating was more a matter of accurate shooting than having gold or silver in your pocket.

What would happen to her when she ran out of things to sell? she wondered. Would she have to go West like the others? What would Henry and his family do? Where could Agatha go? And Richard? Richard didn't have any family. Paralyzed from the waist down, every day was a challenge for him. To even think of him trying to make an overland journey to a new life . . .

A soft knocking against wood brought her from the gloomy morass of her thoughts. Ben stood in the open doorway. At her arched brow, he said, "Mr. Vanderhagen is here and requests a few moments of your time. He says it's a very important matter."

The family attorney had come to *them*? If Otis Vanderhagen had thought it necessary to leave his office . . . The look of stoic resolve on Richard's face wasn't reassuring. Her stomach cold and knotted, Lindsay rose and smoothed her skirts, saying, "Please show him in, Ben."

With a crisp nod, Ben backed out of the doorway. He'd barely disappeared when Otis Vanderhagen all but rolled into the room. At nine in the morning he reeked of cigar smoke and hair tonic. Tugging his waistcoat down over his considerable girth, he called out their names in a deafening roar. Lindsay couldn't keep from wincing and looking for an avenue of escape.

She started as she realized that a second man stood in the doorway. *Filled* the doorway, actually. Height and, at the shoulders, width. He wore a dark charcoal-colored suit, and while the lines of it were a season or two past truly fashionable, it clearly spoke of a good tailor, conservative taste, and a powerful physique. Heavy-heeled boots, she noted. They'd been polished, but no amount of lampblack would ever cover the scuffs on the insides of each. He held a large, relatively flat-brimmed black hat in his hands and the expression on his face told her he didn't want to be there. She knew how he felt.

"Allow me to present Mr. Jackson Stennett," Otis said too loudly, turning to wave the man farther into the room. "Mr. Stennett is a citizen of the Republic of Texas. Mr. Stennett, may I present Miss Lindsay MacPhaull and Mr. Richard Patterson."

He had dark hair and intelligent brown eyes, she noted as he stepped toward her. High cheekbones, too, and a solid, square jaw. *Definitely handsome,* Lindsay thought as he barely nodded.

"Ma'am," he said, the word rolling off his tongue in a way that was somehow both lazy and hard-edged.

From somewhere deep inside her a voice whispered, *and dangerous.* Puzzling the notion, she watched Jackson Stennett step forward and extend his right hand across the desk toward Richard Patterson.

"You're a long way from Texas," Richard observed pleasantly, shaking the offered hand. "What brings you to this part of the world, Mr. Stennett?"

Stennett took a step back from the desk and squared his massive shoulders. His chin came up and Lindsay thought she saw anger flash briefly in his eyes.

Otis Vanderhagen didn't give Stennett a chance to reply. Pulling a thrice-folded document from the inside pocket of his coat, the attorney thundered, *"William's dead,"* and thrust the paper toward Richard. "Mr. Stennett has presented a copy of a recently dated Last Will and Testament."

As Richard opened the document and began to read, Lindsay turned the announcement over in her mind, searching for her feelings regarding the news. Her father was dead. Seventeen years ago she would have cared. His death now was no more final than his departure had been then.

She'd grieved his loss when she'd been eight years old, crying herself to sleep at night and offering God whatever He wanted in exchange for her father returning home. But her father hadn't come back, and her life had gone on without him. Now . . . She didn't have any tears left to shed for William MacPhaull.

Jackson watched the emotions play across her face: mild shock, a wistful sadness, and then cool, deliberate detachment. His gut, already tight, clenched another degree as what had been a niggling suspicion moved closer to certainty. If Billy had done what he thought he had . . . *Better to get it all out in the open and know for sure,* he told himself. Shifting his hold on his hat, Jackson met Lindsay MacPhaull's gaze and said quietly, "My sincere condolences on your father's passing, ma'am. He was a good man."

She studied him, her blue eyes darkening, her heartbeat pounding along the slender column of her neck. After a long moment, she arched a slim brow and said, "Good men don't abandon their families, Mr. Stennett."

Jackson shifted his gaze to the window and gritted his teeth. Damn Billy to hell and back. How many more ugly surprises were out there waiting for him to find? First had been the revelation in the Will that Billy had lived his last seventeen years under an assumed name. The second had been Vanderhagen's announcement just over an hour ago that Billy had three children. And now to learn that Billy had burnt the bridges when he'd headed off to Texas. Jesus. A *mess* didn't even begin to describe what Billy had left behind.

Anger crawled through Jackson's veins. Of all the god-awful predicaments he'd ever been in, this one ranked right near the top of the list. Billy had given him the means of saving the ranch—provided he was willing to take a legacy that wasn't rightfully his.

Jackson glanced back at the crippled man carefully reading the Will. Patterson obviously hadn't gotten to the part where Billy handed the family livelihood over to a complete stranger. When he did . . . Jackson considered the woman. Her porcelain skin, delicate features, and slim build—all wrapped up in pale pink silk and ivory lace— might lead a man to think Lindsay MacPhaull was one of those fragile flowers of womanhood. But she had Billy's eyes and Billy's way of studying a man. If she had Billy's temper, too, things were going to go to hell in a handbasket real quick.

Jackson looked back at Patterson. The man's face was reddening by the second, the speed of his reading rapidly accelerating. Jackson silently swore, and braced himself. At the edge of his awareness, he heard Billy's daughter draw a deep breath.

"This is preposterous!" Patterson cried, flinging the document down on the desk as though it had soiled his hands. The muscles in his neck corded, and Jackson had the distinct impression that, had he been physically able, Richard Patterson would have vaulted over the desk, swinging his fists to beat the band. A sound of fury strangled low in the man's throat and his face twisted with rage. He sputtered, pushed his upper body forward and up in the chair, and roared, "We'll chal—"

His eyes widened like a crazed steer before rolling back into his head. And then he collapsed, his right side slumping and giving way like a tallow candle with an off-center wick. Spittle ran from the corner of his mouth as he fell back and over the arm of his chair.

Lindsay watched Richard collapse, her heart slamming into her throat even as time slowed to a crawl. As though from a great distance, she heard herself shout, "Ben! Send for Dr. Bernard! Hurry!" Her feet seemed to move of their own accord, taking her behind the desk and to Richard's side. Wrapping her arms around his well-muscled shoulders, she tried to move him upright and failed.

Tears welled in her eyes, blurring her vision. He couldn't be dead, she told herself. He couldn't. She needed him so badly. She wasn't ready to face it all alone. "Richard," she whispered, the plea broken and ragged.

"Step aside, ma'am."

Relief flooded through her. Everything would be all right. Jackson Stennett was calm, in control. His hand on her shoulder was warm and steady, his presence at her side large and solid and so very reassuring. When he guided her away from Richard, she didn't resist. Through her tears, she

watched him effortlessly lift Richard in his arms and carry
him toward the divan. Her presence of mind somewhat re-
stored by Stennett's certainty and command, Lindsay dashed
around and ahead of him to arrange a pillow to cradle
Richard's head.

"Now obviously isn't a good time to discuss business
matters," she heard Otis Vanderhagen bellow from behind
them. "Perhaps we should return later."

Placing Richard gently on the divan, Stennett replied
firmly, "Now obviously isn't a good time to leave Miss
MacPhaull alone, either. Go on back to your office, Vanderhagen. If I need you for anything, I know where to find you."

"Are you certain? You'll need my assistance to—"

"I can manage on my own," Stennett assured the
lawyer gruffly while quickly untying Richard's stock and removing his collar. "It's impossible to mangle this matter any
worse than you already have. Go on." He glanced up at
Lindsay and quietly added, "We need to cover him. Can
you find a blanket?"

There was gentleness and compassion in his eyes. Lindsay nodded and dashed to the cloak rack for her pelisse. She
was just turning back when Otis heaved a deep sigh and announced, "Ah, here comes Dr. Bernard up the sidewalk,"
then chugged out of the room as fast as his fat little legs
would carry him.

"The bastard," Stennett muttered as Lindsay reached
his side. "Actually waddles and slithers at the same time."

Lindsay nodded in silent agreement as, together, they
arranged her pelisse over Richard. He was so pale, so suddenly old and fragile-looking. Tears welled along her lashes
again and she reached out to brush a lock of white hair off
Richard's forehead. A tear fell onto his cheek and Stennett
used the sleeve of her pelisse to carefully dab it away.

Dr. Bernard entered the room, his black bag in his
hand, and the tails of his unbuttoned coat flapping behind
him. "What happened, Lindsay?" he asked even before he
reached his patient.

"He groaned and his right side gave out," she answered
as Dr. Bernard dropped to his knees at Richard's side. She
quickly brushed her tears away, adding, "He's had a dull

headache for two days and then he just slumped ov—" Her voice broke again and she couldn't swallow down the lump lodged high in her throat.

"He was agitated at the time," Stennett supplied, taking Lindsay gently by the arm and easing her out of the physician's way. "Actually, he was furious. He collapsed while trying to push himself up out of his chair."

Richard had been reading the copy of her father's Will, Lindsay remembered, numbly watching Dr. Bernard work on the too-still form of her mentor and friend. Something in the Will had . . . Her heartbeat quickened and she became acutely aware of Jackson Stennett's hand wrapped around her arm, of the warmth of his body next to hers. Stennett knew the contents of her father's Will. And in all likelihood, he knew very well what had sent Richard into a rage. Pulling her arm from Stennett's grasp, she took a step back and looked up into his coolly assessing gaze. Yes, he knew. She could feel the truth of it vibrating in the air between them. Jackson Stennett *was* dangerous; far more dangerous than he was handsome.

Dr. Bernard sighed and pushed himself to his feet, saying softly, "It appears to be a stroke, Lindsay. A severe one."

The pronouncement struck her like a physical blow. She felt the air leave her lungs in a hard rush, felt her knees weaken and her legs tremble. Richard was going to die. Slowly, horribly. She saw the sad look in Dr. Bernard's eyes, saw Stennett start to reach for her. Anger and pride brought her chin up. Resolution drew her shoulders back. She locked her knees and willed herself to manage the situation with cool dignity. Richard would expect nothing less of her.

"Given Richard's paralysis," Dr. Bernard said quietly, "it's not unexpected. If you'll ask for his carriage to be brought around, Lindsay, and a couple of your staff for their assistance, I'll get him home."

"Don't bother the staff," Stennett declared. Nonchalantly clapping his big hat onto his head, he added, "If you'll see to the carriage, Miss MacPhaull, I'll manage Mr. Patterson into it."

She was tempted to decline his assistance, but remembering the gentleness of his earlier care for Richard, she bit back the words. "We'll take him to my house, Dr. Bernard," she declared, finding a measure of strength in the evenness of her own voice. Stennett wasn't the only one who could calmly command. "It's closer and I can take better care of him there." She turned and headed toward the office door, calling, "Benjamin!"

The clerk appeared as if by magic. As always, his demeanor was calm and his appearance absolutely unruffled by the commotion of the moment. He held his small traveling desk in one hand and a glass ink pen in the other. "I've already ordered the carriages around, Miss MacPhaull. And I sent a runner to tell Mrs. Beechum to prepare the guest room. What else may I do to help?"

"You're a godsend, Ben," she said, picking up her bonnet and gloves. She heard Stennett taking Richard back into his arms. "If you'd be so kind as to bring the chair out, I'd be most appreciative."

"He won't need it, Lindsay," Dr. Bernard said gently.

He's going to die. The unspoken words echoed through her heart. She wouldn't crumble. Not here. Not now. Not in front of Jackson Stennett. She carefully put the bonnet on her head and tied the ribbons, saying, "Please put today's correspondence in Richard's valise, Ben. I'll need it all."

Ben nodded and quickly set to the task. As Lindsay pulled on her gloves, Dr. Bernard picked up his bag and started toward the door. Jackson Stennett followed, carefully cradling the unconscious Richard Patterson in his arms. She watched them go, knowing with absolute certainty that her world had shifted on its axis and that the Texan was to blame.

Accepting the valise from Ben, she strode after the men, mentally ordering her priorities. The first was to care for Richard, to do whatever she could to make sure he recovered as fully as possible. The second was to be rid of Stennett quickly. She was certain he factored into Richard's collapse. She needed time to find out how, and form a strategy for dealing with whatever threat he posed.

Cheat God first. Then deal with the Devil. Lindsay lifted her chin. She could do it. She didn't have any other choice.

CHAPTER TWO

*T*HE CARRIAGE WAS SMALL and once he'd carefully placed Richard Patterson on the one seat, he backed out to allow Dr. Bernard to occupy the other. After assuring the physician that he'd carry Patterson out at the end of their journey, Jackson closed the door and strode down the sidewalk toward the second black vehicle. Lindsay MacPhaull stood with one foot inside the carriage and watched him approach. From the defiant tilt of her chin, he could guess the course she intended to take. The trust she'd granted him in the moments following Patterson's collapse had evaporated soon after the doctor's arrival. And in the scant minutes between then and now, she'd drawn a line and committed herself to keeping him on the other side of it. He couldn't really blame her. But he couldn't let her do it, either.

As he drew near, she pasted a false smile on her face and said, "I greatly appreciate your assistance, Mr. Stennett."

"It was the least I could do." He put his hand under her elbow in a not-so-subtle suggestion that she climb into her carriage. Behind him he heard the one bearing Richard Patterson start away.

She glanced after it, but remained rooted to the spot. "I have servants who can assist once we reach the house."

Face it square on, Jack. "I recognize a polite dismissal when I hear one," he said, exerting a gentle force that propelled her forward, "but you and I need to talk, Miss MacPhaull. The sooner, the better."

She dropped unceremoniously onto the seat, her eyes blazing. Tossing the valise on the opposite seat, she said crisply, "As much as I dislike agreeing with Otis Vanderhagen about anything, now is not a good time. Perhaps tomorrow morning?"

"I don't mean to be insensitive, Miss MacPhaull," he countered, following her in and closing the carriage door sharply behind himself, "but the truth is that Richard Patterson could well be dead by tomorrow morning." He shoved the valise aside and sat opposite her, his knees brushing against hers in the small space. "Even if things go reasonably well, he's going to be in no shape to handle the reins of the company for some time to come."

"Forgive me for being so blunt," she replied, the perfect picture of imperial control as she shifted to move her legs beyond the touch of his, "but I fail to see how the conduct of my business is any of your concern."

"That's what we need to talk about. Your business is my business now."

She sat up straighter and looked down her nose at him. "A moment of timely gallantry does *not* entitle you to interfere, Mr. Stennett."

Billy should have stayed in New York, if for no other reason than to tan his daughter's pompous backside. Jackson reined in his anger. "Miss MacPhaull, I realize you've had a difficult morning and I'm trying very hard not to trample your feelings. You're not making it easy for me."

"I suggest that you have Mr. Vanderhagen present your claims against the estate in the traditional fashion. Your bills will be paid in a fair and timely manner."

Damn. She hadn't figured it out yet. "I don't have any claims against your father's estate," he explained, trying to see a way to tell her that wasn't cruel and sensing that—no matter what he did—this would go badly. It was clear that Lindsay MacPhaull wasn't the sort of woman to back up and give a man room to come at things easy.

"If you have no bills to present, then why have you made the trip from Texas, Mr. Stennett?" She didn't allow him a chance to answer. "If you came simply to provide the Will and offer condolences on my father's passing, please leave the effort at what you've already made. William MacPhaull left here seventeen years ago and we haven't heard from or of him since. His passing creates no more of a ripple in our lives than that of a pebble dropped into the sea off the coast of England."

"I'm thinking it does, Miss MacPhaull," he countered a bit more sharply than he intended. "If you'd kindly quit yammering long enough to listen to—"

"Your behavior might pass for well mannered in Texas, but here in New York it's considered insufferably rude."

He bristled and before he could think better of it, said bluntly, "Miss MacPhaull, your daddy not only left you seventeen years ago, he left you high and dry when he died."

She blinked and actually took two breaths before saying with quiet dignity, "I beg your pardon? Is there an English translation for what you've just said?"

There was no need for it; he could tell by the way she eased back into the seat that she finally understood the gist of the situation. Despite that, she maintained her regal presence and it irritated him enough to take another hard shot. "Your father obviously made a new life for himself in Texas. Toward the end of it, he also made a new Will. He left all his worldly property to me." He reached for the valise, opened it, removed the copy of Billy's Will, and handed it to her. "Read for yourself."

She glared at him for a long second, then angled the paper and herself into better light and began to read just as Richard Patterson had, slowly at first and then much more quickly. Jackson leaned back into the corner of the seat and crossed his arms, waiting and watching. The creak of carriage springs and the hollow clomp of hooves against paving stones rolled through the space between them. Her breath caught hard and the color drained out of her face. For a moment he wondered if she was going to be sick. Her hands trembling, she took a slow breath and went back to read the part three times. Then she stopped reading and the paper wrinkled from the tightness of her grip.

Jackson shoved back the pity he felt for her and continued to watch her carefully, trying to anticipate the way she would come at him. Her eyes narrowed slightly and her lips pursed—which he took to mean that she was going to be a bit more rational than Patterson had been. All things considered, that was good. Her chin slowly lifted; she was going to fight him. If he were in her shoes, he'd do the same thing. When she looked up at him, her face a mask of cool disdain, he also knew that she was going to continue on in her regal manner. *That* he wasn't going to take.

Her stomach roiling and her throat thick with suppressed tears, Lindsay folded the document and summoned every bit of her poise. "I'll fight this in court, Mr. Stennett," she told him with what she hoped he heard as calm assurance. "You have no right to anything my father owned outside the Republic of Texas. If you were a decent, honorable man, you'd tear up this Will and pretend you'd never seen it."

He shrugged. "Yeah, well, I'm between a rock and a hard place and don't have room to be a decent, honorable man. I'm a cattleman who needs clear title to half the ranch and with no money to do that unless he sells the property his partner left him. I don't intend to let seventeen years of hard work blow off into the wind just because there were a few wrinkles in Billy's life I didn't know about. Sorry, ma'am."

Lindsay gripped the Will and resisted the temptation to use it to slap the soft smile off Jackson Stennett's handsome face. "How much money do you need?" she demanded tightly.

"A considerable sum."

"In dollars and cents, Mr. Stennett," she snapped, maddened by the ease of his drawl and the nonchalance of his posture. "Exactly how much do you want from me?"

"It's not yours to give, ma'am."

The words struck hard, all the more painful for the truth of it. She was penniless. Made absolutely destitute by her own father's decision. God, what was she going to do? Refusing to fall apart in front of Stennett, she fell back on what had always saved her. "I'm willing to negotiate."

"With what?" he countered, cocking an ebony brow. "I own everything, Miss MacPhaull. From the business holdings to the pots and pans in your kitchen."

Common sense said she couldn't afford to let him know how frightened she really was. Praying that he couldn't hear the thundering of her heart, she managed to ask coolly, "Is it your intention to throw us into the streets with only the clothes on our backs?"

He gave her a quirked smile and a dismissive shrug. "Legally, I own your clothing, too."

Her composure crumbling, Lindsay bit her tongue and swallowed back hot tears of rage. And to think that she'd been so grateful for his presence when Richard had collapsed. What a silly little fool she'd been. He sat there looking at her, the light of satisfaction unmistakable in his eyes, and she wished him—with all her heart—to the fiery depths of hell.

"Cat finally got your tongue?" he asked dryly.

The carriage slowed and rolled to a stop and rather than risk the indignity of screeching and launching herself at him, Lindsay leaned forward, wrenched open the door, and all but leapt from the carriage. Whirling back, she met his gaze and declared hotly, "I'll bring the full weight of the law down on you, Stennett."

"The Will's ironclad; it can't be broken," he countered calmly as he came off the seat and out the door. "If you don't believe me, you can ask Vanderhagen what he thinks."

She had no recourse but to retreat in the face of his advance. Wounded pride kept her from going any farther than absolutely necessary. It proved to be a shortsighted decision. Either she had to crane her head back to look up into his hat-shadowed face or stare at the wide expanse of his chest. Neither choice being acceptable, Lindsay opted for a calculated retreat. Turning on her heel, she said, "I'm sure you'll understand if I don't invite you in."

She had gotten only a single step away when he caught her arm and brought her back around to face him. Lindsay stared up at him, more stunned by the power in his gentle grasp than she was by his presumption to physically detain her.

"If you hope to come out of this with anything," he said slowly, "you'd best be looking for a way into my good graces."

Good graces? Just precisely what was he suggesting? That she prostitute herself? Never! She wrenched her arm from his grasp. "Do you know the meaning of the word 'odious'?"

His eyes glinted hard and bright. "Yes, I do. And it's the perfect word to describe this mess Billy left us. If he weren't already dead, I'd be thinking about killing him." With a bare nod of his head, he indicated the house. "You see to the door and I'll see to getting Mr. Patterson through it."

Lindsay did as she was told, furiously trying to see a way out of the ugly maze that had so suddenly sprung up around her.

HER PACING IN THE UPSTAIRS HALLWAY was no less furious than her entrance into the house had been. And it produced no more answers than she'd had when she'd swept past Mrs. Beechum to lead Dr. Bernard and Jackson Stennett up to the guest room.

The door opened and she froze as Stennett stepped out, his hat back in his hand again. "All ready for you to go in, ma'am," he drawled. "The doc suggested you ask that some of Mr. Patterson's nightclothes be brought over from his place."

Of course. She'd been so preoccupied with her own selfish concerns that she hadn't thought of Richard's needs at all. Ashamed of herself, Lindsay nodded. "I'll speak with Mrs. Beechum about it as soon as I can."

"I'll be glad to speak with her for you, if you'd like. It'll speed matters up a bit."

His presumption to take charge of her household rankled, but she couldn't fault his logic. "That would be most considerate of you," she answered. "Please tell Mrs. Beechum to request that Richard's man, Havers, bring any necessary items for both Richard and himself. I think it best that Havers take up temporary residence here. Assuming he's willing to do so."

"Consider it done, ma'am." He bowed slightly and then strode down the carpeted hall.

Lindsay watched him until he disappeared down the stairs, noting how long his legs were, how purposeful his stride. What a shame that they were adversaries; having an ally of Jackson Stennett's age and with his sense of self-possession might have been a pleasant experience. Lindsay sighed, shook her head to dispel the pointless musing, and entered the guest room.

The light flooding in the windows couldn't cheer the scene before her. Richard lay pale and still in the big four-poster bed, his skin as white and lifeless as the linen sheets, the slow rise and fall of the coverlet the only sign that his soul still lingered in his battered body. She met Dr. Bernard's gaze across the bed. "Do you have any hope at all?" Lindsay asked softly.

"I've seen miracles," he answered, closing his black bag and buttoning his coat. "They do happen."

Not in her life. What good fortune had ever come her way, she'd fought for and willed into existence. "Can you operate?"

The physician sighed hard and long. "It's a highly dangerous procedure. And you know Richard's feelings on such measures, Lindsay. We both know that if he were capable of speaking, he wouldn't allow it. I can't ethically undertake surgery in this case. Please try to understand."

She did, all too well. How many times had Richard railed at his paralyzed legs and cursed the years he'd been confined to his wheeled chair? How many times had he told her that he wished he'd been killed in the carriage accident?

"He's not in any pain, Lindsay," the doctor said softly, pausing at her side on his way out of the room. "Have you sent for Havers?" When she nodded, Dr. Bernard laid his hand gently on her shoulder. "That's good. Send for me if you need to. Day or night."

"Thank you for everything," she managed to say before her throat swelled with tears. The door closed behind him and the sound, soft and final, tore the last stone from the wall of her reserve. Hot tears flooded silently over her cheeks. Her knees went weak and she staggered forward to cling to the ornately carved column at the foot of the bed.

"Oh, Richard," she whispered brokenly. "What should I do?"

Silence. The coverlet rose and fell slowly. Sunlight streamed through the windows and fell full across Richard Patterson's masklike face. The curtain needed to be drawn, she realized, sniffling. That much light would never do.

Surrendering to grief would never do, either. Richard might not feel any pain, but if he had any awareness at all he wouldn't be pleased to have her standing beside his bed, carrying on like a brainless ninny. The situation had to be faced squarely and rationally. And she certainly couldn't go downstairs and face Stennett with red eyes and tearstained cheeks. Any leverage she might have would be completely undermined by such evidence of emotional weakness.

"Richard, I've seen the Will," she said, crossing the room. "And we don't have much room for maneuvering. We could try to break it in court, but at what cost? We're financially strapped already. If we win, it'll be a hollow victory. There'll be nothing left once we've paid the attorneys."

Adjusting the curtains so that they softened the light coming through the windows, she added, "I've talked a bit with Stennett—just on the ride over from the office—but I have a sense of there being more hope in trying to work with him than in fighting him. I don't think he's mean-spirited. Determined, yes. Plainspoken to the point of rudeness, certainly. But he left open a door for negotiation and I don't see that we have any choice but to see what can come of it.

"I don't like it," she admitted, coming to the bed and smoothing the coverlet around him. "You know that. But you also have to know that we don't have any other reasonable course. I'll do my best, Richard. I promise to use every skill you've ever taught me. I'll salvage everything I possibly can. I'll take care of you."

Lindsay smoothed an errant lock of white hair back into place. "You're not to worry about anything, all right?" she whispered. "All you have to do is get well. Leave the rest to me."

She touched his cheek and quietly left him, desperately hoping that she could live up to the promises she'd made him.

· · ·

JACKSON LOOKED AT THE CLOCK on the mantel across the study. Just after ten. It had been one helluva morning and, the hour be damned, he'd earned a good stiff drink. The decision made, it was a short distance to the cabinet and the neatly arranged crystal decanters and glasses. He filled a glass with whiskey, sampled it, and smiled. Miss Lindsay MacPhaull had good taste in distilled spirits. There might be hope for her yet. He'd reserve final judgment, though, until he heard the story that went with the one-armed housekeeper. Mrs. Beechum certainly seemed competent enough, and she was a thoroughly pleasant older lady—not at all like the succession of pinched-faced, humorless women who had passed through the homes of his childhood.

"Who are you?"

The indignation in the feminine voice suggested that the woman was a MacPhaull. But Lindsay, at her worst, hadn't sounded even close to that regal. He turned to find a woman standing in the open doorway. Brunette, passably pretty, tall, and not exactly slender. He chewed the inside of his lip, deciding the polite term was 'statuesque.'

A four-legged mop of long black-and-brown fur was tethered to her hand by an ivory silk cord. At least he assumed the animal had legs; they weren't any more visible than its eyes. Ears were merely suggested by the lumps in the expected vicinity of ears. There was a nose, though. It was little and black and just above tiny white teeth bared in displeasure. He looked up from the dog and into a pair of ebony, utterly disdainful eyes.

He took a sip of his whiskey before answering, "Jackson Stennett, ma'am. From Texas."

She looked him up and down, then rolled her eyes and emitted a disgusted huff. "Have you seen Lindsay?"

He took another sip of the whiskey just to make her wait for the answer. "She's upstairs settling in Mr. Patterson. She should be down directly."

"Mrs. Beechum says the old Buzzard had a stroke. Is that true?"

There was entirely too much hope in her voice. Jackson

clenched his teeth. He didn't know Richard Patterson from Adam, but by God, no man deserved to have someone gleeful over his collapse.

"With my luck, he'll linger for years," the woman went on, clearly taking his silence for confirmation. "That man positively hates me. He goes out of his way to make my life miserable. And Lindsay just bats her sweet little lashes and plays his dutiful minion."

Jackson was feeling a kind of kinship with Patterson and a bit of respect for Lindsay MacPhaull when, through the open doorway, he saw the latter come down the stairs. He didn't hear her make a sound, but the other woman apparently did.

"Lindsay!" she cried, whirling around with such speed that she yanked the little dog off its feet. It slid over the marble floor behind its mistress as she advanced into the foyer to meet her quarry. "I went to Madam Farber's today for a fitting and she told me that the Buzzard had put a limit on my account."

"Not Richard; me," he heard Lindsay say as she swept past the woman and headed into the study. "It's one thousand dollars for the remainder of the year."

"Well, it's not enough!" shouted the woman, wheeling about and coming after Lindsay, her poor little mop skittering in tow. Jackson settled back against the edge of the big mahogany desk and watched Lindsay MacPhaull make a beeline for the decanters. Madam Demanding stopped just across the study threshold and shouted from there.

"You know that a suitable gown costs close to fifty dollars! And that's with no accessories! I'm going to the shore and I want a proper wardrobe. And I'll need new clothes for this fall and winter, too. Last year's are hopelessly out of fashion. I wouldn't be seen dead in them!"

Lindsay was pouring herself a sherry when she replied quite calmly, "The wardrobe you're able to purchase for a thousand dollars will have to suffice. There simply isn't money for more." She turned to face the other woman. "You *could* make what money you do have go further by purchasing your gowns somewhere *other* than one of the most expensive shops in the city."

The woman actually stomped her foot and squealed like a pig stuck in a gate. "You and that beastly Mr. Patterson! I'm going to tell Henry what you've done!"

She gave no indication of heading right off to do that, though, and Jackson shifted his attention to Lindsay, fascinated by the whole exchange and wondering how she was going to respond. She'd been crying; he could see the puffiness under her eyes and her cheeks were red. But at that moment, she was a perfect picture of calm composure. Arching a brow, she asked dryly, "Will you be done tattling before dinner? Or do you plan to dine with Henry and Edith this evening? I need to let Primrose know."

"Ha!" snorted the woman, whirling about yet again and striding out into the foyer, her dog practically bouncing as he tried to get his feet under him and keep up. "What do you care where I eat?" she shouted as she departed. "You don't care if I eat at all! You'd be happy if I starved to death in the street!"

Jackson knew better than to laugh outright. The look in Lindsay MacPhaull's eyes was lethal and he didn't want it directed at him. He fastened his gaze on the floor some three feet in front of him and hid his smile around the rim of his glass.

Lindsay softly cleared her throat, lifted her sherry glass in the direction of the now empty foyer and said, "My sister, Agatha."

"I wouldn't worry about her all that much," Jackson ventured. "She looks to be a good grazer. It'd take a while for her to starve to death anywhere."

She blinked fast and hard, the corners of her mouth twitching. The fire in her eyes turned to sparkles of devilment just before she grinned. Jackson watched the transformation, awed by the radiance and the beauty of this Lindsay MacPhaull. Then she threw her head back and laughed and a jolt of pure desire shot through him as clean and sharp as any knife blade.

Christ, he'd been right, he thought, taking a sip of his whiskey. Things had just gone to hell in a handbasket. Couldn't anything in this goddamned fiasco go well?

CHAPTER THREE

ALTHOUGH THE SMILE remained on his lips, it fled his eyes and Lindsay sobered, mortified. To laugh so boisterously was most unladylike. Heat flooded her cheeks. He was certainly a gentleman for not staring at her or commenting on the disloyalty her amusement evidenced. Like as not, he had some understanding of the stress she'd endured that morning and was granting her a great deal of allowance for the circumstances. Not that she was ready to cry friends, by any means, but she was grateful for his tolerance. Now that she wasn't trying to bring the roof down, though, she had no idea of how to go about filling the silence that stretched tautly between them.

Stennett didn't look up from the floor when he asked, "Who are Henry and Edith?"

The tension broken, Lindsay sighed in relief and answered, "Henry is our brother. Edith is his wife. They have three children, Henry the Second, Elizabeth, and James; all named after monarchs—obviously—and treated as though they were indeed heirs to a royal throne. It's a household in which Agatha's histrionics are hardly noticed."

He looked over to the doorway as if a specter of her remained there. "I gather Agatha isn't married."

"It's long been common knowledge that the management of the MacPhaull properties will pass into Henry's hands at Richard's death. Common knowledge has also been that at our father's death, ownership legally passes to Henry. My father's Will didn't establish a dowry and Henry isn't likely to provide one for her. That lack of financial incentive, combined with her temperament, has tended to limit marriage proposals." Lindsay looked down into her sherry and added quietly, "Common knowledge is about to be turned inside out, isn't it?"

At the edge of her vision, she saw him rub the back of his neck. He abandoned the motion with a hard sigh. "Look, Miss MacPhaull. You and I have gotten off to a rough start. But if you'll agree to stop playing the offended princess, I'll stop playing the hard-hearted ogre. Do we have that much of a deal?"

She'd promised Richard that she'd save what she could, and that didn't give her any choice but to play by Jackson Stennett's rules. She didn't like it and she consoled herself with the assurance that cooperation didn't require a complete and forever surrender. Lindsay looked up to meet his gaze. Even, open, honest, and direct. She nodded.

"Just so you know," he said in that easy, hard-edged drawl of his, "I don't want anything more out of Billy's estate than what I absolutely need. It's pretty obvious that there's not likely to be any discussions with Mr. Patterson. If you'd be so kind as to arrange a meeting with your brother, I'll be about my business and gone as quick as I can."

He'd assumed. Just like every man in the business world, he'd assumed that she was nothing more than a pretty ornament whose only purpose was to pour the coffee and fetch papers. She took a sip of her sherry, tamping down her ire, and wondering how to best approach Stennett's enlightenment. Deciding that it was better to have him know the truth now rather than later, she gave it to him. "The only thing Henry knows about the family assets is how to squander them. If you wish to have a rational, informed conversation, it should be with me."

A dark brow shot up. "You've some experience in the management of the company affairs?"

She drank the rest of her sherry and turned back to the decanters so that he couldn't see just how angry she was. "My father went off on his grand adventure when I was eight years old, Mr. Stennett," she began, pouring herself a second glass. "Richard had long been the manager of the company, but at that point he assumed what he could of William MacPhaull's responsibilities as a father. Richard isn't a demonstrative man by nature and the only way he knew to build a bridge between us was to share the workings of the company. I spent most of my childhood in the office where you and I met today.

"When my mother died, Richard allowed me to take full control of the management. He watches, he listens, he advises, and in the end he puts his stamp of approval on whatever course I think is the best." She stoppered the decanter and turned back to face him. "Yes, Mr. Stennett, I have some experience in the management of the company affairs."

"Are you any good at it?"

"The doors are still open and the staff is paid on time each month."

"How much longer do you think you can keep it up?"

A month? Maybe two? She lifted her chin. "That depends entirely on how much you intend to take out of the business for your own needs and when you intend to do it."

He considered her for a long moment. "Fifty-two and some-odd thousand dollars. And I've got just under sixty days."

Fifty-two thousand dollars? Almost a quarter of the company's current net worth? "It can't be done," she declared, her pulse racing painfully hard and fast. *Sixty days? Oh, my God.*

He gave her that quirked smile of his and lifted his whiskey glass in salute. "Where there's a will, there's a way." He winced and quickly added, "No pun intended."

Her eyes burned and pulsed from the heavy pressure behind them. Her fingertips ached. Lindsay knew that if she remained as she was, she'd soon explode. She began to pace, willing herself to breathe and then calmly approach the situation. "Mr. Stennett," she began after a few moments, "our country's in the midst of a financial panic. Haven't you noticed the deteriorating state of affairs? Or is it that the Republic of Texas is so isolated as to be immune from the economics of the rest of the continent?"

"I raise cattle, Miss MacPhaull. Along with almost every other man in the Republic," he countered instantly, all the ease gone from his voice, leaving only the hard edge. "The beef on your table tonight could well be from a steer that's come off Texas grass. If it is, you can be sure that the cattleman lost money selling it. The Panic's stripped money from every pocket out there and people can't afford fancy food on their tables. That means the demand for beef is down. And when demand's down, so's the price buyers are willing to pay. But the cattleman has bills he's got to pay, and a little money being better than no money at all, he sells for what he can get.

"Now added to that is the fact that Billy was a gambler to the center of his bones. The poker table didn't thrill him nearly as much as the high-stakes risks to be had in land speculation. He bought largely on credit, using his ranch land as collateral. He did all right with it, too. He just didn't time his dying all that well. When he cocked up his toes, he left me with a mountain of debt and a short deadline. I could sell every head I own, and with the market as it is—*because of the Panic*—it still wouldn't be enough to clear the title to the land Billy left me.

"The short answer to your question, Miss MacPhaull, is *yes*. I'm well aware of the effects of the Panic and I'm not the least bit immune to them."

In the silence that fell in the aftermath of his retort, Lindsay realized that not only had she stopped her pacing but that the cause of her racing pulse had shifted. Jackson Stennett was far more intelligent than she'd originally thought. The easygoing approach to matters he'd displayed up to this point was nothing more than a thin veneer. Under it lay a man quite capable of holding his own in any New York boardroom. She'd badly underestimated his business abilities.

And if that wasn't startling enough, she'd also underestimated the effect he had on her physically. Despite the fact that he'd remained perfectly still, his hip propped against the corner of the desk and his whiskey in hand, she was very much aware of his strength, of how dangerous he could be if he decided to unleash it and direct it outward. A small part of her was frightened by the possibility. The larger part of her, though, thrilled at the thought of facing and withstanding it.

There was no mistaking the sensation swelling inside her. The feeling was very much like that of standing in the bow of a ship as a storm rolled in at sea. Exhilarating in its recklessness, it warmed the blood in a way nothing else could. To defy destruction was to feel truly alive.

She arched a brow and asked quietly, "I don't suppose it's occurred to you to simply let the creditors have Billy's land?"

He threw the contents of his glass down his throat. "That's not going to happen while I'm still breathing."

"There's an intriguing possibility," she countered. "Do you have a Will, Mr. Stennett?"

He smiled ruefully. "Actually, I do. It names Billy as my heir. Which I suppose would, when the lawyers are done with their wrangling, put it all back into the hands of whoever controls the MacPhaull Company."

"My hands, Mr. Stennett."

He chuckled and winked at her. "And eventually Henry's, Miss MacPhaull." Heading back to the sideboard, he added, "All things considered, it looks to be in your best interest to be sure I don't step in front of any runaway carriages, doesn't it?"

Lindsay shook her head and smiled at his back. "Whether you strip fifty-two and some-odd thousand dollars from the company or Henry gains control, the end result will be the same: the destruction of the MacPhaull Company. I might as well have the satisfaction of seeing you trampled in the street."

He laughed, set his glass down, and then turned to lean against the sideboard, his arms crossed over his chest. "Do you play poker, Miss MacPhaull?"

An intriguing turn. "I beg your pardon?"

"Billy taught me to play. It occurs to me that facing you across a table and a pile of chips would be a lot like playing with him again."

Very intriguing. "Are you suggesting that the ownership of the MacPhaull Company could be the stake in a game of cards?"

"Not at all. I own it and I'm not about to risk it on the turn of a card," he answered, shaking his head slowly and studying her all the while, a knowing smile tilting up the corners of his mouth. "What I'm thinking is that you have your father's way of coming at a high-stakes game. You've been dealt some lousy cards, but, by bluff and bravado, you're going to make the best of them. You're going to do whatever you have to to keep Richard Patterson alive for as long as possible so that you can keep the reins in your hands. You're not going to let anything happen to me and you're going to do your best to control how I get what I need out of the MacPhaull Company assets."

He was very good at judging character as well. She wasn't surprised. There was one inaccuracy, however, and she wanted it corrected. "Richard Patterson is like a father to me. To suggest that my concern for his life is based on business concerns is not only callous, but intentionally cruel."

"Death is inevitable, Miss MacPhaull," he countered, his eyes just as hard as his voice. "And feelings aside, there are consequences of it that practical people acknowledge long before the actual day of reckoning. Billy was like a father to me, but that didn't prevent me from knowing what his gambling and dying would mean to me in a business sense. It's not callous; it's not cruel. It's life. And you know damn good and well that when Richard Patterson goes to meet his maker, you lose control of the MacPhaull Company. You're Billy's daughter and you'll fight tooth and nail to keep your fate in your own hands."

"You would appear to be equally mercenary in your quest to do the same," she observed.

"I am. And I'll make no apologies for it. Neither am I going to take offense that you understand that. You don't have any reason to take offense, either. There's nothing wrong with being realistic."

"Well, if realistic is what you want, Mr. Stennett," she said, setting her sherry glass on the corner of the desk, "then you might take a look at this morning's correspondence." She motioned to the chair, adding, "Make yourself comfortable. I'm going to have Mrs. Beechum prepare a room for you. I'll be back shortly to answer any questions you might have."

"You're actually going to allow me to stay here?" he asked as she headed toward the door.

"It's your house," she replied without looking back. "And then there's the fact that you never allow a player to leave the table with cards in their hand."

He laughed and called after her. "My bags are at the Dunmurphy. Send someone for them, will you?"

She paused just across the threshold and turned back. "Your wish is my command," she said dryly, dropping an abbreviated curtsy.

Jackson watched her go. Lindsay MacPhaull was a very interesting woman. He'd always respected and admired the man Billy had been. But not once had he ever thought of how he'd feel about Billy's traits turning up in a woman. It was . . . well, both fascinating and a little unsettling. Like her daddy, Lindsay MacPhaull had a whole range of poker acts and could switch between them at the drop of a hat. Who she really was underneath it all remained to be seen. He was fairly certain he'd gotten the foundation right, though. She hadn't so much as blinked when he'd laid the brutal truths about business reality out on the table. No matter how badly things might have gotten, Billy never flinched. It looked as though Lindsay was made of the same stern stuff.

And damn if she didn't have the same sort of attraction to high risk that her father had. Jackson remembered the look in her eyes as he'd expounded on the consequences of the Panic. He hadn't bothered to keep the anger and frustration out of his voice. And she hadn't bothered to hide her fascination with both. It had taken every bit of his self-control to hold the distance between them. He'd been so damn tempted to step up to the unspoken challenge and see just what she'd do about it. It had been the suspicion that she wouldn't back down that had kept him planted against the desk. He'd have pushed and she'd have pushed back and the odds were that they'd have ended up on the carpet together, a snarling tangle of arms and legs and . . .

Jackson expelled a hard breath and sat down in the chair. He needed to focus on the business at hand. He had less than sixty days to figure the lay of the land, get what he needed out of it, and get gone. Lindsay MacPhaull was off-limits. She was Billy's daughter and he didn't need that kind of guilt riding his coattails. Besides, he couldn't afford the luxury of distraction, no matter how pretty it was, no matter how much he wanted it. More often than not, it came with a price he couldn't afford to pay. He'd learned that lesson the hardest way a man could.

Pulling the papers from the valise, he willed himself to focus on the flat, emotionless words of the correspondence.

LINDSAY PAUSED AT the housekeeper's door and drew a steadying breath. Before her resolve could desert her, she knocked and called, "Mrs. Beechum? I'm sorry to disturb you, but I need a few moments of your time."

"One moment, dear," came the instant reply.

The door was thick enough to prevent Lindsay from hearing small sounds from the other side, but she didn't need to. Mrs. Beechum was desperately trying to compose herself so that neither one of them would be forced to acknowledge their grief over Richard Patterson's collapse. Lindsay shook her head and smiled wryly. Richard Patterson was the only matter on which Abigail Beechum kept her silence. Everything else was fair game.

A hard metallic click instantly brought Lindsay back to the matter at hand. The door swung open and, taking her cue from her housekeeper, Lindsay pasted a serene smile on her face and pretended that she didn't know that Mrs. Beechum had been crying.

"As I said," Lindsay began, "I'm sorry to disturb you, but I'm afraid that matters simply won't wait. May I come in?"

"Oh, dear, do forgive my lapse in manners," the middle-aged woman said in sincere apology as she stepped back. "My mind is so scattered this morning. I just brought a pot of tea down to settle my nerves a bit. Would you care for a cup, Miss Lindsay?"

It was a comforting ritual they'd shared over the years; a little ceremony they both used to erase the formal boundaries that normally separated employer from employee. Relief surging through her, Lindsay stepped into the room, saying, "Gladly, and thank you. Shall I pour?"

As was the custom, Mrs. Beechum closed the door, replying, "That would be most kind of you, dear." And as Lindsay fully expected, she added, "While you do, you can tell me about Mr. Stennett and how you happened to have made his acquaintance."

"Satan sent him."

Mrs. Beechum chuckled as she settled into her rocking chair. "Well, I must say that he does indeed have the dark good looks of a true rogue, but he doesn't strike me as being malicious in nature. I found him to be quite respectful and well mannered during our conversation."

"You've met the proverbial wolf in sheep's clothing," Lindsay countered, beginning the ritual of tea.

"Miss Lindsay, I'll respectfully remind you that you tend to view all men as having wolfish tendencies. Perhaps you're misjudging Mr. Stennett?"

"I'll tell you a story, Abigail, and then you can tell me if I'm off the mark." She placed the tea set on the table between the rocker and the wing-back chair. Before them, the fire cracked and popped. "Stennett is from the Republic of Texas and—"

"I was trying to place his accent. I knew it sounded Southern."

"Apparently my father considered Mr. Stennett a son. The favorite son."

"Oh, dear me."

"Abigail, please let me get through this as quickly as I can," Lindsay said, exasperated. "I don't relish having to say it all in the first place and I'd just as soon get it over with."

"I'm sorry. I'll reserve my comments for when you're done."

"Thank you. Now, the important part of it all stems from the fact that my father died recently." Abigail Beechum made a sympathetic noise, but Lindsay didn't give her a chance to offer condolences. "In his Will he left everything to Mr. Stennett, who has come to New York to claim his prize."

"Well, leave it to your father to upset the apple cart. What, precisely, does 'everything' entail?"

"As Mr. Stennett has so delicately put it to me: every bit of property, from the business holdings to the clothes on our backs, to the pots and pans in our kitchen. Which, in terms of our daily lives, makes me your former employer."

"Miss Lindsay . . ."

She heard the hesitation in the woman's voice. Abigail Beechum never hesitated unless what she wanted to say was well outside the bounds of her role as housekeeper. It was always a healthy dose of something Lindsay would have preferred not to hear. "Go ahead and say whatever you're thinking." She leaned forward to pour the tea as she added, "I honestly don't think I can be any more deeply bruised than I already am."

"Whatever the formal nature of our relationship, Miss Lindsay, I'll always think of us as being more than employer and housekeeper. We've shared far too many pots of tea over the years for things to change between us now."

The spout clanked hard against the edge of a teacup. Lindsay quickly set the pot down and checked for a chip in the rim. A nod was all she could permit herself in acknowledgment of Abigail's words. She forced the tightness in her throat to ease and then said, "You know that I can't fight him for control."

"Of course you can't. It would be foolish to try, dear."

"I can't very well let him run around the city loose, either," Lindsay explained, setting a teacup on the table, within easy reach of her housekeeper. "I need to keep him where I can influence his decision-making. It's the only hope we have of coming out of this fiasco with anything."

Abigail Beechum nodded slowly. "So he'll be staying in the house with us. I'll prepare a room for him."

"Now, tell me, Abigail . . ." Lindsay sipped from her own cup. "Have I truly misjudged Mr. Stennett?"

The silence was deafening.

Lindsay looked over to see her housekeeper looking decidedly resolute. "Oh, Abigail! Really!" Lindsay cried, dismayed. "The man's willingly taking something that he has no right to take! Oh, yes, he has a conveniently desperate tale of why doing so is unavoidably necessary, but that doesn't alter the fact that what he's doing is wrong. He hasn't poured his life into the MacPhaull Company."

"Dear sweet Lindsay," Abigail said softly, with a slow shake of her head. "Life is seldom fair or kind. You can only make the best of what it gives you and go on. You know that."

It had been just that attitude with which Abigail had faced the loss of her arm. Lindsay wasn't, however, in the mood to be stoic or resigned. "Just once in a lifetime," she riled at her teacup, "it would be nice to have something go right, to have something happen that produced just the tiniest bit of happiness. I wouldn't even care how long it lasted. To be free of worry and able to smile for a small part of a single day would be so welcome."

Again the silence hung between them. Lindsay slid a glance at her companion; Abigail arched a brow. "What?" Lindsay asked petulantly.

"Are you finished with the self-pity?"

"It's not self-pity. It's anger."

"Call it whatever you like, dear, but it's inappropriate."

"I'll remind you that Stennett could toss us out on the street before luncheon, if he's of a mind to do so. I think a bit of anger is quite justified."

"Mr. Stennett isn't going to do any such thing. He's a gentleman."

"He's a man without a conscience," Lindsay shot back.

"Hear me out, dear," Abigail said, her hand raised to forestall any further comment. "Your world has never been idyllic or happy. Both your family and business circumstances have been deteriorating for quite some time and well you know it. Perhaps Mr. Stennett's intervention will change things for the better. He seems to be a man quite capable of taking charge."

Oh, yes indeed. Lindsay sipped her tea again, tamping

down her anger and deliberately taking refuge in the structure of business affairs. "I forgot to tell you the most important part."

"That's not like you at all."

"My mind's a bit scattered this morning as well," she admitted with a tight smile. "Stennett intends to immediately liquidate the MacPhaull holdings, taking some fifty-two thousand dollars out of the proceeds to pay off the debts on the land my father left him in Texas."

In the stunned silence, Lindsay added the last brick of painful truth. "Things aren't going to change for the better, Abigail. We've been living in a house of cards for years. And Stennett's determined to bring it down around our ears."

Abigail sighed and then quietly said, "And would it not have happened anyway? It's now a matter of sooner rather than later. And I'll be honest and tell you that I think that the company passing into Mr. Stennett's hands is better than it passing into Henry's. And if you were in a mood to be honest, you'd have to agree, wouldn't you?"

Yes, dammit. "You can see silver linings in the blackest clouds."

"It's a gift. I'm thankful for it." Abigail picked up her teacup and took a sip. "And I'd suggest that you might try cultivating a bit of the ability yourself. You'll be a happier person for making the effort."

Lindsay nodded, not because she had any intention of buying herself a pair of rose-colored glasses but because civility required some sort of positive response from her.

Apparently satisfied, Abigail set her cup onto the saucer and then rose to her feet, saying, "Now, I'm off to prepare a room for Mr. Stennett. One for Havers, too. I assumed that Mr. Stennett would be at least staying through lunch and instructed Primrose to cook accordingly. Is there anything else you'd like for me to do?"

"If you see me going for Mr. Stennett's throat . . ." Lindsay said, rising and heading toward the door.

"Stop you," Mrs. Beechum finished.

"No," she corrected. "Turn your back."

· · ·

Jack sorted through the papers yet again, his amazement no less than it had been the first three times through the stack of correspondence. Henry was having renovations done to his house. Agatha wanted to buy some land on Long Island. He knew about western land values, but still . . . At that price there had better be a gold mine on the acreage. Payment on a warehouse in St. Louis was overdue. The MacPhaull Coal Company looked to have all but washed away in a recent flood. And the Todasca Canal Company had collapsed, leaving the investors holding the bag. Jesus. What a mess.

"And there's more."

He looked up to see Lindsay in the doorway, her shoulder against the jamb and her arms folded over her midriff. "How much more?" he asked, tossing the letters aside.

"There was a run, five weeks ago, on the Two Rivers Bank in Frankfort, Kentucky. We had to close the doors when the money ran out. We're trying to call in the outstanding loans to meet depositor demands, but it's trickling at best." She smiled tightly. "And then there's the Macon and Charlotte Road Company, which encountered a not-so-dry creek bed and is having to be rerouted. The investors have been asked to put in another ten thousand apiece. We're in for twenty-five thousand already."

Jackson sagged back into the chair. Deciding he could only take the bull by the horns, he asked, "What's the total net worth of the MacPhaull Company? In today's market."

"In today's market and under today's circumstances . . ." She shrugged. "If you were going to sell off everything by sundown, I'd guess that you'd net something in the realm of two hundred thousand dollars. That would include both houses—Henry's and this one—and all the personal property. And, of course, it's assuming that you can find buyers for any of it."

It was a huge assumption. One he wasn't willing to make. "What was the estimated value of total assets before the Panic?"

"Close to seven hundred thousand," she supplied, coming into the room. She took the seat directly across the desk from him and added, "Our biggest single income source is the mining operation in western Virginia. It's the most reliable as well. If you're willing to consider advice, I think it would be worth whatever it costs to put it back into operation."

Jackson pulled the letter from the mine manager from the stack and considered the figures. "Is this man, Snyder, pretty accurate in his estimates?"

"I usually add another twenty percent and come closer than he does."

"Have you got the forty-eight thousand to put it back to rights?"

"Not in hand. But we can come up with it if we sell off some properties. Richard and I were discussing the possibilities when you and Mr. Vanderhagen arrived."

Jackson studied her, not making any effort to conceal the appraisal. She met it just as squarely as she'd answered his rapid-fire questions. God, the woman had backbone. He wondered how many men had seen only the petite, well-curved package and not bothered to discover the interesting woman underneath all the silk and lace and bows. He'd lay down money that her curves owed precious little to a corset.

Business. Clearing his throat, Jackson rose and put the correspondence back into the valise. "The first order of business needs to be a full accounting. I need to see a list of all the property owned by the company. For each property, I'll need its estimated pre-Panic and current value as well as a profit-and-loss statement. Where do I get my hands on that information?"

"At the office," she replied, rising smoothly. "Benjamin keeps the accounts and he's very thorough. May I accompany you?"

He cocked a brow. "You're asking for permission?"

"You haven't defined the manner in which you expect me to conduct myself."

He was being baited and he knew it, but it was ground they needed to cover anyway. "Are you planning to legally oppose your father's Will?"

She smiled ruefully. "Have you ever heard the expression 'cutting off one's nose to spite one's face'?" When he nodded, she further explained, "Since it would cost more in legal fees to fight you than it will to let you have what you want, I think there's more to be gained in cooperating than in opposing. You promised to take only what you need to retire my father's debts in Texas. I'll believe that you're an honest man until proven otherwise. However, if you give me even the slightest reason to suspect that you're not a man of your word, I'll see that you sincerely regret the day you ever thought to come east."

They had a formal truce. How long it would hold was anyone's guess. But an adversary in constant sight made for a more secure peace. "All right, Miss MacPhaull, if you want my expectations of you defined, I'll oblige," Jackson declared, coming around the end of the desk to stand right in front of her. "You're to consider yourself my aide-de-camp. Where I go, you go. You're to supply me with whatever information I require. What information you don't possess, you're to find for me. When asked for your opinion, you'll render it honestly and completely. Once I've made a decision, you'll support it—no matter your personal feelings on the matter—and see to its execution in a timely and efficient manner. Most importantly, you're not going to sabotage my efforts to bring some sort of order to this chaos. Is all that acceptable?"

Her chin came up. "And if it isn't?" she countered.

"Don't push, Lindsay," he said quietly. "I'll push back. And you might not like where it takes us."

She studied him a long moment, fire flashing in her eyes. "Then it's acceptable," she said tautly. "Do you want to go to the office now or after luncheon?"

It wasn't what she'd wanted to say; he could sense it. For whatever reason, she'd made a calculated decision to back down and he was grateful for it. Having won the first—and a crucial—round in their contest, Jackson decided that he could be a bit gracious. "It makes no difference to me. Which would you prefer?"

"After luncheon. Primrose has it ready now," she said firmly, turning and walking away. "Although, truth be told, I'd much rather go now and get it done. Patience has never been one of my stronger virtues."

He followed her out of the study, watching the seductive sway of her skirts and thinking that her confession didn't bode well. Two impatient people all but tied wrist and ankle was bad enough, but two impatient people locking horns over something they both wanted . . . Jackson knew to the center of his bones that it was just a matter of time before Lindsay MacPhaull decided to see if he'd meant what he said about pushing back. He did, of course. And where they ended up at the end of the match all depended on just how much tolerance she had for risk. Something told him she liked dancing on edges and that the idea of falling didn't frighten her all that much.

For him, though . . . There were certain kinds of falling that he didn't ever want to do again.

CHAPTER FOUR

*L*INDSAY LOOKED OUT the carriage window as they made their way back across town, acutely feeling both the confines of the vehicle and the tension in the silence stretching between herself and Jackson Stennett. He didn't seem disposed to do anything about breaking the latter and she couldn't think of a thing to say that wouldn't come out as a tacit admission of her discomfort in the situation. Better to maintain the appearance of poise, she told herself, than to provide evidence of lacking it. Her predicament was bad enough already without surrendering what little advantage she had. Damn her father. Jackson Stennett would like to kill him? Well, the Texas cattleman would have to wait his turn. All things considered, she had suffered longer and deeper for her father's decisions than Jackson Stennett had or ever would.

The real suffering she'd have to endure hadn't yet begun, though, and she knew it. If Stennett was even half as intelligent and business-wise as she thought, he'd take one look at the books and the true nightmare would begin. He'd ask questions and in the end she wouldn't have any choice but to answer them honestly. By the time they sat across from each other at dinner tonight, she wouldn't have a scrap of pride or a remnant of illusion left to hide behind. If there was a God and He was indeed benevolent, Stennett wouldn't finish shredding the already tattered facade of the MacPhaull public appearances. If God didn't intervene, then she'd have to. And if she failed . . . No, failure simply wasn't an option.

"Got your course plotted?"

Her pulse quickened, but whether from Stennett having so accurately guessed the nature of her thoughts or from the way his easy, amused drawl strummed her senses, she couldn't tell. It didn't matter, she assured herself, meeting his gaze. She couldn't afford to back away long enough to figure it out. Lindsay offered him what she hoped passed for a confident smile. "It happens that I do."

"Would you care to share it with me?"

"No, not particularly."

The corners of his mouth slowly inched upward and an intense light glimmered in his eyes. "Fair enough. I figure I have a pretty good idea what it's going to be anyway. So tell me how come your housekeeper has only one arm. I gather by her ability to compensate that she lost it quite a while back."

"She was in a horrible carriage accident. It's a miracle that she lived at all."

He nodded and then cocked a brow to ask, "And how did Richard Patterson end up in a wheeled chair?"

"A carriage accident."

"Same one as Mrs. Beechum?"

"Yes."

"Now in Texas," he drawled, "a housekeeper and the head of the company together in a carriage wouldn't turn a head or even be cause for a blink. But I haven't always lived in Texas and I'm thinking that New York tongues wagged for weeks when they caught wind of the situation."

His intelligence clearly went beyond business matters. Lindsay considered her options and decided that frankness was the best choice. "Actually, the tongues wagged for *years*, not that it was any of their business. Frankly, I don't see that it's any of yours either, but in the interest of keeping you from inadvertently putting your foot in it and creating an awkward situation, I'll tell you the story."

His smile was appreciative and perhaps just a bit apologetic. "She's a very nice lady. I like her."

"Abigail is a good person and I'm very thankful she came into my life. I wouldn't hurt her for anything in the world. I expect you to keep what I'm about to tell you a closely guarded secret. And please don't let her know that I've spoken of it with you. She'd be mortified."

"I'll take it to the grave with me."

Lindsay studied him and decided that he hadn't made the promise lightly, that he could be trusted. "She was married to a Mr. Elijah Beechum, a banker well known for his miserly ways, both in terms of his affections and his money keeping. I was no more than five when the accident happened, just eight when I asked my father about it and he told me what he knew. I don't know how Richard and Abigail met; no one's ever said. And no one's ever said how or why they came to be in the carriage together that day. Assumptions, however, were made."

"That they were having an affair."

Lindsay nodded. "Abigail was hovering on the edge of death when her husband divorced her, leaving her penniless and homeless. She went away for a year or so; to convalesce at a distant cousin's home in New Jersey. Some have gone so far as to suggest that she gave birth to Richard's child while away, but I think that's just a vicious, groundless rumor. My father claimed to have made discreet inquiries into the matter and he found no proof of a child.

"Regardless, from all accounts, she was only grudgingly welcomed at her cousin's home and she was asked to leave as soon as she was physically able. Richard, once he'd recovered as fully as he could, begged my mother to take Abigail in and at least give her a roof over her head and honorable employment."

"Your mother had a kind heart."

"She didn't do it to be nice, Mr. Stennett. My mother was a very complicated woman and her motives for doing anything were always complex. I doubt very much whether considerations of kindness came into her decision at all."

His head tilted to the side and his brows knit, Stennett quietly asked, "So why did she do it? Your best guess."

"I think she saw in it the opportunity to humiliate someone who had been her social equal."

"That's pretty damn spiteful."

"I'll never forgive my father for abandoning us, Mr. Stennett, but I can understand why he left. In looking back at my childhood, I've often wondered why he stayed as long as he did."

"Why didn't Richard marry Mrs. Beechum when the dust settled?"

"Richard was changed by the accident," she said simply. "I know that he's always considered his survival as a cruel sentence issued by a black-hearted God. Before the accident he was quite the man about town. After the accident . . . It was as though the light in him went out. Even as a small child, I noticed it. As far as I know, he and Abigail haven't spoken since that god-awful day."

"Does he still have feelings for her?"

"Not that I've ever heard him voice."

Stennett nodded slowly and then asked, "Does she still have feelings for Richard?"

"I believe so. While you were going through the correspondence before luncheon, she and I shared a pot of tea. She'd been crying before I got there."

"You didn't ask her why?"

"There's an unspoken rule among the MacPhaulls, Mr. Stennett. We don't talk about unpleasant and upsetting realities. It's one thing to be insulting and demanding. It's quite another to rationally discuss a fundamental truth that challenges our illusions of having a perfect life. In fact, among the MacPhaulls, the former is used to avoid the latter. And very effectively, I might add. Amidst all the screaming and foot stamping, it's utterly impossible to have any sort of calm and logical discussion about financial matters, personal heartaches, the issue of responsibility, or the necessity of sacrifice."

"How do you live with that?"

Lindsay smiled tightly. "Rather uncomfortably. Agatha and Henry, on the other hand . . ."

"So if at dinner this evening I happen to look up and see a group of men carrying the furniture out of the drawing room I should—"

"Ask someone to pass you the bread and mention that you think the weather is quite nice for this time of the year."

"What if they come for the dining-room table? And the plates and silverware?"

"Oh," she replied blithely, "that would force the issue. Having your meal carted away does command attention and would make one wonder why it's happening. And one would naturally suspect that it would be because of finances. Rather than discuss that, though, Henry would likely insult someone and a screaming match would ensue. Agatha would become hysterical for some reason or another. In dealing with the two of them, the fact that the furniture is being taken away would be ignored. And when the final door is slammed, the MacPhaulls will have avoided any discussion of the fact that financial matters are less than perfectly ideal. As I said, Mr. Stennett, we do not talk about unpleasant realities."

He expelled a hard breath and cocked a brow. "The MacPhaulls are in for a rude awakening. There's no way I can pretend that the circumstances are anything other than what they are. Billy died and left me to sweep up the debris. I intend to do it."

Lindsay shrugged and looked out the carriage window, observing, "Then you're in for a few rude awakenings of your own, Mr. Stennett."

BEN TIPTON WAS—although he tried to hide it—vastly relieved to learn that the change in company ownership didn't mean a change in his employment. He produced the books and stood ready to answer any questions Jackson might have. The ledgers were neat, Ben's columns straight and his numbers precisely formed. None of that made looking at the totals any easier. Lindsay had stood at the window for the entire two hours, presumably watching the traffic on the street pass by. Whatever her thoughts on the task at hand, she studiously kept them to herself.

Jackson leaned back in the chair and contemplated the tin ceiling. "Ben?"

On the other side of the desk, Ben tore his gaze away from Lindsay and straightened his spine a notch. "Yes, sir?"

"In your estimation, when did the wagon begin to lose the wheel?"

He blinked, rocked back on his heels for a second, and then recovered enough to cock a pale brow and say, "I beg your pardon, sir?"

"When did the MacPhaull Company begin to move from the black into the red," Lindsay clarified, her gaze still fixed on the world beyond the office.

"I'm the bookkeeper, sir," Ben quickly countered, casting a glance her way. "It's not my place to offer such observations."

Because they're not going to reflect well on my employer's business judgment, Jackson silently added for him. It occurred to him that Lindsay had probably maintained her strict silence because she knew darn good and well what the books were telling him and didn't want to compound her embarrassment. In a perfect world, he would have anticipated the possibility of such an awkward situation and insisted on coming to the office without her. But the world wasn't perfect and he really hadn't expected to see anything approaching the disaster that had been so neatly and clearly laid out in front of him. But since the ugly truth had to be faced and put into words sooner or later, sooner was probably better.

"That might not have been the case in the past, Ben, but now's now and I want your opinion."

The bookkeeper hesitated, glanced at Lindsay again, and then quietly cleared his throat. "I'll have to give it some thought, Mr. Stennett. The matter has never occurred to me and I'd prefer to give you a fully considered speculation later rather than a hastily formed and thus inaccurate one now."

"Fair enough." *And a damn fine job of dodging there, Ben.* "Your books look to be in excellent order. I can't see that I need you for anything else today. I'm assuming that your wife is going to be putting your dinner on the table shortly and would like to have you there to eat it while it's still warm."

Ben Tipton's shoulders went slightly less square and his smile seemed a little less forced than it had been all afternoon. "I'm not married, sir. But Mrs. McAbee, my housekeeper and cook, does expect me to present myself in a timely manner for all meals."

"Then head on out for the day."

"Thank you, Mr. Stennett." He turned toward the window. "Miss Lindsay," he said softly, "I hope that Mr. Patterson improves rapidly. If there's anything I can do, please don't hesitate to ask."

Looking over her shoulder, she smiled stoically. "Thank you, Ben. I appreciate your concern."

With an abbreviated bow to her, Ben took his leave, pulling the door half closed on his way out. Jackson wryly smiled at the gesture; how interesting that Ben thought to balance the need for privacy and propriety.

"He's conscientious and very loyal," Lindsay said quietly. "Thank you for assuring him that his job is secure. Given the times, it would be terribly difficult for him to find another."

"No point in cleaning house just to clean house. He's meticulous and knows the books. Both are assets I can appreciate."

She didn't respond and in the silence he turned the ledger pages until he reached those concerning the drafts against owner equity. The numbers were the same as the last time he'd looked at them. "Lindsay? How do you pay for the food on your table?"

Lindsay leaned her forehead against the window glass and closed her eyes. Why had he started with the personal aspects of it all? The details of business transactions would have been so much easier to talk about. The coward's way was avoidance, though, and so she gave him the plain truth as dispassionately as she could, determined that he never know how big the knots were in her stomach. "I've been discreetly selling some of my mother's personal property, as well as household items we neither need nor want."

"How long have you been doing this?"

"Six months."

"And how much longer do you think you can keep doing it?"

"Perhaps another six, depending on the availability of buyers and the prices I can get from them."

"And at the end of six months or the absence of buyers—whichever comes first—what are you going to do? Have you given that any thought?"

"Then I don't see that I'll have any choice but to begin liquidating some of the less profitable company assets," she answered, giving him the answer she always used to reassure herself. But even as she uttered the words, she realized that her circumstances had changed so drastically that the strategy was no longer possible.

"Or at least that was my thinking when I actually owned them," she amended, unable to hide her resentment. "Now that I don't, I really have no idea what course to take. I'm sure something will present itself; it always does." In her mind's eye, she saw a battered wagon heading west into the sunset, a wind-beaten version of herself urging a pair of raw-boned oxen to take just one more step before dying. Damn William Lindsay MacPhaull. Damn him and his black-hearted minion, Jackson Stennett.

"How does Richard Patterson pay his way? I can see by the books that he hasn't taken a salary in over a year."

Lindsay swallowed back her anger and forced dispassion into her voice and demeanor. "Richard has made some investments of his own over the years. I don't know precisely what they are, but they're apparently providing a sufficient enough return that he hasn't needed his salary from the MacPhaull Company. I've insisted, though, that we keep track of the money due him so that he can be paid in full when the Panic ends."

"How long has he been managing the company? Since Billy hightailed it for Texas?"

"Even before that; years before I was born. As I recall the story, my father hired Richard before Agatha and Henry were born."

"And so he's been riding along, doing his job out of a sense of loyalty to the company?"

She looked over her shoulder at him. As he had when questioning Ben, he leaned back in the chair and stared up at the ceiling. As she had countless times already that afternoon, she tried to see Richard sitting in his wheeled chair behind the desk instead of Jackson Stennett and couldn't. Angry with herself for the betrayal, she answered, "I think, Mr. Stennett, that it's more a case of Richard feeling a sense of obligation to my welfare."

His gaze slipped downward to meet hers. "What about Henry's and Agatha's welfare?"

"Richard and I have a long-standing difference of opinion in that regard," she admitted, looking back out at the street, her heart racing at the intensity of his attention. "Richard's frequently argued that they expect too much and give nothing in return. I, on the other hand, have issues of conscience with which to contend. They are my brother and sister."

"What say do they have in the company affairs?"

"None," she answered crisply. "It's as they prefer it. And to be perfectly honest, it's a blessing that they don't want to be involved. As Richard is fond of saying, neither one of them has the sense God gave a goose. On the one or two occasions when Henry made an effort to be a businessman . . ." She shook her head and quietly sighed. "The Todasca Canal Company is one of his projects. You've seen the report on its current status."

"Do either of them have personal investments to provide separate income, like Richard?"

"Not that I'm aware of." She felt rather than saw his gaze leave her, and her pulse began to slow in the long moment of silence hanging between them.

"I'd like for you to invite Henry to dinner tomorrow night. And make sure Agatha will be there, too."

Oh, dear God. He had no idea what he was truly suggesting. She gripped the windowsill in an effort to steady her nerves as her heartbeat roared in her ears. "A family dinner is not a good idea."

"Good idea or not, it's the best way to go about telling them that their fortunes have changed."

"You can't force me to extend the invitations," she countered angrily.

"No, sure can't," he drawled. "But you can either have them over to dinner so they can be told in person, or I'll dictate a letter to Ben and have it delivered through the post. The choice of how they hear the news is up to you. But hear it they will."

Lindsay closed her eyes and slowly counted to ten. How she hated him for the way he backed her into corners, for how he appeared to give her a choice when there really was none at all. Staring out at the street again, she asked through clenched teeth, "Shall I include Edith and the children in the invitation?"

"Edith, yes, but not the children. I suspect that things are going to be said that children probably shouldn't hear."

That children shouldn't hear? *She* didn't want to hear the things that would be said. "Mr. Stennett," she began, turning away from the window.

"Will you please stop calling me Mr. Stennett?" he interrupted, abruptly rising from the chair. "My name is Jackson. Shorten it to Jack, if you like."

She watched him step around the desk and begin to pace the width of the office, his hands stuffed deep into his trouser pockets. She'd point out later the ramifications of addressing him by his Christian name. At the moment, she had more pressing concerns.

"I realize that the company assets are yours to do with as you please," she said, "but I ask that you take into consideration the fact that Henry and Agatha have absolutely no ability to make a living on their own. They have no skills of any sort. If you were to cut them off from MacPhaull income, they'd be destitute within a mere thirty days. Please have a conscience and remember that Henry does have a wife and three children."

"How old is Henry?"

"Forty," she replied crisply, seeing the direction he intended to go and resenting the inherent soundness of it.

"Agatha is thirty-eight. And in the event that you weren't paying attention in the carriage, I'm twenty-five."

"And if I were to cut you off from MacPhaull income, what would you do?"

Probably die somewhere on a godforsaken piece of prairie. The idea was too full of hopelessness and self-pity and she rebelled against it. "I've developed a sufficient number of business relationships over the years that I could prevail on the kindness of someone for employment as a manager," she countered defiantly. "I'd find a modest home to purchase and take Mrs. Beechum with me. I'll do quite well on my own. You needn't strain your conscience on my behalf."

He stopped his pacing and considered her, his head tilted to the side. One corner of his smile quirked up. "How is it that you turned out to be so independent, while Henry and Agatha didn't?"

"That's a puzzle whose solution has always eluded Richard," she supplied, deliberately sidestepping the issue. "If you should happen upon the answer, I'm sure he'd love to hear it."

His smile faded. "The odds are that he's not going to get better, you know," he said gently. "I've seen this before. He'll likely just lie there in that bed, fading a little bit every day until he and everyone else is praying for the end to come."

Her throat closed, leaving her able only to nod in mute agreement and understanding of the only real certainty that lay ahead.

"Does he have any family?" Stennett asked softly.

Lindsay swallowed and forced words past the bruised and aching tightness. "None that I know of. If he has brothers and sisters, I've never heard him speak of them."

"No children?"

"He never married."

"Well, not to be indelicate," he drawled, "but having children doesn't necessarily depend on taking a walk to the altar, you know."

Lindsay clenched her teeth, angry at the very suggestion

that Richard could be so callous and irresponsible. "To my knowledge," she replied icily, "no claims of patrimony have ever been made against him."

He paused for a second or two, studying her, before he slowly asked, "Does Otis Vanderhagen handle Richard's personal legal matters?"

She stared at him, stunned, as his words echoed through her brain. "You're a ghoul!" she declared, stepping forward, her hands balled into fists at her sides. "Richard lies dying a hideous death and you're eyeing his estate!"

His eyes darkened to hard ebony as his temples pulsed with the hammering of his quickened pulse. Slowly, his hands came out of his pockets. "We've already had a conversation about facing hard truths and being honest about it," he said with sharp precision. "You can look at the books just as well as I can. You know damn good and well that without liquidating tangible assets, you're dead broke. You need a miracle and it'd be right nice of Richard to leave you one in his Will. If he does or he doesn't, it effects how I go about putting to rights this god-awful mess. Whether you like it or not, whether you think it's appropriate or not, I need to know what's in Richard's Will."

No one had ever spoken to her in such a way! And about something so utterly reprehensible. She folded her arms and broadened her stance. "I have absolutely no intention of asking Vanderhagen anything about it. I refuse."

He snorted. "I wasn't suggesting that you do. I'll make the inquiry."

The greedy leading the tactless and insensitive. She instinctively took another step forward as her hands again went to fists at her sides. "You'll do no such thing!"

His shoulders went ever so slightly back as he grinned. "Just out of curiosity, how do you think you're going to stop me?"

She would. If she had to crash something heavy over his head, she'd do it.

A measure of his amusement went out of his smile, but not all of it. In his eyes she clearly saw the spark of challenge ignite. "You decide to a take a swing at me, Lindsay," he softly taunted, "you'd better make it the best one you've got. If I can get up, I'm going to set aside the fact that you're a woman and make you pay for it. Understood?"

Oh, she understood perfectly and she was sorely tempted to take another step forward. The battle between that temptation and common sense was as swift as it was decisive. Lindsay lifted her chin. "You are the most odious and contemptible man I've ever met."

"Yeah, well," he said, still taunting, "right now I'm just real damn grateful that Billy didn't make my inheritance conditional on marrying you. I'd give up the ranch first and not think twice about it."

The cut stung deeply, abrading an old wound that had never fully healed. "I can see why my father left everything to you. Birds of a feather, as they say. Bastards to the bone, both of you."

"No," he countered, his amusement gone, replaced by steely coolness. "It's a case of like father like son."

"He wasn't your father."

"More mine than yours."

It was the truth, but that didn't dull the pain. Instead, it opened the doors to memories she had thought forever locked away. With them came a surging tide of emotions that threatened to undo her. "Dinner is served promptly at six," she declared, turning on her heel and heading for the coatrack to retrieve her pelisse and bonnet. "We don't want to be late."

"I'm not hungry. My apologies to Primrose and Mrs. Beechum."

Lindsay didn't look back, but said, "Very well. Suit yourself," as she gathered up her belongings and left him.

Jackson watched her go, silently swearing at himself. He'd never, even as a child, had an exchange as childish as that one had been. What the hell was wrong with him? He'd seen the hurt in her eyes when he'd thrown out the barb about being glad he didn't have to marry her for her money. And then he'd turned right around and deliberately wounded her again, reminding her that Billy had left her behind and in the end chosen him over her.

Raking his fingers through his hair, he considered the door she'd left wide open in her wake. If he had an ounce of decency in him, he'd close up the office, find his way back to the house, and spit out an apology of some kind or another before Primrose brought out the soup course. And in doing so, he'd be handing Lindsay a victory he couldn't afford to give her.

With a heavy sigh, he dropped back into the chair behind the desk. There was work to be done and it had rightful first claim on his time. Patching things up with Lindsay MacPhaull was something that could wait until tomorrow. Today had been long enough and full enough for both of them already. It was going to take everything left in him to look at the books again and try to see a way out. Nothing made tomorrows look better than being able to face the sunrise with answers and something that resembled a fairly logical plan of attack. If you had that much, then everything else generally fell into place on its own.

As for Lindsay . . . Jackson scrubbed his hands over his face. Jesus. She was pretty, lusciously curved, and intelligent. When it came to business, she was apparently rational and levelheaded. But he'd been wrong about the woman who lay beneath that come-hither surface. Down deep Lindsay MacPhaull was still very much a little girl whose daddy had walked away from her and never looked back. Billy ought to burn in hell for doing that to her. And he, Jackson Stennett, Texas rancher and now New York businessman, was destined for the same fate if he didn't scrape together enough self-control to treat her a bit more gently.

Hopefully his apology for hurting her feelings this evening would be one of those things that just happened on its own tomorrow. If not, he'd have to find the grit to do it straight-out. She deserved that much from him. The books said the odds were that, when all was said and done, she wasn't going to get much of anything else.

LINDSAY HESITATED, one foot on the sidewalk and the other on the coach step. Jackson Stennett had claimed that her father was more his than hers. In a sense it was true. But in another, she was proving herself to be her father's daughter to the marrow. She was running from difficulties in the tradition that was William MacPhaull's legacy. If she had any strength of moral fiber, she'd turn around and march back into the office and . . . and . . .

Do what? Simply stand there to prove that she could? Tell Jackson Stennett that her father had been a coward and that she was made of sterner stuff? Why would Stennett care? Given his nature, he'd probably feel compelled to point out that turning around and coming back wasn't proof of anything except a foolish devotion to pride. And he would be right.

Lindsay climbed into the carriage, pulled the door closed behind her, and, with a rap on the wall behind her, signaled the driver to take her home. Today had been very long, she told herself; a day filled with wholly unexpected and unpleasant events. She'd done the best she could under the trying circumstances. Tomorrow would be better. And, of course, running home for dinner wasn't at all like running away to Texas for life. They were two very different actions, committed by two very different people.

Weren't they?

Lindsay sighed, pursed her lips, and decided that, whether it was running away or not, she couldn't afford to hide in MacPhaull House. There were decisions that had to be made, and made both quickly and firmly. And she wanted to talk them out with someone whose judgment and experience she trusted, someone she could call an ally in the days ahead.

She crossed to the opposite seat in the carriage and slid open the window that allowed her to talk to her driver.

LINDSAY STOOD AT THE PARLOR HEARTH and watched the flames dance in the grate. It really was most unseemly to be in a gentleman's house without a proper chaperone. Especially so in the evening. If anyone had noted her arrival, there would be tongues wagging all over town by tomorrow morning. Not that she cared for her own reputation. God knew it wouldn't be the first time her behavior had been the subject of public comment. But Benjamin Tipton certainly didn't deserve to have his name sullied by the gossips. Had there been another way to meet with him without Jackson Stennett being aware of it . . .

"Miss Lindsay," Ben declared, coming into the parlor, his smile large but somehow edged with a shadow of wariness. "To what do I owe the honor and pleasure of your visit?"

"Nothing dire, Ben," she hurriedly assured him. "And I promise that I won't keep you from your dinner. But if you wouldn't mind, I'd truly appreciate hearing your thoughts on . . ." She shrugged and then shook her head as she finished, "Well, I suppose 'the upheaval' is really the only way to put it."

His shoulders visibly relaxed and his eyes brightened. "I'm flattered that you've asked, Miss Lindsay. I'll gladly help in any manner I can." He gestured to a pair of upholstered chairs flanking the hearth. "Please, let's have a seat and be comfortable."

Yes, Ben did like his comforts, she admitted as she smoothed her skirts and settled into the chair. He had exquisite taste in furnishings and appointments. Ben sat across from her and crossed one leg casually over the other, lacing his long slender fingers to clasp his trouser-clad knee.

"First, if you would," she began, meeting his gaze squarely, her hands folded primly in her lap, "tell me what you think of Jackson Stennett."

Ben shrugged one shoulder in a characteristically dismissive gesture. "He certainly seems to be an intelligent man with a reasonable amount of business experience."

"I've gotten the same impression," Lindsay admitted. She moistened her lower lip with the tip of her tongue and plunged into the more complicated aspects of the situation. "In the explanation of things we gave you this afternoon, one important detail was carefully omitted, Ben. Stennett intends to liquidate a considerable portion of the MacPhaull Company holdings within the next sixty days. What are your thoughts on this?"

He gazed into the fire for several long moments, pursing and unpursing his lips. "Well," he finally, slowly, said, "as we know, there are some holdings that really do need to be disposed of. Mr. Patterson's last instructions to me this morning were to prepare a list of properties that could be sold without reducing income." His gaze slid up to hers as he added, "If Mr. Stennett could be persuaded to focus his efforts on selling those, I don't see that he'd be doing anything that Mr. Patterson hadn't intended to do anyway."

She nodded, remembering the conversation she and Richard had been having about Henry's boat and Agatha's cottage at the shore.

Ben softly cleared his throat and waited for her attention to come back to him before commenting, "I'd have to say, Miss Lindsay, that my feelings on the matter depend on what Mr. Stennett intends to do with the revenue the sales generate. If he were to put them into some of the more profitable ventures—say, the coal mine, for instance—then I think his course is a very sound one and one Mr. Patterson would heartily approve."

Lindsay smiled ruefully. "If that's what he intended to do, Ben, I wouldn't be concerned at all. However, he's planning to take almost fifty-three thousand dollars in cash to Texas and retire debts my father left encumbering the title to the ranch they owned in partnership."

Ben's pale brows knitted. "Does he intend to run what remains of the MacPhaull Company from that backwater?"

"He's assured me that he'll title back all the properties that he doesn't have to sell," Lindsay supplied. "Once he has the money he needs, he says he'll return to Texas and be done with us."

"Do you believe him?"

"Surprisingly, yes," Lindsay admitted. "Although, if you pressed, I wouldn't be able to give you a logical reason as to why." She sighed. "However . . ."

"Yes?"

She took a deep breath and plunged ahead. "As you're well aware, we don't have the financial resources to fight the Will in court. We're not without other options, though. Mr. Stennett may be the sole beneficiary of my father's Will, Ben, but until his ownership is recognized by the probate court, he's really powerless to take any action on his own.

"If I were so inclined, I could sell the entire company so that—when the court orders the property to be given over to him—there's nothing to be given. I have this niggling feeling that if Richard were physically able, he would be scrambling to do just that. I value your experience and perspective, Ben. You've been with the company for a very long time. What do you think I ought to do?"

"I assume you want a candid opinion."

"Please." She smiled. "I was quite impressed by the way you evaded Mr. Stennett's questions earlier. It really was masterfully done and I appreciate the attempt to shield me from embarrassment."

He bowed his head in courtly acceptance of the thanks and then replied, "My loyalties are not subject to your father's Will, Miss Lindsay. I'll continue to serve the interests I always have."

God, what would she do without Benjamin Tipton? Where would she be? "Now for your honest thoughts about selling everything before Mr. Stennett can. Do you think it's the course Richard would want me to take?"

He didn't hesitate long enough to blink. "I think Mr. Patterson would counsel you against such a plan."

Lindsay arched a brow.

Obligingly, he added, "I'm sure Mr. Vanderhagen could wrap it all up in a very lengthy legal explanation, but the gist of it would be that liquidating the assets at this point wouldn't go over well. Mr. Stennett would cry foul and the courts would probably agree with him. You're selling assets in a deliberate effort to circumvent the spirit of your father's Will. I'm afraid they'd frown on that and order you to give Mr. Stennett all the proceeds from the sales."

Relief flooded over her. Ben saw the same pitfalls as she did. It was so comforting to know that her thinking wasn't absolutely muddled. "And with all the assets having been liquidated into cash, Stennett could well take it *all* back to Texas with him, as opposed to just a portion of it," Lindsay observed. "Just for revenge."

"Indeed. And I'll add that his having to sue for the inheritance will only keep him here that much longer. I think your original instincts on the matter are the correct ones to follow, Miss Lindsay."

"My original instincts?" she repeated, wondering if she really was as transparent as Ben seemed to think she was.

"If I'm interpreting your actions of today correctly," he supplied readily, "you're inclined to assist him—while subtly influencing his decisions—so that he can be satisfied and thus removed from the situation as quickly as possible."

She'd always known that Ben was an intelligent and perceptive man, but the keenness of his insight was startling nevertheless. "You know me very well, Ben."

His smile said, *Of course.* He tilted his head to the side and cocked a brow. "May I ask a question of you, Miss Lindsay?"

"Certainly."

His gaze went back the flames in the hearth grate. "You said that Mr. Stennett has promised to title back those holdings remaining after he has the money he requires. And that he intends to end his involvement with the company at that point."

Lindsay nodded. "That's my understanding of his intentions."

"To whom does he intend to leave the control of those remaining assets?" he asked, not looking at her. "You or Henry? Or does he plan to place it into a trust for all three of you?"

"I have no idea," she admitted. She thought, given the general nature of the questions Jackson Stennett had been asking, that it was likely he'd either leave what remained of the company under her management or in a trust. But, since she didn't know his thinking with any certainty, she kept the observation to herself.

"In my opinion," Ben went on, "that will be the most important decision Mr. Stennett makes. It—more than anything else—will directly determine your future."

"True enough," Lindsay replied. *And obvious, too,* she silently added. "I'd prefer not to have my finances in Henry's hands. The prospect of being at his mercy has always frightened me. If there's a silver lining to Stennett's inheriting the estate, it's the possibility that he may save me from Henry's stupidity."

"Silver linings," Ben said softly, his smile rueful as he shook his head. His gaze came from the flames to meet hers again. "You have some formidable tasks ahead of you, Miss Lindsay. I don't envy you at all. I am, however, willing to assist you in any way you might require."

"Thank you, Ben," she replied, rising from her seat, reassured by his loyalty and commitment. "At this point, all I ask is that you guide Stennett toward the list of properties Richard asked you to prepare."

"Consider it done," he said, also rising. He gestured toward the back of the house. "Would you care to stay for dinner? I'd be honored."

He'd be pilloried by the gossips. And then they'd start on her. Again. "I'm afraid I can't," Lindsay said, hoping she looked suitably regretful, "but thank you for the invitation. Perhaps some other evening, Ben."

"I shall look forward to it," he said, bowing slightly at the waist and then offering her his arm as he added, "Allow me to see you to your carriage."

She walked at his side and allowed him to hand her into the carriage that sat waiting in the circular drive. It was an oddly disconcerting experience, she decided, as the carriage started to roll and she waved good-bye to him.

She'd known Benjamin Tipton all of her adult life, but there was something about being with him outside of the office that didn't feel at all right. And, despite the sense of betrayal she felt, she couldn't keep from comparing him to Jackson Stennett.

In appearance they were both handsome men, although in very different ways. Ben was fair and finely molded, a creature of parlors and cultured events. Stennett had dark hair and eyes, his skin burnished tawny-gold by life under the sun. Where Ben was delicate, Jackson Stennett could only be described as chiseled.

And while they both were quite capable of exhibiting courtly and mannerly behavior, there was an obvious difference in the underriding tone of it. Ben's manner was tightly controlled and gave her the sense of being based on cool calculation of the advantage to be gained in playing by the expected rules. In fact, now that she thought about it, the politeness was almost like a mask behind which Ben hid the more personal side of himself.

Jackson Stennett, on the other hand ... Lindsay chewed on her lower lip. Stennett struck her as the kind of man who didn't care enough about rules to even bother learning what they were. His manner—his respectful treatment of those around him—was as natural a part of him as breathing. He wore his social station with ease and didn't seem to care what anyone thought of him or what he said or did.

He was a remarkably baronial man, Lindsay admitted. And in comparison, Benjamin Tipton seemed decidedly shallow. It was a shame that Ben's sense of duty and loyalty weren't obvious at a casual glance. They were his best qualities and so few people knew he possessed them.

CHAPTER FIVE

IR?"

Ben. Jackson opened his eyes. Yep, it was Ben Tipton standing beside him. "What time is it?" he asked, easing up and into the back of the chair.

"It's eight o'clock, sir. In the morning. Do you take sugar or cream in your coffee?"

"No, just black and strong." His forehead felt six inches high and a good four thick. And sweet criminey, his shoulders were stiffer than planks. "Pour yourself a cup and have a seat, Ben. We need to talk."

Ben poured from the silver pot, saying, "I think you should know that Mr. Vanderhagen has sent his card announcing that he intends to call at nine."

Wonderful way to start the day. Jackson began working the kinks out of his neck. "Then we have an hour and we'll make the best of it."

"Perhaps you'd like to shave while we talk," Ben suggested while handing him a dainty cup and saucer. When it had been safely transferred, he motioned toward the far wall. "I've seen to the dressing table. If you'd care for breakfast, I'll order whatever you'd like to be delivered."

Coffee, a shave, and the offer of breakfast. Ben sure had the routine down pat. "Thank you. I take it that Richard often spent the night here."

"He did, sir. Especially in the last year."

The coffee was hot and strong. In searing a path all the way down his throat, it succeeded in clearing the cobwebs of sleep from his brain. Ben was at the washbasin, lathering the brush in the heavy shaving mug. Jack considered him. The bookkeeper was what they called a pretty boy back home. For some reason, age never made any difference for men like Ben Tipton. They were handsome and stylish and popular with the ladies—working real damn hard at it all—and about as deep as a hoofprint on rock. All the ones he'd ever run across hadn't liked working for a living and had avoided it if at all possible. Ben struck him as working not out of necessity or because society expected him to be productive, but because it amused him. Ben Tipton was—no doubt about it—good at his job, but he was still an odd kind of critter.

Jackson took another long swallow of coffee and then, leaving the saucer on the desktop, forced his body upright. "Tell me, Ben, have you ever thought about giving up bookkeeping and becoming a manservant?"

"I'm much more comfortable spending my day with books and figures than I am people, sir."

"Why's that?" Jackson asked, setting the coffee cup down beside the washbasin and looking at himself in the mirror. *Rode hard and put away wet.*

"Numbers are numbers," Ben explained, handing him a steaming towel and setting down the shaving mug before stepping back. "They are what they appear to be. People seldom are and I always seem to be disappointed by what I find beneath the surface of them."

Jackson considered the observation as he pressed the moist, heated towel over the lower half of his face. Tossing it aside, he picked up the shaving mug and slathered his chin with soap, saying, "Until recently, I would have disagreed with you, Ben. Now I'm beginning to think that you may be right. I sure as hell never expected Billy to be who he turned out to be."

He set down the mug, accepted the razor from Ben, and began to shave. "And I never in my wildest nightmares thought I'd be in New York trying to figure out how to salvage the business and personal disaster he left behind. The least he could have done was give me a hint that all this was waiting down the road. It would have been nice to have just a bit of warning instead of walking into it all blind as a bat." He met Ben's gaze in the mirror. "And if you breathe so much as a word of my grousing about Billy to Lindsay, I'll have to cut your tongue out for it."

"Of course not, sir," Ben murmured. "Never."

"I'm kidding, Ben." Jackson rinsed his blade for the last time and laid it aside. "I really wouldn't cut your tongue out. It's just an expression."

"Oh."

"Look, Ben," he said, wiping the last traces of soap from his face with the towel. "Maybe it might help you to know that I'm a simple man; what you see is all there is to me. I like a lot of things, but above all else I appreciate honesty and directness. If I ask a question, I want a straight from the hip answer. I can't stand pussyfooting or beating around the bush or excruciatingly polite attempts to avoid the issue. You can deal with me square up and not worry about losing your job or your head."

"That's good to know. If I might ask . . . Do the same parameters apply if Miss Lindsay is present?"

God, he felt halfway human again. He picked up his coffee cup and quickly drank what remained. "If she can't take it, then I'm prepared to throw myself between you and her. I won't let her hurt you."

In the mirror, he saw Ben blink and purse his lips. After a moment, he ventured, "Miss Lindsay is a very good woman, sir, and while I'm grateful for her willingness to employ me, I feel obligated to point out that she does have a temper and that she can be quite headstrong."

"A little like a comanchero," Jackson muttered.

"I beg your pardon, sir?"

"Never mind," he said, heading back toward the desk and the siren call of the coffeepot. "Just understand that I'm bigger and meaner than she is and that I can handle her."

Ben beat him to the silver service. Refilling Jackson's cup and fighting a smile, he said quietly, "I've never seen anyone 'handle' Miss Lindsay."

"I'm selling tickets. Want one?"

Ben smiled. "It should be a spectacular show, sir. I do believe I'll take one—since you offered. How much are they?"

"The price is honesty. And a slight shift in allegiance."

Instantly, Ben sobered. He took a step back and met Jackson's gaze for a long moment as the thoughts and choices paraded through the clear depths of his eyes. Jack noted that they darkened as the decision was made.

"You may well be my employer now, Mr. Stennett," he began, slowly, deliberately, "but Miss Lindsay has been my employer a good many years. There will be some matters that I will never feel comfortable discussing with you and you'll have to accept that." He paused and drew a deep breath. "I also understand the reality of Miss Lindsay's business situation and I feel honor bound to do whatever I can to ensure that she emerges from the situation with as much of her world intact as possible. What I share with you regarding the business will be offered in that spirit. Is that acceptable to you?"

"And on the assumption that I'm a fair and decent man who will do right by her," Jackson added.

"Yes, sir."

"I failed to mention how much I value loyalty, Ben. Your terms are admirable as well as acceptable."

Benjamin Tipton sighed in apparent relief and smiled. "Yesterday you asked about the wheel coming off the wagon. I think the slippage began about fifteen years ago. I see certain patterns in the books that have always intrigued me."

"You have my attention, Ben. Keep going."

As Jackson leaned back against the desk, Ben continued, choosing each word carefully, "If you go back through the records for the last fifteen years, you'll see that a considerable number of businesses and properties have been purchased and sold over that time. This, in itself, is commonplace. But what I see in the numbers is that some properties do very well for a time and then show sudden and precipitous drops in revenues."

"Let me guess. At which point they're sold for a net loss."

"Yes, sir."

"It happens in business." Jackson sipped his coffee. "What makes you look twice at it?"

"There are roughly thirty-seven such sales."

Thirty-seven? I'd've looked more than twice. "That's too many; a little over two a year," Jackson mused aloud. "The law of averages doesn't usually work that hard and long against a good manager."

"And all thirty-seven sales have been fairly evenly divided between only four purchasers."

Just four? As patterns went, they didn't get much easier to see. "So are they turkey buzzards waiting to swoop down on an easy meal or are they gallant white knights responding to the cries of a sweet damsel in distress?"

"Miss Lindsay sees them as knights."

"She contacts them, offering the property for sale?"

Ben nodded. "That's been my observation, sir. Mr. Patterson developed the strategy years ago and Miss Lindsay adopted it when she became responsible for conducting the company affairs."

"And these good-hearted fellows come into the office with pennies on a plate and take the dying critter off their hands."

"Actually, the transaction is done by correspondence," Ben clarified. "I don't recall ever seeing or hearing of a face-to-face meeting."

The hairs on the back of Jackson's neck prickled. Never in all his life had he bought or sold anything without looking the other man in the eye. It had never occurred to him that any other way was acceptable. Trust was a good thing, but it only went so far and it was best to back it up with a sure and certain knowledge of who you were dealing with. Conducting business blindly could—and usually did—lead to costly mistakes in judgment. Surely Richard Patterson knew that, had passed the lesson on to Lindsay. "Do you get the impression that Lindsay knows these gentlemen personally?"

"No, sir. I do believe, though, that Mr. Patterson knew them many years ago. However, all of his day-to-day relationships ended with his injury in the accident. He rarely goes anywhere but here and his home."

Jackson saw the seed of reassurance in the answer, but didn't find any sense of ease in it. "Three questions, Ben. Answer them in any order that you'd prefer. Are these businessmen here in New York? Have you tracked down what happens to the businesses they've bought? And are there any transactions currently pending?"

"In the order in which you asked, sir: no, no, and yes."

Ben had picked one helluva time to try a bit of humor. Jackson smiled wryly. "I'd appreciate it if you'd back up your pony and take it through the gate again."

Ben blinked repeatedly and then his mouth formed an O of understanding. "Do all Texans have such wonderful twists of speech?"

"I suppose so," Jackson answered as patiently as he could. "I don't seem to recall anyone ever stopping in their tracks to admire someone's words as unusual, so I have to think that we all speak pretty much the same way."

Ben contemplated this for a moment, then nodded and seemed to resolutely set aside his wayward thoughts. "One of the companies is located in Philadelphia, one in Richmond, one in Charleston, and another in Boston. Looking into what happens to the various properties after their sale would require a great deal of time and some expense. I haven't had the resources to satisfy what has been, to this point, an idle curiosity. As for pending transactions . . . Miss Lindsay has recently sent out letters to all four companies offering them land she holds in St Louis and—"

"That would be the property where the warehouse burned," Jackson mused.

"Yes, sir. Mr. Patterson and she concluded that there were insufficient financial resources to rebuild it. If one of the gentlemen doesn't respond with an offer, she'll let the bank have it. The second property on which she's requested an offer is the bank in Kentucky. I don't know what she thinks to do if an offer isn't tendered on it."

Jackson didn't either and he made himself a mental note to ask her. He'd also ask her why the hell she was doing business not only blind, but over long distances. "Tell me something, Ben," he ventured. "While she waits for the mail to move back and forth between here and the other cities, the value of what she's offering declines even further, doesn't it?"

"That is generally the case, sir."

"Why doesn't she sell the properties to someone here in town? It would be faster, easier, and she'd make more money in the transaction."

"You'll have to ask her, sir," Ben replied. He leaned forward before he added quietly, "I suspect that it's a case in which she doesn't want her dealings to become public knowledge in the community in which she lives."

"In other words, she doesn't want people to know that the MacPhaull horse is lame, blind, and wheezing."

Ben smiled tightly. His gaze darted to the window and he grimaced. "I see Mr. Vanderhagen's carriage drawing up."

Jackson quickly rose to his feet, finished the last of his coffee, put the cup on the tray, and handed the entire service to Ben, saying, "Here, take the coffeepot with you. I don't want that weasel here long enough to have a cup." As the bookkeeper dutifully turned away with his burden, Jackson added, "One more thing, Ben."

He stopped and looked back over his shoulder. "Yes, sir?"

"Actually two things. First I want a list of all the properties currently owned that are consuming rather than producing income. When you're done with that, I want a list of the MacPhaull properties sold in the last three years, the price Lindsay paid for each and what she got out of it when she sold it, as well as the name and address of the buyer. Not just the name of the company, Ben, but the names of the individuals who hold major interests in it. I also want to know the present status of each of those properties they purchased. If they've been sold, I want to know to whom and for how much."

The corners of Ben's mouth tightened. "I expected that you would want that information, sir. I've already begun. Will there be anything else?"

"Naw. I figure that'll keep you busy for a week or two."

"At the very least, sir," Ben said with a taut smile. He started for the door, adding, "I should mention that it's Miss Lindsay's custom to arrive here at nine-thirty."

"Thanks for the warning, Ben."

Jackson raked his fingers through his hair, buttoned his shirtfront, and then found his tie where he'd tossed it aside the night before. Otis Vanderhagen's voice was booming through the outer office as Jackson pulled on his suit coat. Thanks to Benjamin Tipton's honesty, he had a few more answers than he'd had yesterday. If he could get a few out of Vanderhagen in the next thirty minutes, the day could be counted a success. If he could actually get Vanderhagen gone before Lindsay came sweeping through the door, it would be cause for celebration. The less reason he gave her for swinging a fist at him, the easier it was going to be to set things right with her.

"It's good to see that you've taken the helm so quickly and firmly, Stennett," the lawyer declared, advancing into the room, his hand extended, the door standing wide open in his wake. From the other room, Ben glared briefly at the lawyer's back and then turned away to take care of the coffee service.

Jackson noted the bookkeeper's apparent animosity and then, with no other polite choice, shook Vanderhagen's hand and began. "Circumstances haven't allowed for the luxury of wasting time."

"Yes, poor Patterson. So tragic," Vanderhagen wheezed as he dropped down onto the sofa. "But I'm glad that you're a man of clear and decisive purpose. It will make my task this morning much less awkward and more easily concluded."

Jackson eased down into his own chair, asking slowly, "And that task would be?"

Pulling a handkerchief from inside his coat, Vanderhagen began mopping his face as he answered, "I've spoken with Dr. Bernard this morning at MacPhaull House. Although he didn't come right out and say it, I think it prudent to conclude that he doesn't expect Richard to recover from his lapse of yesterday. Under the terms of William MacPhaull's first Will, Richard's death would set into motion the transfer of company management. Henry, Mr. MacPhaull's eldest child and only male heir, would take the helm."

"But Billy's later Will changed all that," Jackson supplied to prod the conversation along. "I own it all and who manages it is my decision."

"Indeed," he said, his voice actually dropping to normal volume. "Which brings me directly to the matter we need to discuss today." He sucked a deep breath that drew his waistcoat up over his girth. He tugged it down, saying, "Mr. Stennet, you have inherited considerable wealth. As the attorney who has represented the interests of the MacPhaull Company for over two decades, I feel that it's my responsibility to see that there exists some mechanism by which the assets are protected should something—God forbid—happen to you."

"You want me to make a Will stipulating . . . what precisely?"

"Do you have any heirs who you feel properly deserve the proceeds of your estate?"

"Let me save you a race around the course, Vanderhagen," Jackson said, feeling precious seconds ticking by. "I have a Will already; legal and proper, drawn up under the laws of the Republic of Texas. In it, I name Billy Weathers—whom you knew as William Lindsay MacPhaull—as my sole heir. Now, my lawyer back home is a meticulous sort of fellow and he insisted on covering all kinds of impossible possibilities. Long story short, Vanderhagen, because Billy's dead and dead men can't inherit, all my property goes to any legal heirs Billy might have."

"The MacPhaull children," Vanderhagen all but sighed. "I assume in equal parts?"

"I'd guess. Since I didn't know Billy had any children, I didn't see a reason to go about dividing things up."

"Do you intend to modify the bequeath? Or are you planning to let it stand as it is presently worded?"

"I think it's a mite early for deciding something like that," Jackson countered, wondering just how Vanderhagen would divide the assets if given the opportunity. "I'll let you know what I've done in the end."

"I'd be glad to see to the creation of any legal documentation you require. A codicil is all that would be necessary. It's a very simple thing to draw up."

"Like I said, I'll let you know what I decide."

Vanderhagen apparently had enough sense to recognize that he wasn't going to get anywhere by pressing the matter and so he nodded, appeared to mull a moment, and then said, "Regardless of your decision on the particulars of the matter, Mr. Stennett, I'm relieved to hear that you intend to do right by William's children. It's a great weight off my heart and shoulders."

The tone of his voice suggested that he was preparing to leave, forcing Jackson to delay him by asking, "Is there anything else you'd like to talk about? I'd hate for you to haul around any more weight than necessary. As the company attorney, do you need a copy of Billy's Will?"

"You're a good man as well as purposeful, Mr. Stennett," he responded, wiggling forward on the sofa so that he could effectively leverage his body off it and upright. Puffing from the exertion, he mopped his brow again and added, "No, there's nothing else I need from you. I secured the copy of William's Will from Miss Lindsay this morning while I was at the house. I'll be filing the appropriate documents with the court for the legal acknowledgment of your ownership."

"Well," Jackson drawled, leaning back in the chair and steepling his fingers, "if you wouldn't mind holding up for just a minute, I have a couple of questions for you, Mr. Vanderhagen."

"Yes?" he asked, clearly wary about having the shoe put on his foot.

"I have some decisions to make regarding the company assets and it would help if I knew the terms of Richard

Patterson's Will. Do you happen to know them? Do you know if he plans to leave anything to Lindsay?"

The wariness evaporated. He stepped closer to the desk and—though it seemed impossible—actually said quietly, "I can't discuss the terms in any specific sense; attorney–client privilege, you understand. I think you may make reasonable assumptions. He values loyal service and the memories of those he's cared for in the course of his life. He is, however, above all else, a compassionate man who remembers his own beginnings and those who haven't been as fortunate in life as he."

"Thank you," Jackson offered, not liking the answer, but accepting that the choices were Richard Patterson's and not his to make. "Second question: How long is the court going to take before it formally recognizes my right to make business decisions and execute them?"

"Getting such matters through probate usually takes some time; months at best," Vanderhagen replied, moving away now that the topic had moved into a less sensitive area. "Were the heirs to contest the provisions of their father's second Will, you might have some difficulties in conducting business, but Miss Lindsay assures me that she has no intention of standing in your way and that she'll execute decisions in your behalf until such time as the court formally recognizes your right to do so."

Lindsay could make his life a living hell. And she would if she had the money to fight him. Thank God she didn't. Of course, Lindsay wasn't the only card in the deck. "Have you said anything to Henry about the second Will and the unexpected change in his circumstances? Have you said anything to Agatha?"

"My responsibility and primary concern is for the continuation of the MacPhaull Company, Mr. Stennett," Vanderhagen explained, mopping his brow again. "Henry isn't a particularly intelligent or farsighted man, but he does understand the power to be had in getting access to the company coffers. Agatha will see that in Henry losing control of the company, she'll be losing an ally with similar attitudes toward money. Neither one of them will have any comprehension of the costs involved in contesting their father's Will. I'm willing to let Miss Lindsay inform and deal with her brother and sister. Should either Henry or Agatha come to me wanting to battle you for control, I'll do my best to dissuade them from the course."

"And if you can't? Or if they go to another attorney?"

"In either situation, I would hope that you would feel comfortable in allowing me to represent the interests of the MacPhaull Company in court."

Snakes weren't always bad, Jackson mused. They were good to have around for varmint control. Still, the idea of deliberately putting his fate in Vanderhagen's hands didn't set well. "It'd sure be easier just to shoot Henry and be done with it," Jack observed dryly.

"You can't!"

Clearly Otis Vanderhagen thought the idea had been seriously suggested. Just as Ben had taken the threat to his tongue. Sweet Jesus. What kind of world did these people live in? What kind of people did they know? "Just kidding, Mr. Vanderhagen."

"Oh," he breathed, his entire body sagging downward. He recovered enough to wipe the rivulets of perspiration from his face. Stuffing the handkerchief back into his pocket, he managed a weak smile and said, "One hears stories about Texans, you understand."

Jackson nodded slowly. "One hears them about New Yorkers, too."

Vanderhagen puffed up, yanked his waistcoat down, said coolly, "Mr. Stennett," and then spun on his heel—an amazing feat of balance for a man of his proportions, Jackson thought as the lawyer half-waddled, half-rolled toward the door.

"Good morning again, Miss Lindsay," he boomed as he crossed the threshold. "And good day, again."

Jackson winced and hung his head, softly swearing at his miserable luck. So much for keeping Lindsay from knowing that he'd had a chance to meet with Vanderhagen. He wondered if she'd believe him if he told her that the subject of Richard's Will had never come up. Maybe it would be a kindness to keep her from learning that, while she might get a small bequeath, the bulk of Patterson's estate would be going to charity. Then again, maybe not. Honesty might hurt sometimes, but it was always a better course than lying.

"What stories does one hear about New Yorkers, Mr. Stennett?"

He looked up to find Lindsay standing in the doorway. She was wearing a pale blue dress today and a matching pelisse. The sunlight streaming in the office window glinted off the golden curls peeking out from under the crown of her bonnet. He'd have thought her an angel from on high if it hadn't been for the cool resolution in her eyes.

If a fight was unavoidable, he reminded himself, sometimes it was smarter to fight over something that didn't matter rather than something that did. "Well, I'll tell you," he drawled, rising from the chair. "Mostly one hears that, aside from taking everything said quite literally and having no real sense of humor, they'd sell their own mothers for a dollar."

"Actually, the going rate is three dollars," she countered with the smallest of smiles. "Mothers are in short supply these days."

"Good ones even more so, I'd guess," he ventured, wondering why she'd decided not to take offense. "A man could probably get five dollars for one of those."

She chuckled softly and nodded.

He saw in her softening an opening, and he seized it. "Lindsay, about yesterday afternoon," he began.

She held up her gloved hand, her palm toward him. "Let's not talk about it. It had been a horrible day and neither one of us was at our best. Today's a new beginning and I propose that we not start it by looking back."

"If that's the way you want it," he acceded, feeling an odd mixture of disappointment and relief.

"Henry sent a message to the house this morning," she said, her manner easy and light. "Agatha told him about Richard's collapse. He's planning to come by the office at ten to discuss with me the transfer of management. I sent a return note with the messenger, asking him and Edith to dinner this evening and suggesting that we discuss the matter then."

Ten o'clock? Damnation. "Think he'll hold off?"

"I rather doubt it."

"Then we need to be somewhere else when he gets here," Jackson announced, picking his hat up from the corner of the desk with one hand while closing the ledger with the other. "I'm not about to give him the advantage of picking either the time or the place for a showdown. Where would you like to go?"

"I have a social call to make. The junior bookkeeper, Jeb Rutherford, and his wife had their first child very late last night. Jeb sent word to the house this morning. I've made gifts for Lucy and the baby and want to deliver them in person."

Baby. Fragments of crushing memory stabbed at his awareness. Jackson resolutely blinked them away. Settling his hat on his head, he observed, "Seems it was a busy morning at your house, what with messengers bringing notes from Henry and Jeb, and Vanderhagen snooting around."

"That's only half of it," she said lightly, shaking her head—whether in amusement or utter resignation, Jackson couldn't tell. "Richard's cook, Emile, also arrived this morning, vowing that only he can adequately prepare food for him. When I left, he and Primrose were standing in the kitchen, back-to-back, holding rolling pins and preparing to count off paces.

"Then I passed Agatha on the front walk as I was leaving. She spent the night at Henry's and doesn't know if her calendar is free for dinner at home this evening or not. She has a dress fitting at two and an appointment with a jeweler at four."

"A jeweler," Jackson repeated quietly. "Where does Agatha think the money for jewelry is going to come from?"

Lindsay raised both hands in a gesture of surrender. "I have no idea and I didn't pause to ask. I simply wanted to come to the office."

Suddenly he understood the way Lindsay was feeling about it all. You could either scream for nothing or you could stand back and see the utter ridiculousness of the whole thing. At least the latter course offered some degree of entertainment in what was otherwise a very frustrating situation. Interesting that she'd come to him, though. Why? "So you're saying that you see me as a calm haven of sensibility and reason?"

"I don't think I'd put it quite that way, Mr. Stennett," she countered, her smile tight. "Perhaps more along the lines of seeing you as being the lesser of all the present evils."

And one of those evils was Henry, due to arrive at any moment. "Well, evil man that I am," he rejoined, pulling a sheet of parchment from a desk drawer, "before we leave here, I want you to write a note to Agatha. Ben can see that it's delivered. Tell Agatha that she'll clear her calendar and be at dinner this evening or she'll come home to find the locks changed and her belongings on the street."

"You can't do that!"

"Yes, I can. And I will. Evil does as evil pleases." He hefted up the accounting book and started toward the door, saying as he passed her, "I'm taking the ledger to Ben. Get busy and write that note so we can get the hell out of here."

He was back in seconds, returning through the doorway to the sight of Lindsay leaning over the desk and scribbling away. It was a wondrous combination of curves and draped fabric.

"There will be an ungodly scene at dinner, you know," she advised him as she continued to write.

Jackson blinked and swallowed. "Which, in accordance with the MacPhaull code of conduct, I will ignore." *And hopefully more effectively than I am your backside. Lord have mercy.*

"I'll wager you ten dollars that you can't."

What on earth were they talking about? Oh, yes, ignoring Agatha's scene. "You're on. Any other bets you want to make about tonight?"

She straightened, holding the note in one hand and gently wafting her other above it to dry the ink. "Another ten says that you contemplate killing Henry before dessert is served."

"Collecting would require me to be honest," he pointed

out. "I could lie and tell you it never crossed my mind and you couldn't prove otherwise. Not a very smart bet."

"All right," she countered confidently. "Then my second ten dollars says that you'll actually try to kill him before dessert. How's that?"

"It's your money," he replied with a shrug. "I think I ought to tell you, though, that I don't exactly have a hair-trigger temper. It takes a lot to push me over the line."

"Be that as it may, Mr. Stennett, I know my brother and sister and just what behavior they're capable of." She folded the parchment in half. "I'm putting my faith and money on them."

"Nudging them along isn't allowed," he clarified as she handed him the note.

"I won't have to."

She walked past him and the scent of roses drifted in her wake. It occurred to him that she was certainly less prickly today than she had been yesterday. He followed her, wishing he knew what had led to the slight change in her manner. Whatever it was, he hoped its effects were permanent. Passing sixty days in the company of a woman like this one wouldn't be all that hard to endure.

"The morning mail just arrived, sir."

"Thank you, Ben." He accepted the packet and then handed Lindsay's note to her bookkeeper. "Please see that this is delivered immediately to Miss Agatha at MacPhaull House. And if Mr. Henry MacPhaull should make an appearance here at the office, please extend our regrets at missing him, and tell him that we look forward to seeing him and his lovely wife at dinner this evening."

Ben nodded in acknowledgment and Jackson led the way to the door. Lindsay murmured her thanks when he opened it and then proceeded him out onto the walkway. Her small black carriage sat waiting for them, her driver sitting in the box, reins in black-gloved hands. She paused, looked back over her shoulder, and called to Ben, "If there's an emergency, we'll be at Jeb and Lucy's."

"I hope we haven't been too long, John," she called up to her driver as she started toward the waiting vehicle. "It seems that there is always some small detail that can't wait attention."

He smiled down at her, opened his mouth to reply, but got no further than that.

"I distinctly recall having sent a message that I would arrive at the office this morning at ten."

The voice was male and haughtily indignant. Jackson saw the driver look away, saw Lindsay stop in her tracks, grab a deep breath, and then slowly turn in the direction from which the voice had come.

A man only slightly taller and less rotund than Otis Vanderhagen stood a mere arm's length away from Lindsay. He wore a finely tailored suit, his graying temples accentuated by the blackness of his bowler hat and the silver threads of his embroidered vest. Fair skin marked him as a man who lived his life indoors, the thin red veins coloring his patrician nose as a man who liked strong spirits. His chin was lifted high so that he surveyed the world from what he obviously considered a position of superiority.

A message that he'd call? Then this had to be Henry, Billy's eldest child and only son. Jackson gauged the distance between himself and Lindsay, between Lindsay and her brother.

"And you did so," Lindsay said calmly, "on the presumption that I would be here and that a meeting was convenient to me. Unfortunately, by the time your note arrived at the house, I'd already sent one to my junior bookkeeper, Jeb, promising to call on his wife and newborn child this morning. I mentioned that in the note I sent back with your messenger. Did you not receive it?"

"I did," Henry replied, cocking a brow reproachfully. "That's why I've come earlier than I'd originally planned. There are some matters we must discuss, Lindsay."

She squared her shoulders and managed a tight smile. "Now is not the time, Henry. I'm sorry."

Henry went on as though she hadn't said a word. "My architect is demanding payment for his design and for the purchase of building materials. I want a bank draft so the project can begin."

Jackson watched Lindsay's jaw tighten, watched her

draw a long, deep breath. He glanced over at Henry, but the man seemed oblivious to his presence.

"I'm sorry, Henry," Lindsay said again, more slowly and clearly than before, "but that's impossible. As I've explained before, recent business developments have—"

"I'm not Agatha," Henry interrupted with a huff, "and I will not tolerate being put on an insultingly meager budget. I am the heir of MacPhaull Company and I won't be denied what is rightfully mine. Neither will I live in a home beneath the standards that accompany my social position."

Jackson cocked a brow. Apparently the man had absolutely no understanding of reality; he didn't see that his social position was no more substantial than a wisp of smoke and that his financial resources were all but gone. How could a man go through life wearing blinders? Jackson wondered. It was going to be one helluva shock for ol' Henry when he learned that he wasn't the heir of all that he imagined to exist.

Lindsay's smile looked painfully taut as she said, "Standing on a public walkway is no place to discuss business or family matters, Henry. I've invited you and Edith—"

"Never mind," Henry replied with a dismissive wave of his hand. "I'll take care of the matter myself next week. Agatha told me all about The Buzzard's collapse. It's long past due and welcome news."

Lindsay's hands balled into fists at her sides and her blue eyes flashed with furious fire. Her lips compressed into a thin line, she glared at her brother and said nothing. Jackson stood planted where he was, torn between wanting to pound some sense and good manners into Henry and respecting Lindsay's right to deal with her brother in her own way.

"I want you to clear your belongings out of the office, Lindsay," her brother went on blithely. "And give Ben his notice. I'll be taking charge two weeks from today. I'd do it sooner, but I have social plans that I don't want to cancel or miss."

"There are circumstances," Lindsay countered coolly, "of which you're unaware, Henry. But as I said before, now is neither the time nor the place to properly discuss them. I think that—"

Henry snorted and rolled his eyes. "I'm the heir of the MacPhaull Company. *I don't have to care what you think*."

Lindsay sighed, nodded once, and then half-turned to gesture toward Jackson, saying as she did, "Henry, I'd like to intro—"

"All the brainless brawn in the world isn't going to keep me from taking control," Henry said, his smile confident, his gaze raking Jackson from hat to boots and then looking away dismissively. "Two weeks, Lindsay. No, make it three; there's a boat race that slipped my mind. Three weeks and then you and your household of misfits and cripples will be the ones on a miserly allowance. What a delightful change that will be."

With that pronouncement, he turned on his heel and swaggered away. Lindsay chewed on the inside of her lower lip as she watched him go.

Studying her, marveling at her grace and fortitude, Jackson quietly drawled, "I don't much care for your brother."

Still watching Henry's progress down the walkway, she answered, "I suspect that very few people do."

"And he doesn't have the slightest inkling about the company's finances."

Lindsay turned her head to look at him. Arching a slim brow, she smiled ruefully. "I recall having mentioned that to you yesterday."

"That you did," Jack freely admitted, stepping to the carriage door and opening it. "Does he always speak to you like that?"

"I must say that it was a fairly typical exchange." She accepted his hand and assistance into the vehicle. "My sincerest apologies for having subjected you to the unpleasantness of it all."

"Seems to me that if anyone needs to apologize for anything," he said, settling onto the seat opposite her, "it's your brother for his lack of manners. And me, for not shaking some into him."

Her smile trembled and she looked away to take another fortifying breath. Staring out the uncovered carriage window, she said blithely, "The air's a little heavy this morning. I think it may rain within the next day or so, don't you?"

Jackson nodded and sat back, knowing with absolute certainty that Lindsay MacPhaull had never had a champion of any sort, and that she didn't have the vaguest idea of what she was supposed to do with one.

He'd had a champion once; a brother, a friend, a fellow rowdy. They'd laughed together, cried together, and, from time to time, even pounded fists on each other. But no matter what, they'd always been there for each other when they were needed. His first and deepest lessons about loyalty and friendship had been learned at Daniel's side. And when Daniel died, the pain had been immeasurable, all consuming, and so deep that he'd wanted to die, too. He'd been truly orphaned that day. It still hurt to think about it. And so Jackson looked out the window and thought about the day that lay ahead.

Jesus. Damnation, he was a glutton for pain this morning. He was on his way to congratulate a man he didn't know on the birth of his first child. He was going to see Jeb's wife holding their child and remember how he'd once stood at a bedside and watched the shadow of death steal over his happiness. He'd remember the pain of loving and losing, of being utterly powerless to change the course of life and death, of how his pleas and offerings had been worthless in the eyes of God.

But, Jackson sternly reminded himself, he'd traveled a lot of roads since that dark day. He'd learned how to hide the bruises of his heart. He'd mutter something appropriate right at the first and then get as far away as he could. He'd think about the MacPhaull Company ledgers instead of his ghosts. He would pretend he didn't know the lifelong, inescapable heartache Jeb Rutherford was courting.

CHAPTER SIX

*L*INDSAY STARED OUT the window and desperately tried to collect her scattered wits. It had been a shock to walk into the office and find Jackson Stennett seated behind Richard's desk. She'd resented the ease with which he occupied the space, the books open before him, and the scent of Richard's shaving soap lingering in the air around him. Her world had been rudely upended by this stranger a mere twenty-four hours ago and he didn't have the good grace to pretend to be even the slightest bit uncomfortable about it all. Neither had he shown any hesitancy in getting on with the task of dismantling what little order there was in her small universe.

And yet, despite every good reason to loathe the man, despite her determination to remain disdainfully aloof, she'd found herself bantering with him in the office and then reassured by his presence during the ugly confrontation with Henry. His apology for not having taken Henry to task for his behavior had been as thrilling as it was startling. Even now, her heart was still racing.

What was it about him that so disarmed her? What was

it about herself that allowed him to do so? The answers were important, she told herself. She needed to keep a clear head and sense of purpose, to keep a distance between them not only for the sake of her own financial survival but also that of those who were her responsibility to care for.

The key to keeping a safe distance, she quickly decided, lay in learning all she could about the man, in discovering how and why he thought and behaved as he did. She knew that Richard would encourage her to ferret out a vulnerability that could be used to her advantage. As always, part of her felt guilty at the manipulative course. The more pragmatic side of her remembered all the discussions she and Richard had ever had on the subject of business ethics. Richard maintained that all was fair in love and war and business. She didn't like it, but as Richard had frequently pointed out, it was the reality in which they had to survive. Since Richard wasn't able to employ the strategy himself this time, she had no choice but to undertake it on her own.

"It would seem, Mr. Stennett, that you've had some experience at being the lord of the manor," Lindsay observed, as the carriage made its way into the crowded, noisy stream of city traffic.

He gave her an offhanded shrug while replying, "In Texas, every man is a lord."

It was a diplomatic statement if she'd ever heard one. It was also evasive. "But I doubt that every man in Texas commands with the ease and grace that you do," she pressed with equal diplomacy. "Your instructions to Ben were masterful. There are very few in New York who could do as well. How did you come by the skill, Mr. Stennett?"

He studied her for a moment and then said quietly, "My mother grew up with a certain degree of wealth. Then she married my father and while his wealth trickled away, her patrician manner remained. She always saw her sons as growing into men of power and privilege and saw to it that we were taught how to exercise it properly."

"Do your brothers excel at it as you do?"

His gaze went to the world passing outside the carriage window. "I had only one. Daniel. He died when I was thirteen. He was breaking horses and they broke him instead."

"I'm sorry," Lindsay said softly, sincerely.

"It was a long time ago."

But not long enough that he'd forgotten the heartache. "I can't imagine any pain worse than that of losing a child. It must have been difficult for your parents."

"They were already gone," he answered, his gaze coming back to hers. The sadness that had tinged his voice in speaking of his brother was replaced by a matter-of-factness. "My mother to a snake bite. My father in a comanchero attack two years before that. Texas is a hard life. Pretty much the only guarantee it gives you is that you'll learn how to dig graves."

And he'd learned how as a child. It was a miracle that he could smile at all. "Why did you stay then?" Lindsay asked. "Wasn't there family elsewhere to take you in when you found yourself alone?"

Again he shrugged. "My mother's family disowned her when she married beneath her. My father's was never close and the winds scattered them all. And I wasn't really alone anyway." He smiled and the corners of his eyes crinkled. "Billy took me in and managed, against considerable opposition, to whip me into a fairly decent man."

"What a very sad life you've had, Mr. Stennett. I'm sorry."

"Sad?" Jackson Stennett repeated, his brow cocked. "I've never considered it that. With the good comes the bad. It's the same for everyone, no matter where they live or how much they've got. That's just the way life is. You remember the good times and try to learn something from the bad."

"And what have you learned from the bad?"

"Not to get too attached to the folks who pass through my life," he answered readily. "It makes standing over the grave a mite easier. What have you learned from your hard times?"

It was one thing to ask questions of someone. It was entirely something else to have someone ask them of you. "I don't know that I've ever given it much thought," she lied. "It seems as though there's always another crisis to be faced and resolved. Having to look forward doesn't allow one to look back very often."

He nodded and then *tsk*ed before saying, "It doesn't make for much of a life either."

She heard the unmistakable notes of censure in his comment. "Oh, I disagree, Mr. Stennett. There's a great deal of satisfaction to be found in meeting one's obligations and in fulfilling one's responsibilities."

"That's admirable. Definitely."

The unmistakable tone of derision edged his words. Anger shot through her. "But?"

"But nothing."

"What you're so artlessly trying to avoid saying," Lindsay persisted, "is that you see my determination to meet my responsibilities as a lesson learned from my father's having run away from his. You're absolutely correct, Mr. Stennett. While I don't know much about his other personal characteristics, I can at least assure you that when it comes to cowardice, I'm not—nor will I ever be—my father's daughter."

She regretted the outburst the instant it was done. It was too late to call the words back, though; too late to consider what they revealed about her. Stennett studied her, and rather than bear his scrutiny, Lindsay looked out the window of the carriage. Now was a fine time, she silently groused, to wish that she'd listened to her mother and cultivated the self-discipline necessary to keep her emotions carefully hidden. The controlling of such impulses had been just one among many of her mother's expectations that Lindsay had failed to meet. The one thing she *had* learned well was the value of a timely apology.

Lindsay turned back and met his gaze squarely. "I regret my remarks, Mr. Stennett," she offered with every bit of poise she could muster. "It was unseemly and indifferent to your feelings."

His lips parted, but he apparently reconsidered whatever he had been about to say. After a slight pause, he said, "You know, the road between us seems to get a little rocky when we talk about Billy. I'm thinking that it's a subject we'd be better off to avoid whenever possible."

"It might be the wisest course," she ventured, "but given our circumstances, do you really think that's possible?"

"I think," he answered, exhaling hard and long, "we

ought to agree to disagree on the man's personal qualities and not discuss them again. As for the mess he's left us to sort out, we'd do best by dealing with the specific business issues in a purely businesslike way. Can we do that?"

"I'm certainly willing to try." And more than willing to find a less distressing subject of conversation than the one they'd been pursuing. "So what do you think of New York so far, Mr. Stennett?"

"It's big and tall and packed close together," he said, once again watching the world outside the carriage. "I can kinda appreciate now how a cow feels when squeezed in a chute. And then there's the fact that a man can't see enough of the sky, the air burns your lungs, and you couldn't hope to hear a prairie chicken warble over the general din of so many people doing so many things all at once."

In short, he detested her city. How provincial. How irritating. "I don't believe we have any prairie chickens in New York."

"They're smart birds." He seemed to hear the undercurrent of derision in his comment and quickly added, "Tasty, too."

The belated effort didn't do much to dull the barb, but in the spirit of accommodation, she let him sidestep without challenge. "I'll have to see if Primrose can find you one at the market. How do you prefer to have it prepared?"

Jackson wasn't at all sure that he'd want to eat any prairie chicken that turned up this far east. The odds were good, however, that one wouldn't and so he could afford to be open to the idea. "Baked or fried; either way's fine," he said as the carriage angled out of the flow of traffic and began to slow. For the first time since climbing into the vehicle, he looked out the window with actual interest. The carriage was drawing to a halt in front of a large, squarish, wooden structure badly in need of a new coat of whitewash. The numbers painted in black above the entrance, while only slightly darker than the surrounding wood, were still visible.

"I remember seeing that number on the holdings list," he said, opening the door and stepping out in one smooth motion. He extended his hand to assist Lindsay, asking, "Do you own this building?"

"Yes," she said, picking up two gaily wrapped packages from the seat with one hand and putting her other hand in his. "My grandfather bought it, making it one of the oldest properties we have in the portfolio. Though in recent years, it's become a bit costly to maintain. And one can only charge so much for rents and still have a clear conscience, so the profit to expense ratio has been narrowing. Richard's suggested that we should begin thinking about selling it before age converts it from an asset into a liability."

"So why haven't you sold it?" he asked, thinking that it was the most animated response she'd given since they'd left the office. But then it was a business rather than personal subject. It didn't take a genius to know that Lindsay found the former far less threatening than the latter.

"I haven't been able to find a buyer willing to meet my price," she said, standing beside him on the walkway, her hand still in his as she looked up at him. He could feel her pulse racing in her fingertips. Was that business or personal? he wondered.

"Once the Panic ends, though," she went on, easing her hand from his and exhaling, "the market will turn and you'll have no problem disposing of it. I'd recommend that you put the proceeds toward the cost of getting the coal mine up and running again."

Sometimes her business sense was brilliant. And sometimes he wondered how Richard could have slept at night knowing he was letting her make the decisions. "Judging by the books," Jackson said, "the mine is your chief source of income. It seems to me that getting it up and running can't wait until the Panic ends."

She arched a brow and her smile was knowing. "You've learned quite a bit in a very short amount of time."

Had she really been testing him? The notion amused him. "While there's a difference between buying and selling cattle and buying and selling businesses and property, the basic principles are the same. It's a matter of opening the books, lining up the assets and the liabilities, and knowing what your priorities are."

"And the first one is to make a profit," she added, turning toward the steps of the building.

"Profits are all well and good," he countered, taking the packages from her so that she could manage her skirts with both hands, "but they don't mean much if you're spending more than you're making."

"True."

He cupped her elbow in his free hand as they started up the stairs.

"Well, hello, Lindsay. It's been simply ages since I've seen you."

He felt her start, felt her body go taut. She took a quick, deep breath and pasted a false smile on her face just before she turned in the direction from which the voice had come. "Winifred," she said, her voice musical and light and belying her tension. "It's always a unique pleasure to see you. How are you?"

"I'm quite well, thank you," replied a rather large-boned woman in a bright yellow dress and a hat of matching feathers. Her gaze flicked between Lindsay and Jackson and her smile took on a sardonic edge. "I'm sure you've heard that Edward was made vice president of the bank last year. Little Edgar is the first in his class and Mrs. Glasgow says that Myrtle is the best harp student she's ever had. And how are you doing, Lindsay?" She pointedly glanced between Jackson and Lindsay again, clearly expecting a polite and customary introduction.

"Very well, Winifred. Thank you for asking. It was as lovely as always to see you."

Pleasant, musical and light and deliberately cutting. Lindsay didn't like this woman at all. Why? Jackson tilted his head so that the shadow of his hat brim concealed his eyes and his interest in the puzzle.

Lindsay turned away, obviously intending to continue her course. Winifred arched a brow, then hastily said, "We're gathering at the boathouse this Saturday afternoon to watch the races. Would you care to bring your new companion and join us?"

Jackson sucked on the inside of his cheek. *New* companion? There was a story here and he was the only one who didn't know it. And Lindsay was determined to get him away before Winifred shared it with him.

She paused just long enough to look over her shoulder and give Winifred another false smile. "I'm afraid that we have other commitments. Perhaps some other time, Winifred." She turned away again, adding offhandedly, "Please give my regards to Edward."

Jackson touched the brim of his hat in a quick parting gesture, knowing that Winifred probably missed seeing it; her gaze was raking him up and down, making him feel like a prize bull up for auction.

"What other commitments?" Jackson whispered as they went up the steps and Winifred all but ran down the sidewalk.

"I don't know," Lindsay answered, "but I'm sure we'll think of something."

"You two don't like each other, do you?"

"No, we don't. And it's a very long story."

One she clearly had no intention of telling him. He suspected that it probably had something to do with her *old* companion. Maybe Winifred and Lindsay had once battled for the affections of banker Edward and Winifred had won. Which, of course, meant that Edward was deaf, dumb, and blind, and so not worth having in the first place. "Why did she invite us to the boathouse?"

"Because she thinks that I'm stupid," Lindsay said hotly, coming to a halt in front of a door just inside the entrance and beside a narrow set of interior stairs leading to the upper floors. "And because she thinks that I'm naively trusting."

Jackson reached over her shoulder, gently rapped his knuckles against the panel, and then drew back. Lindsay certainly wasn't stupid. As for naively trusting . . . The jury was still out on that one. But even a deaf, dumb, and blind man would have known that the memories Winifred had stirred up were painful ones and that Lindsay's scars were thin and tender.

She'd said she didn't look back at the bad times, and while he'd suspected the claim had been a lie, he knew it for certain now. Lindsay was looking back and remembering right this moment. What lesson was she mulling? he wondered.

The door opened, abruptly ending his musing on the subject. The powdery scent of newborn baby wafted past the tall, angular young man happily greeting Lindsay. Jackson clenched his teeth and swallowed hard. He'd gotten through this ordeal before and he'd get through it again. It had been a while since the last time, he reminded himself. It might be easier than he thought. At least he hoped so as he smiled and shook the hand of the proud father Lindsay introduced as Jebediah Rutherford.

FIRST HAD COME the exclamations over how beautiful and fair the baby was. Then Lucy had opened the packages from Lindsay, first protesting the necessity of gifts at all and then gasping words of gratitude and reverently trailing her fingers over the fine crochet stitches of the blanket Lindsay had made the baby and the shawl she'd made for Lucy. And in the course of things, Lindsay put the encounter with Winifred out of her mind and began to relax.

She noticed that the same couldn't be said for Jackson Stennett as Lucy wrapped the baby in the new blanket. The Texan stood on the far side of the tiny apartment with Jeb, looking pained—almost as though he had something caught high in his throat and couldn't get it swallowed.

"Would you like to hold her?" Lucy asked.

Lindsay accepted the squirming, plump bundle, saying, "She's beautiful, Lucy. Truly beautiful. A tiny little angel."

Jeb came forward. "You should have a baby of your own, Miss Lindsay."

Out of the corner of her eye, Lindsay watched Stennett hesitate and then stoically follow in Jeb's wake. It was obvious that he was uncomfortable being there and she couldn't help wondering why he was behaving so oddly. He'd glanced at the baby when they'd come in, offered a polite comment on it being pretty, and then retreated as fast and as far as civility and the room would allow.

The baby smacked its lips and then began to fidget in earnest, interrupting her musing. The fair pink face began to slowly darken as the brow wrinkled. Lindsay lightly patted the well-padded bottom, hoping the contact would ease the infant's apparent distress.

"Yes, Miss Lindsay," Lucy chimed in. "You should have a whole houseful of your own babies."

"Given my circumstances, I don't think that there's much hope of that," she countered, smiling at the new parents. "And it's probably for the best. I'm not at all sure that I'd be a very good mother." Unbidden, an image of her own mother came to her; tight, thin lips and a hard frown, the air around her resonant with words of anger and condemnation. Lindsay instinctively drew a deep breath and held it.

Jeb saved her, his voice calling her from the past and into the present. "My mama always says that you learn just as much from watching someone do something wrong as you do in seeing it done right. I think you'd do just fine, Miss Lindsay."

Bless Jeb. He'd heard the tales of her mother and he'd known just what she'd been thinking. She smiled at him gratefully and wished she had his faith in her ability to surmount her upbringing. The baby chose that moment to emit a deafening, bellowing cry. Lindsay looked down, startled. The sweet-tempered cherub was no more. In her arms she held a decidedly unhappy bundle of demand. She quickened the tempo of her patting. It had no effect and so she made little shushing sounds that produced equally ineffective results.

"See?" she said, giving Lucy a chagrined and weak smile. "I'd be a terrible mother. I can't make her quit crying."

"She's hungry."

Jackson Stennett's simple pronouncement was the first words he'd spoken since his earlier retreat. The quiet confidence in it prompted her to look up at him and ask, "And how do you know that?"

He shrugged. "Calves bawl for two reasons; they've either lost track of their mamas and they're scared or they're hungry."

Lindsay had no idea whether or not he was right, but did understand that if he was, there was nothing she could do in either case. She handed the child back into Lucy's arms.

"Do you have any children of your own, Mr. Stennett?" Lucy asked, draping the new shawl over both her shoulder and the crying baby cradled in the crook of her arm. Her free hand disappeared beneath the cover.

"No, ma'am," the Texan answered, his gaze discreetly fastened on the wall behind the settee and just above Lindsay's head.

"Well, I've been praying that Lindsay will find a husband," Lucy said as the baby's cries abruptly ceased. "If you don't mind, I'll ask the Good Lord to bless you and your wife with children."

He nodded, but kept his gaze fixed on the wall. Lindsay saw the pulse pounding in his temples, could see the tightness of his jaw and the difficulty with which he breathed and swallowed. "Much obliged, ma'am," he said tightly.

Lindsay felt as though her heart had been struck. Realization and understanding came with the blow. Jackson Stennett had once had a child. She knew it in her bones. And it had been lost, placed in a little grave beside all the others he'd had to dig in his life. And standing there watching others hold a newborn had brought back his memories of it all. She'd been right in her earlier observations. He was in pain.

"We should be going and let you and the baby rest," Lindsay said, rising, determined to spare Jackson any further suffering. "Jeb, whenever you think they can manage without you, come back to the office. But not until then, understood?"

"Thank you, Miss Lindsay," he said. "And thank you for the pretty blanket and the shawl. It wasn't necessary, but they're very much appreciated."

She placed her hand on her employee's forearm. "It was my pleasure to make and give them, Jeb." She gave him a quick and friendly pat before turning to Lucy and adding, "If you need anything, anything at all, please ask. I'd be happy to do whatever I can."

"I will, Miss Lindsay," Lucy answered politely. "Thank you for coming today."

Jackson Stennett offered his own parting pleasantries,

clapped his hat on his head, and followed Lindsay out the apartment door. He got to the outside door first, wordlessly opened it for her, and just as silently followed her out onto the sidewalk.

The carriage was nowhere in sight. Lindsay looked up and down the street. "My driver apparently had to move on and is circling the block. He should return for us shortly."

"Sounds reasonable," Jackson remarked, expelling a long breath as he stared unseeingly at the buildings on the other side of the street. God, didn't the memories ever fade? Didn't the pain ever go completely away? Was he ever going to be able to look at a new mother, at the baby in her arms, and not remember what he'd had and lost? No, he answered himself. He'd failed them, and forever remembering, forever aching was his penance. He'd earned it.

Lindsay watched the shadows of pain pass over Jackson's features and her uncertainty increased with each passing second of silence. She didn't dare make any comments about the Rutherfords or their baby. To do so would be cruel. "I didn't realize that you're a married man, Mr. Stennett," she said in a desperate effort to end her own tension. "You've neglected to mention that there's a Mrs. Stennett."

He shrugged. "That's because there isn't one."

"Then why did you let Lucy think that you were married?" she asked, and then suddenly saw the blunder in taking the course of conversation she had. If there had been a child lost, then it was likely that the wife and mother had been lost as well. Dear God, what had happened to her good sense? Heat fanned across her cheeks, even as her stomach went leaden cold.

"One, because, while I don't hold with praying to get what you want," he answered, studying the buildings across the crowded street, "I understand that some people do and that they honestly believe it will work. If Lucy Rutherford wants to pray, I figure there's no harm in letting her have her sense of working toward a good end." His gaze came to her. "And two, I figured that if I mentioned that I wasn't married, Lucy'd be hitching my name to yours in her prayers the very next time she got down on her knees."

"And we aren't the least bit suited for one another," Lindsay quickly added.

"No, we aren't. I'm not about to live in this city and I can't, in my wildest dreams, imagine you living on a ranch in Texas." Looking over her shoulder at the apartment house, he sighed and added, "It's no place for fragile flowers."

Lindsay considered her options. She could pretend she didn't notice his pain and blithely chatter away about something utterly trivial and meaningless in the hope of distracting his thoughts. Or she could be honest and give him a chance to share the burden he so obviously bore. There was kindness in both courses. Which way should she go?

The decision was made for her when Jackson asked, "Didn't I see a coal stove in Jeb and Lucy's apartment?"

"Yes, why?" she replied, seeing John bring her carriage around the corner and waving to him. He wasn't going to be able to maneuver the carriage to stop precisely in front of them. They were going to have to walk a half block down to meet it.

"That's how the building's heated, isn't it? By coal stoves in each apartment?"

"Yes, but it's too warm now for anyone to use the stove for heating. Just cooking. The carriage will come to the walk a bit—"

"Well," he interrupted, "either someone's got one stoked way too high with the flue closed or there's a fire in the back apartment."

Lindsay whirled about. Thick black smoke roiled from around the edges of a window on the ground floor at the rear of her building. "Oh my God!" she cried, instantly gathering her skirts and starting forward.

Jackson caught her arm and pulled her back, saying, "Get in the carriage and I'll go see." He released her and quickly strode toward the ominous clouds.

Lindsay was right on his heels, her hem well above her ankles as she all but ran to keep up with him.

"I thought I told you to go to the carriage."

"I don't listen very well."

"Lindsay," he growled, taking her hand and drawing

them both to a halt midway down the side of the building.
"I meant what I—"

The explosion rocked the ground beneath their feet.
She felt Jackson pull her to him and shield her just as the
rolling wave of heat and smoke and sound knocked them to
the paving stones. She laid there, knowing that she was
gasping for air, but unable to hear herself. The only sound
in the world was the raucous, laughing roar of the flames.

"Are you all right, Lindsay?" Jackson shouted above
the noise as he scrambled to his feet.

"I'm fine," she assured them both as she sat up. Jagged
bits of glass littered the stones all around around them.
"Yourself?"

"Righter than rain." He extended his hands and she
took them, allowing him to pull her upright. Glass shards
tumbled from her skirts. As soon as she had her feet beneath her, he turned, and still holding her hand, sprinted for
the front of the building.

"Get Lucy and the baby out," he commanded as he
dragged her up the steps and into the entry vestibule. "Tell
Jeb to spread the word on this floor. I'll see to the others."
He let go of her hand and started up the stairs. Only two
steps up, he paused and leaned over the railing to add,
"And once you're out, Lindsay, stay out!"

She nodded and breathlessly pounded her fist on the
Rutherford's door.

CHAPTER SEVEN

*J*EB! JEB!" she shouted, slamming the side of her fist against the wooden panel. "Open the door! Hurry!" The door swung open, an already concerned Jeb standing on the other side. "The building's on fire," Lindsay announced, pushing past him and into the apartment.

"Where's Mr. Stennett?" Jeb asked from behind her as Lucy struggled to rise from the settee with the baby in her arms.

"He's gone up to warn the others in the building," Lindsay said, moving to the dining-room table and gathering up what infant items lay there. "He asked to have you warn those on this floor."

"You see to Lucy and the baby," Jeb instructed as he stepped out into the smoky hall. He paused just long enough to add, "Mrs. Kowalski on the third floor's almost deaf; she'll never hear him knocking on her door. Send someone for the fire brigade!" and then he was gone.

Lindsay nodded in wordless agreement as she tossed the baby items into the center of the coverlet of the double bed. At the edge of her vision she saw Lucy, struggling, one-handed, to pull a large book from a high shelf on a rickety corner cabinet. "You don't have time to take anything, Lucy. It's burning fast. Things can be replaced!"

"I have to have my mama's Bible and the family christening gown," Lucy cried, stumbling toward her and thrusting the baby into Lindsay's arms. "Take the baby while I get them."

Lindsay watched, her heart racing, as Lucy snatched the black leather-bound book from its place on the cabinet shelf. Lucy had so little and to lose it all . . . As the young woman dashed to the low chest of drawers, Lindsay moved quickly into the kitchen area of the apartment. With the baby held securely in the crook of one arm, she pulled linens from the drawers and flung them toward the bed. The tinware followed.

Above her head came the heavy thudding of running footsteps and Lindsay looked toward the open door of the apartment, suddenly aware of the cacophony of sound around her. People were moving up and down the staircase and past the Rutherfords' door. Judging by the shouting, some weren't moving as swiftly as others would have preferred. Through the front windows, Lindsay could see a noisy crowd gathering to gawk from the opposite side of the street. Traffic was snarled in the street itself and drivers were shouting at one another and making rude hand gestures. Horses whinnied and shied in their traces. On the walkway in front of the building, people were racing around like agitated ants. Mothers searched for children, husbands for wives, and everyone sought to protect the haphazard piles of belongings they'd managed to haul out with them.

Over all the sounds of chaos was the billowing crack of flames. Surely someone had already thought to summon the fire brigade.

Lindsay took the baby back to Lucy and handed the infant into her mother's care while shouting, "Out! My carriage is half a block down. I'll bring the bundle."

Lucy went as instructed, pulling first the blanket over the baby's face and then her shawl over her own nose and mouth as she stepped across the threshold and into the smoky chaos of the vestibule. Lindsay dumped the contents of the dresser onto the coverlet, yanked the corners of the bedding into the center, slung the whole lumpy thing over her shoulder, and lugged it toward the door.

The vestibule was crowded as men pushed their way through it, raced up and down the stairs, jockeying and jostling past each other with vicious oaths and desperate anger. Lindsay reeled as a shoulder connected against her own. Her balance already made precarious by the weight of the Rutherfords' belongings, she staggered back into the wall and caught a heel in the hem of her dress. She was bumped again and righted just before she fell.

"Jack!" she called, leaning against the plaster wall for support and searching the sea of faces rushing past her. "Jack!"

No one answered. He had to be upstairs still. He wouldn't have gone out without first looking for her in the Rutherfords' apartment. He wouldn't leave without checking on her. She knew that to the center of her soul.

Her heart racing, her lungs and eyes burning from the acrid smoke, Lindsay lurched forward into the tide of bodies. Arms and shoulders impacted her upper body as she pressed forward. Her hat was knocked askew and long stands of hair slipped from their pins. With a whimper of relief, she reached the current of humanity sweeping out the front door and let it carry her along.

She caught her heel in her hem again as she was all but pushed down the front steps. Unable to catch her balance, she slung the bundle ahead of her as she pitched forward. It largely cushioned her fall, preventing her upper body from fully impacting against the wooden walkway. Her lower body, however, took the full brunt. Her knees struck hard and she heard the cloth of her skirt tear. The wind knocked out of her, Lindsay struggled to get a breath, vaguely realizing that her hat had slid farther sideways on her head and more hair was tumbling out from underneath. She saw a hairpin bounce on the walk ahead of her, but in the din, it made no sound. Someone kicked her ankle as they rushed past and the sharpness of the pain drove her to her feet.

With a deep breath, she hefted up Jeb's and Lucy's belongings again and turned down the sidewalk, choking back a cry of relief when she picked out her carriage and driver among those parked a short distance away. Lucy stood beside John on the walk, clutching her baby and frantically searching the melee. John darted forward the instant he caught sight of Lindsay, taking the bundle from her as though it weighed nothing.

"In the carriage, John. If you'd be so kind," she gasped as she made her way through the crowd to Lucy's side.

"Jeb," Lucy half-cried, half-whispered, her gaze riveted on a spot beyond Lindsay's shoulder.

Lindsay turned, looking back for the first time. The smoke was a dense, roiling, wide column of black rising from the back of the building to twice the structure's height. Red-orange tongues of flame roared upward, leaping and snapping at the smoke, casting an eerie light over the black the world had become. Still, men moved in and out the front door. In the distance Lindsay heard the insistent clang of the fire bells. A cheer went up from the onlookers. Lindsay closed her eyes and sighed, knowing the effort would be far too little, far too late.

"It'll be all right, Lucy," she said, rallying herself. "You'll come to my house and stay there until you and Jeb can find another place to live."

"Jeb," Lucy half-sobbed.

"He's helping others get out. He'll be along shortly. So will Jack," she assured the younger woman as they both scanned the crowd, searching.

It was several long moments before Lucy let out an excited yelp and then exclaimed, "There's my Jeb! And he's got Mrs. Kowalski and her cat." She strained up on the tips of her toes, waving her free arm over her head.

Jeb saw them, but didn't have a free arm to wave back. With one hand, he toted a bundle over his shoulder just like the one Lindsay had brought out with her. His other hand was grasping the elbow of a tottering, heavyset, older woman who was struggling mightily to keep her hold on a yellow-striped cat who seemed equally determined to escape her clutches.

Lindsay signaled the driver to open the carriage door, saying, "Get in, Lucy. You're on your way out of here."

Lucy started to obey, then stopped, her eyes brimming with tears. "Mrs. Kowalski doesn't have any family. She's old and hard of hearing and I don't think she has anywhere to go."

"She'll come with us, then," Lindsay promised, removing her hat and blindly tossing it into the shadowed interior. "Get in the carriage and I'll have Jeb bring her over." She didn't wait to see if Lucy finally did as instructed, but gathered her skirts firmly in hand, lifted them well above her ankles, and plowed her way forward through the crowd.

God, it was noisy. And why weren't these people moving away from the fire instead of running around back and forth in front of it? It was only a matter of time—Lindsay looked up at the building. The smoke was blacker and higher. The flames wider and brighter and louder. A *short* time before the building was fully engulfed. This wasn't the first structure fire she'd seen and she knew how it would progress. Once the floor joists burned through, it would collapse. If it came down on the sidewalk . . . Her heart rose, hammering hard against her breast, and she quickened her pace, jostling and pushing with a fervor every bit as forceful as those around her.

"Jeb!" she called above the noise as she reached her junior bookkeeper. "Lucy and the baby are in the carriage." She pointed in the direction from which she'd come. "Take Mrs. Kowalski and the cat and join them. Have the driver take you all to my house. Tell Mrs. Beechum what's happened and that you all are staying with us until we can make other arrangements. Where's Mr. Stennett?"

"He's right behind me!" Jeb shouted back, taking the cat from Mrs. Kowalski and unceremoniously stuffing it into the bundle. "Sean O'Malley's got a busted leg and has to be helped out."

"We'll wait here for the carriage to come back for us. Get out of here before it all comes down!"

"I'll be back as soon as I can!" Jeb called as he pushed his way down the walk with Mrs. Kowalski lumbering in tow.

"Jack, where are you?" Lindsay asked softly, still holding her skirts above her ankles and watching the smoke

thicken and darken as it rolled out the front door and down
the steps. "It shouldn't be taking this long."

SWEET JESUS AND ALL THE SAINTS, Jackson silently swore.
The son of a bitch with a broken leg would have to live on
the third frickin' floor and weigh at least three hundred
pounds. Slinging him over his shoulder and carrying him
down the stairs had been out of the question. They were
mincing their way downward, the smoke thickening around
them by the second, the sound of the flames getting ever
louder and punctuated by the long, groaning wails of the
joists and beams.

His eyes were burning; the tears running down his face
doing nothing to lessen the painful stinging. Holding his
forearm over his nose and mouth wasn't doing much good
either. His lungs hurt and he couldn't get enough good air
to keep his head from spinning.

Lindsay. Had she gotten out and then stayed out as
he'd told her to? He wasn't going to have the time to go
looking for her if she hadn't. Surely she had a healthy sense
of self-preservation. Hopefully. Good sense he wasn't so
sure about.

The man beside him missed a step and lurched sideways, slamming Jackson's body into the plaster wall and
bringing his thoughts back to the immediate situation.
Good God Almighty. If he didn't get the man moving any
faster, they were both going to die on a second-floor landing
in a New York City apartment house. He could think of a
lot better ways and places he'd rather go. Maybe he should
just pitch the Irishman down the last flight and tell him that
a second broken leg was better than dying—because it sure
as hell was.

Jackson glanced over his shoulder and up the stairs.
The smoke was too dense to see very far, the sounds of the
flames and popping wood too loud to hear anything beyond
them. What he needed—and needed desperately—was a
second pair of hands to balance and haul the burden. He recalled the backs of the men who had pushed past him as he
and the Irishman had started down the stairs. No one had

paused to so much as offer to help. Jackson gritted his teeth and looked at the expanse of steps leading downward. How far they had to go, he couldn't tell. The bottom and the vestibule lay somewhere in the blanket of darkening black. It could be two steps. Or it could just as well be a hundred for all he could see. What he *could* see was the faint light coming in the front door and it drew him down like a beacon.

Please let Lindsay be outside. Please let Jeb come back in and help him get this man out.

The smoke before him rolled backward and as a human shape took form and emerged from it, Jackson's heart slammed hard and wildly hopeful against the wall of his chest. It wasn't Jeb, he realized as the man reached the other side of the Irishman. Jackson didn't care.

The man didn't stop, though; he kept on going. Jackson turned, "No!" he shouted. "There's no time! I need—"

The blur made him blink and flinch. The pain in his head washed the world in a wave of white and then red. Jackson heard the Irishman scream, felt him tear away from his grip, and then he heard and felt nothing at all.

LINDSAY STARTED EACH TIME as three men ran in quick succession from the building. None of them were Jackson Stennett. She paced, breathing hard and never taking her eyes from the doorway. Something was wrong. She *knew* it. Jeb had said Jack and O'Malley were right behind him.

She saw a glimmer of paleness near the threshold to the vestibule in the same instant that a man standing nearby shouted for help and dashed forward. Two others ran with him and together they dragged a large, sooty man down the front steps. Lindsay swallowed a cry when she saw that his left leg was wrapped in grimy plaster.

"Are you Mr. O'Malley?" she asked the man as he was dragged past. "Where's Jack Stennett? The man who was helping you."

He gestured with his head, indicating the front door of the building and the cloud of smoke. He coughed violently and through it managed to gasp, "Stairs."

Lindsay's heart lurched as she stared at the entrance to hell.

HE COULDN'T BREATHE. He was choking to death and the heat was inching closer by the second. He could see the glow of it over his head, rolling down the underneath side of the stairs above him. The rush of fire was so damn loud. And his head . . . Jesus. His head had to be in two pieces. He couldn't think, couldn't move past the pain.

"Jack, where are you? Answer me!"

A soft voice, desperate. Lindsay. Oh, God. Lindsay. She was in here somewhere. He tried to move and couldn't and he wanted to cry. A sensation penetrated his pain; a touch, a grasp by something small and weak. It moved by inches up his legs, his torso, his chest. It touched his neck and then came to rest on either side of his face.

"Jack! Wake up! Talk to me, Jack!"

"Lindsay," he whispered, forcing his eyes open. Through the shimmering of his tears he saw a curtain of light amidst a cloud of black. Not Lindsay. An angel. He coughed and struggled to draw another breath into his lungs.

"You've got to get up, Jack!"

"Where's the man—"

"He's crawled out on his own." The sweet angel suddenly grabbed the lapels of his coat and yanked him upward as it shouted in his face, "On your feet, Jack! Get your feet under you or so help me God I'll roll you all the way down the stairs and drag you into the street by your pant legs!"

It *was* Lindsay. "I told you to stay out," he said as he felt his head being hefted off the stairs.

"And I told you I don't listen well."

If she dropped him, his head would come off his shoulders; he was sure of it. Jack desperately struggled to get his legs under himself. He felt her shift her hold on his coat, felt her body come fully against his side. "Lindsay, get—"

"Put your arm over my shoulders," she commanded, roughly taking it and accomplishing the task for him.

He clung to her because he had no other choice, because he believed in her strength. They careened down the stairs, at the edge of out of control, only a half-breath away from falling. The pain in his head blinded him, made him sick to his stomach. They stopped when they careened into a wall.

"Jesus."

"One foot . . . in front . . . of the other," she gasped, coughing and choking as she pulled him forward. "We can . . . do . . . this."

He went, no longer breathing, just moving because Lindsay MacPhaull wouldn't let him lay down and die. It was beginning to rain fire.

"Few . . . more . . . steps."

They pitched forward. He sensed it rather than felt it, and there was nothing he could do to save them. He heard their bodies hit wood, but there was too much pain to feel any more. His awareness began to gray around the edges and Jackson welcomed it, knowing that inside the mist, pain ceased to matter, ceased to exist.

Lindsay moved against him and he vaguely understood that she was trying to crawl from beneath his arm. If she had the strength to struggle, then she had the strength to get out alive. He had to give her that chance. Jackson focused his attention on the arm pinning Lindsay down, on getting his body to move at his command. He willed movement and nothing happened. And then there came the sound of distant voices. Lindsay stilled and in the next second he was being borne upward. He went without resistance, surrendering to the sweet promise of the mist and knowing Lindsay was free.

THE RESPITE FROM PAIN was too short by a thousand years. He came to as a fresh wave of searing red shot through the back of his head. He'd just barely clawed his way through it when his chest heaved and smoke scraped its way upward and out. There was no stopping the inevitable. He gagged and choked and coughed, finding some meager solace in the fact that he was still alive and had the physical wherewithal

to roll onto his side before he unceremoniously threw up in
the gutter. And when it was done, he lay there, his eyes
closed, breathing and thinking wildly that he needed to find
Lindsay, needed to be sure that she'd gotten out, too. He
knew he had to get to his feet. Actually doing anything
about it, though, seemed to take more mental acuity than
he could marshal.

"Oh, Jack. You're bleeding."

Lindsay. And she was right there. Judging by the even,
calm sound of her voice, she was faring better in the aftermath than he was. He breathed a sigh of relief. A realization slowly nestled around his brain; she'd called him Jack.
He touched his tongue to his parched lips and managed a
small smile.

"Let me see where you're hurt," she said, touching the
side of his face and then running her fingers ever so lightly
through his hair. A lover's touch.

Jack frowned and, reminding himself that Lindsay was
Billy's daughter, said, "It's my head."

"Yes, I can see that much already."

"Prob'ly isn't as bad as it feels. Or looks. Heads bleed
like a son of a—" He bit off the rest, reminding himself that
he really needed to watch his language around her. Lindsay
was a lady, and his mother had taught him manners. He
carefully rolled onto his back. Lindsay knelt beside him, her
golden hair tumbling over her shoulders and made bronze
by the smoke and soot, her face smudged and tearstained.
Her dress was torn and singed and blackened with ash. She
was the most beautiful woman he'd ever seen. If he'd been
capable of moving with any deliberate speed, he'd have
pulled her into his arms.

"You need stitches. We'll get you home and send for
Dr. Bernard. In the meantime, though . . ."

Jackson watched as she rose to her feet. Had she pulled
the back hem of her dress between her legs and tucked it
into the front of the waistband? How'd she know that
washerwoman trick? As he contemplated the mystery,
Lindsay pulled the skirt edge free from her waist. She
didn't, however, instantly drop it for the sake of modesty
and propriety. No, not Lindsay. Instead, she shoved the

dress fabric out of the way, grasped the flounce of her petti-coat with both hands, and pulled in opposite directions. The seam gave way with a loud protest. She repeated the process until the flounce separated completely.

"I can't very well let you bleed all over the inside of the carriage," she explained, smiling as she once again knelt be-side him on the walkway. She folded the strip of cloth in half and then placed the end against his forehead, adding, "The stains would never come out of the upholstery."

Billy had been a goddamned fool to leave her behind. She was made of the stuff that made a man proud to call her his own. It served Billy right to have lost that pleasure, that admiration from other men. She'd been left behind to fend for herself and she'd done all right. She was good and strong and brave. And if it weren't for Lindsay MacPhaull's grit, he'd be deader than a damn doornail right now. He owed her and he owed her big.

"I'll do right by you, Lindsay," he said. "I swear it on Billy's grave."

She kept her attention focused on wrapping the strip of petticoat around his head as she answered quietly, "Thank you. But I never doubted that you would."

CHAPTER EIGHT

*L*INDSAY OPENED THE FRONT DOOR of the house and stood aside as Jeb and her coachman half-guided, half-carried Jackson Stennett inside. The Texan was, without a doubt, the most pigheaded man she'd ever met. Perhaps "pigheaded" wasn't the right word, she mused, as he tightly thanked the men for their assistance and stepped out from beneath their arms. "Prideful," she decided, was the right word, as he stood swaying on his feet and tried to look as though nothing was wrong with him. She wondered how long he could maintain the charade before he fell flat on his face. Not long, she guessed. Under the coating of soot, his face was very pale.

Blood had dried on his shirt and the bandage had soaked through above the wound. It needed to be cleaned and she needed to do what she could to ease his pain before she did anything else. There was no way to count the number of lives he'd saved that morning, no way to tell him what a decent and honorable man she considered him to be. He deserved to be treated well and kindly.

She was about to suggest that they retire to the kitchen

so that she could see to his head, when Lucy came running down the stairs to throw herself into Jeb's arms and shower his face with kisses. A long familiar sadness settled into Lindsay. There were some who were destined for love and happiness in life, she told herself, turning away politely, and there were some who were put on earth to serve selflessly and responsibly. There was no sense in regretting destiny. It was a waste of time and effort. She knew that.

Mrs. Beechum provided a welcome diversion, entering the foyer and saying crisply, "What a morning you've had, Miss Lindsay! What a sight you are."

"You don't know the half of it," Jackson said, scrubbing his face with his hand and managing a smile.

"We need baths," Lindsay said. "Desperately. And would you send someone for Dr. Bernard? Mr. Stennett needs stitches in the back of his head."

"I'll see to fetching the doctor," her coachman offered as he headed for the front door.

"Would you care for the detailed version of how I've dealt with it all?" Mrs. Beechum asked her. "Or would you prefer the summary?"

"Is any of it pressing?" Lindsay asked, eyeing Jackson and thinking that he needed to be off his feet as soon as possible.

The housekeeper sighed. "I'm afraid that all of it demands immediate attention, Miss Lindsay."

"I suppose details would be better," Lindsay admitted, resolving to get through matters as quickly as she could. "And don't think to spare me the problems. They have to be dealt with sooner or later."

"Mrs. Kowalski and her cat have been put in the lavender room. She won't let the cat out. She says that it will run away if she does."

This was more important than taking care of Jack? "It probably would."

"Need I point out the potential unpleasantries in having the animal confined?"

Deal with it and go on, Lindsay. "We need to get a large pan of some sort from the kitchen and have the gardener fill it with dirt and take it up to Mrs. Kowalski's room. That should take care of any potential problems in that regard. We'll just have to say a prayer for the curtains and upholstery and hope for the best."

"Mrs. Kowalski is of the Jewish faith. She's informed me—quite nicely, I'll admit—that she keeps kosher."

This *was* something of a problem—at least as she understood the practice of keeping a kosher kitchen and diet. "Oh, dear. Does Emile know anything about how this is done?"

"He swore—in French, I believe—and then suggested lying to her."

Out of the corner of her eye she saw Jack lean his shoulder against the wall, fold his arms across his chest, and cross one booted ankle over the other. The light in his eyes told her that he was finding the situation amusing. If he was feeling well enough to enjoy it all, she decided, then perhaps he wasn't hovering as close to death as she'd thought. Buoyed by relief, she said, "We'll think of something, Mrs. Beechum. Next problem?"

"Mr. and Mrs. Rutherford and their child have been placed in the blue room. I'll see to having your old cradle brought down from the attic later today. It will need to be cleaned and bedding found for it, of course."

"Of course." This wasn't a problem in the least. It was a simple matter of housekeeping. She'd send Jeb up for the cradle later.

"Outside of your adventures this morning . . ." Mrs. Beechum sighed again. "Miss Agatha had departed before your message to her arrived here. I don't know where she went and so couldn't send it on. Mr. MacPhaull sent a second message. I placed it on the desk in the study. Mr. Rutherford brought the mail packet in from the carriage on his first arrival here and it's with the message from your brother."

"Very good." Were they done? Could she get on with taking care of Jack's head?

"Havers has announced that his accommodations are inadequate and suggests that if you hope for him to remain in service you will have to refurbish his room. He also wants to know how he will be paid since Mr. Patterson is incapacitated and can't authorize his monthly salary."

Lindsay gritted her teeth. Havers' concern about his salary wasn't unexpected, but his sense of necessary style was, and it irritated her. She knew that she should allow herself some time to rationally think the matter over before dealing with his expectations. "I'll have a talk with him," Lindsay promised.

"Primrose is threatening to quit," Mrs. Beechum went on. "I'm afraid that cooking of any sort has been a casualty of the contest she and Emile are waging."

"Meaning that there's no luncheon."

"And that there are no efforts under way for supper, either," the housekeeper confirmed.

Lindsay was hungry and knew that the others had to be as well. "I'll have a talk with both her and Emile. Immediately," she declared, flipping loose tendrils of hair over her shoulder as she eyed the far end of the dining room and the swinging door that led into the kitchen.

She'd taken a single step forward when Mrs. Beechum said, "There are reporters from both the *Sun* and the *Herald* in the kitchen, waiting to speak with you about the building fire."

"Wonderful," Lindsay groused, stopping and turning back. Jeb and Lucy, Mrs. Beechum, and Jackson Stennett all watched her, waiting to see how she was going to handle the small mountain of difficulties before her. She moistened her lips with the tip of her tongue while she looked between them all and decided. "First things first," she said decisively. "Mr. Stennett is going up to his room to lie down before he falls down. I'll be up to take care of his head as soon as possible."

"I'm fine," Jackson offered quietly, wincing slightly as he pushed away from the wall to stand squarely on his feet.

Oh, yes, she could see that. "Humor me, please," she countered. "I have too many things to do without having to stop to pick you up off the carpet. Jeb," she added, addressing her junior accountant, "if you'd be so kind to see that he makes it, I'd be most appreciative."

She didn't give either one of them a chance to speak before turning to her housekeeper and saying, "Now, Mrs. Beechum, please extend my apologies to the reporters and ask them to return later today when I can devote proper attention to answering their questions. Then have Primrose start heating water for our baths. While you're seeing to those two tasks, I'll speak with Proctor about the pan of dirt for Mrs. Kowalski's cat.

"When the reporters are gone, I'll be in to straighten out the difficulties between Primrose and Emile. Tell them that I expect to find them preparing something for us to eat when I get there."

"And Havers?" Mrs. Beechum inquired, her brow raised.

"Havers can wait a bit. I don't know quite what to tell him at this point."

"How about telling him to go to hell?" Jackson suggested.

"It's tempting," she admitted with a weak smile, "but I need him. He's been with Richard for years. I couldn't find anyone to replace him who would be even half as capable in caring for him." To Mrs. Beechum, she said, "Please tell Havers that I'm aware of his desires and extend my apologies for not being able to discuss the matter with him until later."

"Talk to me before you promise him anything," Jackson instructed, making his way toward the stairs. Jeb stepped forward, but Jackson shot him a look that stopped him in his tracks. "I can make it on my own, Jeb. Much obliged for the concern, though."

Lindsay watched Jackson Stennett haul himself up the stairs. She wouldn't be long, she silently promised him. And she promised herself that she'd apologize for putting a cat pan and kitchen squabbles ahead of him. It wasn't right. But it was very much the usual nature of her world.

THE WATER IN THE PITCHER was cold, but it was clean. Jackson studied his reflection in the mirror. He looked like hell. There was some consolation to be had in the fact that he could see that fact clearly. No blurred edges, no half-transparent, slipping, double images. He had a god-awful headache and his shirt was ruined, but his brain hadn't been scrambled. He'd live. All things considered, it could have been a lot worse.

Jackson poured some water into the basin, then stripped off his jacket and opened the neck of his shirt. He'd washed the worst of the grime from his face before a knock came at the door. "It's not locked," he called out, dropping the wash rag into the bowl and thinking he might feel human again one day soon.

In the mirror, he saw the door open. It wasn't Lindsay who stood on the other side, but Mrs. Beechum.

"Miss Lindsay asked me to tell you that she'll be along directly to tend to your head."

Jackson smiled wryly. "Did she ask you to extend her apologies for not being able to do it right now?"

"Of course, sir," the housekeeper answered.

Jackson turned and faced her, his arms folded across his chest. "Tell me something, Mrs. Beechum, is there anything in this world she *doesn't* apologize for?"

The woman quietly replied, "You've noticed."

"It's rather hard not to, ma'am. With her, every other sentence either begins or ends with the words 'I'm sorry.' Why does she do that?"

Mrs. Beechum contemplated the floor for a second and then lifted her face to meet his gaze squarely. "Lydia MacPhaull—her mother—was somewhat difficult to please. She had very high and exacting expectations."

"Of Lindsay."

"Especially of Miss Lindsay, sir. And especially so after the senior Mr. MacPhaull left home."

If he was reading between the lines correctly, Billy's wife had made the daughter pay for the father's sin. It wasn't right and it wasn't fair. And it had been damn small of Billy to have let it happen. "What about Henry and Agatha?" he asked. "Did Mrs. MacPhaull hold them to the same standards?"

"Unlike Miss Lindsay, they seemed to have no difficulty in being and doing as their mother wanted. But Miss Lindsay is cut from a different kind of cloth, sir. Which of course made constantly failing all that much more difficult for her."

"Billy should have taken her with him when he left."

"I've always been of that opinion."

He started, not realizing that he'd spoken the thought aloud. At least he'd managed to commit the error with someone who shared his view on the matter. He wondered how Lindsay felt about it. Had she wanted to go with her father? Had she missed him? Or had staying with her mother been of her own choice?

"Is there anything I can get or do for you until Miss Lindsay gets here, Mr. Stennett?"

"I'm fine, Mrs. Beechum. Thank you for offering."

"Very good, sir."

He mentally subtracted the years. Lindsay had been eight when Billy had walked out of her life. How long had she endured, alone, with her mother's animosity? "Mrs. Beechum?" he called just before the door closed. The housekeeper looked around the edge, her brow arched. "How long has Mrs. MacPhaull been gone?"

"Three years, sir. It will be four this fall."

He suspected, just from the way she said it, that the woman could have told him the exact number of days, hours, and minutes. "Thank you."

She nodded and quietly closed the door. Jackson resumed his mental calculations. Billy had been gone seventeen years. His wife had been dead for the last three of them. Which made it fourteen years that Lindsay had lived apologizing. Maybe more.

Jackson rubbed his fingertips hard against his brow. Billy had tossed the financial mess into his lap knowing that he'd do right by the children Billy had never mentioned having. And Jackson would do what was expected of him. But Lindsay had risked her own life to save his and that debt couldn't be settled by handing her money or property deeds. It went deeper than that. He didn't have a whole lot of time before he went home, but maybe he could use what he did have to undo some of the damage that Lindsay had suffered at the hands of her parents. It was a tall order he was setting for himself. And there was a distinct possibility that Lindsay might not appreciate his efforts. But he knew that if he didn't try, he wasn't any bigger a man than Billy had been.

. . .

LINDSAY PAUSED IN FRONT of the hall mirror, the heavily laden tray carefully balanced in her hands. She'd done the best she could to wash the grime from her face. Time hadn't permitted her do much more than finger-comb her hair and use the few remaining pins to pull it all back off her face. Her dress was a disaster, destined for the ragbag.

She pasted a soft smile on her face, thinking it would outshine her otherwise bedraggled appearance. It didn't. She rolled her eyes, sighed, and gave up the attempt. Hopefully Jackson Stennett would be too concerned with his own condition to notice hers, and too much of a gentleman to comment on it if he did. It was the best she could hope for. Her mother would be appalled that she was even taking the chance; a lady never allowed a man to see her as anything less than feminine perfection.

With a deep breath, Lindsay lifted the tray and turned to the closed door across the hall. Her hands full, and the tray too awkward to shift, she was forced to knock by tapping the toe of her shoe against the lower edge of the panel.

"One second," he called from the other side.

Lindsay's heart began to race. She called herself a fool and was drawing a steadying breath when Jack opened the door. Her breath caught, almost choking her. He stood before her smiling, his eyes bright, and his shirt closed by a single button midway down his chest. Even smoke-shaded, the linen contrasted sharply with the bronze and darkly furred expanse of skin. She swallowed hard, and mindful that she was gawking, deliberately met his gaze, lifted the tray and said, "I brought hot water and soap." Pleased with the composure she heard in her voice, she added, "I thought that we'd get your wound cleansed before Dr. Bernard gets here. It will make his work easier."

Stepping aside to allow her to enter, he asked, "Have the crises of the cat, the cooks, and the newspapermen been averted?"

"For the moment," Lindsay supplied, carrying the tray to the window table. "The reporters will be back with their questions this afternoon." She looked back as she set down the tray. Jack was studying the doorway as though trying to decide whether to leave the door open or close it.

"If you'd be so kind as to leave it open," she said, "and then come over here and have a seat; you're too tall for me to work with you standing up."

He slid a glance at her, his smile quirked and his eyes twinkling. Her pulse quickened another degree. Pushing the door almost, but not quite closed, he came toward her, asking, "How is it that a woman who tucks her skirts up one minute can be concerned about open doors and propriety the next?"

"Necessity of the moment can be granted forgiveness," she answered, angling a chair for him. "Deliberate flaunting and shortsightedness don't merit such latitude."

He tried to nod, but the pain in his head flared with the effort. Without another word he walked to the chair and sat obediently. Lindsay carefully removed the scrap of petticoat from around his head, then tried to gingerly peel back the wad of fabric she'd pressed over the wound itself. He sucked a breath through his teeth and Lindsay winced.

"I'm so sorry," she whispered, just before she yanked the bandage off with one swift motion. He made a strangled sound deep in his throat and gripped the arms of the chair so tightly his fingertips went white. Lindsay wanted to put her arms around his shoulders and hold him, to assure him that the worst was over. She took a step back. The distance didn't help; her mind filled with an image of Jackson Stennett wrapped in her arms, his head nestled against her shoulder as he feathered kisses along the side of her neck. Her breath caught and heat suffused her cheeks.

"Please don't tell me how awful it looks. I have a weak stomach."

Lindsay blinked and the vision vanished. "I wasn't going to," she hurriedly said, busying with the medicinal items on the tray. "In fact, I was going to say that I've seen worse paper cuts."

He turned sideways in the chair so that he had a full view of her. "You'd out and out lie to me?" he asked, grinning.

He had a smile that could melt ice at fifty paces. Her

knees were decidedly shaky. "Yes," she said, looking away from that very dangerous sparkle in his eyes, "but only to make you feel better." She focused intently on laying out the items she needed. A soft cloth, cinnamon soap, clean compresses. Would she need the razor?

"Lindsay?"

The softness of his voice was compelling. She met his gaze. His eyes were dark and somber and she felt herself being drawn into the depths of them. She stopped breathing.

"Thank you for coming in after me, for dragging me out."

It would be so easy. All she would have to do is lean forward and down a little bit. His lips would be soft, the kiss simple and light and delicious. "It was an impulse," she said, desperately going back to the organizing of her supplies. "I've always had difficulty controlling them. In hindsight, I could have saved myself a great deal of money and frustration if I'd have left you in there. It wouldn't have been nearly as satisfying as pushing you in front of a carriage, but . . ." She shrugged and poured the hot water from the little pitcher into the bowl.

"Would you have really rolled me down the stairs and dragged me into the street by my pant legs?"

"Of course I would have." She soaked the cloth and then took up the bar of cinnamon soap.

"It wouldn't have been very ladylike of you."

She could feel his smile bathing her. *Keep busy, Lindsay. Don't give your mind the chance to wander.* She lathered the cloth, saying, "And not a soul in the entire city would have been the least bit surprised to hear that I'd done it." She laid aside the soap and squeezed the excess moisture from the cloth. With no other choice, she faced him. "How many fingers am I holding up?" she asked, trying to take command of the situation.

"Two," he answered, his smile broadening. "And just so you know . . . Everyone always holds up two."

She motioned for him to turn in the chair so that she could work on the back of his head. As he complied, she observed, "I take it that you've been rendered unconscious before?"

"Yeah. And often enough that it's a wonder I have any sense left at all."

She arched a brow and said dryly, "I think that's a debatable conclusion."

He chuckled and then groaned.

"Are you all right, Jack?"

"It hurts to laugh."

"Then don't," she instructed blithely. "And brace yourself. I'm going to start." She tenderly dabbed at the gash along the base of his skull. As much to distract herself as him, Lindsay said, "Dr. Bernard will be here any minute now. You know what he's going to say, don't you?" She didn't give him a chance to guess. "He's going to say that you should take to your bed and not tax yourself for the next several days."

"Well," he said, his words sounding as though they were being forced through clenched teeth, "Dr. Bernard hasn't invited your brother and his wife to dinner tonight. And Dr. Bernard hasn't threatened your sister with destitution if she doesn't make an appearance at the table, too."

"Henry declined the invitation. That was his second note of the day."

"Oh, really? What was his excuse?"

"He and Edith have tickets to a play this evening. They happen to have tomorrow evening free, though." She rinsed the cloth in the bowl, squeezed it out, and then poured fresh water over it.

"What about Agatha?"

"Henry and Edith had an extra ticket," Lindsay explained as she rinsed the antiseptic soap from his wound. "Henry said they've invited her to go with them. She'll accept, of course. Agatha loves the theater." She tossed the rag into the bowl with a soft sigh. "I don't see that there's anything we can do to force them to come to dinner this evening."

"Considering the general chaos going on in the house and the hellacious headache I have, it's probably best to postpone it all a day anyway. Are you done with your doctoring back there?"

"I still have to put iodine on the wound."

He came out of the chair in one swift, determined motion and then turned to face her squarely, his grin wide. "Let Doc do that. I'd feel a lot less guilty about hitting him than I would you."

She laughed, realizing even as she did that she'd laughed and smiled more in the last two days than she had in the last two years. Maybe longer. Considering the upheaval going on in her life, it was a decidedly odd way to behave. But there was something about Jackson's way that made her feel good, made her feel as though her problems weren't nearly as looming as they had been before he'd walked into Richard Patterson's office. It was all an illusion, she reminded herself, sobering. If anything, the troubles besetting her had been made even greater by Jackson Stennett's arrival. *The power of a handsome face and a disarming smile,* she silently warned.

"What's wrong, Lindsay? What are you thinking about?"

She started. In an effort to disguise the involuntary movement, she began to organize the tray again. Unwilling to be candid with him, she fell back on the tried and true. "That I'm very sorry."

"About what?" he asked, settling down on the arm of the chair, his arms folded over his chest.

She shrugged and gave him the most obvious reasons. "Your injury, the chaos in the house, the fact that your plans have fallen apart."

"Did *you* crack me in the back of the head?"

She knew where this was going and it rankled to face the fact that Jackson Stennett was right about anything. Having to admit it aloud . . .

"Answer me, Lindsay."

If he thought he could back her into a corner and force her to meekly admit that he was right and she was wrong, then he had a lesson to learn. She lifted her chin and said, "I should have foreseen that you could have been injured in the fire. I should have kept you from going any farther than Jeb and Lucy's."

He seemed to chew on the inside of his lip for a moment. "You might have tried, but I'd have done it anyway. And why are you apologizing for being kind to people who have lost everything they own and have nowhere to go?"

Having seen the tack of his course, she was ready with an answer. "I could have found rooms at a boardinghouse for Jeb and Lucy and the baby, for Mrs. Kowalski and her cat."

"You don't have the money to pay for their lodging and neither do they," he countered just as quickly. "Your only other choice was to leave them standing in the street. I'd have been real disappointed in you if you had. You're a better person than that."

The unexpected compliment warmed her. It also flustered her and tied her tongue.

"Now," Jackson went on, apparently unaware of his affect on her, "tell me just exactly what you did—or failed to do—that caused my dinner plans to fall apart?"

She was going to lose the contest; she could sense it. Jackson was cool and logical and determined to methodically destroy her every point. All she could do was finish it out with all the dignity she could muster and hope that he was a gracious winner. "I should be stomping my foot and insisting that Henry and Agatha cancel their plans for the evening and come here for dinner."

"Sometimes things don't work out like you thought they would, Lindsay. It's no one's fault. You learn to roll with the punches and make the best of it. One day, one week, one month—It won't make a bit of difference in what I'm going to say to your brother and sister and how I'm going to say it."

Dear Lord. What *was* he going to say to Henry and Agatha? She needed to know, needed to prepare. If it was horrible, she had to try to change his course.

"So, I'll ask you again, Lindsay . . . ," he drawled. "What do you have to be sorry about?"

"I'm sure there's something," she said offhandedly, her mind still focused on the likely conversation to be had with her brother and sister.

"Nope."

She managed a smile, but only because she knew that it would imply that she was actively participating in the conversation. "You're being very kind."

Her attention hadn't been wholly on their conversation and Jackson knew it. He'd mentioned her siblings and her mind had wandered off down a path of its own. He knew enough about her already to guess that she'd been fretting over how to keep him from upending their little versions of Eden. Apologizing wasn't the only bad habit she had. Misplaced loyalties appeared to be another. As long as he was going to tackle one, he might as well take a shot at the other while he was at it.

He only knew one way to go about the tasks. Learning another one had never been necessary. There were ladies and there were cantina girls, but, under the differences of money and social class, they were all female. And he'd long ago discovered the incredible power of a wink, a smile, the promise of a kiss. Hell, he hadn't done his own laundry in at least fifteen years. But there was one big difference between Lindsay MacPhaull and all other women. She wouldn't be drawn to a suggestion of intimacy. The personal frightened her. As for himself . . . Kissing Lindsay MacPhaull didn't seen like it would be at all painful.

"No, I'm not being kind," he said, his course charted. "I'm being honest. If there's ever anything I think you need to apologize for, I'll let you know."

The concerns for Henry and Agatha were swept aside by the sudden tide of anger. "And what if I don't care to apologize on cue?" she retorted.

He slowly rose from the chair and his grin turned devilish. "It would be a welcome change. I might even applaud."

"It's a very old habit—my apologizing," she responded tightly. "I'm afraid that it might take some time to end it."

"Tell you what," Jackson drawled, liking how the anger sparked in her blue eyes. "Every time you needlessly say 'I'm sorry,' I'm going to kiss you."

As he fully expected, her eyes instantly widened and she took a full step back. "You wouldn't dare!"

He closed the distance she'd put between them, saying, "No matter where we are, what we're doing, or who's there to see. I figure that ought to motivate you to think before you slip into being needlessly contrite."

"Wouldn't you rather punch me in the shoulder with your fist?" she asked, holding her ground. "Or perhaps pinch me? Either would accomplish the same end."

"Hardly. You could take those without blinking and you'd probably hit or pinch me right back. But a long, sweet kiss . . ." Jackson started as the light in the depths of her eyes flickered and changed. His pulse tripped at the re-alization that Lindsay wasn't as angry as she was intrigued. Good God. He'd picked the threat because he'd thought it would be enough to force a change in her behavior, but now . . . How intrigued was she? How much tolerance for risk did she have? "I'll bet money that you wouldn't even think about kissing me back," he whispered.

Lindsay deliberately ignored the instinct that urged her to escape. She wouldn't run from him, wouldn't retreat in the face of such a blatant challenge. "This is a most un-seemly conversation," she declared regally.

His smile was roguish. "Are you sorry you walked into it?"

"No."

"Good girl."

"I'm not a girl," she retorted. "I'm a woman full grown."

He caught the inside corner of his mouth between his teeth as he struggled to bring his grin back under control. "I kinda noticed that already." He cocked a brow. "More than once."

Her cheeks darkened the way they had the last time he'd complimented her. And, as last time, she struggled for words in the aftermath. He let her find them this time.

"I think your brains were rattled loose when that beam came down on your head," she finally said, her defiance still there but clearly wavering. "At the very least, your sense of decorum was knocked out of kilter."

It hadn't been a beam that had taken him down, but for the moment he let her keep the illusion. "It doesn't have anything to do with the gash on the back of my head. My devotion to propriety shifted when I opened my eyes and you were standing over me with my lapels in your fists. You called me Jack."

"I shouldn't have," she said on a sigh. "Another impulse I wasn't able to resist."

"But you crossed the line and there's no going back."

"I think we should try. The less you give people to talk about the better."

"People like Winifred, for instance?" he guessed.

Anger once again coursed through her. Bitter, painful memories came with it. "Winifred Templeton is a prime example of a tongue hinged on both ends."

"That's not very nice," he chided. "Neither was refusing to do the polite thing and introduce us when we were all standing there. It was very awkward."

Jackson Stennett thought that it had been awkward? He didn't know the half of it. "Well, I'm—" She bit the rest off, her heart lurching. He grinned knowingly, forcing her to hastily protest, "That doesn't count. I didn't actually say it."

"You thought it, though. It counts."

"And I was speaking facetiously, not sincerely."

He reached out and trailed a fingertip along the curve of her jaw and Lindsay's heart rose into her throat. Of its own accord, her body leaned into the caress, thrilling to the gentle touch. Her mind reeled, remembering, warning. She didn't have the good sense to resist handsome men with dark intentions. She'd proven that in the past. If she allowed him to kiss her, even once, it would end in disaster. She was too hungry, too needy, too desperate. And above all else, she was afraid. Better to be forever alone than humiliated.

"This is utterly childish, Jack," she said, turning her head even as she stepped beyond his reach.

Jackson let his arm fall back to his side. There wasn't a doubt in his mind that Lindsay wanted to be touched. But it was just as obvious that her fear was stronger than her desire. Why was she afraid of him? Even as he wondered, the answer came, crystal clear and sharp-edged. Damn fool that he was, he was trying to plow his way across a bridge he had no business crossing. He was here for the next sixty days and then he'd be gone. He was going to walk out of her life just as permanently as her father had. Lindsay had every right to be afraid. She knew the pain to be had in being abandoned by someone she cared about.

And he knew the pain to be had in losing them. The secret to surviving it all lay in keeping a safe distance, in making all relationships passing friendships. Anything more than that was asking for trouble. "I'll let you off the hook this one time," he offered. "On one condition."

"Which would be?"

"You never call me Mr. Stennett again. From now on I'm Jack, and the Winifred Templetons of the world be damned."

"Fair enough," she agreed with a small sigh of relief. Her gaze darted to the door. "I hear Dr. Bernard downstairs. Since he'll be up in just a minute, I'll leave you. I need to check on Richard." She turned on her heel and headed for the door, adding as she went, "And not to worry. I won't promise Havers anything I can't afford to give."

As he watched her slip out, it occurred to him that Lindsay had spent her entire life giving. How deep was her well? How much more did she have left? He knew for a fact that her bank accounts were damn near dry. Adding Mrs. Kowalski, Jeb and Lucy and the baby to her household was going to empty them within a week. As for the well of her heart . . . Jackson dragged his fingers through his hair and reminded himself that it was none of his business.

LINDSAY LEANED A SHOULDER against the wall outside of Richard's room and closed her eyes as she tried to settle her mind. She'd escaped—albeit narrowly—Jackson's advance. She should be relieved and steadfastly committed to staying well out of his reach in the future. But intellectually knowing that and actually feeling it were two very different things. There were just too many feelings inside her right now, all jumbled up and twisting around each other. Sorting it out was necessary, but so daunting a task. All she wanted to do was lock herself in her room, curl up in a little ball, and cry. She wanted to stay there until someone knocked on the door and told her that it had all been fixed and that she didn't need to do anything but come out and be happy.

Tears slipped from beneath her lashes. No one was going to rescue her, take care of her. No one ever had. What order there would be in her life, she was responsible for imposing. Her father had dealt her a cruel hand and all she could do was make the best of it.

Lindsay straightened, brushed the tears from her cheeks, and took a deep breath. She'd check on Richard, then placate Havers. And then, while she was still filthy from the fire, she'd climb up into the attic for the cradle. There was no point in having Jeb do it when she needed to see what among the stored goods could be sold to pay for the food this week anyway. Next week . . . The tears welled in her eyes again. Lindsay blinked them away and rapped her knuckles firmly against Richard's door.

The door opened within seconds and the slim, small, impeccably attired George Havers started at the sight of her. He recovered his composure quickly, however, and bowed slightly at the waist. "Miss MacPhaull," he said, pulling the door wider and stepping aside. "Your housekeeper led me to believe that our meeting was to be postponed until tomorrow."

"I would be most appreciative if we could put it off until then, Mr. Havers," Lindsay replied, entering the room. Richard lay just as he had the last time she'd seen him. She managed a smile for the manservant and added, "This morning has been the longest day of my life and I'm afraid that, at present, I wouldn't be able to give your concerns the full and considered attention they deserve."

"I understand, Miss MacPhaull," he said with another bow. "Tomorrow will be quite acceptable."

"Thank you." *And thank Abigail for smoothing my way.* "I was tending to Mr. Stennett's head wound and thought that, since I was nearby, I might sit with Richard while you see to the preparation of his luncheon and to having your own."

"That is most considerate of you," Havers replied, easing toward the door. "I shan't be gone overlong. Mr. Patterson seems to be resting comfortably."

And how would they know if he was uncomfortable? Lindsay wondered, watching the slow rise and fall of Richard's chest. "Please take what time you need, Mr. Havers," she said absently as the manservant pulled the door closed behind him.

The bedcovers were smooth, the drapes drawn, and a small fire was burning in the hearth. Richard had been shaved that morning and his hair had been combed in its usual manner. There was nothing that needed her attention. Lindsay stood at the lower corner of the bed and leaned her shoulder against the carved bedpost. Did he know that she was there? Was he aware of anything going on around him?

Part of her yearned to hear his voice, to share her burdens with him and receive his wise counsel. And yet part of her sensed that there were things she wouldn't have been able to tell him, things he wouldn't have been able to understand. She had learned long ago the necessity of acceptance, of making the best out of the less than ideal. Richard, despite being paralyzed from the waist down, had always believed in his ability to eventually mold circumstance to his will.

"I know what you expect of me," she said softly. "And I expect it of myself. I should be making it difficult for Mr. Stennett to exercise control. Legally, he doesn't have the power to make decisions yet.

"But he strikes me as being a good man, Richard. He risked his life to bring people out of the burning apartment building. How many men can you name who would have done that?"

There was no answer and Lindsay watched him for several long moments before beginning again. "He's intelligent, too. It took him all of an hour yesterday afternoon to look at the books and see that the company is in desperate straits.

"You'll be pleased to know," she offered with a weak smile, "that one of his first priorities is to put an end to Henry's and Agatha's spending. The caterwauling will be ear-piercing, of course. I've warned him and he isn't the least bit deterred. Nothing seems to give him pause, Richard. Nothing. In terms of resolve, he's really a most admirable man.

"I know," she admitted, staring into the dancing flames of the hearth fire. "I'm letting myself be distracted. I should be focusing my attention on his less than redeeming qualities and my efforts on doing everything I can to keep him from taking his fifty-two thousand dollars out of the company."

And yet?

The unspoken question hung in the still air of the darkened room, heavy and quietly demanding. She looked at Richard, lying so still and pale. He'd spent the last twenty years of his life confined to a wheeled chair and never let the disability deter him from his responsibilities. He'd adapted and compensated and held to his purpose. How could she tell him that she was weary of struggling against the tide of circumstance? Her body was whole and sound. She was almost forty years younger than he was. How could she tell him that she found comfort in Jack's strength and determination? That the real reason she couldn't hold the fight against Jackson Stennett was because she couldn't fault either the soundness or the logic of his actions? That she knew instinctively that his course was the necessary one and that he was an honorable man? How could she explain any of that without hurting Richard's feelings, without denigrating all that he'd put into the maintenance of her world?

She couldn't. And so she kept the truth to herself. Instead, she told him about the encounter with Henry that morning and how he and Edith and Agatha couldn't come to dinner that evening because they were going to the theater. She told him about Jeb and Lucy Rutherford's baby and the apartment fire and Mrs. Kowalski and her cat. She asked him what he wanted her to do about Havers and his yet unanswered demands for better accommodations.

Richard remained still and soundless and Lindsay kept talking in order to push away the condemnation she imagined in his silence. She was still rattling on, painfully aware of how forced her conversation was, when a knock on the door mercifully spared her further effort. She opened it with a tight smile, expecting to find Havers on the other side, a tray in his hands.

It was Abigail Beechum who stood there, though, and

Lindsay's forced smile eased as she gestured the house-keeper into the room; there was no need to pretend with Abigail.

"I was passing in the hall and couldn't help hearing," Abigail said, her gaze drifting past Lindsay to Richard's still form. "I thought perhaps . . ." The light in her eyes went out and a deep sadness softened her features.

"It was just me," Lindsay supplied gently. "Trying to convince myself that I'm doing what's right, what Richard would expect of me."

Abigail pursed her lips and, after a moment, softly sighed and turned to face Lindsay squarely. "You have good instincts and exceptional judgment. You'll do what you must, child. And, in the end, it will work out for the best."

Lindsay swallowed back the threat of tears and managed a tremulous smile. "You have a great deal more confidence in me than I have in myself."

"I have no more faith in you," Abigail whispered, reaching out to touch her cheek, "than Richard has always had."

Tears welled in Lindsay's eyes. There was no holding them back this time, and as they spilled down her cheeks, she wrapped her arms around Abigail, burying her face in her housekeeper's shoulder to quietly sob, "I am so grateful to have had you both in my life. So very grateful."

"It will be all right, Lindsay," Abigail crooned, holding her tight. "Trust yourself. And know that I'm here for you. Always."

CHAPTER NINE

A BATH, CLEAN CLOTHES, clean hair, and knowing you could afford to buy food . . . The simplest of things were the ones that gave the greatest pleasure, Lindsay mused as she came down the stairs. Her sense of satisfaction would be complete if she found Primrose and Emile actually cooking the evening meal. The study door stood open and a movement within caught her attention. Lindsay altered her course.

Jackson sat behind the huge mahogany desk, frowning slightly as he contemplated something in the papers spread out before him. He, too, had experienced the wondrous joy of a bath and clean clothes. She saw no bandage of any sort on his head. Of course. He looked up with his eyes, meeting her gaze only briefly before he slowly assessed her from hairpins to hem and back again. His frown changed to an appreciative smile that sent an exquisite shiver through her.

Alarmed by her reaction, she seized the conversation, determined to keep it directed away from herself. "I distinctly recall Dr. Bernard telling me that he'd ordered you to bed rest for a couple of days."

"He suggested it. I've decided to ignore it." He motioned her into the study, saying as he did, "An offer's come in on the St. Louis property."

At last, a bit of good news. She advanced, coming to a halt in front of the desk and accepting the document he handed her. It was from Percival Little, the prospective buyer in Boston and the senior partner of Little, Bates and Company. His was usually the last of the offers to come in. Interesting that his had been the first this time.

"How much did you ask for it?" Jackson asked.

She looked at the numbers and her heart sank. "Twice this much," she supplied, handing the paper back. "I detest the offer–counteroffer process. It takes so much time."

"Not to mention that it would be so much easier if everyone were direct and honest right from the start about what they wanted and expected."

For some reason she felt that he wasn't speaking about just business transactions, that he was also making a veiled reference to personal relationships. If she were to be honest and direct with him about their relationship, what would she say? With no clear answer, she opted for a general truth, "Unfortunately, that's not the way the world works."

He considered her for a long moment and then began to sort the papers as he drawled, "No, it's not, is it?"

And he was disappointed by that fact. Lindsay battled the impulse to apologize. "The reporters are going to be here soon, Jack. They're going to ask about the fire. There will also be questions about the MacPhaull Company in general."

He leaned back in the chair, his gaze steady and direct. "And what do you intend to tell them?"

"I don't know," she admitted, feeling her pulse quicken. His eyes were so dark and yet so soft. As before, she felt her soul being drawn into the depths of them. Her thoughts didn't scatter; they softly drifted to the edge of her awareness.

"Lindsay?"

She drew a deep breath and with great effort pulled her mind back to business. "There's no avoiding the fact that Richard is incapacitated," she said, settling into a chair and gripping the arms to ground herself. "If the reporters don't already know it, then it's only a matter of days before someone in the business community notices his absence and the questions will begin in earnest. There are two ways to go from that point, both having distinct advantages and disadvantages. Which to choose depends on what you intend to do with the assets and how you want to go about it."

"What are the choices?"

It was a straightforward business question. Why did she hear it as being wrapped in black velvet? Lindsay tightened her grip on the chair. "In the first one, I say that while Richard is indeed ill, he's expected to recover fully and that he continues to advise me as he's always done. The circumstances of the MacPhaull Company remain essentially unchanged and business is being conducted as usual."

"All of it a bald-faced lie."

"Yes," she admitted, hearing the censure in his voice. Again, she fought back the urge to apologize. "I don't like it, either," she offered instead. "But in making it our official truth, the vultures can be kept at bay. What assets you need to dispose of can be sold for higher prices if the buyers don't know that the company's in both turmoil and desperate straits. The drawback is that if you intend to tell Henry and Agatha the truth, the reporters will soon be back here knowing that they've been lied to. My brother and sister are not very skilled at keeping cards close to their vests. If they know something, all of New York soon knows it."

"The other choice?"

"Basically, we tell them the truth," she answered. "I tell them that Richard's health is immaterial because, in my father's recent passing, both the ownership and the management of the company came into your control. I then paint you as a paragon of business acumen. I'd probably even go so far as to tell the tale of your heroic rescues in the midst of the fire. I would, of course, neglect to mention that your objective is to dismantle the company as quickly and efficiently as possible."

"That keeping the vultures at bay concern again," he observed, watching her intently. "And what would be the advantages and disadvantages of this course?"

"The primary advantage lies in it being the truth. Honesty is always easier to live with than lies, don't you think?"

"Oh, definitely."

Again, she had the distinct impression that he was referring to relationships outside of business. "With the truth, we wouldn't have to explain why you're involved in the decision-making when people ask. And ask they will, Jack. Secondly, if people know that you're decisive and brave as well as a competent businessman, you'll have their respect even before you go into any buy–sell negotiations with them."

"And the disadvantages?"

"In a business sense, people are going to be watching your actions very closely. There will be some who'll assume that you do indeed intend to dismantle the company. While you'll have their respect, you won't have the element of secrecy or surprise for very long. Once you actually make the first move to sell the first property, they'll know, and the vultures will circle.

"And in a more personal sense," she added, "Henry and Agatha are going to know with the next edition of the paper that their circumstances are drastically changed. You won't have a chance to tell them yourself or in the way that you'd prefer. Today's fire will seem a minor thing in comparison to how they're going to react."

He grinned. "We'll have to barricade the doors."

"And Primrose will have to boil the oil," she added, her heart suddenly and insanely light. How easily he made her troubles laughable. It was a gift, truly. One she appreciated very much.

"What would you prefer to tell the reporters, Lindsay?" he asked, his grin still broad, his eyes bright.

That Jackson Stennett is in charge and none of it is my problem anymore. God is good and merciful. "If you'd delay saying anything to Henry and Agatha," she suggested, opting to be rational, "I'd prefer to go the first way. You can get more for the assets with that strategy."

His smile faded as he considered that, and then he cocked a brow to ask, "What about the living with a lie?"

"All of this is a lie, Jack," she said, gesturing to the room and accoutrements around them. "What's one more?"

"A lot," he instantly countered. "Tell the reporters the truth, Lindsay."

Her stomach clenched. "But Henry and Agatha—"

"Will sure as hell regret they didn't show up to dinner when they were invited, won't they?"

"Oh, God," she quietly moaned, imagining the scene Henry and Agatha would create. "You don't know what you're unleashing."

"I don't really care."

She did care, and the looming confrontation was something she didn't want to witness. MacPhaull Rules weren't that strong; they'd be blown to itty bitty little pieces. "I have an idea," Lindsay offered. "You stay here and deal with my brother and sister. I'll go to Texas and herb your cattle, or whatever it is that you do with them."

He laughed. "It's *herd*, Lindsay. *Herd*."

There was a quiet knocking from the door. Jackson looked that way and Lindsay turned in the chair to do the same. Mrs. Beechum stood circumspectly on the other side of the threshold, her empty dress sleeve tucked into the waistband of her skirt. In her hand she held a large rectangular box. Lindsay instantly recognized the signature color of both the box itself and the ornately tied bow. Goldsmith was the finest and the most expensive jeweler in the city.

"Pardon the intrusion, Miss Lindsay," she said, "but this package has just arrived for Miss Agatha and I presume it to be of sufficient value to deliver straight to you for safe-keeping."

Lindsay rose from the chair and went to her house-keeper. The box was weighty and Lindsay clenched her teeth. Damn Agatha.

"Also," Abigail Beechum said, "the reporter from the *Herald* is here. I've put him in the parlor. Primrose is preparing the tea."

"Thank you, Mrs. Beechum," Lindsay replied as she yanked an end of satin ribbon and gathered the loosened binding into her fist. "Please tell him that I'll be there in a few moments."

The housekeeper nodded and left as Lindsay went to the desk, tossed aside the ribbon, set the package in front of Jackson, and opened the lid. A black velvet box lay inside, nestled in golden tissue. With a deep sigh of certainty, Lindsay lifted the case and popped open the hinged top. An ornate diamond-and-ruby necklace glinted brightly from a nest of midnight-blue satin.

"Is it pretty?"

She looked over the top of the case to meet Jackson Stennett's gaze. "No one can fault Agatha's taste," she answered, turning the case so that he could see the purchase for himself. As his brow shot up, Lindsay smiled thinly and added, "Unfortunately, she just can't seem to grasp the notion that she doesn't have the money to go with it."

"What do you intend to do about it?"

Lindsay closed the case and placed it back in the delivery box as she replied, "I'll return it, of course. And with it will be a letter apologizing for the fact that it's being returned, as well as informing Mr. Goldsmith and his staff that all of my sister's future purchases will have to have my prior approval."

"I'm guessing," Jack drawled, "that Agatha isn't going to be too happy about that."

"No, she's not," Lindsay admitted, thinking that Jackson Stennett had a true gift for understatement. She gave him a reassuring smile as she squared her shoulders and added, "I'll see to writing the letter this evening. It's too late in the day to send anything to Goldsmith's, but I'll see that it's done in the morning. But first things first. I need to meet with the reporter sitting patiently in the parlor."

"I'll give you five minutes, Lindsay, and then I'll join you."

"You don't trust me," she accused, instantly hurt and angry.

"It's not that at all," he said softly. "This isn't exactly a pleasant task and you shouldn't have to go it alone."

Despite herself, Lindsay was shocked. This was not the natural order of things. Richard would take tasks from her because he insisted that he could do them better. Her mother had taken them because Lindsay was incapable of doing them to her satisfaction. Mrs. Beechum would take them because they were within the realm of her housekeeping duties. Never had anyone offered such a kindness. It made her throat tighten uncomfortably. "If you think you must," she replied. "But please know that I'm perfectly capable of handling the situation without assistance. From you or anyone else."

He nodded and countered, "I don't doubt your abilities at all. But just because you can carry the load by yourself doesn't mean that you should have to. I'll be in in a few minutes."

She left the study knowing that, despite her best intentions and Richard's unspoken expectations, the scales on Jackson Stennett were beginning to tip. While she resented his having inherited all that she'd worked for, she also knew that she wasn't feeling her usual sense of being overwhelmed. It was hard to place a dollars and cents value on the comfort to be had in sharing a burden, but if she emerged from the company reorganization reasonably close to being financially sound . . . What was money compared to knowing that for a time you weren't alone in facing difficulties? In that regard, Jack was well on his way to proving himself priceless.

THE BACK OF HIS HEAD POUNDING, Jackson stood just outside the parlor door, listening to Lindsay paint him as the greatest hero since Hercules. It was almost embarrassing to enter the parlor following all that praise, but he managed it with aplomb and then neatly turned the tables on her, telling the very young Mr. Horatio Wellsbacher of the *New York Herald* of his rescue by the daring and fearless Lindsay MacPhaull. Wellsbacher scribbled notes furiously. Lindsay's cheeks turned the most delicious-looking shade of rosy peach. And it took every bit of restraint Jackson possessed to keep from wrapping his arm around her shoulders, drawing her close, and tasting.

And when the telling of the fire stories was done, Wellsbacher thought to gather some details for the whole thing. He asked what sort of business Jack was in that had brought him to New York. Lindsay answered beautifully, as though she'd had months to rehearse the lines. Jack picked up his cue and took the conversation from there, laying out the story of Billy's death, his own inheritance of the MacPhaull Company, and his determination to see that the hard work of Billy's youngest daughter hadn't been in vain.

Wellsbacher took notes the whole time, rarely looking up from his notepad, and only occasionally asking a question for clarification or expansion. Lindsay sat with her hands folded demurely in her lap, the perfect picture of a circumspect lady. When she slid Jackson a look, silent laughter in her eyes, he felt an intense desire to see just how much of a proper lady she wasn't.

As he struggled with the impulse, it occurred to him that he did a lot better resisting it when she wasn't around. Whenever she was near, his brain seemed to quit listening to his common sense. Focusing on the business task at hand was exceedingly difficult, but Lindsay—bless her—kept his attention from going too far astray by supplying bits of information and prompting him to add his own contributions.

When Jackson declared that there was nothing further to be said, the young man jumped to his feet, extended his hand, and furiously pumped Jackson's while gushing about the incredible journalistic opportunity he and the lovely, lovely Miss MacPhaull had just given him.

Lindsay offered to have Mrs. Beechum show him to the door, but Horatio Wellsbacher couldn't be delayed by such unnecessary social niceties. Declaring that he remembered where the door was, he managed to keep a dignified pace until he reached the foyer. From there, he ran, his notepad clutched in his hand, his gaze obviously fixed forward and on the wondrous story he dreamed of handing his editor.

Jack grinned in amusement as the front door slammed closed with enough force to rock the pictures on the parlor walls. His amusement was replaced by pleasant surprise when Lindsay touched his arm and, smiling up at him, asked, "Did Dr. Bernard say anything to you about not drinking for a while?"

His reaction was without thought; Lindsay's hand lay

on his forearm and he covered her fingers with his own. Her smile warmed and he felt his heart lurch. "No. Why?"

"I feel the need for a celebratory sherry and my mother always maintained that it is in exceedingly poor taste to drink alone."

He thought he heard a small voice suggesting that he not allow her so close, but the words were muffled and seemed to come from a great distance. "I wouldn't want you to sin," he said, leading her out of the parlor and back to the study, where the liquor was kept. And because he was tired of controlling his impulses, he added, "Not without me anyway."

She laughed softly, genuinely, and he had a hard time swallowing. Speech was momentarily beyond him and so they arrived at the beverage cart without another word. Lindsay slipped her hand from beneath his to pour their drinks and he felt the loss of her touch with a sharp pang of regret. God, he was in trouble. Deep trouble. He had to get a handle on himself before he did something fatally stupid.

"What are we celebrating?" he asked as she handed him a glass of whiskey.

"A masterfully controlled interview," she replied, lifting her glass of sherry in salute. "You did beautifully, sir."

Again he reacted without thinking, lifting his hand to touch his hat brim as he smiled and said, "Thank you, ma'am." Only there wasn't a hat on his head. Where had he left it? He'd been wearing it when they'd left Jeb and Lucy's. With a wince, he remembered when and where and how it had been lost. At Lindsay's questioning look, he asked, "You didn't happen to drag my hat out of the fire with me, did you?"

Her shoulders sagged and then she said softly, "It didn't even occur to me to look for it. I'm sorry."

Sweet Jesus, now she'd done it. She'd gone and apologized.

"Oh, dear," she gasped, her eyes widening as she, too, realized what she'd done and what the consequence would be. Then, just a quickly, she took a deep breath, closed her eyes, said, "All right. Get it over with," and tilted her face up, presenting him with her lips.

Kissing her was what he wanted to do, what he'd threatened to do. And if he did, it would be a giant first step down the road of regrettable endings. How the hell could he get them both out of this gracefully?

"Have you ever been kissed, Lindsay?" he asked, noting her firmly set lips and thinking that he might be able to plead chivalry. She nodded, her eyes remaining closed. Jackson silently swore as he dropped his gaze to his whiskey glass. The notion came out of the blue and he seized it, not knowing whether it was wise or not, but willing to take the chance. It was better than certain disaster. He dipped his finger into the glass then reached up, gently trailing it over her lower lip.

The firm line softened at his first touch and his heart raced. Then her lips parted and she lightly touched the tip of her tongue to his fingertip. His knees went weak as his breath caught and his blood went hot. Even as he told himself not to, he traced the curve of her lip again. Lindsay's sigh was pure seduction and he pulled his hand back before she could feel the trembling in it.

Her eyes fluttered open and a soft smile touched the corners of her mouth. "I've never been kissed quite like that."

"I'm not sure that kissing you any other way is a particularly smart idea." *Not that this was particularly smart, either,* he silently added.

"You were the one who set the penalty," she reminded him. "Perhaps you'd like to reconsider. I'd certainly be willing to allow a change in the rules."

Jackson was about to agree when she slowly trailed her tongue over her lower lip. If she knew what she was doing to him, she was an extraordinary seductress. If she didn't, then she had incredible natural instincts for the art. Either way, she had a siren's call.

"I've never tasted whiskey before," she said, her voice a sultry whisper of discovery. "It's rather nice in a smoky sort of way, isn't it?"

His common sense whimpered once and surrendered. Jack dipped his finger in his whiskey again. "The fellow who kissed you wasn't any good at it, was he?" he asked, slowly painting her lower lip again. Her eyes remained open this time, her gaze fastened on his.

Lindsay's heart raced. Inviting Jackson Stennett's kisses was beyond foolhardy. But never before had a man's touch stirred her as Jackson's did. It made her feel alive and wildly, wondrously free. The feeling was too heady to deny, too luscious to refuse a deeper taste. Whatever the price of asking for more, she'd pay it and pay it gladly. Let others think whatever they would. "He had the reputation of being a very skillful lover."

Lover? "Oh, yeah?" Jack drawled, intrigued by the possibilities and casting aside any notion of propriety. "Did his performance live up to the advance billing?"

She gently licked his fingertip again and an exquisite jolt of pleasure shot through him. As he struggled to find a sliver of good judgment, Lindsay whispered, "A lady doesn't kiss and tell, Jack."

It was an invitation if he'd ever heard one. "That's good to know," he said, trailing his fingertip down over her lip, her chin, and then slowly up the line of her jaw. Such very delicate lines, such acceptance in her eyes. She wasn't going to change her mind. God only knew why she was courting his advance, but the temptation was too strong to resist. He slipped his hand to her nape, cradling her head as she lifted her lips to his.

Lindsay closed her eyes and drew a slow breath, her heart racing. It wouldn't go the way it had the last time, she reassured herself; she was much wiser now. And she knew that Jack wasn't going to stay. Besides, being with Jack wasn't at all like it had been when—

Sensation swept away all conscious thought. Feather-light and gentle, his kiss whispered promises of sweet, dark mysteries and slow, wanton revelries. She abandoned herself in the pleasure of the caress and was rewarded by the luxurious deepening of the kiss. His tongue traced the path that his finger had blazed over her lip and she met it with her own, melting into him and sighing in welcome as he drew her closer and tasted her more deeply still.

She was molten and weak, soaring and stronger than she had ever been. Heady sensation and wonderment, the heat and potent tension of timeless instinct. . . . Then there was only the lingering shadow of what had been. And she hungered for more of what was gone.

Jackson, his breathing ragged, stepped back from her, back from the brink of too late. She was so damn easy to kiss, so damn delicious. He'd only thought he was a goner before. He hadn't known just how intoxicating her lips were, how sweetly she could surrender. And as she looked up at him now, her lips still dewy from his kiss, her blue eyes softened by yearning . . .

God help him; all he wanted to do was lean down, begin again, and let her finish seducing him. But wanting and doing what were smart were two different things and he knew it. Neither one of them needed the complications inherent in taking a lover.

She blinked and then looked away, but not before he saw the shadows of doubt and regret pass across her beautiful features. Part of him wanted to assure her that she had done nothing to be ashamed of. Another part of him recognized the advantage of letting her put some distance between them. She'd tell him that she had reacted inappropriately and that she was appalled, that she would never let it happen again. And, if he were any sort of gentleman, he'd apologize for taking advantage of her inexperience and swear to never touch her again. *If* he were a gentleman. She drew a steadying breath and Jack braced himself.

"Jack, I should tell—"

"I think dinner's being served," he interrupted as the faint notes of a bell sounded from the dining room. Silently blessing Primrose for the timely reprieve, he offered Lindsay his arm, saying brightly, "Shall we?"

She took it and allowed him to guide her from the study. In the foyer, it crossed his mind to forget dinner, to turn and go up the stairs, and give her a choice between her room or his. Good judgment for once prevailed. It chafed, but he endured.

They were seated opposite each other at one end of the huge table when she next spoke. "Jackson?"

"Yes?"

Apparently having thought better of whatever it was

she'd intended to say, she shook her head and with a soft smile said, "Never mind."

Even in the candlelight, he could see the color flooding her cheeks. "You were going to say that you liked my kiss better, weren't you?" he teased.

She met his gaze, her smile tentative. "Well, yes. Among other things."

It was those *other things* that he didn't really want to talk about. Facing the matter square on meant having to close the door. It had been a helluva long time since a kiss had singed that hard and deep. For the moment, it was nice having possibilities in front of him—even if he knew deep down inside that in the end he was going to have to turn his back on them. He smiled at her and winked, and then, with all the grace and social elegance of a three-legged plow horse, deliberately changed the direction of their conversation. "When do you think Henry and Agatha will see the paper?" he asked, cutting into his steak.

Lindsay barely kept her shoulders from sagging with relief. Jack clearly didn't want to discuss anything of a personal nature, mercifully sparing her the ordeal of confessing her past sins in order to explain her current ones.

"The evening edition of the paper has probably already been typeset," she answered, eagerly attacking her own steak. "I doubt that the news of the MacPhaull Company's new ownership will be cause to stop the presses. Given that, I think it's safe to assume they'll see the story in tomorrow morning's edition. They'll charge forth immediately, of course."

He took a sip of wine. "If you'd prefer to be elsewhere for the confrontation, I'd certainly understand."

Jackson Stennett was a prince among men. But as tempting as it was to let him take charge, she still wore the yoke of obligation. "I think whether or not I'm there depends on what you intend to say to them."

"In a nutshell, I'm going to tell them that they're going to grow up and be responsible for themselves and their own finances. They aren't your responsibility anymore."

"They don't know how to be responsible," she calmly pointed out.

"Then it's high time they learned."

"Jack . . ."

"I've looked at the books, Lindsay," he countered, cutting himself more meat. "I understand what the numbers are saying. You make money and your brother and sister spend it. They don't contribute anything to the MacPhaull coffers except bills for payment. Agatha's new necklace being a prime example. Their free ride is going to come to an end, Lindsay; an abrupt and permanent end."

Her appetite gone, Lindsay laid her fork aside. "But how will they survive? Henry has children whose welfare has to be considered."

He chewed slowly and swallowed before answering, "I'm going to take out of the business just what I need to clear the loans on the land Billy left me. Then I'll equally divide what's left between the three of you so that each has income-producing assets in your own name. What Henry and Agatha decide to do with theirs is their business. It's none of mine. Most importantly, it's none of yours, either."

Oh God. It was a good plan; equitable and sound, except for the fact that Henry and Agatha would be bankrupt within a very short period of time. The only hope they had of remaining solvent was to let her manage their assets for them. Which is exactly what they'd insist upon, she realized. Jackson could divide, but he wouldn't be able to conquer. The minute he went back to Texas, the management of the MacPhaull properties would revert to the way it had always been done. It was probably best to let him have his illusions, though. The less conflict between the two of them, the better.

"It's fair, Lindsay."

"I know," she agreed, her mind considering the other likely consequences of his intended actions. "I also know that Henry is going to see getting a third as considerably less than what he was hoping for."

"He can be grateful for a third or get nothing at all."

"And if he challenges the Will, Jack? What will you do then?"

He shrugged and sampled his wine. "He won't have grounds to contest it, Lindsay. Ever. The MacPhaull Company was Billy's to do with as he pleased and he gave it all to me; lock, stock, and barrel. Elmer Smith, the lawyer in Texas, might not be able to punch his way out of a rotten flour sack, but he's got a mind like a steel trap. He made sure the will was sound, Lindsay. It can't be broken. Otis Vanderhagen knew that the minute he laid his eyes on it."

"But what if Henry decides to contest it, just to be difficult?" she persisted. "Or to force you into giving him more than you intend to?"

"It'd be a real stupid thing to do for whatever reason."

"Why?"

With a sigh of tried patience, he laid down his silverware. "First of all, Henry has no say in the MacPhaull Company operations. Added to that is the fact that Billy's last Will hasn't been formally recognized by the New York courts yet and so the ownership of the MacPhaull assets hasn't been officially transferred. Billy is still the owner of record and Richard is still the manager."

She knew that and she nodded. "Which means that, legally, nothing has changed at all. I can still buy and sell and do whatever I deem necessary to keep the company fiscally sound."

"Exactly. Henry can pitch all the fits he likes, but it's not going to get him anywhere."

"But if I were to pitch a fit about helping you dismantle the company . . ." she ventured, watching him.

His gaze was dark and somber. Quietly, he said, "You could put a real big knot in my rope for a while."

Yes, she could. And very easily. If she were of a mind to. The larger question was why she wasn't. "If I were going to fight you for control, you and I wouldn't be sitting here eating dinner together tonight."

"No, we probably wouldn't," he drawled, going back to his steak. "I'd be in a hotel somewhere and you'd be scrambling to sell whatever you could for whatever price you could get, just so that you could hand me an empty bag when the courts made you give it to me."

"I could still do that." *I should be doing that.*

"But you won't."

He was so confident in his victory. The ease with which he'd apparently achieved it rankled her pride. "How can you be so sure?" she asked tauntingly, hoping to ruffle his composure.

"You're a good and decent person, Lindsay MacPhaull. You play fair and deal square. If you had it in you to be even just a little bit ruthless, you'd have cut Henry and Agatha off a long time ago. You'd have left me in the fire this morning."

"I could decide that it's time I learned how to be ruthless."

Again he sighed and laid down his silverware. "You could," he agreed softly, staring down at his plate. He looked up at her. "Or, for the first time in your life, you could decide to hand over the reins, sit back, and let someone take care of you for a while."

Her heart skittered. "That would require a great deal of trust on my part," she observed as tendrils of fear snaked through her.

"Yep," he replied, pushing back his chair and rising to his feet. "Just as much as I have in you. Good night, Lindsay. Let me know in the morning what you decide."

Lindsay watched him go, torn between knowing what she knew Richard would tell her to do and what she wanted to do. Yes, she could—as Jack had so descriptively said—put a knot in his rope for a while. In terms of her own financial interests, it was what she should do.

If her mother were still living, the lecture on responsibility to family would have already begun in earnest. Interwoven with that tirade would have been another one on the importance of feminine virtue and how its sacrifice should be considered only in exchange for significant business concessions.

But she wasn't her mother, and she wasn't Richard, either. She was Lindsay MacPhaull and she was tired of struggling through the turmoil on her own. She could sell off property and keep what pennies she got or she could let Jack do it and hope he could not only get more for it, but that he was also a man of his word. Would it really be all that horrible to let someone else be the rock of the MacPhaulls for a while?

For a while was the key, she reminded herself. Jack would go back to Texas, and when he did, her life would go back to normal. The real question, then, was whether she could temporarily surrender control and still have the strength to stand on her own again when the time came and she needed to.

Just how long was the respite Jack offered? He'd said he had to have it all done within sixty days. Lindsay mentally subtracted the time it would take for him to return to Texas and then the days necessary to actually pay off the creditors there. What remained was just over a month. She knew people who considered that span of time to be barely enough for a suitable holiday.

But, she sadly reminded herself, allowing Jack to manage the reorganization of the MacPhaull Company without hindrance wouldn't result in a complete abdication of her responsibilities. Jack would be shouldering only part of them. It could be a real holiday only if she somehow escaped the expectations of her brother and sister. That, she knew, was never going to happen. And there was absolutely no reason for Jackson Stennett to relieve her of that daunting burden. In fact, Jack's intention to make Henry and Agatha responsible for their own finances added to the weight she already bore for them.

Swallowing back tears, Lindsay placed her napkin beside her plate and rose from the table. She needed to write the letter to Mr. Goldsmith and then put it and the necklace into the study wall safe before she retired for the evening and Agatha returned home from the theater. If Agatha could get her hands on her newest bauble, there would be no prying it free. It would be yet another horrendous debt heaped on the mountain of those Lindsay already couldn't afford.

Maybe, she mused as she headed toward the study, she should consider running away to some far corner of the world where Henry and Agatha couldn't find her. It was what her father had done. And she could, on days like today, truly and honestly understand why he'd surrendered to the temptation.

JACKSON STOOD AT THE WINDOW of his darkened room and absently gazed over the moonlit garden at the back of the house. Even in the relative darkness, he could tell that the formal plantings needed tending, that the whole of it was suffering from the effects of the Panic and the demands on Lindsay's limited resources. In the grand scheme of things, gardens couldn't rightfully claim to be a priority. God knew Lindsay had more to be concerned about than the fact that new gravel needed to be put down on the pathways.

Jackson thought back over the course of the day and all that he'd learned about the snarl Billy had left him to untangle. With a wry smile, Jack consoled himself with the certain knowledge that no matter how hard his day had been, Lindsay's had been considerably more difficult. There had been the unexpected meeting with Henry the Imperial Lord, the fire, the complications of unexpected houseguests, and then the necessity of facing the reporter.

And the necklace. Jesus, he couldn't forget the necklace. The thing had to be worth thousands of dollars, and it was a sure bet the jeweler hadn't just given it to Agatha out of the goodness of his heart. His own heart had damn near rolled over when he'd laid eyes on it.

How Agatha thought Lindsay could afford to pay for it was a mystery. Just yesterday morning, he'd stood in the study and very clearly heard Lindsay tell Agatha that she'd been put on a clothing allowance because their funds were limited. Apparently, Agatha had chosen to ignore the dose of reality. He'd bet the necklace that Lindsay had been just as honest with Henry about their financial situation. And given the expectations Henry had declared that morning, her effort had gone to pretty much the same pointless end.

He'd have brought Lindsay's brother and sister to heel a long time ago. Why hadn't Richard Patterson? Because Lindsay protested and protected them, he answered himself with a slow shake of his head. Why did she defend them? From what he could tell so far, they were both rude, self-centered, and ungrateful people. God, Lindsay MacPhaull either had the patience of a saint or she actually enjoyed being abused.

A distant high-pitched noise suddenly intruded on his thoughts. Jack let the curtain fall back into place. It came again, accompanied by the sound of a crash. Was someone breaking into the house? He'd left Lindsay downstairs alone. His heart racing, Jack strode across his room, tore open the door, and started down the hall. He was halfway to the top of the stairs when Lindsay's voice rang out clear and strong and firmly calm.

"I meant what I said, Agatha. It goes back to Mr. Goldsmith in the morning. We barely have enough money to pay for the food on our table."

They were both in the foyer. And judging by the noise ringing up the stairwell, Agatha had just flung the silver calling card tray against a wall. Jack drew a deep breath. Should he step into the sisters' confrontation? Or should he just stand back and let Lindsay handle the situation? The former seemed likely to make matters even worse than they already were. But the latter course seemed downright cowardly. He reached the top of the stairs and froze, gazing in amazement over the scene below.

"You can't tell me what I can and can't have!" Agatha yelled, stamping her foot.

Lindsay, near the far wall, straightened, the silver calling card tray in her hand. "We can't afford such extravagances," she deliberately replied, returning the tray to the center table and placing it back beside the vase of flowers.

Agatha suddenly snatched up the crystal vase and lifted it above her head. "Give me my necklace, Lindsay. Give it to me or I'll smash this to bits."

"Put it down," Lindsay commanded with deadly calm, tapping the top of the table with a finger. "If you break it, *you'll* be the one going without the food it would have bought. I swear it."

Agatha gasped, blinked a full dozen times, then slammed the vase down on the tabletop. Her compliance was fleeting, however. In almost the same instant that she put down the vase, she grabbed the flowers, flung them to the floor, and then proceed to kick them around the foyer as she squealed in outrage.

Jackson watched in slack-jawed astonishment as Lindsay leaned her hip against the edge of the table, crossed her arms, and said quietly, "When you're through with your tantrum . . ."

Agatha didn't even so much as pause to gasp for more air; not that Jackson had expected her to. Instead, she reached for the silver calling card tray.

Lindsay, her cheeks flooded with color and her eyes blazing, moved with lightning speed to swat her sister's hand.

Jack choked back his laughter as Agatha jerked her hand back and blinked at Lindsay in stunned, sudden silence.

"I'm sorry, but enough is enough, Agatha. You're behaving childishly."

Agatha lifted her chin with a huff, said, "I'm going to tell Henry what you've done," and then turned on her heel, yanked up the hems of her skirts, and strode toward the front door. "He'll make you give me back my necklace."

The sound of the slamming door reverberated through the entire house. Lindsay's shoulders slumped momentarily, but she quickly recovered her resolve. "You were right," she said quietly and without looking up at him. "She wasn't happy about the necklace being returned."

He stood there, not knowing what to say, but wishing there was something he could do to make Lindsay smile.

She scrubbed her palms over her face briefly and then sighed before saying, "I suppose there's nothing to be done at this point but clean up the mess. Good night, Jack."

"I'll help you," he offered, starting down.

"Thank you, but no thank you," she declared, looking at him for the first time. "If you don't mind," she said quietly, her voice strained, "I'd prefer to be alone right now. I hope you can understand."

He didn't, but he nodded anyway and retreated out of respect for her wishes. As he slowly made his way back to his room, Jack realized that he now knew the answer to his earlier pondering. Lindsay didn't enjoy being abused. Neither did she have the patience of a saint. Unfortunately, it appeared that she deeply regretted that she didn't. All things considered, though, there was hope for her in the long run.

She had a backbone of steel and her head was firmly set on her shoulders. She was a damn fine woman. A damn fine woman desperately trying to control a stampede of idiots.

THE MOON WAS BEGINNING to set and Jackson stood at the window of his bedroom, watching, puzzling the dream that had ended his sleep. He'd been at his house in Texas and walked out on the front porch at dawn. Right by the front steps, he'd seen a rosebush that hadn't been there before. Its flowers were a thousand shades of pink and the fragrance that wrapped around him had been as velvet as the petals had been to his touch.

And as he'd stood there, wondering where it had come from and who had planted it, it had begun to grow. Fast. He'd thought of that as he'd stood there in amazement and watched its canes wind around the porch railing, wrap up the post, and then stretch across the opening to spill across the railing on the other side.

The color and the fragrance had been magical and he'd breathed deep and grinned like a schoolboy. Until the rose reached the other end of the porch and he saw it twine around the straggling morning glory vines Maria Arabella had planted years ago. He'd started forward, determined to save the only thing he had left of her, but he'd gotten no farther than a single step when he realized that there was no saving to be done. The morning glories twined with the rose and were lifted higher, their blue cups tiny but soft islands in the riot of pink. He liked it. It seemed to be the way it was supposed to be. Right, somehow. It was all so wondrous, so unexpected. It made him happy. And just a little sad, too. As though he was giving up on something that had once been important.

And it had been that realization that had brought him from his sleep and kept him awake since. Dreams were the strangest things, he mused, shaking his head. There were some folks who believed that they were chock-full of important meanings and that you were supposed to spend hours trying to figure them out so you could change your life for the better. He'd never been particularly good at understanding what he was supposed to, though.

It was pretty obvious that this one had something to do with Maria Arabella, but God only knew what. She'd planted morning glories, but they hadn't survived the first summer's heat. And he'd held her in his arms as she'd died that winter. The rose growing so beautifully was just flat-out impossible. His mother had tried to grow them, but Texas had proven to be tougher than their thorns.

"The women in my life haven't been gardeners?" he guessed with a wry chuckle, heading back to his bed.

With his head cradled in his hands, Jack closed his eyes and focused on the memory of the roses running riot over his home in Texas. He still didn't know what it meant, but he liked it nonetheless. Roses. Wild roses. So impossibly, remarkably wondrous.

CHAPTER TEN

$\mathcal{J}$ACKSON PULLED ON HIS BOOT and then paused, straining to hear the noise that had caught his attention. It came again a few seconds later from behind a dark tapestry hanging on the inside wall of the room Lindsay had given him. He rose from the chair and strode across the thick carpet. Pulling back on the edge of the tapestry, he found a plain wooden door hidden beneath. Connecting rooms, he realized instantly. And someone was in the one on the other side. Who?

The noise came again and this time he was close enough to hear it more clearly. It sounded like wood striking wood; perhaps a dresser drawer or an armoire door being closed. Had Agatha returned to go through her morning dressing routine? Was it Mrs. Kowalski looking for her cat? Lucy or Jeb Rutherford? Or maybe it was Lindsay. Jack half-smiled. There was a keyhole beneath the cut-crystal doornob; it would be a simple matter to look and satisfy his curiosity.

Shaking his head, Jackson pulled the tapestry farther back and then knocked lightly on the door. There was no answer, no further sound from the other room. He knocked again and after waiting for a few seconds, indulged his curiosity. Surprisingly, the door was unlocked. The hinges squeaked only slightly as he inched it open and peered through the narrow opening.

The morning sunlight coming through the windows barely illuminated the room, but he could see enough to note that the carpet, wallpaper, draperies, and bed hangings were the color of dark, dark red roses. Here and there were touches of ivory—the rumpled sheets, the padded seat on the bench before the dressing table, some pillows in a high-backed, burgundy chair beside the fireplace. It was as though someone had tried to force a bit of light and feminine ease into the cavelike room.

Jackson considered the dressing table. The items on it were simple and few; a silver-backed mirror, a brush-and-comb set, a single perfume bottle, and a small silver jewelry box. Jack stepped back and pulled the door closed. The things were too nice, too expensive to belong to either Lucy or Mrs. Kowalski. And he was willing to bet that they were too simple and few to belong to the Agatha he had met his first day here. Mrs. Beechum's room was downstairs. That left the room to be Lindsay's.

He looked around the one he'd been given. It was just as dark as the other—as the whole house, for that matter—but more masculine. It was done up in dark greens and browns and plums and reminded Jackson, just a bit, of the main room in the house Billy had built his fourth year in Texas. That house wasn't dark, though. Billy had refused to put curtains of any sort on the windows. He'd once said that he didn't have any secrets.

Jackson snorted. Billy had had some damn big secrets; they just weren't in that house in Texas. They were in New York and waiting to take a bite out of Jack's hide. Taking his coat from the dressing tree, Jack glanced back at the tapestry. It didn't take a great mental leap to figure out that Lindsay had put him in what had been Billy's room. And it didn't take any greater leap to guess that Lindsay's room had once been her mother's.

How long had it been since the door between the two

rooms had been opened? Jack wondered. Billy had walked away seventeen years ago. Had the wife he'd left behind been a chaste martyr of abandonment? Had Lindsay given this room to the man who had been the not-so-accomplished lover? The latter possibility rankled. Telling himself that it wasn't any of his business if she had, Jack crossed to the door leading into the hallway. There was business to tend, decisions to make and see executed. Thinking about Lindsay in any respect beyond that wasn't in either of their best interests.

"I shall be gone only a few minutes, sir."

Jackson stopped, halfway across the threshold, and watched as a short but slender, crisply dressed man stepped backward out of the room into which Jackson had carried Richard Patterson's limp form two days earlier.

"I'll bring you some tea when I return," the other man said, pulling the door closed. He turned away, never seeing Jackson, and walked off toward the servants' stairs.

Havers, Jackson thought. Havers of the extravagant expectations. How'd he come to have them? Servants didn't usually feel so secure in their employment that they were comfortable in making demands for the continuance of it. What kind of leverage did he have on Patterson? Or was the leverage on Lindsay? So many questions . . . Jack glanced toward the back stairs and then moved resolutely toward the other door.

The drapes were drawn and the room was as dark as night. Jackson closed the door behind him and gave his eyes a moment to adjust. When they did, Jack found Patterson lying exactly where he'd been placed when he'd brought him in. The slow, shallow rise and fall of his chest was the only sign of life. Jack walked to the end of the bed and stood there in silence for a long moment.

"Lindsay thinks you're a paragon of business, you know," he said quietly. "And a wonderful human being who's taken care of her all these years. Is it the truth, old man? Are you really that kind, that astute? Or are you like everyone else in her life, sucking everything you can out of her?"

There was no answer, of course, and Jack settled his

shoulder against the carved post of the footboard. "Damn convenient for you to have that stroke when you did, by the way. Keeps you from having to answer some tough questions. Four buyers—just four and the same four—for fifteen years. Now that's interesting. Seems to me that they've got to be real grateful to you for selling them failing properties that they could so quickly turn around. If they weren't damned good friends of yours to begin with, they sure ought to be by now."

In Patterson's continued silence, Jack began to slowly pace the width of the room, talking more to himself than to the other man. "You know, the books are telling me that something's way off the mark here. I know what you took as an annual salary before the Panic set in. In my mind, it wasn't enough to pay for the kind of life that includes a manservant and a French chef. And you've managed to keep them employed the last year and a half even though you haven't taken your salary. Where's the money coming from, old man?

"I'm going to figure it out, you know," he said, pausing to study the ghostly white face surrounded by white linen. "I see three possibilities right up front. In one, you're a gullible old fool who's been taken time and time again. Frankly, I'm not going to put any money on that one. Lindsay's an intelligent woman and she wouldn't have gone along with you all these years if she thought you weren't pitching from a full loft. It takes someone smart to con someone smart.

"Which means there's really only two possibilites left to consider," Jack said, resuming his pacing. "In the first one, you're deliberately sabotaging a property, selling it low to one of your friends, then either taking a kickback or getting a percentage of the profits when they start to come in again. In the second one, you're playing a shell game, sabotaging the properties and then selling them to businesses you secretly own. That way *all* the profits are yours. In both cases, all the losses are Lindsay's.

"Yeah," Jack drawled quietly, stopping and facing his silent adversary. "I think you're a conniving, thieving son of a bitch, Richard Patterson. And by the time I'm done digging and sorting through this mess, I'm going to know the truth of it. If I'm wrong, I'll apologize. But I don't think I'm going to be wrong. Do you?"

Silence.

"And I figure you didn't manage all this on your own," Jack went on. "You had to have had some help, one way or the other. Someone had to do the dirty work of sabotage for you. And if it's a shell game, someone has to be at the other end of the post road and someone had to do the legal work in setting up the companies. Otis Vanderhagen comes to my mind on that last one. How about yours?"

He waited a second, knowing that there wouldn't be a reply, and then said, "You know what the worst thing is about all this? It's not the money. It's that there isn't any way that I can keep Lindsay from knowing that you've betrayed her trust. Billy left her behind and that was cruel and it was wrong. And Billy sure pulled the rug out from under her feet when he left the MacPhaull Company to me. On the surface of things, that looks to be just as mean-spirited as his having walked out on her all those years ago.

"But as an aside and just between us, I think he thought he was going to be upending Henry's world, not Lindsay's. Now why he'd want to do that to Henry is an intriguing question, but it's more of a curiosity than it is pressing in the big scheme of things.

"The whys of what Billy did can't be known for sure. What I do know is that when all the dust settles, Billy's sins are going to be nothing compared to yours. At least Billy didn't pretend to be the cornerstone of Lindsay's life, didn't pretend to have her best interests in mind. And handing the MacPhaull Company to me is going to turn out to be the wisest decision Billy ever made, whether he knew what he was doing or not. I'll salvage something for Lindsay out of all this. You can bank on that."

Jackson sighed and shook his head sadly. "But her heart's going to be broken when she learns that you've betrayed her more blackly and deliberately than her father ever did. I can't do anything about healing that wound, Patterson. All I can do is be satisfied with the certainty that your soul is going to rot forever in hell."

Richard Patterson remained still and deathly quiet, wholly unaffected by the sureness of his fate. Jackson watched him breathe for a while, willing the old man to rouse from his oblivion and answer all the accusations and suspicions that had been laid before him. In the continuing silence, Jack turned to leave, but paused, his hand on the doorknob, to quietly, earnestly add, "Just so you know, Patterson . . . I'll see justice done. When I have sufficient proof of what you've done to Lindsay, I'm going to put a pillow over your face and send you on your way."

Jackson had barely pulled the door closed when he heard the slight rattle of china on the back stairs. He stepped squarely into the hallway and waited. Havers appeared only seconds later, bearing a tray with a tea service.

"Sir," Havers said as he became aware of Jackson's presence.

"We haven't met, Havers. I'm Jackson Stennett."

Havers continued to advance, saying, "It's a pleasure to make your acquaintance, sir."

"Allow me to disabuse you of that notion," Jack countered. Havers instantly stopped. Jack nodded briefly. "I understand that you have a list of demands regarding the continuance of your service to Mr. Patterson and that you expect to communicate them to Miss Lindsay. Kindly put them in writing, submit them to me, and be advised that *I* will be the one making the decisions about them. Henceforth, should you have any concerns, you'll come to me with them and not Miss Lindsay. Understood?"

In the long-standing tradition of servants the world over, Havers quickly stuffed his shock behind a mask of cool indifference. "Yes, sir," he replied blandly. "You will have my list this afternoon."

"Have Mrs. Beechum put it on the desk in the study."

"Yes, sir."

"Good day, Havers," Jack said, stepping around the man and walking away without a backward glance. One bit of order on the way to being imposed, he told himself as he went. Now to see what kind of chaos and crisis awaited him downstairs this morning. God knew there would be one. In Lindsay's world, it was guaranteed.

. . .

LINDSAY CAME INTO THE DINING ROOM to find both a covered plate and Abigail Beechum waiting for her. The look on her housekeeper's face didn't bode well.

"Good morning, Miss Lindsay."

"Is it?" Lindsay asked, taking her seat and reaching for her napkin.

"Well, let's see," Abigail mused aloud as she lifted the silver dome off Lindsay's plate. "Primrose and Emile have managed to find a degree of cooperation sufficient for preparing a decent breakfast."

"It looks good," Lindsay offered, as she began to cut the thick slice of ham.

"Mrs. Rutherford thought it the most wonderful food she'd ever eaten," Abigail contributed, setting the cover on the sideboard. "Mrs. Kowalski, however, after inspecting the kitchen, decided that she couldn't bring herself to consume foods prepared in a manner that doesn't meet her religious proscriptions. She and her cat left just a little while ago, saying—Mrs. Kowalski saying, not the cat—that she would prevail upon the kindness of the synagogue for her bodily sustenance. I do believe that she's going to see if she might prevail upon its members for lodging as well."

Lindsay nodded. It had been the ham. Mrs. Kowalski had seen the ham and the culinary prospects before her and decided to take her chances in the wider world. It was probably for the best.

"While at breakfast," Abigail went on as Lindsay ate, "Mr. Rutherford received a note from Mr. Tipton, asking him to return to work, if at all possible. He left immediately."

Yes, Ben probably needed another set of hands at the office. Jack had requested the gathering of a great deal of information. The task would be accomplished more quickly with Jeb's assistance. "Anything else?"

The housekeeper took a deep breath. "Mr. Vanderhagen is in the parlor, clutching this morning's edition of the *Herald* and trying to wear a rut in your mother's Persian rug."

God love her, Abigail had certainly saved the best for last. Maybe. If Vanderhagen had seen the news story, he wasn't the only one. Lindsay took a sip of coffee before she broached the worst possibility. "Any sign of Agatha or Henry?"

"Not yet. Your sister apparently spent the night at your brother's. Thank God."

Lindsay nodded, remembering the ugly scene with her sister the night before and grateful that a reprisal of it would, apparently, be delayed for a while yet. She managed a smile for her housekeeper and said, "If you'll show Mr. Vanderhagen into the dining room, I'll deal with the first of today's fire-breathing dragons."

"Once I do that," the older woman said, heading for the door, "I'll be in the kitchen with a full bucket of water. Call if you need assistance in putting him out. It would be my pleasure."

"Thank you, Abigail," Lindsay replied, laughing and wondering how Abagail could manage, with one arm, to throw the contents of a bucket with any force. "If you hear the crash of the coffeepot followed by a particularly loud bellow of outrage, that'll be your signal to bring the bucket in. I'll take the assault from there."

"He's not worth the cost of a new coffeepot," the housekeeper pronounced as she disappeared from sight.

Lindsay quickly ate her eggs and ham, determined to be done with breakfast before Otis Vanderhagen steamed into the dining room.

"Why did you tell them all this? What were you thinking?"

Lindsay didn't bother to look at the bellowing blob of attorney as he crossed from the doorway to the table. Instead, she laid down her fork, blotted her lips with her napkin, then reached for the coffeepot and freshened her cup. With all the serenity she could muster, she said, "I believe that honesty is always the best approach. Sooner or later the truth is bound to come out anyway. Being truthful from the first spares one embarrassment later."

The paper hit the table beside her. Vanderhagen jabbed at the newsprint with a stubby finger as he yelled, "You should have sent the reporter to me and let me issue any statements to be made!"

"It wasn't Lindsay's decision; it was mine and I take full responsibility for it."

Jack. Gallant Jack. Interfering Jack. Lindsay met his gaze squarely. "I don't need to be defended, Jack. My actions were reasonable. I can take care of myself in the present situation."

"We covered the difference between 'can' and 'should' yesterday," he countered, settling into a chair. His gaze met hers and she saw anger flash in his dark eyes. "If we need to go over it again, I'd be happy to."

It was a challenge, clear and unmistakable. She bristled, but before she could utter a word, Vanderhagen made a snorting sound and barked at Jack, "You can't be honest in this town. They'll eat you alive!" Then he pointed a stubby finger at Lindsay and bellowed, "You of all people should have known that. Need I remind you of—"

"Tell me how all this is going to affect the legality of Billy's second Will," Jackson interrupted, ignoring the man's ire and pouring himself a cup of coffee.

"It's not," Vanderhagen admitted petulantly.

Lindsay momentarily set aside her irritation with Jack. Now wasn't the time. "Ham, scrambled eggs, and toast," she supplied as she lifted the silver dome from his plate. "Mine was quite good. Let me know if yours has gotten cold and I'll have it heated for you."

He nodded his thanks for the offer and, putting his napkin across his lap, said, "Tell me, Vanderhagen, just how the truth's going to affect the operations of the company."

"There will be assumptions that the company's approach will change. People won't know what to expect, how to read your actions. They won't know your long-term objectives and what positions to take in reacting."

"And how is any of that bad?"

Otis Vanderhagen was quick and empathic. "It creates uncertainty and uncertainty creates volatility and volatility always leads to chaos."

"And out of chaos frequently comes opportunity and

advantage," Jackson countered calmly just before he took a bite of eggs and ham.

"Or disaster," Vanderhagen shot back, pulling his handkercief out of his pocket and mopping his brow.

Lindsay watched as Jack slowly chewed, swallowed, and took a sip of his coffee. "You're thinking that things can actually get worse than they already are. They can't." He looked over at her and said, "It's all a little cool, but still edible. Coffee's nice and hot, though."

"And this!" Vanderhagen said, snatching the folded paper from the table and shaking it at her. "Lindsay, you are far too valuable to the company to be blithely running into burning buildings and pulling out injured men!"

Appreciating the manner in which Jack was dealing with the man, she copied him. "I did not run *blithely*," she corrected, serenely pulling the crust from her toast. "I gave it considerable thought. And since the alternative was Mr. Stennett's certain death, there was no other choice. If the situation were to occur again, I would make the same decision." She popped the bit of toast in her mouth as though she had nothing other than eating on her mind.

At the edge of her vision she saw Vanderhagen look between her and Jack, open his mouth, and then promptly snap it shut. He looked again, stuffed the newspaper under his arm, and asked, "How is Richard this morning?"

Jack replied before she could. "Much the same as yesterday and the day before."

"I'll go up and see him before I leave," Vanderhagen declared, turning on his heel. At the doorway he turned back. "As the company attorney, I am strongly advising both of you to issue no further statements to the press."

Jack's rebuttal was quiet, but nothing less than final. "I'll do as I damn well please and think necessary. I'm not going to hide behind your skirts."

"Educate him, Lindsay! Before he brings the house down around your ears!"

Lindsay listened to him storm through the foyer and up the main stairs, her gaze fastened on the gold-fringed, navy brocade draperies framing the doors that led from the dining room to the back terrace and the formal gardens beyond. "In all honesty, I wouldn't mind if this house did fall in on itself," she said. "I've always felt as though I'm living in a shrine to pretension."

"Why haven't you changed it?" Jackson asked, forking up the last of his eggs and ham. "Make it into something you like being in?"

"It was my mother's home until she died and so it wasn't mine to change," she explained with a shrug. "Since her death, I haven't had the money necessary to gut it and start over."

"Do you like these curtains?" he asked.

"No," she admitted, reaching for her coffee cup. "They're too heavy and too dark. They make the room feel like a cave."

He made a contemplative sound, put his napkin beside his plate, and rose from his seat. Lindsay watched as he stepped across the room, lifted a side panel, and peered up under the yardage. "What are you doing, Jack?"

He didn't say a word, but stepped back, took the fabric in both hands, and yanked. Lindsay heard herself gasp over the sound of straining wood and cracking plaster. The draperies came down as one massive wall of blue, landing on the floor at Jack's feet in an embarrassingly substantial cloud of dust. Brilliant sunlight flooded the room. The gardens beyond had never seemed so large or beckoning.

Jack turned to face her, his smile broad and his eyes just as bright as the morning. "And it didn't cost a dime."

Her bedroom draperies faced the garden, too. If one hard pull was all it took . . . The plaster could be repaired easily enough. No. She needed to be practical. One just didn't run around the house pulling the draperies off the windows on a mere whim. "What do you intend to replace them with that will be equally inexpensive?"

"I don't see that they need to be replaced," he supplied, coming back to the table and picking up his coffee cup. He turned back to the doors, took a sip, and then said, "No one's out in the garden trying to peer in."

"There is the gardener to consider," she felt compelled to remind him.

Jack looked at her over his shoulder. "And does he routinely try to peer in your windows?" he asked, his smile quirked.

Lindsay laughed. "I don't suppose it would make much difference if he did. Proctor's almost blind. I doubt that he can see anything that's more than a foot beyond the end of his nose."

"Your next objection, then?"

She didn't have one. At least not one that wasn't founded on a hidebound devotion to living in a fashionably decorated tomb. "I suppose I could exist with it for a few days and see how I feel about it."

"There you go," he pronounced, saluting her with his coffee cup. "And when you decide you like it, you just point to the next set of curtains and I'll pull them down, too."

The ones in my bedroom. The thought of actually inviting Jack into her room sent her pulse skittering; not with trepidation, but with anticipation. Startled by the realization, she instinctively sought refuge in putting some distance between them. "Speaking of deciding . . ."

"Have you?"

She nodded and took a sip of her coffee. "I understand the difference between 'can' and 'should' very clearly, Jack. I think our association will run much more smoothly if you'll bear in mind that I'm not only quite capable of taking care of myself, but accustomed to doing so. I appreciate the fact that you're motivated to protect me by a sense of gallantry. But, however kind your intentions, the effort isn't necessary. I'm not a child and I'm certainly not helpless. I don't like being treated as though I am."

"I didn't mean to imply that you are. If I somehow did, I'm sorry."

She nodded in gracious acceptance of his apology. "I gave the present situation some thought last night and it occurred to me that a reorganization of the company and personal assets is necessary regardless of anyone's secondary motives. Since I've never taken on a task of this magnitude and scale, and since Richard isn't able to advise me in the process, I'm willing to accept your counsel. I think we'll be a good partnership."

The single word reverberated in his mind. *Partnership.*

Every partnership he'd ever entered into had ended with his being alone. Everyone had died. He didn't want Lindsay dead, too. Neither did he want her holding any expectations he didn't want or couldn't meet.

"It's just temporary, you know," he said, watching her face, looking for the slightest sign that she didn't understand the nature of things. "When it's over and done, I'll head back to where I belong and I won't so much as glance over my shoulder. You'll be on your own once I leave. What I parcel out goes without any strings of any sort."

"I understand completely," she answered swiftly and surely. "But in the meantime, I still think we'd make good partners."

Just what kind of partners do you have in mind? he wanted to ask. Just business? God, he wanted to ask, wanted to know. And he knew better. "You're comfortable with the idea of making Henry and Agatha responsible for themselves?" he asked instead.

"Yes. Absolutely."

Crisp and certain. In a way it was an answer to his other questions; Lindsay's mind was clearly focused on the business aspects of their association. His needed to remain there. "Speaking of your brother and sister, if Vanderhagen had time to read the paper and get here to lamblast us, I'm wondering what's keeping the other shoe from dropping."

"You should be counting your blessings. I suggest we go about our day as we normally would and make them wait until dinner this evening."

"Our normal day isn't exactly something I'd like to have another of right away," he countered with a chuckle. "So far we've had a surprise Last Will and Testament and a stroke, followed by a fire and a household turned upside down. If it's all the same to you, I'd just as soon have an oddly uneventful day today."

"And how do you propose to accomplish this?" She grinned, her eyes sparkling with a merriment that made him ache to hold her, to kiss her as he had the night before.

"We'll just keep moving," he answered resolutely, setting his coffee cup down in its saucer with a solid *clink*. "Trouble will have to hunt us down and catch us."

"My bonnet and gloves are on the foyer table." She tucked her napkin beside her plate and rose, adding, "I'll get them as we tear past."

Jackson followed, thinking that if he had any real choice in how to spend the day, he'd go upstairs, tear down the door between their rooms, and then see where that bit of absolute insanity might take them. Thank God Lindsay wasn't going to give him the opportunity to find out. At least not today, anyway. Down the road, though . . . He remembered the way she'd licked his fingertip the night before and his blood heated.

The truth was plain and simple; Lindsay didn't have much more resistance to temptation than he did. Their relationship would likely be a glorious, breathless, memorable affair. A *short*, glorious, breathless, memorable affair. It was the likely end of it that could prove to be ugly, though. Lindsay needed to know that he wasn't going to offer her anything beyond the moment. If he could be certain that they could come together with a mutual understanding and then part amiably, he'd be willing to take the ride.

Which meant that there was another plain and simple truth; sooner or later he and Lindsay needed to have a blunt conversation about where they were headed. Jesus. He never learned.

CHAPTER ELEVEN

*L*INDSAY WATCHED THE WORLD passing outside the carriage window and pretended that she didn't know that Jack's knee brushed against hers every time the wheels rolled over a rough patch of paving stone. The first time it had happened, it had occurred to her that she could—and probably should for the sake of propriety—turn on the seat and avoid the contact as she had the very first time they'd shared the carriage. She remained just as she was seated, however; largely because Jack knew that they were touching and made no move to end the contact, either. Instead, he watched her with a knowing smile, giving their contact an element of danger that she found so exhilarating, it was irresistible.

At what point in her life had she become such a wanton? Lindsay wondered. Her mother's instruction on the art of seducing a man had been embarrassingly direct, but Lindsay had proven herself so inept at implementing the principles that her mother had finally declared her utterly hopeless and ceased trying to educate her. Apparently the lessons had been stored somewhere in the deepest recesses of her brain, though. They'd surged to the fore, unbidden, last night when

Jack had traced her lip with his whiskey-coated fingertip. And now she was alone in the carriage with him and brazenly welcoming the touch of his leg against hers.

There was only one thing that Jack could reasonably think: that she was agreeable to his physical advances. Oddly enough, given her romantic misadventure of the past, she did indeed enjoy Jack Stennett's touch. She liked the way it made her heart race, and the sense of daring that came with inviting it. It hadn't been at all like this before. As for the almost certain consequence of being so bold with Jack . . . Lindsay was very well aware of where it would lead. She was also well aware that she'd reached the point where she either needed to stop flirting with him or quit pleading propriety and let matters progress as they would. It wasn't fair to give Jack contradictory messages.

What to do? Withdrawing behind the facade of a prim and proper lady was a safe course. It was also lonely and allowed no room for pleasure of any sort. More than anything else, it was false. She wasn't prim and proper by nature. It took conscious effort to remember how she was supposed to behave. On those occasions when she chose to ignore social convention, she always felt a wonderful sense of being both liberated and honestly herself.

She hadn't felt anything like that with Charles, of course. Every step she'd taken with him had been a duty, an obligation, and very much a calculated surrender. There had been no sense of being free, of daring exhilaration; just a nagging hope that her performance would meet his expectations so that she could accomplish her mother's business goals. She'd failed miserably on every count and vowed never again to subject herself to such humiliation.

But it was all very different with Jack. There was an undeniably powerful quality to being with him, to his advances. For the first time since the debacle with Charles Martens, she was tempted to risk her pride. But what if it turned out this time just as it had before? She certainly didn't want to experience such a humbling again. Once had been quite enough.

What a dithering little ninny she'd become, Lindsay silently groused. It wasn't like her at all. She was quite accustomed to lining up the advantages and disadvantages of any situation, and then making a clear and definitive decision on the action to be taken. Her mother had fervently maintained that the physical relationship between a man and a woman was merely a business one, and should be approached with the calm rationality one used in negotiating interest rates with a banker. One should consider the merits of the association, negotiate for concessions greater than your own—typically in the form of expensive gifts—and then honor the agreement with a dutiful and silent surrender.

Of course, her mother had been abandoned by her father and while there had been a procession of—as her mother had put it—"companions" afterward, not a one of them had been companionable for very long. To Lindsay's mind, her mother's approach, while certainly profitable, had always seemed to lack true substance. She'd tried her mother's way and found that it didn't suit her in the least. Her own way was something she'd never thought to discover. Until now.

As though he knew of her internal debate, Jack shifted on the seat, taking up sides in the contest by deliberately stretching his legs out so that his calf rested firmly against her own. Her pulse quickened as a delightful warmth spread through her limbs. Maintaining her pretense of being unaware, she reminded herself to breathe. She could feel Jack's gaze on her and knew without looking that his smile was quirked and knowing.

Perhaps she ought to face him and squarely address the issue of their relationship. Her mother had held that there was no need to actually talk about relations; that men could be trusted to *know* where matters were headed. It seemed less than honest to Lindsay. But where and how did one begin such a conversation? And it could be that her hesitancy was a sign that she wasn't as comfortable with the notion of being seduced as she'd thought.

Dithering again, Linds, she silently admonished. *Make a decision one way or the other.*

The slowing of the carriage, however, ended the immediate necessity of doing so, and she felt a surge of relief for the timely reprieve. "We have arrived," she announced unnecessarily, making a production out of smoothing her skirts and flouncing her hems. In the process, she casually put space between their lower limbs.

Jack made a humming sound of agreement and straightened in the seat. "Sooner or later, you always do," he said softly, giving her a wink as the carriage stopped and he reached for the door handle.

What was it about him that made her feel as though there were layers to the things he said? she wondered, watching him smoothly exit. She accepted his hand and allowed him to assist her out. Even through the fabric of her gloves, she was aware of the warmth of his skin and she missed it when he slowly released his claim to her.

He chewed the inside of his cheek as he considered her and then, with an almost apologetic smile, turned to look at the smoldering remains of the apartment building. "Was it insured?" he asked.

Lindsay quickly gathered her wits and reminded herself that discussing business matters was a blessedly safe and certain haven. "Unfortunately, no," she supplied. "There was a horrible fire in the city four years ago. The water supplies were insufficient and millions of dollars of insured property was lost north of Harold Square. We suffered some damage to our properties, but it was minimal. Payment of the loss claims bankrupted every insurance company in town. Our carrier was among those who failed. The rates from companies in other cities nearby were prohibitive and we decided to take our chances. The cost of insurance will come down once the construction of the aqueduct is finished, but that doesn't mean much to us now."

Jack nodded as though he were contemplating all of it and then turned to look at the traffic moving past them. "This looks to me like it's a pretty busy street," he finally observed.

He was seeing his way to an action; she could sense it in her bones. "It is," she answered warily. "Twenty-third is a major east–west route."

"And the city doesn't have any direction to grow but northward."

Ah, he was considering future property values. "Well, there is out to Long Island," she reminded him.

He brought his gaze to hers and grinned. "Where Agatha wants to buy some land at an outrageous price."

"There is a certain appeal to her being isolated by the ferry schedule."

He chuckled before turning away from her yet again. This time he surveyed the entire block. After a long moment he asked, "Want to know what we're going to do?"

"Ship Agatha and her belongings out on this evening's ferry?" she ventured only half facetiously.

He laughed outright. "The motion's on the table for consideration." He sobered slowly. "*After* we've put this chunk of land up for auction. Who do we see about handling it for us?"

It made sense to do so. Lord knew there wasn't any money available to rebuild. And it was on the list of those properties Richard was considering selling. But there was something in Jack's manner that suggested he was thinking on a larger scale. "By 'chunk,' just what are you referring to? The lot?" Lindsay asked, indicating the pile of charred lumber.

"You own half the block, don't you?" He didn't give her a chance to answer. "The whole thing goes up for sale."

She glanced down the row of apartment buildings and small storefronts, mentally calculating the rents that would be lost and reckoning that against the probable receipts from their sale. The scales didn't come close to balancing. "No one wants to buy aging apartment buildings, Jack," she said gently in the hope of educating him without battering his pride. "They're expensive to maintain and the rents are always difficult to collect."

"I'm not selling the apartment houses," he countered quickly. "I'm selling the land under them. That's what's valuable, Lindsay. Whoever buys it all will probably tear down the apartments and build something new."

Richard had mentioned that course, but it had been a long-range plan. Jackson's intent to shorten the timetable instantly triggered the objections Lindsay had always harbored about the strategy. "Where will the tenants go, Jack? Where will they live? Where will they do business?"

Jackson shrugged. "That's their problem, not yours."

"What a *horribly* selfish attitude!" Lindsay declared,

thoroughly appalled by it. "I can't believe that you think I'm capable of such a callous and—"

His hands on her shoulders stole not only her words, but her breath. His gaze was dark and somber and regretful. "You can't mother the whole world, Lindsay," he said softly. "And you have to take care of yourself before you can take care of others. It gets sold to the highest bidder. All of it. Now, I'll ask again, who do we see about setting up the auction?"

"Samuel Gregory," she supplied reluctantly, knowing that Jack was right and that she had to put common sense before emotional considerations. Still, she wanted to cry, to bury her face in his chest and sob great big tears. Lifting her chin, Lindsay drew a steadying breath and gathered her composure to add, "He's reputed to be the best. There are others, of course, but I think we might as well start at the top and work our way down, if necessary."

LINDSAY SAT PRIMLY in the straight-backed chair, her hands folded demurely in her lap, knowing that Samuel Gregory's huge cherry-wood desk prevented him from seeing how Jack's crossed legs had resulted in the toe of his boot coming to rest against her leg. Unlike in the carriage earlier, this touch wasn't deliberate. The office was small to begin with—not much larger than a broom closet—and Jack's height and the width of his shoulders had all but filled it. He'd apologized for bumping her as he'd settled in the chair beside hers and tried to make himself comfortable in the cramped space. Whether his touch was intentional or not, the effect was just the same. Lindsay could only hope that the tiny, incredibly cluttered office was sufficiently dim that the auctioneer was unaware of how quickly her pulse raced.

"I charge fifteen percent of the gross receipts for my services," Gregory said, studying the paper Jack had handed him after the introductions and explanations had been completed.

"I'll pay you ten percent on the first fifty thousand dollars," Jack drawled, slowly rubbing his foot against her leg, "and an additional one percent for every twenty-five thousand over that."

All right. The contact might not have been as unavoidable as she'd thought. Lindsay tried to pay attention to the conversation in the hope that she'd be less aware of Jack's touch and the heat consuming her.

"That's ridiculous," Gregory snorted.

"Look at the property list again," Jack countered calmly, drawing a line up her calf with his boot toe.

Lindsay swallowed. She couldn't physically move away; there wasn't room to go anywhere. Not that she really wanted to end the contact. Here and now, in the presence of Mr. Gregory, Jack's touch was even more daring than it had been in the carriage. And so much more exhilarating. When she got Jackson Stennett out of here, she was going to repay him for putting her through such an exquisitely brazen form of torture.

Gregory nodded and said quietly, "These are certainly well-situated properties, but still—"

"You can make as much money as you can squeeze out of the sale—which I'm thinking may just be considerably more than your usual fifteen percent," Jackson drawled, "or you can make nothing at all. Miss MacPhaull," Jack said, looking over at her, smiling, and drawing a deliberately slow trail down her leg with his toe, "assures me there are several auction agents in town. All with solid reputations."

What was left of *her* reputation wouldn't be enough to fill a thimble if she didn't summon a scrap of propriety and put an end to Jack's advances.

"Five percent for every twenty-five thousand over the base fifty."

"Two and a half," Jackson lazily countered, trailing his toe upward again, watching her eyes.

Moth to a flame.

"Done. Let me consult my calendar." The auctioneer opened a book and quickly began turning pages. "How does four weeks from today sound to you, Mr. Stennett?"

"Too far away," Jack said, winking at her and turning his attention to the businessman. He stopped moving his foot, leaving it pressed lightly against her calf. "Shoot for two at the most."

"But I have to have time to generate interest in the properties," the older man protested, blinking furiously. "I have to have time to agitate the competing interests."

Jack shook his head. "Too much time and those competing interests have a chance to get rational," he said, his speech no longer a slow and easy drawl, but certain and crisp. "I want them waving fistfuls of money without thinking beyond a gut level, wanting to beat out the other guy. Two weeks at the outside."

"Impossible. My calendar is completely full," Gregory declared, indicating his open book with a sweeping motion of his hand. "Three weeks I *might* be able to do, but not any sooner."

"Then we'll find another auctioneer," Jack said, firmly. He rose from his chair, adding, "Thank you for your time."

Lindsay looked between the two men and silently groaned at the prospect of having to endure the process a second time in another tiny office with another auctioneer. "Perhaps, Mr. Gregory," she quickly ventured, catching Jackson's hand to stay him, "one of your already-scheduled clients would be willing to move their auction date to create an opening for Mr. Stennett?"

Gregory blinked and then furrowed his brows as he quickly perused his book again. Jack lightly squeezed her hand and let it go.

"The Theorosa family might. They've been waffling since the beginning," Samuel Gregory said to his book. He looked up and met Lindsay's gaze. "His mother's house, you understand. The old lady's been gone two years and it's been empty ever since. It's sound, but fairly small. Probably won't go for more than a few thousand, if that. Not really worth my time, but Mrs. Theorosa—the one still living—is a member of my wife's reading club and I couldn't say no."

"Where is the house?" Jackson asked casually, standing beside Lindsay's chair.

"Just outside the city. It used to be a dairy farm, but the

cows and the land were sold off to neighbors after the senior Mr. Theorosa's death some years ago."

Jackson extended his hand and Lindsay placed hers in it, allowing him to help her rise as he said, "Tell the Theorosas that if they'll remove the property from auction, you'll guarantee a buyer and a fair price for them."

Samuel Gregory snatched up a pen from the desk stand. "Two weeks from tomorrow it is, Mr. Stennett," he said, crossing out an entry—presumably the Theorosa name. As he scribbled in another, he added, "I assume the sales are to be on a cash basis?"

"Current letters of credit from reputable banking institutions will also be acceptable," Jackson corrected, leaning back to push open the office door. "I'll rely on your judgment to know the honorable and serious bidders from those wasting our time. If you have any questions regarding the properties or the sale itself, please don't hesitate to ask. You can find either myself or Miss MacPhaull at the company offices."

"Very good, Mr. Stennett," Gregory said perfunctorily as he reached into a basket at the edge of his desk. He handed Lindsay an iron key, the ringed end tagged with a string and a small square of white paper. "Here's the key to the Theorosa property—in case you'd like to take a look at it beforehand to estimate your bid. Go north on Broadway five miles beyond the edge of the city. It's a small, white clapboard structure on your left. You won't have any problem finding it."

"Thank you. We'll do that," Jackson said, drawing Lindsay out from between the closely spaced chairs. "And thank you for your time today. I'm looking forward to a most profitable relationship."

"As am I," the auctioneer declared as they slipped out of his closet and into a slightly larger anteroom. They nodded in acknowledgment of the secretary as they passed, but said nothing further until they were outside on the walkway.

"That was an absolutely masterful manipulation," Lindsay offered. "Congratulations."

"You didn't do too badly yourself," he offered, opening

the carriage door for her. He offered her a hand in, but when she took it, he drew her to halt. His smile was roguish and his eyes bright as he gazed down at her. "And thank you for allowing me to distract myself along the way. I didn't want Gregory to think that I was too in need of his services. It's always to your advantage to have an opponent think you've got more important things on your mind than them."

"Then your attention was purely a negotiation ploy," she observed, arching a brow in patent disbelief.

"I didn't say that," he countered, his smile brilliant and so warming that she was tempted to step closer and invite him to slip his arms around her.

"Might I ask what do you intend to do with the Theorosa house?" she asked in an attempt to keep from embarrassing herself.

He shrugged. "I don't know. I wanted the opening in the schedule and was prepared to pay for it. A couple of thousand will be of little consequence by the end of the auction."

The auction. Now that they weren't sharing their conversation with Samuel Gregory, there were a few questions she felt compelled to ask. "I caught a glimpse of the properties listed, Jack. There were quite a few. And while I dislike appearing petty and self-absorbed, I can't help wondering—if you sell so many, what will be left to divide between Henry, Agatha, and me?"

"None of you are going to be rich, but you'll have steady incomes to live on and to invest."

"You're not going to tell me the specific details, are you?"

He handed her into the carriage, saying, "Only because I haven't exactly decided on them yet. You'll be the first to know when I do, though."

"Thank you." Arranging her skirts and taking her seat, she asked, "So where are we going next? To the office?"

"Nope, Henry and Agatha will be looking for us there. Let's go see the Theorosa house." He turned to look up at her coachman. "John? Take us out of the city, if you please. Five miles north on Broadway."

She waited until he was settled opposite her before implementing her plan to pay him back. "My," she said with a sigh, plucking at the front of her pelisse, "it's certainly warm for this time of year, don't you think?"

"I don't know," he said, watching her fingers. "It's my first time in New York. I have no idea what the weather's usually like."

The carriage worked its way into the northbound traffic.

"Then you'll just have to believe me when I tell you that it's unseasonably warm." Using both hands, Lindsay slowly opened the top button of her pelisse as she said, "I hope you don't mind the boldness, but I simply can't endure being so uncomfortable for another minute."

"Not at all." He touched his tongue to his lower lip as though he were parched. His voice sounded decidedly tight and dry as he added, "By all means, please be comfortable."

"Thank you, Jack." She opened the top button of her dress front. "You're such a gentleman."

THEY WERE, WITHOUT DOUBT, the longest miles he'd ever traveled in his life, Jackson decided as the carriage pulled off the dirt road and into a short, rocky drive. They'd managed a semblance of polite parlor conversation, offering comments on the weather and observations on the various places they passed. Lindsay, bless her, had carried the larger portion of the burden. He'd spent the majority of the trip alternately remembering the light in her eyes as he'd touched her in Samuel Gregory's office, wondering just how many buttons she was going to undo, and tamping down one wild impulse after another. By far the tamest of the bunch had been the one where he'd thought about leaning across the carriage, putting a finger gently across her lips, and then quietly asking her if she'd ever considered the merits of making love in a carriage. In the wildest of his imaginings, she'd crossed to straddle his lap, twined her arms around his neck, and between bone-melting kisses, offered to show him all kinds of wicked pleasures to be had in such a liaison.

Jackson knew that he needed some space and a chance to have his mind sufficiently occupied with other thoughts so his blood could cool down. The carriage had barely come to a halt when he opened the door and bounded out. Lindsay exited right after him, before he could remember his manners and offer to assist her.

"This is Samuel Gregory's idea of fairly small?" she said, looking past him and shaking her head.

Jackson, realizing that he hadn't even noticed the house, looked up. It was every bit as big as MacPhaull House, two stories high, but made of whitewashed clapboard instead of brick. It sure wasn't his idea of small, fairly or otherwise. His house in Texas would have fit in it twice.

"I love Mrs. Theorosa's front garden," Lindsay said softly, walking past him and up the front walkway. "It's so informal, so welcoming."

"And so very different than the front walk at MacPhaull House," he observed, following.

"Ours isn't a very inviting house, is it?" Lindsay bent to sweep dried leaves from the new growth beside the front steps. "Perhaps when you're done tearing down curtains, I'll have you rip out the landscaping."

"Or maybe," he countered, watching her tend the plants, "you could sell your house to someone who likes that sort of formality and move into this one."

"What about Agatha?"

"Maybe you could offer to include her with the house at no extra charge."

Lindsay laughed and straightened. "No one in their right mind and who knows her would consider that an incentive, Jack. No, I'm afraid I'm stuck with her."

"Well," Jack drawled, looking up at the house again, "I'm thinking that she'd decide to move in with Henry rather than live in such squalor with you."

"It isn't squalor; it's a charming house."

"Maybe we ought to take a look inside before you render judgment. Still have the key?"

With a flourish, she produced it from her reticule, gathered her skirts in hand, and skipped up the front steps. Jack smiled and went after her. He'd been right; time and other matters had been just what he'd needed. His blood had cooled and he could look at Lindsay now without being battered by carnal fantasies. And that was good; very good. While she might be intrigued by his flirtations and daring enough to hold her ground in the face of them, beneath it all, she was still sweet and gentle and absolutely inexperienced. If she did indeed want to be seduced, she deserved, at the very least, a man willing to make it a slow and tender affair.

Chapter Twelve

*T*HE CURTAINS WERE LIGHT, lacy things and early afternoon sunlight flooded through them. Jackson watched as Lindsay walked into the center of the front room and stopped. Turning a slow circle, she said, "Surely the family intends to take the furnishings out before the sale."

"Seems to me that if they'd wanted any of it, they'd have taken it before now," he observed, closing the door behind them. "Gregory said Mrs. Theorosa had been gone two years."

"How sad."

"Why do you say that?"

"To have the possessions of your lifetime not wanted by anyone," she whispered. "It's sad, Jack. Poor Mrs. Theorosa."

"She probably doesn't know," he countered rationally. "And if she does, she probably doesn't care."

"Well, I care," Lindsay retorted, with a degree of passion that caught him by surprise. "She had beautiful things and no one's even bothered to cover them with sheets to protect them from the dust."

Jackson looked around the room, noting the mis-matched furniture, the hardwood floors covered in places by hooked wool rugs, and the wide array of little mementos scattered across the tabletops and the mantel. A thick coating of dust covered everything. He squinted, trying to imagine what it would look like cleaned up. Unfashionably colorful, he decided.

"Let's go see what's upstairs, Jack."

Bedrooms. There always were. And while his curiosity didn't particularly demand a trip to see for sure, the tone of Lindsay's voice was that of a woman on an exciting adventure of discovery. If it made her happy, he'd go along without a negative word. Jackson darted ahead of her and led the way, pushing through the cobwebs that had been allowed to drape the stairwell. The steps were uncarpeted and solid oak; not a one of them creaked.

The flooring upstairs was of the same oak, and a long wool carpet lay the length of the central hallway, which was barely a third of the width of that at MacPhaull House. A window at the end of the corridor allowed light in, making the small space feel more cozy than tight. Four doors opened into the hall; two on each side and opposite each other. Lindsay was making her way from door to door, opening each, pausing to study each room's interior, smiling, and then gently closing the door before moving on to the next.

"The roof must be in fairly good shape. I don't see any water stains on the ceilings," he offered. "And the walls don't show any cracks. Whoever built this place apparently built it well."

"Four bedrooms. Lovely, all of them. Mrs. Theorosa liked her flowers, didn't she? The pansy room is my favorite," she declared, opening a door and, with a gesture, inviting him to look for himself.

He dutifully stepped to the door, prepared to nod and mutter something suitably agreeable. It was, however, impossible to say anything at all for the first few moments. He'd never seen anything like it. Despite the coating of dust, he didn't need to squint to see the colors. The walls were purple; not a sedate deep plum as those in his room at

MacPhaull House, but a brilliant royal shade. Lace curtains the color of lilacs, tied back at the sides with big bows of yellow satin, adorned the two windows in the room. The pale purple color was repeated on the ceiling, making it look like a soft dawn sky. A double-sized oak four-poster bed with a high headboard and a rolled-edge footboard commanded almost one entire wall. The coverlet was a quilted affair of yellow, with appliqued pansies running riot across the surface. Wool area rugs ran the length of the bed on both sides, each a series of huge purple and yellow pansies seemingly laid out side by side.

What did the other rooms look like? he wondered. One would be roses, he'd bet money on it. Another would likely be peonies. The fourth, only God knew. Tulips maybe? Irises?

"The colors are so bright and bold, don't you think?" Lindsay asked happily.

"That they are," he admitted. "Mrs. Theorosa certainly wasn't a slave to decorating fashion, was she?"

"No, she wasn't, and I think she's to be commended for it. Once you're done with refurbishing the MacPhaull House draperies and the landscaping, perhaps—"

"Perhaps not," he interrupted with a chuckle, knowing where she was going. "I'm a terrible painter. I tried to help Billy when he built his place, but halfway through the front room, he threw me out. If you're thinking of repainting MacPhaull House, you'd be better off to hire it done. Whatever it costs, it'll be worth it."

"You and my father didn't live in the same house?" Lindsay asked, tilting her head to study him. "Somehow, I assumed that you did."

Jackson shrugged before leaning his shoulder against the doorjamb. "I lived with him for a few years after my mother died, but eventually moved back to the house my parents had built. It's nothing fancy. Four rooms and a single story. Billy's house, though, is a lot like this one. By Texas standards, it's considered a palace."

"Does anyone live in it now that he's gone?"

"Nope. But you'll be glad to know that I did put sheets over the furniture."

"What do you intend to do with it? Sell it?"

"Selling it would require selling a good-sized piece of land for the new owner to make a living on. I can't—and won't—do that. So I guess it'll just sit empty."

"You won't move into it?" she pressed quietly. "Since my father left you everything, he surely left you his house, too."

"He did." Jackson pictured the big house in his mind. As always, Billy stood on the wide front porch, his hands stuffed deep in his pockets as he stared off into the hills. "Maybe down the road," Jackson said softly, "I'll think about hauling my gear over that way. But doing it right now wouldn't feel right." He gave her a rueful smile. "Just a little too quick to pick the bones, if you know what I mean."

"I do," she said, nodding. "I wanted the larger space of my mother's room for a long time before I actually moved my belongings in there. And there are times when I regret acting on the notion. The issue of picking the bones aside, there's also the matter of exorcising the shadows of those who lived there before." She looked around the pansy room. "Mrs. Theorosa left good shadows; the kind that invite you to pick up life where she left off."

He'd never thought of it that way before. But since Lindsay had made him think of things in that way, he could see that Billy's house did have its shadows, the kind that said he hadn't been quite finished with living yet. Finishing Billy's work would be the price of living easily within its walls. Just what Billy expected him to do was a complete mystery, though. It wasn't the everyday kind of work around a ranch; it was something special. You could feel it even if you couldn't precisely define it.

Lindsay moved past him, bringing him from his musing. "Where are you going?" he asked, pulling the door to the pansy room closed and following her toward the head of the stairs.

She didn't look back. Holding her skirts above her ankles, she moved down the stairs resolutely. "There's bound to be some oil and dusting cloths in the pantry."

"You're going to clean?"

"I know how." She reached the main floor and turned

toward the back of the house, adding, "Just because I have a housekeeper doesn't mean that I haven't taken my turn at the work."

Jack stopped in the main room. "This isn't your house, Lindsay."

"I know you were teasing," she called from the kitchen area, "but maybe I *will* sell MacPhaull House and move in here. I like it. I feel welcomed by it."

That was a twist he hadn't expected. MacPhaull House would bring a tidy little sum of money. "But what about all your mother's possessions?" he asked, gauging the depth of her commitment to the notion. "The ones she spent a lifetime acquiring. You won't have room in here for hers and Mrs. Theorosa's, too."

"Agatha and Henry can have them," she answered, stepping from the kitchen into the dining room with a rag and a small bottle of pale yellow liquid. She set both items on the sideboard and, unbuttoning her pelisse, continued, saying, "Besides, nothing was special to my mother. She never put her heart and soul into purchasing anything. She simply stopped by a store, described the space she was filling, and told them to send whatever they had that would be fashionably suitable."

"How do you know Mrs. Theorosa didn't do the same thing?"

"Because nothing matches," Lindsay explained, tossing her pelisse over the back of a dining-room chair. "That tells me that each piece has a unique story, a special history of how it came to be here."

"You're sentimental."

"And that's bad?" she asked, pulling her dress sleeves back from her wrists.

"No. Just surprising."

She arched a brow and smiled. "Because I'm a hard-edged businesswoman?"

"Lindsay, sweetheart," he retorted, chuckling softly, "you're not hard-edged if you consider where your tenants will move should you decide to sell a property. You're certainly intelligent, but I think you've also got the biggest heart in all of New York."

"Which isn't necessarily good," she added, picking up her cleaning supplies.

He watched her douse the rag as he said, "It has its drawbacks in your world—as Otis Vanderhagen so clearly pointed out this morning."

"So if you know I'm softhearted," she asked, setting to work on the dining-room table, "why are you surprised to discover that I'm sentimental?"

"How you came to be so nice is something of a puzzle."

She stopped and looked over at him, her brow arched higher than before and her smile bright. "I beg your pardon?"

"Well," he drawled, feeling a desperate need for the distraction of movement, "I'm thinking that from the bits and pieces I've heard about your mother, she wasn't the one who passed it on to you." Heading for the dining-room windows, he continued his observations, saying, "It sure wasn't Billy; he didn't stick around long enough. Agatha and Henry are clearly out of the running." Opening a window and letting fresh air into the house, he added, "Was it Richard?"

"No, not really," she supplied, going back to her task as he continued to open windows. "Richard's always been frustrated by my tendency to, as he says, think with my heart first and my head second. No, if anyone deserves the credit for shaping me, it's Abigail Beechum. In many respects, she's been more like a mother to me than the one to whom I was actually born."

"So if you were to move here, she'd come with you."

"I'd ask her to, but the decision would be hers. I think she'd like this house as much as I do."

"What about Primrose? Would you bring her, too?"

"If she wanted to come along, yes. But I doubt that she would. She's very active in her church and all of her family members live within just a few miles of MacPhaull House. I don't think she'd like living so far away from those comforts. They mean a lot to her."

"Do you go to church?" Jackson asked, gathering the antimacassars from the backs and arms of the parlor upholstery.

"The last time I went was to my mother's funeral," she replied brightly. "It was a very tasteful affair—the hired mourners weeping to perfection—and was attended by the city's first and foremost citizens. The musicians played a wonderful selection of dirges and the mercy meal was catered by one of the finest restaurants in the city. No expense was spared."

The loss of her mother didn't seem to affect Lindsay too deeply. It was almost as though she were talking about the passing of a complete stranger. He remembered his own mother's funeral and how he'd embarrassed himself by sobbing like a baby in Billy's arms. God. Deliberately pushing his memories aside, he observed, "Sounds like you put on a fine affair."

"All I had to do was take the right dress out of my closet, put it on, and get there on time. Mother did all of the planning and made all the arrangements herself."

"So she knew she was dying."

"No, actually the end came quite suddenly," Lindsay said matter-of-factly, as she moved into the main room with her oil-soaked rag and started to work. "Mother didn't trust me to make her final social appearance the graciously memorable occasion she envisioned. Rather than taking a chance at being the guest of honor at an utterly botched affair of my making, she spent *years* planning her own service down to the last detail. There were even invitations to be sent out. All I had to do was write in the date and time."

Invitations? To a funeral? "You're kidding," he laughingly accused, shaking the antimacassars out an open window.

"I am not," she countered, chuckling. "I didn't post them, though. I thought that was going too far. I fully expect, however, to have her meet me at the Pearly Gates, determined to have me barred for disobeying her edict."

The more he heard about Lydia MacPhaull, the less he liked her. And the more he understood why Billy had left and why Lindsay had spent her life in the offices of the MacPhaull Company. "She even had the family mausoleum spiffed up and expanded for her arrival, didn't she?" he guessed.

"How did you know?" Lindsay asked, laughing outright.

"It just figures that she'd've done something like that."

Sobering, Lindsay paused in her dusting. Staring down at the tabletop, she said softly, "I always understood why my father left and never came back. Even though I was a child, Jack, I knew that he wasn't happy and why." She lifted her gaze to meet his. "I would have left, too. If I could have."

Damn Billy for leaving her alone. "But you eventually got old enough to walk out the door," he reminded her as gently as he could. "You didn't have to stay."

"I suppose you're right, in theory," she admitted with a shrug, and went back to her work. "In a practical sense, though, the circumstances have never allowed it."

Watching her and thinking that she was the very picture of contented and efficient domesticity, he pointed out, "You could have gotten married. You can't tell me you've never had a proposal."

"Three, in fact. But none of them were matches Mother approved of and so they were more firmly than politely declined. The one potential match Mother did approve of and encouraged me to pursue"—she paused and then made a small *tsk*ing sound—"didn't end quite the way she thought it would."

"That would be the fellow who was supposed to be a Romeo and wasn't," he contributed carefully, not at all certain how much she wanted to tell him about the ill-fated affair, but sensing that it rested heavily on her shoulders and that the burden would be eased if she could bring herself to share it.

"That would be the one," she replied flippantly. "And as it turned out, he wasn't much of a gentleman, either."

"Oh, yeah?" he drawled nonchalantly, even as his mind raced along the tracks of myriad possibilities. "I hope Richard or Henry called him to task for you."

"The lapse in judgment—among the various and sundry other shortcomings—was perceived to be mine, not his." She laughed and added, "Abigail did, however, sincerely offer to hunt him down and beat him to death with an umbrella for me."

Lapse in judgment? Just what great social sin had Lindsay committed? Had she held the man's hand in public? And what shortcomings? Jack hadn't known Lindsay all that long, but certainly long enough to know that she didn't have any flaws that would inspire a man to run in the other direction. Whoever Romeo was, he'd been a damn fool for walking away from Lindsay MacPhaull. She was better off without him. Jack was about to tell her that when she suddenly stopped working and looked out the living room window.

"Jack, it's going to storm. If we don't leave before it starts raining—"

"The road back to town will be impassable and we'll be stuck out here," he finished for her. "I'm ready to go any time you are."

But he wasn't ready, he realized, as he watched her glance around the room, her expression wistful. He wanted to stay here. With her. The storm could pound down and he wouldn't care if they ever got back to MacPhaull House. They'd clean house and talk some more and he'd find some wood in a pile out back and build them a fire in the main room when the sun went down. And they'd talk into the night, and when it got late, he'd build a fire for her in the hearth of the pansy room and he'd make love to her until the sun rose.

God, he was losing his mind, had been all damn day long. Theirs was a business relationship and needed to remain only that. Mixing business and personal was never a good idea and he knew it. It clouded judgment and made for poor decisions. Why the hell couldn't he keep that bit of hard truth in the front part of his brain? Why was it so damn easy to slip into forbidden fantasies? There wasn't a thing he was willing to offer Lindsay beyond a decidely temporary and purely physical affair. She wasn't a cantina girl; she was a lady and an innocent and deserved to be treated accordingly.

And in spite of cool reason and common sense, he chafed at that reality and was angry at being unable to have what he wanted. Yep, he was losing his mind. All he required for a final surrendering of it was for Lindsay to look up at him and say that she didn't want to go back to MacPhaull House tonight. He'd set aside wisdom and common sense and all of his memories if she'd only ask him to.

She sighed and gave him a regretful smile. "I suppose that since Henry and Agatha are to be at dinner, we don't have any choice but to leave. Let me put my supplies back in the cabinet. I'll only be a minute."

She walked away as he said, "I'll close up the windows," and shook his head. Henry and Agatha. He'd forgotten all about her brother and sister and dinner tonight. Not a good sign at all.

He picked the key up off the end table while she slipped her arms into her pelisse. "I want to stop by the office on our way back to the house, if you don't mind," he said, watching her button it all the way to the top. "Ben's working on getting me some information I need and I also want to get him started on a reply to the offer we got from Little, Bates and Company."

"Are you going to accept it?"

"I'm going to counter it and see what happens."

"I can tell you already," she said with absolute certainty. "Percival Little will counter with the same amount he originally offered. In the meantime, the others Richard queried will respond with offers fairly similar to Percival's and you'll have to accept one because you'll be out of time to negotiate any further."

He gave her a quick smile. "No, I won't. The St. Louis property was on the list to be auctioned. The minimum bid is the balance of the bank note on it. Anything we get above that is profit and more than ol' Perce is willing to pay."

"Then why are you even bothering to respond to Little's offer?" she asked as they left Mrs. Theorosa's house.

"He's wasting our time and it's only fair that we waste some of his in return."

"You can be quite vindictive, can't you, Jack?"

"You haven't seen me at my best," he said, winking. "I'm just getting warmed up."

Lindsay managed a smile because she knew she should, but the better part of her awareness was involved in watching Jack lock the door and knowing that she had only a few minutes left in which to change her mind. She didn't want to go back to MacPhaull House. Not tonight. And maybe never. There was something about Mrs. Theorosa's house, something about being in it with Jack, that made the rest of the world and all of its concerns disappear. It didn't matter that they'd brought no food with them. It didn't matter that Henry and Agatha would dine alone. It all paled beside the temptation to reach out, lay her hand on Jack's, and ask him to take her back inside and kiss her until propriety ceased to matter, too.

"There," he said, putting the key in his pocket. He offered her his arm and a tight smile. "Ready to go?"

"Duty calls," she replied, laying her hand on his forearm. "We must obey."

CHAPTER THIRTEEN

*T*HE FIRST DROPS OF RAIN had arrived as they'd left the porch and headed to the carriage. John, already in his raincoat, had smiled down at them and told her not to worry about him, that he wouldn't melt. It was pouring now, coming down in wind-lashed sheets, and the carriage rocked so hard that she couldn't imagine how John was staying in the box, much less controlling the team of horses and making forward progress. Lindsay clung to the corner strap and tried to look as though she wasn't concerned.

Jack had simply braced his feet on the supports for her seat and crossed his arms over his chest. She couldn't help but wonder if he wasn't also trying to conceal his concern. If he was, he was doing an excellent job of it.

"Does it rain like this in Texas?" she asked, as the carriage rocked hard to one side and then quickly righted.

"Oh, yeah," he drawled. "And we can get hailstones the size of a man's fist, too. Of course, it's all right as long as you don't have hard rain followed by the hail. On the back side of the hail line is where you'll get your tornado."

She hadn't thought about that possibility. The deadly

columns of wind weren't terribly common in her world, but neither were they unknown. While she'd never actually seen one, she'd read newspaper accounts of them. It was an experience she hoped to never have for herself.

"Do you think there's a chance we might be having a tornado now?" she asked, trying to sound as though it was a casual question.

"Nope." He chuckled and added, "The air doesn't feel right. It may be wet, but it's not heavy. And we haven't had any hail, either. I'd say the odds aren't particularly good for one."

"That's good to know."

He tilted his head to the side. "Are you afraid of storms, Lindsay?"

"No, not really," she answered truthfully. "But I do prefer to be inside a strong house during the worst of them. I hate this rocking and pitching we're doing. I don't know how John's managing."

"He's a good driver. I suspect that he's looking for a place that's a bit sheltered and once he finds it, he'll pull off and wait out the worst of the weather."

"Poor John. He deserves a bonus for having to drive in these conditions."

Jack made a contemplative sound and then said, "I didn't notice if Mrs. Theorosa's place had a carriage house or not."

"It does," she supplied readily. "I saw it through the kitchen window. It's for one carriage and has living quarters above." She smiled, knowing what his next question would be. "And yes, I'll bring John with me if he'd like to continue in service."

He grinned and then slowly sobered as he studied her. "Are you seriously considering moving up there, Lindsay?"

She nodded, the decision having been made almost the moment she'd walked in the door of Mrs. Theorosa's home. "How much do you think MacPhaull House would bring at sale? There's no mortgage on it."

"It's hard to say," Jack answered. "Mr. Gregory can probably give you a fairly accurate estimate."

"I think that once Richard's gone, I'll have Mr. Gregory

offer it. I'll send him a note tomorrow and let him know that it will be coming on the market. That way he can make discreet mention of it to parties who might be interested."

"You don't *have* to sell MacPhaull House, Lindsay. There'll be money to support it."

Lindsay started at the tacit suggestion. "It never crossed my mind that I wouldn't be able to afford to live there, Jack. I know you won't sell the roof from over my head. The honest truth is that I don't want to live there anymore. I want to live at Mrs. Theorosa's. If keeping Richard close to Dr. Bernard weren't important, I'd move in tomorrow."

He grinned and the corners of his eyes crinkled. "I should probably remind you that I haven't bought it yet."

"All right, quibble over the details if you like," she laughingly countered as the carriage rocked in the wind. "I'll move in the day the deed is transferred."

"Maybe you should hold off on the decision to sell MacPhaull House, though," he suggested, his smile fading. "Live at Mrs. Theorosa's if you want and think it over for a while. It's a pretty big step you're thinking about taking. Once MacPhaull House is sold, you can't change your mind and undo it."

"Why would I want to undo it? A choice between living in a bright and cheerful house and living in a dark and dreary mausoleum is no choice at all. No, my mind is made up." She smiled at him. "Nothing in my life has changed for years and years, Jack. And then you walked into the office and . . . and . . ."

"All hell broke loose?" he supplied.

"Well, yes, in a manner of speaking," she agreed, still searching for the right words. How could she explain how very different everything had become in those few seconds? "At first the changes were so disconcerting, but as time goes on, I'm becoming more comfortable with the notion. I think I'm actually to the point of enjoying it all."

"Enjoying having your world turned inside out and shook loose?" he asked dubiously.

"I know!" she exclaimed, suddenly seeing how she could make sense of it for him. "This morning when I woke up, my

first thought was 'I wonder what's going to happen today.'
Now, it wasn't the first time that's been my first waking
thought, Jack. Before, it's always been a dreadful thing to contemplate and I've wanted to pull the blankets over my head
and hide. But this morning it made me smile and want to
hurry out of bed and get on with the day so I could find out.

"It's as if I've stumbled into someone else's life. And
I've become a different person as a consequence. Life is interesting in a way it's never been before. I owe you a great
debt of gratitude," she offered sincerely.

"Oh, I don't know," he drawled, his smile quirked.
"Maybe you were just ready to break out of your old way
of doing things when I came along and gave you a shove."

"For which I'm most appreciative." The coach lurched
to one side and she held her breath while it slowly righted.
"I don't think that time will change how I feel about selling
MacPhaull House, Jack. It doesn't have especially happy
memories in it, and while the decision to dispose of it may
seem impulsive, I'm certain it's the right thing to—"

The carriage lurched again, more violently that it had
before, pitching forward and to the left. Into the wind, she
realized. In the same fraction of a heartbeat, she knew the
cause and that the carriage wasn't going to right itself; they'd
lost a wheel. Gasping, Lindsay clutched the corner strap
with both hands in a desperate attempt to keep herself from
being thrown off the seat.

Across from her, Jack bellowed, "Hang on!" as he
wedged himself into the downside corner and shoved his
feet hard against her cushion. The sounds and sensations
were a jumble, wrapped and tumbling around one another;
the wind, the rain, the whinny of horses, Jack's swearing,
and the thundering of her heart.

And then there was only the horrendous, jolting im-
pacts of wood and metal against stone. Lindsay was flung
upward and down and then upward again, the force and
speed rattling her teeth and blurring the world around her.
She felt the leather strap wrenched from her hands, heard
herself cry out as she pitched forward. Her heart hammering wildly, Lindsay instinctively put her hands out to break
her fall and closed her eyes, unwilling to see.

An iron band clamped around her upper arm in the same second that she heard Jack growl, "Gotcha!"

The impact was hard, but it wasn't uncontrolled. The pressure about her arm instantly eased, replaced just as quickly by wide bands that encircled her shoulders and her waist and held her securely. Lindsay pressed herself hard into the circle of salvation and drew a deep breath of relief. The erratic movements of the carriage ceased as abruptly as they'd begun, allowing the luxury of conscious recognition. She was sprawled over Jack, his arms wrapped around her, the lapels of his coat fisted in her hands.

"Jack," she whispered against his chest. "Oh God, Jack." Lindsay lifted her head to look up into his eyes. "Are you all right?"

"I'm fine," he assured her with a tight smile. "How about you?"

Lindsay did a quick mental evaluation and blinked in realization. She was lying along the entire length of him, one leg on either side of his outstretched ones. She could feel the hard heat and power of him from her cheek to the insides of her thighs. His pulse thundered into her body, igniting her blood. In her mind's eye flashed an image of lying with him like this on soft linen sheets. Her breathing caught as her pulse danced. Now wasn't the time or the place to indulge in fantasy, she sternly reminded herself.

"Fine," she managed to say, her voice taut. *In a most general sense.* "And this is the second time we've had this conversation," she added, trying to climb off him with some semblance of poise and grace.

"That's occurred to me as well," he said, gently taking her upper arms in his hands. He lifted her up with ease, saying, "Let me slide out from under you here and I'll go check on your driver."

"John," she whispered as she was gently settled into the corner. God, what a selfish person she was; she'd been thinking of making love to Jack when she should have been concerned for her coachman's well-being. He could be lying on the roadway—or in a flooded ditch—injured or dead, and all she'd been aware of had been the feel of her body against Jack's. She was a miserable human being, a horrible person who—

"Stay put."

Lindsay blinked, startled from her silent self-flagellation. She looked around the dim interior of the carriage to find herself alone and the downsloping door open just enough to permit exit. Rain splashed up from the paving stones. The sight triggered something inside her and suddenly she became aware of the pounding of it on the roof overhead. The wind was still blowing; it whistled and blustered through the openings of the door. Beyond it all, she heard the muffled sounds of two men talking. Two men meant that John was at least alive and able to speak. Lindsay slumped back against the squabs, relieved.

There were matters to be tended, she reminded herself. And to sit inside the carriage while others saw to them was unconscionable. At the very least the wheel had to be put back on and Jack and John certainly didn't need to attempt the task with her weight added to it. Grasping the edge of the open door, Lindsay pulled herself out of the slope of the seat and slipped outside.

The rain came down in torrents, making the roadbed a shallow but quickly running river of water that swirled around her ankles and instantly soaked both her shoes and the hem of her dress. The wind caught the brim of her bonnet and snapped it down over her face. A curtain of water poured off it and onto the bodice of her pelisse. Lindsay undid the ribbons beneath her chin and tossed the ruined straw hat into the open coach door behind her.

The afternoon light was leaden and dull, but there was sufficient light for her to see that the left front wheel was, as she had guessed, missing. She turned and looked back, searching along the deserted road for it and finding no sign of it anywhere. The sound of voices came to her on the wind. Lifting her skirts above the swirling water, she made her way around the back of the carriage and to the other side. John sat in the water, seemingly oblivious to it, but hugging his right arm close to his body.

"Dammit, Lindsay!"

She turned in the direction of Jack's voice and found him crawling from beneath the carriage itself. He was drenched to the skin, his clothing molded against his body, his hair plastered around his face, and the water streaming down his cheeks.

"Oh, hush," she said, realizing that she was in much the same condition. "You didn't really expect me to stay in there, did you?" He scowled, but she ignored him and knelt down beside her coachman, saying, "John, how badly are you hurt?"

"It's my arm, Miss Lindsay. I think it's broken."

"I'm afraid you're right," she said, noting the odd angle at which his forearm drooped from the elbow. "Not to worry, though, John," she added briskly. "We'll get you to Dr. Bernard just as quickly as we can. He'll set it and you'll never know it was once broken."

"First things first," Jack declared, dropping down beside her in the water. "We've got to get the wheel back on the carriage before we can go anywhere. Can you manage just a bit with one arm, John?"

The coachman nodded, said, "I'll give it my best, sir," and leaned forward to gain his knees. He cried out and sagged back with a strangled moan. Jack caught his shoulders and kept him from collapsing completely.

"Don't try to move again," Lindsay admonished, sweeping his legs with her gaze, searching for some sign of further injury.

"It's my side, Miss Lindsay," John explained through clenched teeth. "I'm afraid some of my ribs are broken as well."

"Then you'll stay right here and *I'll* assist Mr. Stennett."

Jack snorted. "You will not."

"You have two choices, Jack Stennett," she declared, meeting his gaze over John's head, her hands fisted on her hips. "You can stand out here waiting for an able-bodied man to happen along to help you put the wheel back on—and hope we don't drown while we wait for what amounts to a miracle—or you can accept my help so we can get out of here before we look more like wharf rats than human beings."

"Have you ever put a wheel on a carriage?"

"Of course not," she retorted. "But I'm quite capable of following instructions. Tell me what you want me to do."

"Get back in the carriage."

"I won't," she declared, vaguely aware that John was looking back and forth between them, following their conversation with an amused smile. "Think of something else; something that might actually be a step toward getting the wheel on."

"Wheels are heavy and they're greasy. You'll ruin your dress."

"It's already ruined," she countered, holding her arms out from her sides so that he could see the truth of it for himself. "So are my gloves and my bonnet. And just in case you're wondering, I don't care."

"And if I might point out the unfortunate obvious, sir," John said with a decidedly pained and rueful expression. "You don't have any other immediate choice."

Lindsay watched as Jack looked down the road and then back the way they'd come, then at the carriage. After a long moment he made a sound somewhere between a growl and a sigh and climbed to his feet. Extending his hand, he helped Lindsay rise as he said, "See what you can find to bandage John's midriff and arm. The less he moves it all, the better. I'm going to unhitch the horses so they don't bolt on us and make things even worse."

He hadn't offered his surrender outright and Lindsay accepted it in the same manner. As Jack strode to the front of the carriage, Lindsay touched her coachman's shoulder and said, "I'll be back in just a moment, John."

"I'll be right here when you do," he quipped. His effort to laugh was broken by a gasp that made Lindsay wince in sympathy.

Lifting her skirts again, Lindsay made her way to the rear of the carriage. Once there, she removed her pelisse and draped the sodden mass over the rear wheel. Free of its weight and bulk, she began the struggle to gather the rear of her skirt upward so that she could reach the ties of her petticoat. As she fumbled with the wet silk ribbons, it occurred to her that for the second time in as many days, she was faced by circumstances forcing the sacrifice of a petticoat. It said something about Jack Stennett; that accidents seemed to follow him around, waiting for a chance to happen. First the beam falling on his head in the middle of a raging fire. Now it was a lost wheel in the middle of a torrential downpour. Lindsay smiled, undid the lower lacings of her corset so she could move and breathe at the same time, and then shook her head as she peeled the drenched petticoat down her legs. What would befall him—and her—next? An explosion amidst a wave of pestilence?

She paused, remembering. There had already been an explosion—when the windows of the apartment at the rear of the building had been blown out, knocking them to the ground and showering them with glass. Three potentially fatal accidents in a mere two days. It boggled the mind. Either Jackson Stennett was the unluckiest or the luckiest man she'd ever met. Which it was, she couldn't tell. But, she decided, tearing her undergarment into wide strips, life since his arrival had been anything except boring and predictable. She could only hope that she survived his stay. And all the others around them did too, she mused, heading around the carriage, fabric strips in hand.

As he'd promised, John was exactly where she'd left him minutes earlier. Jack was still working on the couplings and harnesses. Lindsay made a mental note to someday ask John to show her how it was all assembled. Had Jackson Stennett not been with them, she'd have had to manage the horses and the repairs on her own. In a driving rain—as night was coming on—was not the best time to approach the tasks for the first time.

Lindsay knelt down beside her employee, wondering how she'd managed to survive all of her twenty-five years so blissfully ignorant of the workings of her everyday world. *Because you're dependent on others, Linds,* she silently groused. If there came a day when she couldn't afford cooks and coachmen, she was going to be largely helpless and at the mercy of people kind enough to explain such simple things to a formerly wealthy and spoiled woman. It would certainly be difficult, but above all else it would be humiliating. Better to learn before she actually needed to know.

"It'll be all right, Miss Lindsay," John assured her as she made a sling for his broken arm. "Mr. Stennett's already checked the axle and he says that it's not bent. If the wheel's in one piece and can be got on, she'll roll just fine all the rest of the way home."

It occurred to her that there were a large number of *ifs* in the situation. "Well, let's hope for just a sliver of good luck and a sound wheel, shall we?" Lindsay replied, wrapping a wide strip of cloth around his body, just above the elbow, effectively pinning his arm to his side. She pulled it tight and tied the ends together. "Is that too tight, John?"

"No, ma'am. Mr. Stennett's right; the tighter and stiller, the better." He looked down at the configuration of bandages and then said, "I think you'd best put another one around me, over the break, to hold that half in place."

She did as he asked, flinching when she pulled it too tight and he sucked a breath through his teeth. When she'd finished, she left John where he was and rose to her feet, realizing that the last two days of misfortunes had forced her to develop medical skills she'd never guessed she possessed. Heaven only knew what she'd be capable of by the time Jack went back to Texas. The way things had gone lately, she might well be a surgeon.

Lindsay wiped the water off her face with wet hands and shoved cascading tendrils of hair off her shoulders. Jack was leading the horses to the side of the road, the ends of their reins and harnesses trailing in the water behind them. She turned, lifted her skirts, and walked off in the direction from which they'd come, determined to start being useful. It would be nice to have found the wheel and have it back to the carriage by the time Jack finished with the horses.

She found it a quarter mile away from the carriage, lying half on the road, half in the water-filled ditch, and blessedly, mercifully in one piece. It took every measure of her strength to drag it fully onto the road. Once she had it there, she had to summon yet more strength to heft it up and onto the rim so that she could roll it back. She was breathing hard and the muscles in her arms, back, and shoulders were burning by the time she'd managed the task. She was soaked. The rain was still coming down in sheets, whipped and driven by the wind. The discomforts paled beside her sense of accomplishment as she neared the rear of the coach.

"Jesus, you're a stubborn woman."

Lindsay halted the wheel and looked up. Jack leaned against the carriage, one booted ankle crossed casually over the other and his arms folded across his chest. His smile was wide and amused and infectious. "Yes, I am," she admitted, lifting her chin and grinning. "Thank you for noticing."

"Capable, too."

"So you're willing to concede that I might be trainable? And of some practical use?"

"All right, Lindsay," he said, laughing and straightening to take the wheel from her. "You win."

"I'll do whatever you tell me to," she promised, walking beside him in the rain as he rolled the wheel toward its axle.

"For starters, don't ever open a door that wide for a man, sweetheart. We're predatory creatures to the bone. Even a half-invitation is sufficient to get you into a whole lot of trouble."

Lindsay laughed, and scoffed, "You're not predatory, Jack."

"Remind me," he said, maneuvering the wheel close to the side of the carriage, "when I haven't got my hands full to prove you wrong."

She nodded, but she doubted that he saw the gesture; his attention was focused on the axle. And then he removed his jacket. His shirt was plastered hard against his arms and torso and Lindsay couldn't resist the temptation of looking. "Nicely sculpted" was the most benign of the observations that occurred to her. The rest were as decidedly wicked as the hand that had molded the ripples and planes of Jack Stennett.

And he'd said men were predatory creatures? Judging by her own reaction to the mere sight of him in wet clothing, they didn't have exclusive rights to the claim. Women were, she decided, simply less bold about it. She averted her gaze, but not enough that she couldn't see him at the edge of her vision. Jack was just too magnificent, too inspiring to ignore. She'd probably go to hell for ogling him, no matter how discreetly. At least it would be a quick and happy trip.

"Here's the plan, Lindsay," he said a few moments later, forcing her to abandon her reverie. "I'm going to lift up the carriage and you're going to shove the wheel hub onto the axle. You're going to have to put your hands here and here," he said, showing her where he wanted them. "And you're going to have to throw your entire body into the push in order to get the wheel into place. It's got to go all the way on, Lindsay. Halfway won't do. Understand?"

"Yes." She'd managed to get it out of the ditch, on its side and back here, hadn't she? And she'd bet Agatha's wardrobe allowance that he'd tamped down his gentlemanly impulses and watched her do it, knowing that she wanted the satisfaction of doing it by herself, and willing to let her earn it.

"Now," he went on, "I don't know how long I'll be able to hold the axle where it needs to be, so please move as fast and accurately as you possibly can. If I yell for you to let loose of the wheel and get back, for once in your life, do exactly as you're told, when you're told. I don't want you to get hurt. All right?"

"All right, Jack," she said, stepping forward to take the balancing of the wheel into her own hands.

He moved to the corner of the carriage and studied it for a moment before squatting down and fitting his hands beneath the lower edges. "Ready?" he asked, looking up at her. His smile was reassuring and she thought that he was the most handsome man she'd ever seen.

She placed her hands on the spokes as he'd shown her. "Whenever you are."

"On the count of three." He seized a deep breath. "One . . . two . . . three!"

Lindsay held her breath, awed by the speed and apparent ease with which Jackson hefted up the corner of the carriage. In one smooth motion, the axle left the road and swung upward in a quick arc. As it neared the hole in the hub, she leaned into the wheel and started to push it forward and onto the mating part. Even as she did, the axle rose higher. She tried to lift the wheel, but didn't have the strength. "It's too high, Jack!" she cried. "Lower it a couple of inches."

He swore through his clenched teeth and bent slightly at the knees.

Lindsay sighted the alignment quickly and then shoved with all her might. She was rewarded by the the sound of metal sliding and then impacting metal. "It's there, Jack! It's on! I heard it hit something hard on the back side!"

"Stand back," he growled through his teeth.

Lindsay obeyed instantly, her hands fisted in her skirts, dragging the sodden mass with her as she scrambled backward. Jack eased his grip with a heavy sigh and then stepped back as well, flexing his fingers as he studied the wheel.

"Well done, Mr. Stennett! Well done, Miss Lindsay!"

Lindsay turned to find her coachman leaning against the rear wheel of the carriage. Even in the rain and fading light, she could see the effort it took for him to stand and the pain he suffered in breathing and talking. "Oh, John," she said sadly, moving toward him. "You shouldn't be on your feet."

Jack stepped to her side, slipping his arms back into his coat, and said, "I'll pin the wheel in place and see to hitching the horses back up if you'll get John inside. There's no way he can do the driving as busted up as he is."

"Can you drive, Jack?" she called over her shoulder as she opened the door.

"I've been driving wagons since I can remember anything at all. See to John."

She did so, trying to assist him up the step and into the seat as best she could and as much as his pride would allow. It was a slow process, his breathing labored and his movements painful both for him to bear and for her to watch. When at last she had him tucked into a corner and a large wool blanket over his lap, she left, closing the door. Jack was hitching the horses and she stepped silently forward to watch and learn what she could.

He didn't look up from his task as he said, "What are you doing out here? Get inside with John before you catch your death of cold."

"Do you know the way to Dr. Bernard's house?" Lindsay asked calmly.

He hesitated. "No."

"Then you're going to need someone riding up there with you who does, aren't you?"

He went about his task muttering under his breath. Lindsay smiled and watched as he efficiently fastened buckles and pinned things into place. She had no idea what was what and why it was all done the way it was. She had the distinct impression, though, that Jack could have done it all in his sleep. How wonderful it must be, she thought, to have the skills necessary to take care of yourself in any circumstance.

When he was done, he straightened and motioned toward the driver's box with a jerk of his chin, saying, "I'll give you a lift up."

She managed it with his gallant assistance, but not without silently cursing those who thought women weren't properly clothed unless they were swathed in sixteen thousand yards of fabric. Settling into the box, Lindsay noticed that the rain was finally beginning to lighten. She smiled wryly. Of course the rain was easing—now that they were as soaked as people could get. But where there was one positive, there was an accompanying negative; the sun was setting, and as it dipped, so did the temperature. Drenched to the bone, Lindsay was all too aware of the chilly edge to the gathering night air.

"Have you ever ridden shotgun before?" Jack asked as he nimbly climbed into the box beside her.

"Shotgun?" she repeated warily.

"The man—or in this case the woman," he explained, grinning, "who sits beside the driver and fends off any would-be marauders."

"With a shotgun," she guessed.

"Yep." He flicked the reins along the backs of the horses and made a clicking sound. As the animals started forward, he continued, saying, "Personally, I prefer a rifle;

it's more accurate and gives you a longer range. But some men couldn't hit the broadside of a barn with a big stick and they need all the scatter they can get."

"I've never fired a weapon of any sort," Lindsay admitted. "I gather that you're proficient at it."

"Proficient? Naw," he drawled. Then he looked over at her and smiled broadly. Devilment sparkled in his eyes. "I'm damn good."

Lindsay laughed. "Somehow, Jack Stennett, I don't doubt that at all." The wind gusted, cutting through her sodden clothing and scraping cold fingers along her flesh. Lindsay couldn't contain the shiver.

"I'd offer you my coat, but it's so wet it wouldn't do you a bit of good."

"I'm all right."

Still smiling, he made that quick motion with his chin again. "Scoot on over here."

There was something so right about it that Lindsay closed the distance between them without hesitation. Snugged up against his side, she slipped her arm around his near one and all but wallowed in the warmth of his body. God, what she wouldn't give to spend forever like this. It felt so good. "This is highly improper," she said, just to assuage a sudden twinge of conscience.

"But it's warmer than sitting there all by your wet and lonesome self, isn't it?"

"Yes," she admitted freely, snuggling even closer.

"Don't worry," he said with a wink. "There isn't anyone out and about to see you choosing sensibility over propriety."

"I've been thinking lately that—as virtues go—propriety is vastly overrated."

"I decided that a long, long time ago." He chuckled. "My mother pitched a blue fit."

"Speaking of mothers, my mother would be appalled at how late we're going to be for dinner. Have I mentioned how very much like her Henry and Agatha are?"

"No, you haven't, but I sorta gathered that all on my own. Your brother and sister are just going to have to understand that they're not always the first priority."

The notion had been posed for their consideration before. It hadn't gone over well. Maybe Jack would have better luck at it than Richard had.

"Lindsay?" Jack said softly. He didn't give her a chance to reply, before continuing, "You did beautifully back there. I can't think of anyone I'd rather have help me replace a wagon wheel."

A warmth, deep and settling, bloomed inside her and filled her completely. Words were impossible. Lindsay hugged Jack's arm in silent thanks. Life was good; better than it had ever been. With a contented sigh, she leaned her head against Jack's shoulder and wished that it could go on like this forever.

Chapter Fourteen

*J*ACK PAUSED AT THE DOOR on his way out of Dr. Bernard's house. Behind him he heard the good doctor talking to John in low, soothing tones. Ahead of him sat the carriage at the curb, Lindsay ensconced in the box just as he'd left her. It had taken a brutal description of the process of bone-setting to get her to stay there. He'd had some second thoughts about leaving her alone until Dr. Bernard had grasped the lower half of John's arm and asked him to hold the upper half immobile. John had strangled on a scream of pain before passing out, and Jack had been eternally grateful for the foresight to insist that Lindsay remain behind. She had grit, but there was no need to test it any more than necessary. She'd been through a lot in the last couple of days.

He pulled the door closed and bounded down the steps, remembering the determination with which she'd dragged the wheel onto the road and gotten it on its edge. He'd never considered her a fragile flower, but watching her had given him a whole new appreciation for the way she went at life. Nothing daunted Lindsay for long. He grinned. She just loosened her corset lacings and tackled whatever came her way. God, she was so like her father in so many ways. The good ways, he amended, climbing up into the box.

She'd scooted to the far side of the seat again. He glanced around, noting that the sky had cleared and that other drivers had ventured out onto the wet, moonlit streets. Ah, so much for warmth being more important to her than the opinions of strangers. "You're still here," he quipped, settling in. "I thought maybe you might have taken the carriage and driven off into the night."

"I thought about it. How's John?"

"Fine, and the bone's set," he supplied, picking up the reins. "So why didn't you?"

"I don't know how to drive. I was afraid I'd wreck the carriage and hurt the horses."

While her tone was lightly bantering, he thought he heard an honest wish and a regret beneath the surface of it. "Would you like to learn?"

"To drive?"

"Well," he drawled, "I figure most folks can probably crash and maim without being taught." She shot him a look of good-natured censure and he laughed. "Yes, Lindsay, to drive. I'll show you how."

She glanced at the horses, and when she looked back at him, her face was bright with anticipation. "When?"

"Right now's as good a time as any," he declared. "You hold the reins like this." He held up his hands for her to see how the leather strips were threaded through his fingers. She leaned close, studying them from several angles, and he couldn't help smiling at the intensity she brought to the task.

"I don't know, Jack," she said slowly, leaning back. "What if—"

"I'm going to be right here," he promised, laying the reins in her lap and giving her no further choice in the matter. She drew a deep breath and, as he'd fully expected, squared her shoulders and picked them up.

"Nothing bad is going to happen," he gently assured her, as she carefully threaded the strips through her fingers. "We'll take it slow and easy and I'll talk you through it one step at a time. You've got good horses; they're not going to get ornery on you."

"You'll take the reins back if they do?"

"Absolutely. Whenever you're ready, give the reins a little flick and make a clicking sound like I did earlier."

She drew one more deep breath and then committed herself to the attempt. Jackson, true to his word, kept up a steady, softly spoken stream of instruction, explaining each of the terms he used and the mechanics of making the horses go where and when she wanted them to. Navigating the very first corner without hitting it or any of the other carriages in the street produced a sigh of relief and a noticeable relaxing of her shoulders. The second one elicited a giggle of delight deep in her throat. The sound strummed all along his senses and quickened his pulse.

There were no two ways about it; Lindsay MacPhaull was one helluva woman. There had been three marriage proposals, she'd said. And then the one man—The Fool—who'd courted her and walked away. Four men wasn't very many, all things considered. Why wasn't he having to plow his way through a line of men that stretched down the front walk of MacPhaull House and around the block?

Physically, she was the kind of woman that turned male heads when she walked past. No china doll had ever been made that could rival the delicate beauty of her face. And her body . . . Jackson let his gaze caress the sweep of her curves. Her clothing molded to her and left precious little to his imagination. Jesus, her body was perfection; the kind that invited a man to slip his arms around it, draw it close, and hope to God he could drown himself in the sheer and uncommon pleasure of making love to her.

And yet Lindsay seemed completely unaware of her effect on him. Him and every other man on the face of the earth, he realized. And so he was back to his original puzzle. Why was she unmarried? Why were there no suitors fuming over the fact that he'd walked into her life and claimed her every waking moment as his?

The physical attraction of her aside—which wasn't something to be lightly discounted—she had a cartload of other qualities that were every bit as alluring. Surely he wasn't the only man who appreciated intelligence, a quick wit, refined tastes, and social graces. She was damn resilient, too. When she smiled, she lit up the world. And her laughter was so genuinely happy and unrestrained that a man couldn't help but realize that she wasn't bound all that tightly by the notion of propriety. All it took to free her was a little nudge and a playful wink. Lindsay was, when she was being unguardedly herself, a woman of passionate impulses.

And what intriguing impulses they were. How could a man not be fascinated by a woman who didn't have a submissive, passive, reticent, or retiring bone in her lusciously curved body? There was no controlling Lindsay MacPhaull. You either accepted the fact that she was your equal in every sense or you ran for your life.

Jackson smiled. He wasn't the running sort. But there were a surprising number of men in the world who were. And that, he supposed, was the answer to his questions. One look into her dazzling blue eyes and most men would instinctively understand that they were going to have to surrender any notion of being the king of their domestic castle and lord of their financial dominion. It wasn't in Lindsay's nature to back down. Whatever the contest, she'd stand toe-to-toe with a man and give back every bit as good as she got. The greater the risk involved in the battle of wills, the more she'd be drawn to it. And, like Billy, she'd be likely to up the stakes all along the way, confident that the opposition would soon fold under the pressure.

He didn't run and he wasn't the kind of man to fold either. It didn't bode well for the two of them. He didn't seem able to keep from thinking about making love with her and she didn't seem inclined to play the modest maiden. It would be much easier for him to cling to the remnants of gentlemanly conduct if she were to try clinging to propriety, though. As it was, she'd met his every advance without flinching and then calmly bettered him before walking away. At the rate they were going, they'd one up each other into a bed before the month was done.

And would that be so damn horrible? Jack asked himself. Lindsay was a big girl and knew what she was getting herself into; The Fool had apparently taken her for a ride aways down Carnal Road. Jack had been right up-front with her, telling her that he wasn't about to stay in New York one day longer than he absolutely had to. Lindsay knew that he wasn't a Forever and Always man. If she tumbled into his bed, then she'd be tumbling with her eyes just as wide-open as his were.

And he'd make damn sure they were. There wasn't going to be any bastard child and there wasn't going to be any tearful farewell scene on the docks. And Lindsay needed to understand very clearly that whatever happened between them personally wasn't going to be allowed to affect the business aspects of their relationship in any way. The two areas had to remain separate at all costs; to let them merge, even accidentally, would tarnish all the pleasure they might otherwise have in their companionship. There were lines in the sand and then there were lines in the sand. While some of them were getting mighty blurred, the one separating business and personal was deep and and well-defined. If she couldn't accept that, well, he'd just have to resign himself to being celibate. And acutely, painfully miserable.

"You're being awfully quiet over there," Lindsay said, gently interrupting his internal diatribe. "Has my driving scared you speechless?"

There was no point in delaying the necessary and the inevitable. "You're doing just fine," he assured her, turning in the box so that he sat angled toward her, allowing him to easily watch her face. "I'm just wondering about a few things."

She arched a brow, but didn't take her eyes off the road. "Are there any answers you think I might have for you?"

"It depends on how honest you want to be."

"Oh, that sounds ominous," she said lightly. "Are your ponderings of a business or a personal nature?"

"Purely personal. How brave are you feeling, Madam Coachwoman?"

"Very," she replied, smiling. "I haven't even come close to hitting anyone or anything. And no one has felt obliged to point their fingers at me and laugh. Ask whatever you'd like, Jack. If you ask a question that makes me uncomfortable, I'll let you know. Until that point, you'll get the truth as I know it."

"All right." *Take the bull by the horns, Jack.* "This afternoon, on our way to Mrs. Theorosa's . . . Was it really unseasonably warm?"

"No."

She hadn't hesitated so much as a fraction of a second. "I thought so," he drawled, wondering if he was as brave and forthright as she apparently was. "You were getting even with me for the game I played with you in Gregory's office, weren't you?"

"That was the general intent." She turned her head to smile at him. "Was it successful?"

"Extremely." He held his hand up between them, holding his thumb and index finger a scant half-inch apart. "You came this close to getting an indecent proposal."

She laughed and went back to watching the road, saying, "But, being a gentleman, you restrained the impulse."

He had the distinct impression that she regretted his nobility. "Would you have accepted it?" he asked, incredulous.

"Honestly, Jack, I don't know what I would have done." She smiled wickedly and arched a brow. "I think it's quite likely, though, that I would have undone another button while I contemplated the matter."

She could light his fires so damn easily. The fact that she was truly a good and decent person was the only thing that kept her from being a very bad girl. And that made her one helluva interesting woman. "Didn't Abigail Beechum ever tell you that it's cruel to tease?" he asked.

"It seems to me," she retorted saucily, "that the shoe fits your foot just as well as it does mine, Jackson Stennett. I seem to recall that it was your foot tracing delightful patterns up and down my leg in Mr. Gregory's office."

"Delightful, huh?"

"Be that as it may," she offered, the tone of her voice suddenly soft and serious, "I shouldn't have deliberately teased you as I did and I'm sorry, Jack. If you'll promise to avoid tempting me, I'll promise to—"

"It won't do any good," he interrupted with a chuckling snort and a dismissive wave of his hand. "You'll only undo it all by apologizing."

She instantly looked over at him, her brows knit and and her lips pursed in a little O of good-natured aggravation.

"You dance, you pay the piper, Lindsay."

"Well," she said on a quick exhale as she turned back to watch the road, "if you intend to kiss me for that particular lapse in self-control, you'll have to wait, because we've reached MacPhaull House and I have to get the carriage not only through the gate, but around back and into the carriage house. Do you have any idea of how small the doors are on the carriage house? John's always complaining about them."

Wonderful timing and a nice sidestep, he thought. "Would you like me to take it from here?"

"Absolutely not. There's no satisfaction to be had in saying I managed to drive halfway home but gave up the reins when it got the first bit difficult."

"And satisfaction is everything."

"It is indeed," she agreed, "and I intend to fully earn mine. If you want your kiss, then you'll have to give me sufficient driving instruction to insure that you're alive and whole enough to collect it."

She was too damned cavalier about inviting his advances. To his surprise, he discovered that it rankled. He was going to collect that kiss the minute they climbed down out of the box, and he was going to make sure that it singed her all the way to her nonchalantly daring little toes. This was going to be the last time she contemplated one of his kisses without a sizable tremble of anticipation.

"There are limits to what a man—gentle or otherwise—can tolerate," he felt compelled to warn. "You're courting trouble, Lindsay. You need to know that."

"I do," she answered solemnly. "I don't, however, seem to be able to resist temptation where you're concerned. Good judgment disappears like a wisp of smoke in a gale wind. Now," she added, her tone back to being blithely buoyant, "tell me how I'm supposed to maneuver this huge black box through those narrow little gates."

Lindsay knew that she'd been too honest, had pushed him too far. She could feel the tension vibrating out of him, could hear it in every taut syllable he uttered as he told her how and when to pull the reins. Pay the piper? Oh yes, the reckoning loomed in the minutes ahead, a certain, inescapable fate. This kiss wasn't going to caress her soul as his last one had, though. If she was reading him correctly, he intended for this kiss to be rough and perhaps even a bit frightening. Which it was, even in considering the prospect. Deliciously frightening. She didn't have the sense God gave a goose. Amazingly, given how thoroughly distracted she was, she managed to get the carriage through the gates and into the carriage house without wrecking it.

Even as she drew the horses to a halt, he was swinging down out of the box, saying as he did, "Sit right there and I'll come around to help you down."

Laying the reins aside, she watched him stride around the front of the horses. Long, hard strides. Her heart skittered and it occurred to her that a reasonably prudent woman determined to save herself would summon a haughty manner and cry propriety at this point. She couldn't do that in good conscience, though; the predicament was of her own making. Staging a well-timed faint was a possibility. But not a good one, she decided as Jackson reached her side of the box. Given the look in his eyes, he'd deliberately drop her on her head. He lifted his arms and Lindsay knew that she was out of time and options. There was nothing to be done but lean out, put her hands on his shoulders, and let him exact his rough justice.

His gaze, dark and hardened with the determination of intent, met hers and held it captive. Lindsay felt her breath catch, her pulse quicken. She was courting the storm, inviting it to do its best to destroy her. And she'd never felt happier or more wondrously alive. She had to be insane. Her heart racing, Lindsay leaned out and down, entrusting him with her safety, her dignity, and her thrilling expectations.

His clothing was wet and warmed from the heat of his body. And under it, beneath the palms of her hands, she could feel the corded muscles in his shoulders, feel the steely strength of his arms as he slipped his hands around her waist and lifted her free of the box. His hands firm and sure around her waist, he held her above him for a long heartbeat, watching her face, silently promising to wreck slow havoc on her senses.

And then he drew her closer and began to lower her, his gaze holding hers. She gasped at the tantalizing friction of her body slowly moving down the length of his. He was pure muscle and sinew and gloriously wicked intent. He was everything dangerous, the most forbidden of all temptations. The knowing, the waiting, the wanting . . . An exquisite ache blossomed deep in her chest and spread like quicksilver into her limbs. If he didn't kiss her, she'd die; she'd crumple to the straw-covered floor and die of hunger and disappointment.

Jackson forced himself to swallow, made himself take a breath. God, never in his life had he seen such open and innocent yearning in a woman's eyes. Never had he wanted to possess a woman like he wanted Lindsay MacPhaull; totally, deeply, and completely. Right here, right now, and all damn night long. To hell with what he should and ought to do. To hell with her being a lady and his being a gentleman. To hell with dinner and Hen—

Dinner. His common sense rushed to assert itself. They were already late for dinner. If he kissed Lindsay, the odds were they'd never get there. She had a way of making him hungry in a way that had nothing to do with food. If he gave in, they'd both eventually regret the moment of weakness. He needed to be practical, to exercise good judgment.

But goddamn it, he needed Lindsay, too. He needed her in a way that he'd forgotten a man could need. And he'd promised himself that he'd kiss her. He'd promised her, too. If he went back on it . . . Just one kiss, he told himself. One short, quick kiss to satisfy his sense of pride, to show her that he was a man of his word. And that would be it; one brief kiss and then he'd set her aside and walk away. He could do it. He had the strength.

Lindsay blinked in dazed surprise and would have stumbled back if Jack hadn't caught her arms and kept her upright. It had to have been the quickest, most passionless kiss in the history of mankind. She didn't know whether to be angrily insulted or graciously blasé. Confused, she was— and in spades.

He cleared his throat and refused to meet her gaze as he

let go of her arms. "I need to take care of the horses," he said hastily, stepping away.

Lindsay watched him walk off, suddenly aware of just how frustrated and angry she was and how deeply her feelings hurt. "Quite the predator," she muttered under her breath.

He stopped and then slowly turned back to face her. His brow cocked, he tilted his head and studied her through narrowed eyes. A smile flirted at the corners of his mouth. "What did you say?"

Her heart jolted and her pulse raced. Yes, she was wildly, foolishly crazy. And she didn't care one whit. "I was observing—to myself—" she countered lightly, her hands fisted on her hips, "that I was right earlier this evening. You are *not* a predatory man, Jack Stennett."

He moved toward her, slowly and deliberately. He stopped only when he was close enough for her to bask in the warmth radiating from him, close enough that she had to tilt her head up to meet his gaze.

"Is that a dare, Lindsay?" he asked, his voice the lazy drawl that sent tingles racing down her spine.

"No, it's an opinion," she answered with quiet defiance.

He studied her for a long moment and then one corner of his mouth quirked upward. "Hope it's not carved in stone," he said, slipping his arms around her waist and drawing her hard against the length of his body.

His lips brushed over hers once, twice, and then, as though he sensed the craving curling tightly inside her, he claimed her lips fully with his own. He devoured her, his possession as sure and masterful as it was compelling and thorough. Her lips parted at his gentle demand and her knees weakened as his kiss deepened to wrap around her soul. She pressed closer, twining her arms about his neck, abandoning herself to a kind of bold hunger that was heady and all consuming and right; as right as breathing and living itself. Desire sang through her and she rose on the song, eagerly returning the passion of his kiss.

His heart thundered; his blood shot hot and fierce. She

was everything he could want, all that he did want. He couldn't hold her close enough, taste her deeply enough. His hands explored the luscious curves of her waist, her hips, then slid to cup her from behind, drawing her against the hard proof of his desire. She responded instantly, and just as boldly, gently catching his lower lip between her teeth, then teasing his captive flesh with the tip of her tongue. Exquisite sensation swept through him in wave after intoxicating wave. Moaning at the sheer pleasure of it, he tightened his arms around her.

Wrapped in the certain strength of his embrace, wondrously intoxicated by the power of his kisses, Lindsay twined her fingers in the dark hair at his nape as his hands came up to open the buttons of her dress. Whispering her assent against his lips, she slipped her hands to his shoulders and then to the front of his shirt. The buttons opened easily and the warmth of his skin beckoned her touch. She reveled in caressing the corded planes of his chest, in the low, deep groan of his appreciation as he drew his lips from hers.

A protest melded into a gasp of wonder as his lips trailed down the column of her throat and into the hollow at the base. He lingered there, thrilling her senses, teasing the sensitive spot with slow, deliberate strokes of his tongue as his hand glided into the valley of her breasts. He kissed a trail downward as his fingers slipped beneath the lace of her corset and across her hardened nipple.

Deep inside her a flame flared and grew, pulsing and heavy with urgency. Her knees trembling, she clung to Jack's shoulders and arched into his possession, aching and desperate to answer desire's insistent command, to sample its promise of delicious pleasure.

Her skin was heated satin and rich cream, a feast for his senses; her willingness and passion, a potent and heady elixir. He cupped her breast, the curve of her perfectly filling and warming his palm. Hunger surged through him and he bent to taste the bounty she offered him. She moaned softly, arching into the caress of his lips and tongue, sending his senses reeling.

Ageless instincts urged him to know more of her beauty,

her wonder, to lower her into the straw and—*Straw. Not here. Not this way. Not like Maria. God, not like Maria.*

Lindsay felt his decision in every inch of her body, regretted with all her heart the gradual easing of his embrace, the lightening of his possession. Jack's lips lifted from her breast and she shuddered as she drew a ragged breath. God, she missed the touch. It was for the best, she told herself. There was dinner. Henry and Agatha. And the doors to the carriage house were open. Someone could walk in on them.

As though he knew her thoughts, he lightly brushed his lips over hers. Once, twice, ending as he had begun. Lindsay slipped her arms from around his neck, placing her palms against the broad expanse of his chest to steady herself. Her pulse raced and the ache deep inside her throbbed in rhythm with her heart. She'd survive, she assured herself, willing her eyes to open. Lindsay looked up into dark eyes still smoldering with passion.

"I really do need to take care of the horses," he said breathlessly, his smile regretful as he eased his arms from around her.

She nodded in agreement and took a step back. Jack mercifully spared her the need to say something halfway intelligent by winking, turning away, and setting to work. She buttoned her bodice and watched him, only vaguely aware of what he was doing. Learning to hitch and unhitch a team of horses paled beside a greater realization. Society might well consider her an "experienced" woman, but when it came to Jack, she was encountering a wholly new and unexpectedly wonderful world of sensation. There was no sense of duty in surrendering to him, no notion of keeping to her part of a rationally negotiated bargain. There was nothing the least bit rational about being with Jack; he set her senses on fire.

Lindsay smiled ruefully. If he were to ask her for business concessions between kisses, she'd agree to give him anything he wanted and offer to throw in Mrs. Kowalski's cat, too. Lydia MacPhaull was undoubtedly watching from her eternal destination and flailing her arms in disgusted outrage. *For godssakes, Lindsay, can't you do anything right?* Apparently not.

"Why don't you go to the house and start getting cleaned up for dinner," Jack said quietly, interrupting her thoughts. "I'll be along in few minutes."

Lindsay looked out the open carriage house doors and across the yard. The windows at the rear of the house were illuminated with lamplight. Henry and Agatha and Edith were in there and waiting for her. "Truth be told, Jack," she said, turning back to him, "I'd rather take a beating than go in there alone."

"Why do Henry and Agatha frighten you so much?" he asked, pulling the harness off a horse.

She watched the animal amble through its open stall door, as Jack pulled the harness from its companion. "It's not so much that my brother and sister frighten me; it's that every encounter ends with me feeling as though . . ." She shrugged, unable to put a lifetime of feelings into precise words.

"As though what?" he pressed, hanging the tack from wooden pegs.

"I don't know," she admitted. "It's such a jumble of things. Overwhelmed, mostly. And completely inept. If I were even halfway adequate as a manager, they wouldn't have grounds to complain about anything. As it is, though, it seems that I can't do anything right."

He nodded, closing the stall doors. "Do you ever feel angry?"

All the time. "Anger isn't a very productive emotion."

"Try letting it have free rein the next time it comes over you," he countered, coming to stand in front of her. "You might be surprised just how much it can accomplish."

"But it tends to lead to such unladylike behavior." Lindsay smiled up at him. "I've seen Agatha angry. It's not a pretty sight."

"Sweetheart," he drawled, his eyes sparkling, "you'd be downright beautiful all riled up."

"Even if I happen to be angry with you?"

"Now, what could I do that would get you all puffed up?" he asked, all innocence and utterly adorable charm.

"Somehow, Jackson Stennett, I imagine that you could find a hundred different ways to try a woman's patience."

He grinned. "A hundred and fifty-two. I've kept count."

She laughed, certain that the total was even higher than he'd admit and fully equal to the number of times he'd been kissed and forgiven. He could charm the hardest of hearts. She'd bet that there were women all across Texas vying for his attention. And, she realized, sobering, he could claim one in New York as well; one who didn't mean anything more to him than any of the others. She caught her lower lip between her teeth as a bitter memory surged to the fore. *A rather dull little notch in the bedpost.*

Jackson felt an odd twinge in the center of his chest as he watched the light in Lindsay's eyes fade and then go out. She swallowed and lifted her chin, then drew a deep breath as she blinked back a mist of tears. He knew the look of painful memories, and everything in him wanted to pull her into his arms and banish them with sweet, tender kisses.

"We'd better go in, Lindsay," he said, desperate for a way to distract them both.

It took her a moment, but she managed to nod and say, "Through the kitchen. That way we can take the servants' stairs up and avoid being seen looking so . . ." She glanced down at the front of her dress and sighed. "Bedraggled."

"Sounds like a plan," he quipped, offering her his arm. She took it, but the pensive look in her eyes as they left the light of the carriage house told him that her mind had slipped back into the past, that she hadn't shaken the troubling memory. Something—or more likely, someone—had wounded her deeply. Who? How and why? And what had he done to make her remember?

Maybe nothing, he decided, as they neared the back door of the house. It could be that she was simply dreading the coming encounter with her brother and sister. He paused at the bottom of the steps, realizing that he couldn't go inside knowing that he hadn't done anything to ease her heart and mind. But what? God, he was usually more adept than this. She looked up at him and in the moonlight he could see the unspoken question in her eyes.

"You're beautiful when you're sad, too, Lindsay," he said, trying to find his way, the right words. "But when you laugh, when you smile, the whole world gets brighter. You don't do it near often enough. If you'd tell me what I need to do to make it happen, I'd be willing to try."

"Oh, Jack," she whispered, a soft smile curving her luscious lips. "You are the sweetest man I've ever known. And you don't have to do anything beyond being yourself."

Something deep inside his chest swelled. "Jesus, I can't resist you," he admitted quietly, cradling her face gently between his hands. She looked up to meet his gaze, her eyes filled with gentle invitation. "Tell me that now isn't the time or the place for this," he whispered, tracing the fullness of her lower lip with the pad of his thumb.

"Now isn't the time or the place, Jack," she supplied obediently, her words edged with genuine regret. She sighed and graced his thumb with a kiss. "And there are some things that I should tell you before we go any further."

"Save them for after dinner," he said, leaning down to feather a kiss across her lips. "I'm perfectly willing to cover old ground until then."

"Buggering the coachman, I see."

Even as the words registered in his brain, Lindsay strangled a cry and vaulted out of his loose embrace. Anger, instant and roiling, swept through him. Jack let her go and spun about, his hand fisted and aimed with instinctive, deadly precision. The impact of flesh and bone against flesh and bone wasn't nearly as satisfying as he'd hoped. His teeth clenched, his hands fisted in front of him, he glared at the man flopping weakly in the grass at his feet. Henry.

Jack was preparing to order him to stand and apologize when Lindsay stepped forward and, holding her skirt hem well back, smiled down at the son of a bitch. "Henry, meet Jackson Stennett," she said with a gentle sweep of her hand. She met Jack's gaze and smiled. "Jack, you owe me ten dollars."

"I didn't try to kill him," he countered, glaring down at Henry's prostrate form. Reaching into his trouser pocket, he pulled out a gold coin. Handing it to her, he added, "But I think I probably will."

She laughingly took the money from him. "Thank you.

And I'll remind you of the other wager we made. I'm going to win it, too."

"Give me a hand up," Henry growled, struggling to lift his upper body.

Jack bounded up the stairs, opened the kitchen door, and then held out his hand. Lindsay put hers in it and let him draw her into the warmth and light of the kitchen. She laughed when he waved to Henry just before closing the door on him.

There was heaven and there was earth and then there was Lindsay—whose happiness was the closest a man could come to finding heaven on earth. It was an incredibly precious and fragile thing. Henry had just taken the very last free shot at it that he was ever going to get.

CHAPTER FIFTEEN

$\mathcal{L}$INDSAY CHECKED HER HAIRPINS one last time before she hastened to answer the knock at her bedroom door. She found Jackson standing outside, wearing a clean, crisply pressed suit and a tight smile.

"Do I look New York presentable?" he asked, grimacing as he stretched his neck beneath the starched collar of his shirt.

As was the suit he'd worn the day she first met him, this one's cut was years past truly fashionable. And while it fit him perfectly, accentuating the width of his shoulders and the narrowness of his hips, he was clearly uncomfortable in it and she wouldn't have added to his misery for all the money in Christendom. "I'd be proud to be seen on your arm anywhere in town, Jackson Stennett," she declared with utter sincerity, stepping out of her room and pulling the door closed.

He grinned and offered her his arm, saying, "That's most kind of you, ma'am. Any words of wisdom you'd care to impart before we go down to face the lions?"

"Remember the MacPhaull Rules, Jack," she gently admonished as they started down the hall. "Unpleasant realities are to be ignored. Other than that, I can't think of anything."

He slid a glance at her and rolled his eyes. "And how am I supposed to discuss the reason I'm here in town and what I intend to do? I'm thinking that I can sugarcoat it six ways to Sunday, but they're still going to find the taste of the news just a tad bit on the unpleasant side."

"You don't have to tell them a thing," Lindsay assured him. "They read the significant details in the paper this morning. There might be general conversation all around the topic, but no one will come right out and ask you what and how much you intend to give them. You can be as vague as you like in discussing your ideas and no one will back you into a corner over the matter."

"How the hell does anything get done in this family? How do you all ever arrive at an agreement of any sort?"

"We don't. Each of us does what we want and the others make adjustments."

"And if one of you makes a fabulously stupid blunder?"

"Then those it affects have to make fabulously brilliant recoveries."

"Why do I have a sense of you being the one who has to make all the recoveries?" he asked as they started down the stairs.

"Because I am."

"Please tell me that they have the grace to at least feel a bit ashamed of themselves from time to time; that they feel badly for being deadweight you have to haul around."

"Please *try* to grasp the basic idea of MacPhaull Rules, Jack," she laughingly countered. "Being ashamed of oneself or feeling guilty are unpleasant things and so aren't mentioned either directly or indirectly. It's assumed that one is, of course."

"But are they?"

"I think so. Maybe. On occasion. When they pause to reflect on their lives."

He halted them at the base of the steps to quietly ask, "What would happen if I decide not to play by MacPhaull Rules?"

"Frankly, I'd rather you not take the chance," she admitted, her heart skittering.

He made a humming sound as he led her across the foyer, but she was unsure what it signified and there wasn't time to ask. Hoping for the best, she and Jack walked into the drawing room together.

Henry, standing at window with a glass of brandy in his hand, lifted it in salute and observed dryly, "Ah, the prodigal sister arrives at last." His nose was not only mashed, it was shoved slightly to one side. There were dark splotches all down the front of his suit. Lindsay forced herself to nod in acknowledgment of his greeting.

Agatha threw the contents of a sherry glass down her throat with one quick motion and then leveraged herself out of the high-backed chair. For a second she swayed slightly and then found her balance—along with the smile she usually reserved for wealthy elderly men.

"My apologies for our tardiness," Lindsay hastily offered, her stomach leaden as she watched Agatha's gaze move slowly over Jackson. "We were delayed first by the storm and then a carriage mishap in which John was injured. We had to make repairs before we could take him to Dr. Bernard's."

"And this must be the Mr. Jackson Stennett we read about in this morning's paper," her sister said, gliding forward, her hips swaying enough that Lindsay was surprised she didn't feel a breeze. "It said that you were from the Republic of Texas."

"Yes, ma'am. We've met before, although we haven't been formally introduced."

Agatha met Lindsay's gaze and arched a brow in a familiar expression of reprimand and demand.

"Lindsay tends to forget to engage in basic social niceties," Henry offered from his vantage point on the other side of the room.

"I don't see that she's had the chance before now," Jackson instantly, coolly countered, covering her hand with his own.

"Thank you, Jack. Agatha," she began, "may I present

Mr. Jackson Stennett. Jack, my sister, Miss Agatha MacPhaull."

Agatha inclined her head and looked through her lashes in what Lindsay knew she considered to be a coquettish way. Jack softly cleared his throat and told her he'd never been so charmed.

Lindsay gestured toward Henry. "And this is my brother, Mr. Henry MacPhaull. Henry, Jack Stennett."

The two men simply nodded once in a crisp fashion and in the general direction of the other. Lindsay felt the air thicken with tension. "Where is Edith, Henry?" she asked, trying to create the distraction of conversation.

"She sends her regrets. A maid dropped a hot coal on one of the new carpets and dealing with the matter left Edith simply exhausted. She knew that you'd understand and forgive her absence."

"Of course," Lindsay replied, fully aware that Jack was struggling to contain a wry smile. This wasn't going to go well at all. She could feel it in her bones. "Shall we take ourselves to the dining room?" she suggested, anxious to move matters toward a "good night" just as quickly as she could. "I feel horrible about how long we've made Primrose and Emile delay the serving of our meal."

"Servants are to serve, Lindsay," Agatha said as she swept past. "One needn't be concerned for their feelings."

At the edge of her vision, she saw Jack's jaw turn to granite. Henry sauntered past in Agatha's wake, saying, "It had better be worth the wait."

"MacPhaull Rules," Jackson whispered as they followed, "allow people to behave badly."

There was nothing she could say in defense; Jack was right. His tolerance wasn't going to make it through dinner. She'd have be alert and quick if there was to be any hope of avoiding broken dishes and bloodshed.

"Are you having the draperies cleaned?" Agatha asked Lindsay as soon as Jack escorted her through the dining-room doorway.

"No," Lindsay replied, noting that the plaster had already been repaired. "I had them removed. Permanently."

"Mother selected those window coverings herself."

Jack pulled her seat out for her and as Lindsay settled into it, she calmly countered, "Actually, Mother hired a decorator to select them for her. There's a difference."

"All fashionable windows are draped, Lindsay."

"I prefer light to fashion."

"I would think," Henry said, assisting Agatha with her chair, "that you of all people would appreciate anything that prevented people from seeing what you're doing."

Lindsay bristled. Jack considered Henry, his eyes narrowed. "I'm not doing anything but eating in this room," Lindsay explained, forcing herself to chuckle breezily. "The only person who might catch a glimpse of that would be Proctor. And I doubt very much that he would care enough to bother to look."

"But judging people isn't your strong suit, Linds. We all know that," Henry countered, his smile obsequious. He turned it on Jackson, as Emile brought in the first course and Primrose began to serve. "No offense intended, Mr. Stennett. Of course."

"Of course," Jack said tightly, thinking that was the second backhanded slap the son of bitch had taken at Lindsay in just as many minutes. And those had come after the foulmouthed insult delivered outside the back door. Henry didn't seem to be a quick learner. How many verbal assaults, Jack wondered, was he supposed to allow in the name of superficial civility? If it weren't for the fact that Lindsay was a bundle of knots before they'd even come down the stairs, he'd have squared up to her brother again in the drawing room. Henry would have learned the lesson once and for all or he'd have found himself bouncing down the front steps on his backside.

But the night was still young, Jackson reminded himself. They were only on the soup course. Given what he'd seen so far of Henry, the odds favored the man losing a few teeth before dessert. Why in hell's name did Lindsay put up with the way these two treated her?

He glanced back and forth between Henry and Agatha. *Two peas in a pod.* They were obviously brother and sister. Lindsay no more favored them in appearance than she did in disposition. He couldn't help but think that she had to be eternally grateful for those blessings.

"So, if I might be so ill-mannered to ask, Stennett," Henry said in a tone that managed to be both stuffy and nonchalant, "just what do you have in mind for the future course of the MacPhaull Company? I understand from the newspaper article that you have yourself personally invested in agricultural commodities. Will you be diversifying our holdings in that direction?"

Lindsay froze, her spoon halfway between her bowl and her mouth. The color draining from her face, she cast a disbelieving look at Henry and then quickly did her best to pretend that her only interest was in consuming her meal.

"Well," Jack drawled, "I can't say that I've made anything but the most preliminary of decisions at this point. I'll need a little time to get the details nailed down."

"You know what they say: A prudent man is one who travels the well-worn road."

"I don't think I've ever heard that one. And just between you, me, and the fence post, MacPhaull, the road this company's been traveling is pretty well worn-out. It's time to haul the wagon out of the rut."

Henry laughed deprecatingly. "What a quaint bit of speech. Could I get you to translate it into English for me?"

Jackson couldn't recall any other human being whom he'd ever loathed as much as he did Lindsay's brother. Or any other man who so richly deserved to be dropped a dozen pegs. Jack nodded slowly, seeing his course and committing to it. "I'll try," he said lazily. "The MacPhaull Company is on the verge of bankruptcy and if drastic changes aren't made in both the business approach and structure, it will be forced to cease operations and liquidate all assets to pay its creditors." He paused just long enough to let Henry blink once before he added with a smile, "Did you have any problems understanding that?"

Emile entered the dining room with a tray of salad plates and linen-lined silver bread baskets. Primrose came in his wake. Suddenly the only sound in the room was the faint *tink* of china as Emile set his tray on the sideboard.

As Primrose collected the soup bowls, Agatha met her

brother's gaze across the table and said blithely, "Did I mention that I had lunch yesterday with Winifred Templeton?"

"How is Edward doing these days?" Henry asked, reaching for his wineglass. "I've heard the bank is struggling to keep the doors open."

Lindsay smiled her thanks as Primrose set a salad plate in front of her. Jackson nodded his. Henry and Agatha went on with their conversation as though they were the only occupants of the room.

"Winifred says the rumors are wildly inaccurate; that thanks to Edward's keen business sense, this last year has been more profitable than any previous year in the bank's history. Little Edgar is first in his class at school. And little Myrtle is the best harp student Mrs. Glasgow has ever had. Winifred invited me to join her table at the boat races this coming weekend."

"Well, I hope you told her that you intended to wear my colors despite your seating."

"Of course. She said she understood, appreciated my sense of loyalty, and sent you her best wishes for a safe and speedy race."

"How very and typically kind of her. I've always liked Winifred. Edward got quite a prize when he married her."

Both paused to pick up their forks and Jackson seized the conversational opening. "I recall seeing a boat listed in the company assets. Is that the one you're speaking of?"

"Not a boat; a *yacht*," Henry corrected. "A three-masted racer built to my exact specifications just last year in a Providence shipyard. She's magnificent. Are you a sailing man, Stennett?"

Lindsay silently seethed. Her brother knew Jack was a cattleman and not a sailor. He was deliberately trying to make Jack look like a country bumpkin. It was mean and low and so typically, thoroughly Henry.

"Naw," Jack said, his drawl the same slow and exaggerated one he'd affected in Mr. Gregory's office. "The first time I ever boarded a ship bigger than a riverboat was to come here. Can't say that I overly enjoyed the trip. If given my druthers, I'd much rather saddle up and ride."

"How . . . provincial."

Which was precisely what Jackson wanted him to think, she realized. Henry—while flaunting his usual sense of superiority—was being suckered into badly underestimating Jack's intelligence and breadth of business experience. She didn't have a doubt as to how the contest between the two of them would end. While Henry certainly deserved to be shown as the pompous fool he was, he was going to be exceedingly embarrassed when it became obvious that the table had been so brilliantly turned on him. As for Jack . . . How much satisfaction could there be in winning a battle of wits against an unarmed man? She hoped he realized that before matters got out of hand, and that once he did, he'd elect to show Henry a bit of mercy.

"The captain of the ship was a nice enough fellow," Jack went on. "And a reasonably good card player. He told me that any boat was nothing more than a hole in the water that you poured money into."

"Obviously he doesn't have a taste for the finer things in life or an appreciation for the expectations of social position."

"Maybe. But he did know about making money with his vessel. Do you use yours in any commercial way?"

"Purely pleasure, Stennett." Henry laughed and waved his hand dismissively. "Oh, there's the occasional wager on the outcome of a race, but it's really nothing of significance."

"Thankfully, since you so seldom win," Agatha teased.

"But," Henry countered, "you must admit that the races have been getting closer. I've wagered five hundred dollars on myself to win the round this weekend."

Agatha suddenly straightened in her chair, her eyes bright. "Is it too late for me to place my own wager? I hear Jacob Miller's fitting his yacht for a race out of Boston and won't enter this one. I have two hundred dollars I'd be willing to risk on you under the circumstances."

"And if Jacob Miller were sailing against me?"

"Why," Agatha said sweetly, batting her lashes, "I'd put my wager on him, of course. We both know he's the better sailor."

Emile entered the dining room again, this time bearing a large tray on which four large silver-dome-covered plates had been placed. Again, he set the tray on the sideboard as Primrose silently set about collecting the plates from the previous course.

"How much does a boat like yours sell for?" Jack asked, shattering the silence.

Henry started, cast a meaningful glance at the servants, and then found a condescending smile. "My dear Stennett. We have a saying in this part of the world: If you have to ask how much it costs, you can't afford it."

"Oh, I wasn't thinking of buying one," Jack corrected, his drawl lightening with every word. "I was thinking of selling one. Yours." He smiled at Primrose as she set a plate in front of him. "I was wondering how much I could get for it. What would be your best guess?"

"Oh, how you tease, Mr. Stennett," Agatha exclaimed, laughing. "I've heard that Texans like their tall tales and their wild pranks. Why don't you come to the club with us this weekend? I'd simply *adore* showing you off to everyone."

"Well, I've never been one to enjoy being paraded around on a fancy leash, so I think I'll pass on the invitation. Thanks just the same, though. And I hope you enjoy the race. It's likely to be the last in which there's a MacPhaull entry."

Henry's brows came together in consternation. "You're serious."

Jack smiled lazily and reached for his wineglass. "What gave me away?"

Lindsay inwardly groaned. It was the beginning of the end. She'd been right; Jack hadn't made it through dinner before abandoning the pretenses that kept life marginally sane in MacPhaull House. Primrose set a plate of food in front of her and Lindsay desperately seized the opportunity to put things back on course. "This looks delicious. Game hens cooked to perfection. Are these apricots I see in the wild rice stuffing?"

"Yes, madame," Emile said softly from his station at the sideboard. "Bon appétit."

"Emile is Richard's chef," she explained in an effort to fill the silence, as Primrose finished serving the others. "I think, Henry, that you'll find the food well worth whatever wait you've had to endure."

The door was still swinging behind Emile and Primrose when Henry snapped, "Are you planning to sell anything other than my yacht? Or is this the typically heavy-handed manner in which all Texans deal with perceived slurs?"

Lindsay gasped as Jackson's brows went up and his chin went down. In the next half second, his feet shifted and his hands went to the arms of his chair. Henry was about to die. "I've decided to sell MacPhaull House," she blurted.

"What?" her sister screeched. "You can't do that! You can't sell the roof from over my head!"

Bless the predictability of Agatha's histrionics. "Yes, I can," Lindsay blithely assured her, relieved to see that Jackson's attention had shifted. His eyes were slightly narrowed and one corner of his mouth was quirked in a telltale smile. It didn't matter that he knew she'd deliberately incited Agatha. "I'm the manager of the properties," Lindsay went on, "and I can do with them as I think best."

"This was our mother's house!"

"And our mother is gone," Lindsay said with all the gentle calm she could muster. "I've found a lovely house north of the city and Jackson's agreed to buy it for me. You're welcome to move there with me; it's sufficiently large for—"

"Jackson's agreed to buy it for you?" Agatha repeated, her gaze darting between them.

Lindsay saw the suspicion grow in her sister's eyes. Ignoring it, she went on, "It came about as a consequence of arranging the auction of other properties and—"

"What other properties?" Henry demanded. "Are you selling me and my family out onto the street?"

Jackson smiled. "It could be arranged."

"No, Henry," Lindsay quickly assured him. "Your home is not being sold. As I was saying, Agatha, the new house is large enough for the both of us. However, if you don't want to move with me, I'm sure we can—"

"I'm purchasing land on Long Island," Agatha declared,

leaning away so that she was beyond Lindsay's reach. "I'll build myself a house there."

"No, you're not," Jackson said, while using a knife and fork to pull his game hen apart. "And no, you won't."

"Who are you to tell me what I can and cannot do?" Agatha demanded imperiously.

"I'm the owner of the MacPhaull Company. I thought you said you'd read the paper."

"Indeed we have," Henry declared, settling into his chair and looking smug. "And since you and our sister made yourselves so deliberately unavailable today, we took it upon ourselves to visit the law office of Mr. Otis Vanderhagen in an effort to clarify our understanding of the circumstances."

Jackson took a bite of his dinner, chewed, and swallowed. "It's very good, Lindsay." He shifted his attention to Henry. "And did ol' Otis tell you that you're up the creek without a paddle?"

"Mr. Vanderhagen pointed out the legal ramifications and suggested several courses of possible action. I'm a reasonable man, Stennett. I'm willing to compromise for the sake of family harmony.

"Now," he continued with a deep breath and a smile that suggested he was feeling in control of the situation, "I am of the philosophy that owning something doesn't necessarily require one to actually do something with it in direct manner. Richard Patterson was my father's manager and I've long been prepared to take over his responsibilities. Might I suggest that you would be infinitely happier in returning to your quiet little corner of Texas and allowing me to send you a payment once a year?"

Oh God, Lindsay silently groaned. "It's four times a year, Henry," she corrected quietly. "Disbursements of owner equity are made quarterly."

"A minor detail," he declared with a wave of his hand. "One has bookkeepers to handle such petty affairs. So what do you think, Stennett? Does it sound as reasonable to you as it does to me?"

Lindsay took a bite of her food. Henry had absolutely no idea of the kind of man with whom he was trying to strike a deal. Jackson was the last man on earth who would even consider being fobbed off with such an offer. Henry would be the first to accept it. And therein lay the central difference in the two.

"I own the company and I'm going to put it to rights," Jackson said with certainty. "Once I do, I'll walk away and what's left will be yours free and clear."

"What's left?" Agatha repeated, her voice tight and her eyes wide.

"Your daddy willed me the MacPhaull Company assets intending that I use them to clear the title on the land he left me in Texas. I'm selling off just enough of the properties to get the money I need to do that and then I'm going to divide what's left between the three of you and you can do whatever you damn well please with it."

"Equally?" Henry asked, blinking furiously. "You're going to divide the properties equally between the three of us?"

"That's my initial thinking. It's subject to change, though."

"The MacPhaull Company is mine," he snarled, slamming his fist on the table. "I'm the rightful male heir and I'll be damned if I settle for a third of what's been promised to me all my life. I can tie up your claim to the property by challenging the Will, Stennett. You won't be able to so much as sell the garden vegetables from a cart on the corner!"

"Then by all means," Jackson drawled, "trot yourself down to the courthouse and file the papers. But you need to know that if you hire an attorney for all this, you're not submitting the bill to me or Lindsay for payment. It comes out of your own pocket."

Henry sagged back in his chair. The idea was clearly one that hadn't occurred to him. It was so very typical of the way Henry went at life. He brought himself so much grief and aggravation that Lindsay couldn't help but feel sorry for him.

In the lull of his shock, she said gently, "Henry, you can challenge the Will if you like, but you should know that the effort is absolutely futile. Richard may have suffered a stroke, but he's still alive. And according to the stipulations of Father's first Will, as long as Richard breathes, you don't have any say in how the company is managed or any control over the assets.

"There were no such restrictions made in his second Will. Jackson owned the MacPhaull Company the very second our father died. And Jackson has elected to leave the management structure intact and functioning as usual for the immediate future. This—"

"Do you have a point?" Henry snapped, pouring himself more wine with a shaking hand. "Or are you trying to bore me into a stupor?"

Ire shot through her. Lindsay clenched her teeth as she struggled to tamp it down. Simple words for simple minds, she reminded herself. "You can't contest Jackson's control until Richard dies. By the time you do have the right to file with the courts, the reorganization of the company will be done. It will be too late, Henry."

"I'll have Richard declared legally incompetent."

"It won't make any difference," she countered crisply. "Papers were filed years ago giving me the power to act as Richard's proxy on matters relating to company business. In a legal sense, my signature isn't mine, it's Richard's."

"Let me see if I'm understanding this correctly," her brother said hotly. "You're willing to assist this man in depriving me of my birthright?"

Suddenly she was so tired of dealing with the impossible expectations of her life; so very, very tired of carefully choosing her words and trying to cushion everyone's feelings. Let the pieces fall where they would; she didn't have the strength to care anymore. "Jackson isn't exaggerating. The MacPhaull Company is almost bankrupt. Properties have to be sold or we'll lose everything. It's a calculated liquidation and it's absolutely necessary. And I'm sorry, Henry, but you don't have the business sense of a gnat. If I let you have control of the company in its present condition, we'd all be living on the street within a few short months."

"And what," he brother asked, his words dripping poisoned honey, "are you getting in exchange for being the MacPhaull Judas?"

"A house!" Agatha shrilled. "She's getting her own house. She doesn't care what happens to us!"

Lindsay sagged in her chair, mentally and emotionally near exhaustion.

"I've had about all of this that I'm going to take," Jack declared, laying his napkin on the table beside his plate and preparing to rise.

Lindsay roused herself, knowing that only she could avert a truly ugly escalation of the tensions in the room. "Jack, please," she softly pleaded. "Let me deal with this in my own way."

"You've got two seconds, Lindsay, and then I'm pitching them both out the front door."

"That won't be necessary," Henry announced, throwing his napkin into the center of the table and surging to his feet. "We're leaving. Come, Agatha."

Numbly, Lindsay watched chaos erupt around her. Jack vaulted to his feet, his jaw hard and his eyes flinty. Agatha jumped up from her chair, the buttons on her dress catching the edge of her dinner plate, flipping it over and scattering food over the pristine linen tablecloth.

"My things!" Agatha howled, her hands pressed to her cheeks. "I have to get my things or she'll sell them to beggars!"

"Beggars don't have any money," Jack quipped sardonically as Agatha ran for the door.

Lindsay called after her, "Agatha, I'm not going to—"

"I'm impressed, Lindsay," Henry interrupted, his tone sickly, deadly sweet. "I truly am. You've finally come into your own; finally managed to employ Mother's instruction. It's a damn shame, though, that you didn't do it sooner. Of course, Charles Martens was of the Terwilliger-Hampsteads, a family of impeccable breeding and incredible wealth. He was *considerably* out of your league."

Her stomach knotted and dropped to her feet as ugly certainty settled into her.

"Lindsay," Jack said softly, reaching for her.

She stepped away from the comfort of his touch, knowing that to accept it would be playing into her brother's intent. "Get out, Henry," she demanded, her hands fisted at her side, her heart racing with fear and rage.

He smirked and sauntered to the door. "Just out of

curiosity, Linds," he said wryly, turning back. "I know Mother was very clear about the parameters and mechanics of trading your virtue. Despite that, the whole town knows you didn't come even remotely close to meeting Martens' expectations. He was quite candid about it all, you know. Why do you think it worked this time and not the last? Does Stennett have lower standards or have you gotten better in bed?"

The verbal slap and the flood of humiliation that came with it were familiar. Lindsay closed her eyes, enduring, unwilling to see Jack's reaction to the revelation of her darkest truth.

There was a snarl, deep and hard and utterly feral. Lindsay gasped and instinctirely stepped back, opening her eyes and desperately searching for the threat. Her heart skittered and a cry strangled low in her throat. Henry's eyes were bulging from their sockets, his body pinned high against the doorjamb by Jackson's massive shoulder.

"Don't kill him!" she heard herself cry, watching in horror as Henry's face turned red and his nose began to bleed.

Jack stepped back, grabbed her brother by the lapels of his jacket, spun around, and flung him into the foyer. Henry landed in an uncontrolled heap of expensive suit and slid toward the front door. A brilliant thrill of satisfaction rippled through Lindsay at the sight.

Through the tears welling in her eyes, Lindsay saw Jack stride forward, yank open the door, turn, and lift Henry by the lapels of his jacket again. She cried out again, but the plea didn't so much as give Jackson pause. With a snarl, he tossed Henry out onto the front steps.

He turned back and, even through her tears, Lindsay could see the fiery light in his eyes, the deep, quick rise and fall of his chest. "Are you all right?" he asked through clenched teeth.

No, she wasn't. Her heart was racing too fast; it was going to explode. And deep down inside her were coiling the unmistakable, shameless tendrils of desire. Heat fanned through her body and she gasped at the surging impulse to throw herself into his arms. Shaking her head, she backed up, struggling to breathe, struggling to gain control of herself. Jack's brows knit and the fire went out of his eyes. In its place came a soft light of understanding, a shadow of pity.

"Lindsay," he whispered, reaching out his hand.

She retreated another step, her mind reeling amidst a raging torrent of thought and emotion. The heel of her shoe struck the bottom stair, and through the swirl of her confusion she saw a chance to escape. Snatching her skirts into her hands, she whirled about and fled up the stairs.

She met a hysterically screaming Agatha along the way. Her sister's arms were loaded with gowns and spilling jewelry boxes. Lindsay twisted out of her path and kept going, dashing up the stairs and through the path of glittering baubles left in Agatha's wake.

"Yes, Agatha!" Jackson called from the foyer below. "Hurry! Run! The beggars are coming!"

Lindsay heard and felt the front door being shut just as she reached the haven of her bedroom. She slammed her own door closed and quickly turned the key in the lock. She stood staring blindly at the door, the wild chatter of her thoughts still pounding her senses.

She should be doing something, she thought vaguely. She should be analyzing what had happened and trying to see her course. Jack might come upstairs after her and he'd expect—

Jack. What Jack must think of me now. A proper whore.

Tears filled her eyes and spilled over her cheeks. Her strength drained out the soles of her feet. Her knees trembled and she closed her eyes, unable to care about saving herself. Out on the street, a carriage rolled away.

CHAPTER SIXTEEN

JACKSON STOOD in the center of the foyer, staring at the marble floor and shaking his head in disbelief. He didn't even know where to begin to sort out all that had happened. It just boggled the mind. And people said that Texas was a land of uncivilized manners. Jack snorted. In all the saloons and hellholes of Texas, he'd never seen any man who had sunk to the human depths that had been plumbed and mapped by Henry MacPhaull. The things he'd said to Lindsay, of Lindsay . . . Jack clenched and unclenched his fists and regretted to the bottom of his soul not having made the son of a bitch eat teeth.

And Agatha . . . Sweet Jesus. Her boat might be in the water, but both oars had slipped the locks. He couldn't recall having ever met a person—man or woman—who moved from blatantly seductive to vacuous to conniving and into outright hysterical insanity with the speed and smoothness that Lindsay's sister had. Agatha needed a keeper with a strong arm and a stout leash. He could only assume that she'd hauled her armload of valuables to Henry's house.

Which meant that he could almost feel sorry for Henry. Almost. Maybe he should pity Edith. Jack smiled wryly. Edith was the wife exhausted by a maid burning a hole in the rug. Having to get through one of Lindsay's days would kill the woman. Henry's pomposity and condescension under the same roof as Agatha's craziness and Edith's frailty. . . Thank God it wasn't this roof. The upheaval of the Rutherfords, Mrs. Kowalski, her cat, and a kitchen war paled in comparison. Even if you added in a blind gardener, a one-armed housekeeper, and a busted-up coachman, Lindsay's world was still infinitely saner and more predictable than the one swirling around the other MacPhaulls. No wonder she felt as though she had to take care of Henry and Agatha; they were idiots.

But, he silently reminded himself, at some point one had to step back and let others not only make mistakes, but suffer the consequences of them. It was how people learned *not* to be idiots. He'd be willing to bet that Henry would at least hesitate and look over his shoulder the next time it crossed his mind to insult Lindsay. It would have taken only one beating with most men; but then, Henry clearly wasn't like most men.

"If I had two hands, Mr. Stennett, I would applaud."

Mrs. Beechum. Jack turned to the dining-room doorway and found her standing there, smiling at him, her empty sleeve, as always, tucked neatly into the waistband of her shirtdress. Emile and Primrose stood at the door on the far side of the dining room, looking at the table morosely.

"I suppose you heard it all," he ventured.

"Oh, indeed. Henry getting his comeuppance was definitely the high point of the evening. But we," she said, gesturing to the cooks behind her, "thought you telling Miss Agatha that the beggars were coming was particularly entertaining."

"She brings out the worst in me. My mother raised me better."

"Miss Agatha brings out the worst in everyone, sir. So does Henry. I wouldn't let it bother you another moment. May Emile and Primrose clear the table and finish in the kitchen?"

"Certainly," he said, thinking that as long as his day had been, the servants' was going to be even longer. "Miss Primrose, Emile?" They both turned to face him. "The food was excellent and I appreciate the work it took to keep it until we got here. I'm truly sorry that the circumstances didn't allow us to properly enjoy it."

Primrose smiled shyly, Emile bowed slightly at the waist, and then they both stood there looking him. The rules for servant conduct bubbled from the recesses of his memory; they wouldn't move until he formally gave them permission to or he walked away. "Don't worry about cleaning the kitchen too thoroughly," he said, turning to leave the doorway. "Your day's been long enough."

He stopped in the center of the foyer and looked up the stairs, vaguely aware of the clink of china behind him and that Mrs. Beechum moved past him and then bent to pick up one of the baubles Agatha had dropped. He needed to go up and see Lindsay. Just exactly what he was going to say when he got there, he didn't know. He wasn't about to apologize for throwing her brother out the front door on his ass. And while he might be able to utter some regrets for goading Agatha there at the end, his heart wouldn't really be in it. The only things he saw that they had to talk about were, first, why she allowed her siblings to treat her so badly, and second, why she'd been so upset at having justice finally exacted on her behalf.

He could pretty well guess what she'd say; they couldn't help being the way they were and she had to make allowances for their behavior because they were her brother and sister. Nothing he could say in rebuttal would make a bit of difference in how she saw the whole thing. As for the reason she was upset . . . He could guess on that one, too. She thought that he'd gone too far, that he'd overreacted and beaten a defenseless man. He could explain until he turned blue, but it wasn't likely that she'd ever accept the fact that, in the world of men, Henry's mouth was considered a weapon.

Jackson sighed quietly and shook his head.

"Is there a problem, Mr. Stennett?"

He'd forgotten that Mrs. Beechum was there. "You

know Lindsay better than anyone else," he said quietly. "Why does she take such abuse from her brother and sister?"

"It's a very complicated situation," the housekeeper answered, bending to retrieve a glittering ring.

"I'm willing to wade through a lot."

Mrs. Beechum stepped to the central table, dropped the ring onto the silver calling-card tray, and then faced him squarely. "Lydia MacPhaull made no secret as to how she felt about her children," she began, her words so quick and precise that Jackson knew that she'd given the matter a great deal of thought over the years. "As you've no doubt surmised, Henry and Agatha were doted upon. Lindsay, however, was an unwanted and deeply resented child, Mr. Stennett. Despite her every effort, she has never fit in the MacPhaull family. She's spent her entire life wanting only to be wanted. Suffering insults and indignities is a small price to pay for being important to those around her."

"She's not important to them beyond the fact that she controls the MacPhaull money."

"I agree. But you must understand that for Lindsay, being used is better than being all alone in the world."

"She's not alone," he protested. "She has you. And besides, she's a wonderfully intelligent and charming woman. If she went out into the world, she wouldn't be alone for any more than ten minutes."

"We know that, but Lindsay doesn't. The only value that she's ever been granted is that derived from what she can give to—or do for—those around her."

"Even Richard Patterson?" he posed.

"Even Richard," Mrs. Beechum countered firmly.

Jackson stared at the far wall. He was no better than anyone else in Lindsay's life. She was important to him, yes, but only because she knew the workings of the MacPhaull Company and he needed her assistance to get out of it the cash he had to have. He was using her just like all the others. And when he didn't need her anymore, he was going to walk away. In doing so, he'd be adding to all the experiences that made Lindsay believe about herself as she did.

"Mr. Stennett?" He met the housekeeper's gaze and she

went on, saying, "As Lindsay's friend, I want you to know that she had no real choice in accepting the attentions of Charles Martens. Lydia schemed and Lindsay was the reluctant, unhappy pawn. There were no other men before him and there have been none since."

Charles Martens. God, he hadn't even given that bit of the mess so much as a passing thought. Jackson gave the older woman a quirked smile. "Would you believe me if I told you that what happened with Charles Martens doesn't matter to me?"

"Yes, I would, Mr. Stennett," she assured him quietly. "However, you should know that it matters a great deal to Lindsay."

Jackson grimaced and then looked up the stairs. Was that the reason she'd been so upset? Sweet Jesus and all the saints, he silently swore as he started up, taking the steps two at a time. If it was, he should have been up these stairs right on her heels. God, he was going to have to gush apologies right and left for being so incredibly thickheaded and then somehow make her understand that he didn't give a winged-rat's ass about Charles Martens.

"I'll finish picking up the litter on the stairs," Mrs. Beechum called after him. She chuckled and added, "We'll be able to run the house for months on what Miss Agatha left behind."

"Send every last piece of it to her," he instructed without pausing. "Put in a note saying the beggars thought it was all too garish for their tastes."

"With pleasure, Mr. Stennett!"

Jackson strode down the hallway, stopped at Lindsay's door, and quickly knocked. He heard movement from inside, but it didn't sound as though it was heading toward the door. He knocked again and this time there was only silence. Taking a deep breath and willing his heartbeat to slow, he said with all the gentleness he could summon, "Lindsay, please come out and talk to me."

"Leave me alone, Jack," she called from the other side. "I've had enough for one night."

From the sound of her voice, she was on the far side of the room, near the windows. He stood there, his eyes narrowed as he considered the door and his options. Letting Lindsay wallow and brood wasn't one of them. He turned on his heel, went to his room, strode across it, pulled back the tapestry and opened the door connecting their rooms.

"All right," he declared, invading Lindsay's sanctuary, "I'll grant you that it's been a helluva long day on top of a couple others just like it, but—"

"I'm going to lock that door as soon as I find the key," she declared, coming out of the window seat, her dress hem fluttering about her ankles, and her eyes blazing.

"That's probably a really good idea," he countered, standing his ground. "But since it's open now and I'm through it already, we might as well talk."

She whirled around, presenting him with a view of her back. Her arms hugging her midriff, she lifted her chin and said regally, "I suppose you want to know all the sordid details. Not that all that many have been left for the telling."

He hadn't heard that tone in her voice since the first day they met, and he realized that it was the manner she fell into when she felt threatened and uncertain. Jack took another deep breath and then moved to the bench in front of her dressing table. "Sordid?" he said softly, sitting down. "In whose eyes, Lindsay?"

"The world's," she stated, her manner unaffected by the change in his approach. "Do you want me to expand on what Henry already supplied or would you prefer to move directly on to the general analysis?"

"I figure the past is the past," he said gently, "and you're entitled to keep it there, if that's the way you want it. It doesn't make any difference to me."

She chuckled wryly, the sound of threatening tears bubbling along the edge of it. "Scandal is never relegated to the past in New York society, Jack," she said with more fervor than he expected. "Remember the smile on Winifred's face when she accosted us on the walkway? She's smiled at me like that ever since I had the sorry misjudgment to get entangled with the not-so-honorable Charles Martins."

He held to his course. "Lindsay, you don't have—"

"Yes, I do," she snapped, turning to face him. "You have a right to know what people are thinking every time they see us together in public. Your reputation is being tarnished by association."

"They're assuming that we're lovers," he supplied, thinking that these New Yorkers were people willing to take some mighty big leaps. Not that he particularly cared where they landed, beyond the fact that it obviously troubled Lindsay. Texas might not be paradise, but at least people there weren't quick to assume, judge, and condemn.

"Of course they think we're lovers," Lindsay said, her shoulders sagging and the imperial edge easing out of her voice. "I've proven in the past that I have no moral virtue. To assume that I've found some in the intervening years wouldn't be the least bit probable." She sighed and shook her head. "It's amazing how men presume that their advances will be welcomed. And I get very tired of the whispering behind my back. Keeping myself isolated offers distinct comforts."

"So that's why you turned down Winifred's invitation to the gathering at the boathouse," he said, remembering and understanding in a wholly new light. "Do you ever go out socially?"

"No."

"But that pretty much guarantees that you're going to spend your life alone."

"I don't mind being alone," she assured him. "And maintaining celibacy isn't something with which I struggle, Jack. For the life of me, I can't see what there is to recommend the marriage bed."

He hadn't expected her to address the issue so candidly, but since she'd opened the door, he figured he might as well walk boldly through it. "Then ol' Charles Martins, aside from being a first class bounder, was a lousy lover, wasn't he?"

"I wouldn't know," she said, adopting her regal manner again. "I don't have anyone to measure him against."

Slow and steady, Jack. "You and I have taken a couple of steps down the road, Lindsay. How do I compare?"

She turned her back on him again. "This is a most unseemly conversation. I'm not the least bit comfortable with it, and if you were a true gentleman, you'd drop it."

Breathless. His question had triggered memories of

their being together and they'd taken her breath away. Jack smiled and, preparing for the long haul, leaned forward to rest his elbows on his knees.

"Well, I figure dinner pretty much established the fact that I'm not much of a gentleman," he said, watching her intently as he deliberately defied her ultimatum. "As for you being uncomfortable with it, Lindsay . . . In the first place, you're the one who insisted on laying the cards on the table. And in the second place, it's not that the matter's too delicate for your sense of propriety, it's just that dealing with it requires you to admit that your emotions can't be neatly lined up in columns of black and white."

Lindsay stood motionless and silent for a half-dozen long heartbeats. Then her shoulders slumped and, with a sigh, she reached back to massage her neck. Jack wanted to go to her, wanted to gently take the task of easing her tensions into his own hands. Tamping down the reckless impulse, he asked, "So how do I compare to Charles Martens?"

"You don't."

"In a good way or in a bad way?" he pressed.

"In a good way," she admitted. She went to the window seat and sat, her hands clasped tightly in her lap, her lips pursed and a faraway look in her eyes.

Jackson waited, willing to sit there with her for as long as it took for her to sort through it all, willing to accept whatever she could find to give him.

Lindsay watched the memories play across her mind's eye, heard again all the words that had been spoken. It was all so very familiar; she'd relived the debacle a thousand times before. But this time remembering was different in one significant way; she didn't feel anything. No twisting sense of shame. No stab of regret. No wave of stinging humiliation. Nothing. It was almost as though she had opened a trunk of memories that belonged to someone else.

Would the dispassion go into the telling as well? she wondered. She'd never had the courage to speak to anyone about what had happened and how she'd felt about it. Did she have the courage to now?

Lindsay looked up to find Jack watching her, his eyes

dark and somber and infinitely patient. She knew in that instant that if there was ever a person who would listen and not judge, it was Jackson Stennett. And to think that she'd told Abigail that he was the spawn of Satan. She'd been wrong. Whatever else Jack was to her, he was also the best, most genuine friend she'd ever had. She could tell Jack anything.

"At the time, I thought I loved him," she began. "In hindsight, I realize that I didn't."

Jack nodded and gave her a smile that clearly said he'd already guessed that much on his own. Buoyed by his ease and acceptance, Lindsay started again, not truly planning what she was going to say, but trusting it to come out as it should.

"As Henry so gallantly mentioned, there were business considerations involved. My mother's only interest in Charles as a suitor lay in his family's wealth and prestige. She believed that no sacrifice was too great in the campaign to unite the MacPhaull fortune with that of the Terwilliger-Hampsteads. But as much as I'd like to lay the blame for it all at her feet, I can't. She pushed, Jack, but I didn't dig my heels in and refuse to do as I'd been told."

"Why?"

"Such a simple question. The answer is anything but." She caught her lower lip between her teeth as she contemplated how to go about the explanation. Deciding that there wasn't any particular right or wrong way, she shrugged and said, "You see, Charles lavished me with attention and gifts and it was so wonderful to feel special to someone, to think that he was going to take me away from this house, away from all the frustrations and ugliness.

"I let him seduce me, believing the promises, seeing only the rainbow I thought I was going to get, and thinking that I was gloriously in love and equally loved in return. And I was so naive and trusting."

Lindsay smiled ruefully, wondering how she could have ever been so gullible. With a shrug, she went on, saying, "When he proposed to another, I thought I'd die of grief. Only it wasn't grief at all, Jack. It was nothing but wounded pride and humiliation. I'd been a complete fool and everyone in town knew it."

"That's the thing about our first times, sweetheart," he said gently, quietly, staring at the floor in front of him and remembering. "At that age, I think we're not so much in love with the person as we're in love with the notion of being in love. Everyone's made the mistake, including me. Falling out of it hurts like hell." He smiled ruefully and added, "Makes you real cautious about ever trusting that much again."

"But you did, didn't you?" she countered softly.

He started and looked up, his heart racing, to meet her gaze.

"I'm just guessing, Jack, but I think you were married once; that your wife and child died. I think it was very difficult for you to go see Jeb and Lucy that morning and that you struggled to hide the pain of your memories the entire time we were there."

"Apparently I wasn't too good at it," he observed with a tight smile.

"Why did you offer to go with me, Jack? Why did you put yourself through that ordeal?"

"Babies are a part of life," he answered, then paused to swallow down the lump in his throat. "Avoiding them makes people wonder and ask questions. It's easier just to ride it out in silence than it is to try to explain what happened."

"I understand, Jack, and I sincerely apologize for having broached the subject and opened the door to memories that hurt you. I wasn't thinking clearly or I wouldn't have. I knew that day that you were troubled by them."

Telling himself that if Lindsay could dig deep to be honest with him, he couldn't do anything less for her. "Her name was Maria Arabella. I was eighteen. She was seventeen, and a miscalculation on a grand scale," he said, staring blankly at the floor, remembering and regretting. "Like you, she was a lady and I should have had the good sense to keep my distance. But, as you know," he added wryly, "I don't do all that well with resisting impulses."

He exhaled hard and then took another deep breath to begin again. "She was beautiful and educated and when she danced . . . I wasn't the only man who wanted her and there were a lot of others who had better pedigrees and prospects than I did. But I was determined to have her any way I could get her and so I seduced her, hoping that would force her into choosing me over all the others.

"There's no way around the fact that it was a low thing to do. In looking back with older eyes, I can see that it was unforgivable. But at the time . . . When she told me she was carrying my child, I was over the moon. I braved her father's wrath, ignored Billy's misgivings, and happily waltzed her right up the aisle of the church."

He chewed the inside of his mouth for a minute and then made a *tsk*ing sound. "I was still shaking the rice out of my hair when I discovered that wanting and having are two different things, Lindsay. We were so different. In the rush of seduction, that didn't matter and neither of us cared. It did matter, though, in the days and months that followed. We were strangers living under the same roof, sharing the same bed. We were just starting to close the distance when . . ." He swallowed the knot in his throat. "When she died giving birth to our son."

He stared off, his attention clearly focused on the past, the shadows of pain evident in his eyes. Her heart aching for him, Lindsay tried to bring him back to her, calling softly, "Jack?"

"The was nothing the doc could do to save either of them," he went on sadly. "Matthew was born too early, too small. Maria knew before she went that he wasn't going to make it. She asked me to wait to bury her until Matthew could be placed in her arms in the same casket. She said he was too little to go alone, that he'd be frightened without her."

Dear God, how had he endured that loss? How had he gone on living? Tears tightened her throat and then welled in her eyes. She struggled to keep them from spilling over her lashes, part of her sensing that he needed her to be strong and composed so he could share the burden, part of her struggling against the impulse to cross the room and gather him into her arms, to offer him whatever comfort he needed or wanted from her.

"I realized," he said, "as I sat there on the bed beside her, that I had grown to love her and that it was too late. I couldn't bear to ask her if she'd grown to love me, too. I was too afraid to hear that she didn't. In hindsight, I wish I'd found the courage. I'll wonder about that the rest of my life."

"Oh, Jack," she whispered. "I'm so sorry. So very sorry."

He nodded and then looked up from the carpet to meet her gaze. She watched his eyes and saw him close away the painful memories.

"I'll let you have that one without paying the penalty," he said with a wan smile.

"As punishments go," she countered, sniffling and managing a smile in return, "I can think of far worse than your kisses, Jack. I think you misjudged the effect they'd have."

"I've misjudged a lot of things in my time, Lindsay," he countered, sobering and sitting up straight. "But the past is over and done and all I can do is keep from making the same mistakes again. I don't want you added to the list of my regrets. You need to know how I'm thinking and feeling about the two of us and you need to hear it in plain, blunt terms so that there isn't the slightest chance of a misunderstanding. I'm going to shoot straight from the hip with you, Lindsay, whether it bruises your sensibilities or not."

"You think I have tender sensibilities?" she asked, chuckling quietly. "After a lifetime of enduring Henry and Agatha?"

"The way I see it," he said, determined to avoid being sidetracked, "there's pure physical desire, being in love with love, and then real love. One doesn't necessarily lead to another."

He paused, considering the truth and knowing it for that. "Being in love with love is for the young and the hopeful. Ten years ago I managed to survive it. I'm too damn old and battered to tumble into it anymore. And giving someone a piece of my heart isn't something I ever intend to do again. Putting it six feet under hurts too badly. What's left for me is physical desire. Nothing more, nothing less.

"I won't lie to you, Lindsay. I've never been a monk. There were women before Maria Arabella and there have been women since she died. I treated them all well and kindly, but being with them was physical and nothing more.

It's not ever going to lead anywhere beyond that. I won't let it. I hope you can understand that and why it has to be that way. It doesn't have anything to do with you."

"I understand completely," she answered. "And I appreciate your honesty. Truth be told, Jack," she added, "I'd have serious questions about your sanity if you *were* willing to risk your heart. It seems to me that only a fool would ask to be hurt like that again."

He nodded and pursed his lips as he stared unseeingly at the far wall.

"Jack?" she asked softly, tentatively. "*Do* you desire me?"

His smile returned, and when he looked at her his eyes sparkled. "To be real honest, sweetheart, I haven't wanted a woman as badly since I can't remember when. I get around you and my blood heats, my heart races, and my good intentions get trampled in the dust."

"You do the same to mine," she admitted, greatly relieved. "And when you touch me, you take my breath away and make my knees go weak. I never felt any of that with Charles. It makes me wonder about what else I might have missed with him."

Jack smiled, thinking that if she didn't mind being celibate, then she'd missed a helluva lot. "You know what they say about curiosity and the cat," he reminded her with a wink. "You might want to keep that in mind."

"I have no good reputation to protect, Jack," she confidently rejoined, obviously undaunted by the warning. "And I have no prospects for marriage. It seems to me that curiosity is all that I *do* have and that there isn't a price for it that I haven't already paid."

Damn. He hadn't thought about that. He suspected there were a lot of facets to his relationship with Lindsay that he hadn't given the consideration they deserved. "I'm hearing this tiny voice in the back of my head; common sense, I think." He rose to his feet, adding, "It's saying that I ought to get out of here and give it all some serious thought before we set fire to any bridges."

"Then I'll wish you a good night, Jack," she said, rising from the window seat. "Thank you for barging in here and making me think things through. I appreciate it very much. You can't know how much I wish that I'd known you five years ago."

If he'd been around then, Charles Martens wouldn't have gotten within a mile of her. "Just so you know," he said, his hand on the doorknob, "I kissed you before I ever heard the name Charles Martens. And if I kiss you again, it won't be because I think you might give me what you gave him. I'll kiss you because I like the way you taste; because I like the feel of you in my arms, and I like the way you kiss me back. And if I end up losing the battle with good judgment and seducing you, then you damn well better leave Charles Martens outside the bedroom. Do you understand?"

"Yes," she answered, not hesitating for so much as a blink. "And you need to understand that if I decide to go to your bed, it's not because I'm motivated by business interests or because I have illusions of there being a forever for us. It will be because I want my curiosity satisfied. I don't expect anything of you beyond that. It'll be that simple."

Jackson chuckled. "Sweetheart, nothing about you is simple. Good night. Sweet dreams."

The door closed soundlessly behind him and Lindsay sank back down onto the window seat, her legs too shaky to hold her upright. *She* was complicated? Not compared to Jackson Stennett. He was far more vulnerable than she could have ever imagined, far more emotionally battered that anyone could have guessed. Her mother would have called it a weakness and demanded that it be exploited for the benefit of the MacPhaull Company. Richard would have been less strident in his exhortation, but his words would have been an echo of her mother's just the same.

Use him before he has a chance to use you. All's fair in love and business. And there's no such thing as love in business.

Lindsay shuddered and shook her head, studying the door connecting her room and Jack's. Jack wouldn't use her. He was better than that. And she wouldn't deliberately add to his pain for all the money in the world.

There was no denying that she was physically drawn to him. She liked the way she felt when in his arms. But to talk confidently about bedding a man was one thing. Actually sliding under the sheets with him was another matter entirely. She knew that from bitter experience. And she knew the risks of abandonment and public humiliation that could go with it. With a sigh, Lindsay rose from her seat, blew out the oil lamp on the vanity, and then crawled into bed knowing that in the scales of decision, the past still weighed heavily. For her. And for Jack.

JACKSON DRAPED HIS TROUSERS and shirt over the back of the chair in front of the window, then turned to look at the door separating him from Lindsay. God, he was tempted to walk over to it, knock, and ask her if she'd be interested in spending the night with him. His room or hers, it didn't matter to him one way or the other.

What did matter, though, he reminded himself as he turned toward his bed, was accomplishing the task that had brought him to New York. Becoming Lindsay's lover would complicate the hell out of making decisions, and neither one of them needed it to be any more difficult that it already was. And then there was Henry's tendency to insult. To provide the man with ammunition was unthinkable. Added into the ugly mix was the likelihood of social condemnation if word got out that Lindsay had involved herself in another short-term affair.

Jack raked his fingers through his hair and sank down on the edge of his bed. He didn't want to leave Lindsay with more battles to fight than she already had. Of the two of them, he had the clearer perspective on the risks and consequences of becoming lovers. That meant that he was the one who was going to have to exercise self-discipline and restraint. The best way of keeping to that narrow, safe track was to focus all of his energy on business, on figuring out who had been stripping away the MacPhaull Company assets.

He fell backward onto the soft bed and stared up at the ceiling, forcing his mind to analyze what he knew of the Byzantine maze that was Lindsay's world. It was so much less painful than remembering and dealing with the shadows of his own.

CHAPTER SEVENTEEN

$\mathcal{L}$INDSAY CROSSED THE FOYER at an angle that allowed her to see into the dining room well before she arrived there. She saw Abigail Beechum at the buffet, putting silverware back into the velvet-lined storage chest. There was no sign or sound of Jack, and Lindsay felt a curious mixture of relief and disappointment.

"Ah, breakfast smells good," Lindsay said, sweeping into the room. "How are you this morning, Mrs. Beechum?"

"Fine, thank you. And yourself, Miss Lindsay?"

"I had a restless night," she admitted, settling into her place at the table. "I think I went to bed with too much on my mind." Taking the silver cover off her plate and putting it aside, she noted that hers was the only breakfast on the table. "Where's Mr. Stennett's place setting?"

"He's eaten and left for the office already."

"My, he's certainly the early bird this morning."

"He said he was pressed for time and that he had much to do. He also asked me to relay a message for him." She paused just long enough that Lindsay knew she needed to mentally brace herself. "Mr. Stennett requests that you pack a bag for traveling and prepare to be gone for the better part of a week. He suggested that you might want to take simple, comfortably fitting clothes."

Lindsay's mind whirled with possibilities. As with his absence this morning, she felt an unsettling combination of emotions; some exhilarating and some deeply troubling. Telling herself that it was foolish to presume and react before ascertaining the facts, she mustered enough poise to casually ask, "Did he happen to say where I'm going?"

"No. I inquired and he—very apologetically, mind you—told me that your destination must be kept a secret for the time being. And I think I should mention that you aren't traveling alone. Mr. Stennett's accompanying you. His bag is already packed and is to be brought down when yours are. He said that since John is injured, he'll make arrangements to have a hack come by the house for you at ten-thirty this morning."

"At which point I'm to be standing in the foyer, sweetly obedient to his command," Lindsay observed sardonically, her ire the easiest of her tumbling emotions to grasp.

"I believe that's an unfair characterization of the situation, Miss Lindsay."

Her housekeeper's gentle rebuke stung, but Lindsay wasn't going to abandon her pique without putting up a bit of struggle to defend it. "How else would you state it, Abigail?" Even to her own ears she sounded peevish. Why was she in such a difficult mood this morning? The night before certainly hadn't been the first relatively sleepless one she'd had in recent weeks and months.

"I think that Mr. Stennett has a plan of sorts formulated. I have no idea what it is, of course, but I feel it there under the surface of things. He was very firm and deliberate when he gave me the message. I can't help but think that he's given the trip a great deal of thought."

"Do you think this plan of his centers around the proposal of a romantic affair?" Lindsay posed, deliberately trying to lighten her tone of voice.

"Does it matter which of you makes the first overture?"

As usual, Abigail had cut to the heart of the matter and

left Lindsay with no other choice but to face the situation honestly and squarely. Her appetite gone, Lindsay laid down her silverware and pushed her plate away, saying gloomily, "I haven't been very discreet, have I?"

"I don't think it's so much a lack of discretion," the older woman consoled, "as it is your lifelong inability to hide your feelings about anything."

Lindsay sighed and turned in her chair to meet the housekeeper's gaze. "Could we pretend that we're in your room and sharing a pot of tea?"

Abigail smiled and got herself a cup of coffee from the silver pot on the buffet.

"I'm uncertain about what to do, Abigail," Lindsay admitted as the housekeeper took a seat beside her at the table. "On the one hand, there's the expectations of propriety. And while my reputation isn't sterling in that regard, I can at least claim that my past stumble was both a single occurrence and the result of being young and naive. Society might eventually grant me a small bit of forgiveness for it.

"On the other hand . . ." Lindsay considered the tangle of feelings and thoughts ensnaring her and then sighed. "Oh, what a mess," she declared. "It's easier not to think about it and just do what's expected of me."

Gently, but firmly, Abigail countered, "But the easiest way out of a situation isn't necessarily the best course, Lindsay. Sometimes we need to consciously choose to muddle along on the rougher road."

Lindsay couldn't believe her ears. "Are you saying that you think I ought to have an affair with Jack?"

"Oh, Lindsay, my dear child," the other woman said, softly laying her hand on Lindsay's forearm. "Let's begin with an ugly and bitter truth: Society doesn't forget and it never forgives. You can live like a nun, hiding inside these walls and behind your office desk for the rest of your life, and it isn't going to earn you so much as a sliver of social redemption."

"So what you're saying is that I might as well accept my fate and whatever romantic opportunities come my way," Lindsay summarized, again surprised by Abigail's stance on the matter.

"You enjoy Jackson Stennett's company, don't you?"

"Yes, very much."

"And if I'm not mistaken, you find him physically attractive," Abigail pressed.

"I do indeed."

"He strikes me as being a good man, Lindsay. I simply can't see him treating you as Charles Martens did."

The memories surged to the fore, but she shoved them aside, determined to deal with the present situation calmly and rationally. "I can't help but wonder if perhaps he might not be using my attraction to his business benefit. If I'm consumed by thoughts of becoming his lover, it's time and effort I'm not expending in blocking any actions he wants to take."

"It would be very callous, Lindsay. Mr. Stennett doesn't seem to me the sort of man who would use a woman that way. Maybe it would ease your mind to know that he was genuinely concerned for you after the dinner debacle last night. I believe his feelings for you are sincere and would be the same regardless of your particular circumstances."

Lindsay remembered the way he'd come into her room, determined to keep her from stewing in self-pity and humiliation. She smiled and nodded in silent acceptance. "But an affair with Jack would end in essentially the same manner as the one with Charles did; we would each go our separate ways," she pointed out. "Jack has no intention of remaining in New York. And I, of course, have too many responsibilities here to even consider the possibility of going to Texas with him. Not that he'll ever suggest it," she hastily added. "Jack has too many ghosts, too many regrets to allow himself to become emotionally attached to anyone."

"You have your fair share of ghosts and regrets, too."

"True, but mine don't haunt me as deeply as Jack's do him. He's a very complicated man, Abigail."

"Just as you're a complicated woman."

Lindsay chuckled dryly, remembering. "Oddly enough, Jack mentioned something along those lines last night."

"Then I'm adding 'perceptive' to his list of other fine qualities."

Jackson Stennett did indeed have a great many fine qualities. For some reason, that fact only added to her confusion. "Why is this such a difficult decision to make, Abigail?" she asked. Not giving the woman a chance to answer, she went on, saying, "I'm perfectly capable of adding up the respective columns and it's plain to see that there's more to recommend being Jack's lover than there is in clinging to the tattered remains of my reputation. Why can't I bring myself to simply say that I'm willing to accept an offer should he make one?"

"Because," Abigail said, patting her hand, "it's the course your mother would insist upon if she were sitting here instead of me."

"But you've said I should take the chance if it presents itself," Lindsay instantly countered, her frustration mounting. "What's the difference?"

"The difference lies in motives and well you know it," the housekeeper rejoined, her tone that of a woman offering an opinion that had long been considered and was grounded on firm conviction. "Jackson Stennett is not Charles Martens and you are not—thank God—your mother. You tried to live as Lydia instructed and you failed miserably at it. Accept that you aren't capable of the cold, callous manipulation of other people and be grateful for it, Lindsay.

"Life should be lived on your own terms, not those others hold for you. As long as no one else is harmed, life should include all the things that make you happy. Some of life's wonders last forever and some don't. You can't know which will be which before you begin the journey. You have to act on faith, knowing that no matter what happens, it will all turn out for the best and as it should."

Faith. That all would turn out for the best and as it should. If her life had turned out for the best so far, then she didn't want to contemplate what the bad might have been like. Lindsay shook her head. "How can you be so peacefully philosophical about life," she wondered aloud, "when you've had so much heartache in your own?"

"It's all a matter of perspective, Lindsay," Abigail replied cheerfully. "I'm no longer married to a man who mistreated me. I live in a lovely home. I eat well, my bed is comfortable, my days have purpose. And I've had the joy of helping a beautiful child grow into an even more beautiful young woman. I can't think of anything else in life I could have asked for."

"Do you have any regrets?"

Abigail's gaze drifted to the windows overlooking the garden. After a long moment she sighed and looked back at Lindsay with a bittersweet smile. "One doesn't live without making mistakes, Lindsay. Of course I have regrets. But the decisions I made were the best I could make at the time and under the circumstances. If I could go back, knowing what I know now, yes, there are some things I would do differently. But, by and large, I'm content with the paths I've chosen."

"You've never wanted to marry again?"

"No, I honestly haven't. Richard and I . . ." A shadow passed over her expression, making her seem older than Lindsay had ever seen her. Her gray eyes shifted focus and Lindsay knew that she was lost in the memories of another time and place. After a moment the housekeeper sighed softly and blinked.

"Richard was kind to me, Lindsay," she said, her words and gaze now sharply focused, "and his courtship—as clandestine and improper as it was—saved me when I had all but given up the hope of life being anything more than one beating after another. But as kind as Richard was, I felt no great physical passion for him and I had objections to the way he often used the people around him. The last time we were together, he asked me to leave my husband so the two of us could marry, and I had no choice but to be honest with him." She paused, and when she spoke again there was a misty edge to her voice. "He was so horribly angry. Understandably. I hurt not only his heart, but his pride as well."

Lindsay remembered and before she could think better of it, said, "The last time was—" She bit off the rest of the words, but it was too late.

Abigail nodded and finished the thought for her. "The carriage crashed and I lost my arm and Richard lost the use of his legs. It changed both of our lives forever."

"For the better?" Lindsay asked gently, unbelievingly.

"For myself, absolutely," Abigail assured her, her smile genuine and radiant. "My husband divorced me and, after a time, I came to live here. I can't speak with any certainty about Richard, but I think he discovered much about himself and the kind of life he'd been leading to that point. In some respects I think that he used the knowledge to become a better man."

"I consider him to be good man," Lindsay assured the woman, covering her hand with her own. Suddenly, and quite unexpectedly, tears swelled Lindsay's throat. Before they made speech impossible, she hurriedly added, "And as you've been like a mother to me, he's been like a father. I don't know what I would have done without either one of you."

"See? Life does work out for the best, doesn't it?" Abigail said, her smile beatific. She pulled her hand from under Lindsay's and rose to her feet, saying, "Now, shall we go upstairs and get you packed for your trip with Mr. Stennett?"

Lindsay rose and followed Abigail from the dining room. Her thoughts and feelings were slightly more ordered than when she'd come into the room, but she knew in her heart that she remained undecided as to how she'd respond if Jackson asked her to come to his bed.

Abigail was right; Lydia MacPhaull would be firmly in favor of a capitulation. As long, Lindsay silently qualified, as it came only after Jack had offered significant business rewards as compensation. And Richard . . .

Lindsay froze on the stairs, struck by a dark realization. Richard lay on Death's doorstep. If she were to be gone for almost a week, then it could well be that she'd return to discover that he'd passed in her absence.

"What is it, child?"

"What if Richard dies while I'm gone?" she asked, her voice a broken whisper.

"Do you think that remaining here will make him live longer?" Abigail gently countered. She didn't give Lindsay a chance to answer. "It won't. If you were to ask Richard whether he'd want you hovering at the side of his deathbed or seeing to business with Mr. Stennett, what do you think he'd tell you to do?"

Lindsay smiled sadly. "He'd tell me to have my bags in the foyer at ten-fifteen."

Mrs. Beechum nodded then turned and resumed her way up the stairs. Lindsay went behind her, mentally framing the words she wanted to say to Richard before she left the house. She wouldn't be overly emotional, wouldn't tell him how much like a father he had been to her. Richard didn't like open displays of affection or demonstrations of feelings. She'd thank him for teaching her about business and about being stalwart through difficulties and challenges. She'd assure him that she'd exercise good judgment and make the best of the present situation, that he could pass to a better world peacefully and without worrying about her. And maybe, just maybe, as she left his side, she'd whisper that she loved him and that she would miss him terribly.

Tears welling in her eyes, Lindsay blindly made her way to her room and set herself to the task of packing her bags.

JACKSON RAPPED ON THE FRONT WALL of the rented hack, signaling the driver to stop. When it did, he disembarked, saying to the puzzled driver, "I've decided to walk the rest of the way. Keep the fare with my thanks."

The driver tipped his hat and flicked the reins, setting the horses in motion. Jack stood on the sidewalk and watched him move away, thinking that he sorely missed his own hat. He'd never realized the integral part it served in everyday conversation until he'd had to go without it. If he had the time, he'd scour the city until he found one to replace it. That was, of course, assuming he could find a hat in this place that actually had a brim big enough to be of some practical use. Top hats and bowlers were fine. For other men. He'd rather be dead than be seen in either one of them.

It was all a pointless consideration, he reminded himself as he started down the sidewalk. He didn't have time to hunt for a hat. What he did have was a little more than thirty days to figure out a giant, very expensive puzzle. Well, he didn't *have* to figure out what had been happening with the MacPhaull Company assets over the last fifteen years. It was water under the bridge as far as his immediate situation was concerned. All he had to do was sell what properties were left and get the hell out of town with the cash. Who had been stealing the properties—and he was convinced someone had been—was really Lindsay's problem, not his.

But he owed Billy and he owed Lindsay. Finding out who had been thieving and getting the property back would go a long way toward repayment of that debt. Lindsay's financial existence would be more secure and he would have cleaned up the biggest mess of Billy's life. And he was beginning to think that Billy had had a pretty good idea of what kind of business disaster he was leaving behind.

Odds were, though, that Billy hadn't had so much as the foggiest idea about the kind of woman Lindsay had grown into. If he had, Billy would have never sent the likes of Jackson Lee Stennett to rescue her. He'd have sent Elmer; the bespeckled, shy, incredibly logical, unemotional, and safe little lawyer.

"Tough luck, Elmer," he muttered, smiling and reaching for the door handle of the MacPhaull Company offices. "Finders keepers, losers weepers."

"Good morning, Mr. Stennett."

"Mornin', Ben. Hope you've got your pencil sharpened," Jackson said, stopping at the clerk's desk. "I have some things for you to do."

"At your service, sir."

"First off," Jackson said, producing the key to the Theorosa house from his pocket and handing it to the bookkeeper, "there's a house I'm buying north of town. I'll draw you a map of where it is and see that you have it before I leave here today. I want you to find a lady or two to go up there and clean the place from top to bottom. The furniture and the rugs need to be taken out and beaten to within an inch of their lives. The curtains and all the bedding should be washed and put back into place. Also, while you're at it, arrange to have the pantry stocked with nonperishables."

"Yes, sir."

"Second thing this morning," Jack went on, "is a letter

I want sent to Percival Little, of Little, Bates and Company, regarding the offer he's made on the St. Louis property. I'm sure there's an existing protocol for this sort of thing and I think it should be followed. Care to tell me what it is?"

"You tell me the gist of what it is that you want to say," the man supplied crisply. "I then write the letter on company stationary and present it for your approval and signature. After that, I deliver the letter to Mr. Vanderhagen's office for his approval, and he mails it, usually on the same day."

That was an unexpected twist. Casually, Jackson asked, "Why does Vanderhagen have to approve the letter?"

"As Mr. Patterson explained it to me years ago, it's as much a matter of professional courtesy as it is of making sure that the MacPhaull Company isn't in violation of either the law or the common sense of self-interest." Ben shrugged. "I suppose, in essence, that Mr. Vanderhagen serves as another set of eyes and a detached point of view."

"All right," Jack drawled, "we'll do it as it's always been done. The gist of what I want to say to ol' Perce is that a new hand is at the helm of the company, that I find his offer insulting, and that I won't take less than what Lindsay and Richard Patterson originally asked for."

".Yes, sir." Ben shifted his weight between his feet and then cleared his throat softly before asking, "Do you want those sentiments expressed that bluntly? Or would you mind if I stated it all a bit more diplomatically?"

Jackson smiled, thinking that it didn't matter one whit. There wasn't anyone named Percival Little. There wasn't any business in Boston known as Little, Bates and Company, either. "Oh, be diplomatic if you think you must, Ben. It doesn't matter one way or the other to me."

"Very good. I'll have the letter for you within the next thirty minutes."

"Much appreciated. Now for the third thing. What have you managed to find out about the properties that have been sold over the years?"

"It's been very slow going, sir," Ben said. "Jeb spent all of yesterday at the city clerk's office, digging through the records. He found only two, but he'll return today and resume the search. I've prepared a report on the the two he did find. I also wrote the city clerks of Richmond, Boston, Philadelphia, and Charleston requesting the information available in their records. It will, of course, be at least a couple of weeks before we hear anything back from them—if we hear anything at all. There is, after all, nothing to compel them to assist us."

"No milk of human kindness, huh?"

"I wouldn't count on it, Mr. Stennett. You'd be much more certain of their cooperation if it were demanded by a court order."

But he needed proof of theft to get one. This was one of those situations, Jackson silently observed, where the law didn't do you any good until you didn't need it. "Well, then I guess we'll have to be content with what they're willing to give us and with what Jeb can dig out of the records here in the city. If there's a pattern, it might well show up just as clearly in the transactions close to home as it does in those farther away."

"A good attitude to have in a frustrating situation, sir," Ben said with a tight smile.

"Good attitude is my middle name," Jackson countered, turning away. "I'll be in the office."

"This morning's mail is on your desk, sir. Along with the report."

"Thank you, Ben."

Jackson ignored the mail, not wanting to know what new crises had arisen or which of the existing ones had worsened. There wasn't much he could do about them until after the auction anyway. The reports were a different matter entirely. Not bothering with planting himself in the chair, he picked them up, propped a hip against the corner of the desk, and began to read.

The McBride Manufacturing Company, makers of buggy whips and plagued by a long series of equipment breakdowns, had been sold to the MacWillman Company of Richmond for half its purchase price. City records showed that the business had ceased operations a year and a half later. Whether it had been relocated, dissolved, or sold wasn't known.

The story was essentially the same for the Candlish Barrel Company. A year-long combination of material thefts, a collapsed roof, and reoccurring small fires had been its downfall. The buyer had been the Michaels, Katz, and Osborne Company out of Charleston. The purchase price had been only a third of what the MacPhaull Company had invested in it. M, K, and O had held it for almost four years and then sold it to a local company, Brooks and Langan Investments, for seven times the price they'd originally paid for it. Ben, ever thorough, noted that J. Y. Brooks and R. R. Langan were well-known and highly respected in the New York business community.

Jack tossed the report down on the desk, his gut hard with certainty. There was a varmint loose in the MacPhaull Company and it had been steadily chewing away at the holdings for the better part of fifteen years. By now it had to have a very full nest, stuffed floor to ceiling with money that was rightfully Lindsay's.

Henry had a sufficient sense of self-importance to think of robbing the company blind, but lacked the intelligence and long-range thinking capabilities to pull it off for any extended period of time. Agatha would have considered the effort as being too akin to real work and thus beneath her. Ben was a bookkeeper, and while he possessed the mental acumen necessary, hadn't been with the company that long and was far too honest and loyal to consider stealing the company assets. Lindsay had been a child when the game had begun. The fact that she'd never questioned the selling patterns was a telling fact as well. She trusted the thief implicitly. That left only two real possibilities as to who the rat bastard could be: Patterson or Vanderhagen.

His money was on Patterson and the odds were good that he'd have proof of that in as many days as it took for the mail to get from New York to Boston. He intended to be sitting on the doorstep of the address of Little, Bates and Company when the post was delivered. Whoever received his response to Percival Little's offer was going to answer some questions and answer them honestly. And Lindsay was going to be standing right by his side when the truth spilled out. If he thought there was any way he could spare her the pain of discovery, he'd leave her behind and make the journey alone. But he knew Lindsay. She was going to hear the truth with her own two ears so that she couldn't deny it or accuse him of trying to blacken the reputation of the man whom she considered to be more her father than Billy. There was no other way and he'd made the decision.

He looked at the clock on Richard's desk, noting the time. Just an hour before he needed to leave for the docks where he'd meet Lindsay. She'd have questions and since he preferred not to answer them in a crowded public place, he needed a plan for distracting her attention. Jackson scooped up the mail, thinking that a few new quagmires would do nicely for that purpose, and moved around the desk toward the chair, flipping through the packets as he went.

The bank left holding the bag for the Todasca fiasco had written again. There was correspondence from the Two Rivers Bank in Frankfort, Kentucky. What had Lindsay told him about that crisis? Something about a bank run and calling in loans to meet depositor withdrawals? Why did he expect the letter to say that the doors were still closed and that the manager was requesting funds to install barricades? There was also a letter from an architect. Henry's, Jack surmised. He'd have to have Ben draft another letter, he decided, pulling out the chair.

A flash of white caught his attention, pulling it away from the mail. A smallish box, wrapped in white paper and tied with string had been put in the seat of the chair. Jack tossed the mail onto the desk and picked up the parcel. The string loosened with a single tug and the paper fell open. Jack lifted the lid and froze. A rat was inside. Or, more accurately, pieces of what had been a rat. Atop it lay a folded note. Jack carefully removed the note before replacing the lid. The paper was fine vellum, folded in half. Inside, written in clumsily formed block letters, was a simple message: LEAVE OR DIE.

"Damnation," he muttered, thinking back to the fire in the apartment house, the explosion, the man who had struck him on the stairs, and then the carriage crash. Individually, they had appeared to be nothing more than singular events in a run of miserable luck. In hindsight, and taken all together, they seemed much more than mere coincidence. Jack touched the tender stitches in the back of his head. Maybe someone *was* trying to kill him. Or maybe someone was making use of what had already happened to threaten him into turning tail and running.

In either case, whoever it was didn't know Jackson Stennett well at all. Which was everyone in New York except Lindsay, who knew him better than anyone living and who had been with him at every accident. His blood chilled. Jesus, he'd die of guilt if anything happened to her in an attempt to do him in.

Jackson scowled. He sure as hell didn't need another set of *who?* questions right at the moment. Of course, it was logical to think that the someone who wanted him dead or gone was the same someone who'd been stealing the company assets. Which meant that unless Richard Patterson was a consummate actor and shimmying down drainpipes in the middle of the night to hack up rodents, it put a big dent in Jackson's suspicions about the man.

"Damn, I don't need this," he groused, picking up the box and heading toward the office door. "Ben, who sent the package?" he asked the second he entered the anteroom.

Ben didn't look up from his writing. "What package?"

"This one," he said, holding up the box. "I found it in the seat of the desk chair."

Ben crossed a t and lifted the pen away from the paper before glancing up. He considered the box for a moment and then shook his head. "I have no idea, sir. I've been here alone since I unlocked an hour ago. Jeb went straight from MacPhaull House to the clerk's office this morning."

"Who, besides yourself, has a key to the office?"

"Miss Lindsay and Mr. Patterson are the only others that I'm aware of," Ben answered. "If anyone else has one, they've obtained it on the sly."

Jackson handed the note to the bookkeeper, asking, "Do you recognize the handwriting?"

"No, sir," he replied, again shaking his head. He turned it over to look at both the front and back sides before observing, "It would appear that it was either written by a young child or that some deliberate effort was made to disguise the handwriting." Handing it back to Jackson, he added, "May I inquire as to what is in the box?"

"You don't want to know," Jack assured him. "Do you have the stove fired up?"

"Yes, sir. The coffee's on and almost done."

"One more question, Ben," Jack said, his mind clicking through what he needed to do and the time he had to do it in. "Where can I find the nearest gunsmith?"

"MacDavit's is two blocks east and one block south," Ben said. "He's supposed to be the best. It's said that his prices reflect it."

"Money's no object." Actually, Jack mentally amended as he walked toward the stove at the rear of the office, money was the only object of the web in which he'd become entangled.

LINDSAY HURRIED DOWN THE STAIRS, the last of her bags in hand. "I'll get the door, Mrs. Beechum," she called as the knock sounded again. Breathless, she opened it to find Otis Vanderhagen standing on the front step. He whipped his bowler from his head even as his gaze went past her and came to rest on the luggage stacked in the center of the foyer.

"Are you going somewhere, Lindsay?" he boomed.

As always, she answered quietly in the hope that he'd take a polite hint and lower the volume of his own speech. "A brief out-of-town excursion, Mr. Vanderhagen. We'll be gone for just a few days."

"Where are you going?" he asked, his voice still loud enough to carry to the back of the house.

"I have no idea," she admitted. "Jackson didn't say."

"Well, in case you see Mr. Stennett before I do," Otis said, "would you be kind enough to tell him that I've perused the letter to Percival Little, seen nothing amiss in it, and sent it on its way?"

"Certainly. Is there something you need from me this morning?"

"No, I can't think of anything. I was on my way to a

meeting and had some extra time. I thought I'd come visit Richard for a bit."

"That's very kind of you," Lindsay said sincerely. She stepped to the side and gestured into the foyer. "Please come in."

"It hurts to see him in such a condition," Vanderhagen went on, crossing the threshold, "but we've been friends for a good many years and I can't pretend that he's already gone. If he's aware of anything, I want him to know that his associations continue as they always have."

It occurred to her that the negative opinion she'd always had of the man might have come from never having had the chance, before now, to see him as a person, as a friend to Richard. The guilt was compounded by the realization that she could very well have spent a lifetime misjudging the man.

"Ah, I see that the hack's arrived," he announced as the hired carriage rolled to a stop in front of MacPhaull House. "I'll see myself upstairs. No need to trouble yourself with it. I know the way."

Lindsay nodded, still grappling with her new and unexpected perspective of the man. "While the driver's loading my bags, I'll ask Primrose to bring up coffee and some pastries for you."

"That would be lovely," the attorney said, already moving toward the stairs. "I'm starving. Travel safely."

She thanked him absently, watching the driver tie off his reins and climb down from the box. Where was she so blithely going? she wondered. Was traveling safely really the greatest of her concerns? Maybe she should be staying here, letting Jack make the mysterious journey on his own. Why did he need her along?

The driver stopped on the other side of the open door, tipped his hat, and asked if he could begin loading the bags. Lindsay hesitated and then nodded as she deliberately set her doubts aside.

CHAPTER EIGHTEEN

*T*HEIR BAGS SAFELY STOWED, Lindsay emerged from the small cabin area of the packet ship, tilting her head so that her bonnet brim better shielded her eyes from the bright sunlight. Overhead, the crew climbed in the ropes, preparing the vessel for departure from port. Judging by the flutter of her hems and the rocking of the deck beneath her feet, it was going to be a rather quick and lunging jump from berth. All in all, an exhilarating ride, she knew. She'd have to remember to thank Jack for having arranged to make their journey—to wherever it was they were going—by sea. She loved to sail, and the wilder the water, the better.

A crewman rang the hour of noon as she turned a slow circle, scanning the deck for some sign that Jack was going to arrive in time to sail with her. She finally found him, standing at the rear of the vessel, his hands on the rail and his gaze fixed firmly on the wharf as though he was looking for something or someone. Picking her way through cargo and coils of rope, Lindsay made her way to him, her step steady on the gently rolling deck.

As she reached his side, she realized that he wasn't

searching the docks at all. In fact, his eyes were closed and he gripped the rail so tightly that his hands were white. His face was a pale and sickly shade of green.

"You're not looking at all well, Jack."

"I don't do very well the first two or three days on a ship," he said, his eyes still closed. "After that, I'm all right. Captain Morris—on the way here—told me I was one of those who had to get his sea legs the hard way."

"Then why are we sailing? Can we not get to wherever we're going overland?"

"We're going to Boston, and yes, we could go overland, but sailing the distance is faster. I don't want to take the chance of getting there too late."

"Boston," Lindsay repeated, moving around to stand on the windward side of him. "May I assume that this jaunt has something to do with the offer from Percival Little? Are you thinking to meet with him in person?"

He drew a long, slow breath before opening his eyes and turning to face her. "I don't think there's any such person, Lindsay. I think he and Little, Bates and Company are fictitious. They're made-up, just like the stories of ogres and fairies."

Knowing that he could better battle his stomach if he kept his eyes open and focused on something close, she stepped closer and met his gaze squarely. "I'm compelled to remind you, Jack, that the MacPhaull Company has conducted quite a bit of business with the ogre over the years. And that his bank drafts have always been good."

"Lindsay, anyone can sign a letter with anyone's name and banks don't give a damn who owns an account under what name as long as they can take a cut from the transactions."

Recognizing his seriousness, she saw no choice but to counter his assertion with cool logic. "Why would anyone want to hide behind such a facade? What would be the point of it, Jack? The MacPhaull Company has no list of persons we're unwilling to do business with."

"Let me give you a hypothetical situation." He swallowed and took another long breath as his skin tone edged toward ashen. "Let's say that someone wanted to make a whole lot of money without risking any of theirs in the process. Let's say that person knew of a company that owned a bunch of different kinds of companies all over the country."

"Let's call that company MacPhaull," she suggested, wondering how long he'd be able to keep talking, and knowing that he must feel strongly about the matter to make the effort. Despite the craziness of his notion, the least she could do was give him her attention long enough to distract him from the roiling of his stomach.

"All right," he said, barely nodding. "Let's say someone wanted to make money through the MacPhaull Company holdings."

"But they don't own the MacPhaull holdings."

"No, they don't. But if the manager or the owner of the company could be motivated to sell a property for pennies on the dollar, that person could pick up the property, hold it for a while, and then sell it for a profit."

"And how would this person motivate Richard and me to sell a profitable company?" she asked gently, hoping to make him see the error of his assumptions. "It goes not only against logic, Jack, but good business sense."

"They know that," he countered, slowly rubbing his free hand over his jaw. "They also know that good business judgment usually calls for disposing of an unprofitable holding. All they have to do is see that a company turns from a money maker to a financial drain. When you and Richard do the logical thing and decide to cut your losses by putting it up for sale, they're there to buy the property."

"And just how would they be in any position to turn around the fortunes of any particular holding?"

"They see that there are fires, materials are stolen, machinery breaks down, that tools go missing, shipments disappear, roofs collapse, water pipes are broken. The list is endless, Lindsay." He exhaled hard before adding, "A creative man would never run out of ideas."

"Deliberate sabotage," she said.

"With every incident looking like an accident."

"All right, Jack," she said patiently. "Assuming that you're correct—and that's a significant assumption—why would it be necessary for this person to create a false persona? In this case, that of Percival Little and Little, Bates and Company."

"It's not just Little, Bates and Company, Lindsay." His breathing quickened and his skin suddenly took on a telltale sheen. "It's also Michaels, Katz, and Osborne. It's the MacWillman Company, as well as Hooper, Preston, and Roberts, Limited."

"All four? All four of the largest companies with which MacPhaull does business?" she scoffed, laughing. "Jack, your brain is sloshing."

"No, it's not." He cocked a brow and gave her a smile that was both pained and rueful. "My stomach sure as hell is, but my brain's working just fine."

And they hadn't even left the dock yet. He was going to be flat on his face before they ever cleared the harbor. "All right, Jack. We'll finish out the logic of this utterly illogical hypothetical situation. You think that there are four persons out there sabotaging the MacPhaull Company holdings in order to force Richard and me into selling properties at a loss so that they—these four mysterious and unknown persons—can purchase them, hold them, and sell them at an obscene profit. Am I understanding your thoughts on this clearly?"

"There aren't four persons," he corrected, closing his eyes.

"Eight? Maybe ten? And keep your eyes open, Jack. Closing them only makes it worse. You're focusing only on how the world is moving beneath you. Open them and look at me."

"One, Lindsay," he said, doing as she'd told him. While his gaze held hers, he gripped the rail with both hands again. "One person. That's why the facades are necessary. One person owns all four of the companies. If you knew you were dealing with only one person, you'd get suspicious, you'd see the pattern. The shell game depends on your attention being divided so that you don't see the pattern."

"And how is it that *you've* seen this alleged pattern, Jack?" she asked, her anger sparked by his words. "Is it that you're so very much smarter than either Richard or me?"

"I'm looking at the history of the company from the outside, Lindsay," he said blandly, almost as though he wasn't the least bit aware of having stirred her ire. "I don't have the blind loyalties and faith that you do."

Lindsay clenched and unclenched her fists. "No one's ever accused me of being blindly faithful about anything, Jack. No one."

"Well," he countered, his voice edged with frustration. "just because they've never said it aloud doesn't mean that they aren't counting on it, just the same."

"That would imply that this person sabotaging the MacPhaull Company is either someone whom I trust implicitly or someone whom I wouldn't consider capable of such a complicated act of thievery."

"Yep." He swallowed with what seemed to be difficulty and a great deal of thought. "On both counts."

"How long do you think these purported thefts have been occurring?" she asked, her hands on her hips.

"At least fifteen years."

"I haven't accepted your supposition, Jack," she stated, thinking that he looked like he could collapse at any moment. "But I am willing to run with it a bit longer just for the sake of argument. Setting up false companies would take a great deal of thought and legal work; not to mention what amounts to confidence operations in distant cities. Henry might be motivated to steal, but he doesn't have the intelligence to actually do anything on a scale this large or for the length of time you think it's been happening. Ben's certainly capable of actually doing it, but he's the most loyal man on the face of the earth. Otis Vanderhagen, however, meets the requirements on all counts."

"So does Richard Patterson," he offered softly, his eyes full of regret.

"Richard would *not* steal from me."

"And there's your implicit trust and blind loyalty."

"Richard would *not* steal from me," she asserted again, angry and unshakeable in her conviction.

Jack moistened his lips with the tip of his tongue. "If I'm

wrong, I'll apologize. But I'm not wrong, Lindsay. I'm sorry, but I'm not wrong. Richard Patterson's behind it and I'm betting Otis Vanderhagen has a finger in the pie as well."

He was ill. He didn't know what he was talking about, and he clearly didn't understand the depths of betrayal he was suggesting. "You're going to have to give me irrefutable and undeniable proof of Richard's involvement."

"That's why we're going to Boston. You're going to be with me when my letter to Percival Little arrives in the hands of whoever deals with the game on the Boston end. You're going to be there when I ask the hard questions and you're going to hear the answers from the mouth of Richard's shill. I'm not going to give you a choice to believe anything except the ugly, bitter truth."

An order rang out behind them and, in almost the same fraction of time as the mooring ropes were cast free, there was a sudden scrape of unfurling canvas and then the pop and lurch of wind filling the sails. The vessel surged away from its berth in the next heartbeat, its hull plowing and rolling hard against the incoming waves. Lindsay grasped the railing to keep from being pitched off her feet.

"And assuming that this shill points his finger straight at Richard . . . What are you going to do about it, Jack?"

"Theft is against the law," he answered tightly, his breathing growing quicker and more shallow.

"You can't try and imprison a dead man," Lindsay countered, watching in alarm as his face went whiter than the sails over their heads. "At least not in New York."

"But you can challenge the settlement of his estate. If you can prove his property was gained from embez—" He leaned out over the railing and lost the battle to keep his stomach down.

"Oh, Jack," Lindsay said softly, gently rubbing her hand over the width of his shoulders.

"If I die," he half-moaned, "for godssakes don't bury me at sea. Have a heart and find—"

She waited until the second purging episode had passed before she asked, "Do you want me to haul your body back to Texas?"

He laid his forehead against the wooden railing. "Only if you promise to take me overland."

"Where exactly should I take you? I understand that Texas is quite large."

"Little town called Waterloo." He gagged, but managed to keep from having to lean out over the rail again. "Just started up nearby. By the time you get me there, it'll probably be called Austin. Talk was swinging that way when I left."

"Waterloo," Lindsay repeated, still rubbing his shoulders. "As in Napoleon. Or Austin. As in Stephen Austin. I can remember that, Jack. Do you have any special requests for a funeral service? Will I need to hire professional mourners?"

"God, Lindsay." His laughter was somewhat strangled, but she was glad to hear that he was capable of the attempt.

"I just want to do this right, you understand. I need very specific instructions."

"Just get me to the Hill Country. Central Texas."

"I'll ask for directions," she assured him, running her fingers gently through the hair at his nape. It felt like strands of warm, dark silk. "Surely people will point me in the right direction; if for no other reason than to get rid of me. You're going to smell awful by the time I get you there, Jack."

"Oh God." He tried to laugh again, and this time the effort ended with him leaning out and retching again.

"I'll get you a proper headstone," Lindsay promised him when he returned his forehead to the rail. "Of course, I'm going to have HE WAS WRONG ABOUT RICHARD PATTERSON carved in it."

"I'm not wrong," he muttered miserably. "I'm not."

"We'll just have to wait and see." She stepped against his side and, sliding her arm around his waist, tried to draw him away from the rail, saying, "Right now, though, let's get you to the cabin."

"I can't move," he moaned. Even as the words left his mouth, he belied them by sinking slowly to his knees.

"Oh, Jack," Lindsay whispered, easing down onto the

deck and wrapping both arms around him. "We'll come back to New York by coach."

"Doesn't matter," he answered morosely. " 'Cause I'm dying right here."

Drawing him down so that his head rested on her lap, Lindsay gently brushed damp tendrils of hair from his brow. "I'll take care of you," she crooned. "You'll live to see Boston."

He groaned. Lindsay loosened his tie and undid his starched shirt collar. He sighed in relief and nestled his head deeper into the cradle of her lap. After a few moments, his breathing evened and deepened and she knew that he'd escaped his misery in sleep.

Still winding her fingers through his hair, she leaned her head back against the gunwale. Crew members scurried in the ropes overhead and the languages of at least fifteen nations billowed on the wind. When they were well under way and when the frenetic activities of departure were done, she'd get someone's attention and ask them to help her get Jack to their cabin. He'd rest more comfortably in a bunk with a soft mattress under him. She'd open the porthole so that he'd have plenty of cool, fresh air.

"My poor, sweet, deluded Jack," she whispered, looking back down at the massive, vibrant man made so utterly vulnerable by the forces of nature. "How very badly you must want to get to Boston."

How strongly he must believe. Lindsay frowned and thought back through all that he'd told her of his suspicions. Four companies with one owner, whose single purpose was stripping the MacPhaull Company of assets? Using deliberate sabotage to reduce the value of the holdings so that the properties could be acquired for a mere fraction of their real worth? It was, she had to admit, a brilliant strategy, if indeed it was being done.

What would be required for someone to manage the game for the fifteen years Jack maintained it had been going on? Certainly an initial amount of capital would have been necessary. But, if it worked as Jack thought it did, the process would have more than paid for itself after the first one or two purchases and subsequent sales.

The logistics of making it work would be complicated, though. Four companies, each in a different city and some distance from New York, meant that whoever—if indeed there really was someone—couldn't realistically travel between them to conduct the correspondence and business from all ends. They had to have established a system for making it all look real. There had to be people in Boston, Richmond, Philadelphia, and Charleston who were participating in the scheme, who took their instructions from whoever was behind the thefts and were rewarded for their complicity.

Why would someone want to strip the MacPhaull Company? Lindsay quietly snorted in a most unladylike way. Money was always a first consideration. Revenge usually counted among the other most popular motives, too. The desire for wealth was a universal thing, though, and that made for an impossibly long list of persons who could be behind it all. Vengeance, however, produced far fewer possibilities. Unfortunately, she couldn't think of anyone who might think that the MacPhaull Company had done them an injustice.

Perhaps it was a personal vendetta, she mused. Perhaps someone wanted either herself or Richard to be punished for some unintentional or imaginary wrong they were thought to have committed. It was so easy to step on people's social toes, but surely no damage had ever been inflicted that would warrant such a long-term, concerted effort at retaliation. If it had begun fifteen years ago, she would have been just beyond childhood and incapable of hurting anyone to a sufficient degree to bring such a hatred to bear on the MacPhaull Company.

Could Richard have inadvertently stirred someone's wrath? Lindsay sorted through her memories. Richard had been at the helm of the company since long before she had been born. She remembered being a young child—no more than five years old—and sitting at the top of the stairs watching him cross the foyer toward her father's study. Richard had had long strides and she could remember thinking that it said he was a man of concentrated purpose. Everything about him had been larger than life, too. His laugh had been loud and exuberant in those days. His eyes had been bright and quick and he'd had an air about him that said nothing could put so much as a dent in his spirit.

It had been his sense of confidence and resiliency—and the peppermints in his pockets—that had been her harbor in the marital storms that shook the walls and rattled the rafters of MacPhaull House. Those same qualities had been nothing less than her salvation in the days and months following her father's departure.

Richard had changed a great deal in the aftermath of the carriage accident. He hadn't laughed very much after that and the light in his eyes had changed, too. It was deeper and cooler and not nearly as quick. And it had been shortly after the accident that the scheme to strip the company had begun. Or at least that's what Jack thought.

Lindsay sighed. Richard had stepped beyond the bounds of propriety to court Abigail Beechum, a married woman. And Abigail had said that she'd had reservations about marrying him because of the way he used the people around him. Lindsay couldn't imagine Richard being so callous, but she didn't doubt the veracity of Abigail's observation. All in all, Lindsay had to admit that there was a distinct possibility that Richard might have been the one to have committed the sin that had triggered a quest for economic revenge. With adult eyes, she could look back at her childhood memories and realize that Abigail hadn't been the first married woman to have been courted by Richard Patterson. A wronged husband might feel humiliated and angry enough to go a long way to achieve retribution. And a crippled man with a wounded spirit would have been seen as an easy mark.

Lindsay watched as Jack's dark hair slipped through her fingers. He didn't know Richard as she did, didn't know how Richard had devoted his life to the MacPhaull Company. She could understand how Jack had come to the conclusions he had. But when the truth was known, Jack would apologize as he'd promised. He was a good man and a strong one, one strong enough to admit his mistakes.

Calmed and certain, Lindsay shifted her gaze beyond him, catching the attention of one of the crewmen. She motioned him over and asked for his assistance in getting Jack to the bunk in their cabin. It took two burly sailors, but Jack was eventually hefted up and half-dragged, half-carried to his berth. Lindsay followed behind, never more than a step away.

IT WAS DARK, but he could still feel the world rolling and heaving beneath him. His stomach lurched and rose in protest, determined to punish him yet again for his decision to buy passage to Boston by sea. Jackson, lying on his side, drew his knees up, just as determined to hold his own against the inner torment. A chill swept over him from head to toe and he shivered hard, drawing a steadying breath through his clenched teeth.

A soft warmth moved to mimic his own shifting position and then nestled more closely against the length of the back of his body. Jackson felt a nuzzling in the space between his shoulder blades as an arm slipped around his waist and drew him even closer. He didn't dare look anywhere but at the open porthole. To shift his head would be to invite another bout of ignobility.

"Lindsay?" he whispered.

"Are you warm enough?" she asked, her voice soft with concern as she rubbed his shoulder again with her cheek. "I've tried covering you with a blanket, but you keep kicking it off."

"I'm just right," he replied, burrowing back into the curve of her soft body.

"Are you feeling any better?"

"A little," he answered, realizing that there was sudden warmth in the center of his chest and that it seemed to have a settling effect on his stomach. Peace slipped over him and his eyelids grew heavy.

"Is there anything I can do for you, Jack?"

"Just keep hanging on to me."

"I wouldn't let go for the world," he heard her say as he drifted into a blessedly easy sleep.

CHAPTER NINETEEN

*J*ACKSON BUTTONED A SHIRT CUFF and listened to the copper bathtub being taken out of the adjoining room. His own bath had been gone some ten minutes or so; just long enough for him to pull on some clean clothes and make a decision. He waited until he heard the tub bang against the corner of the servants' stairs at the far end of the hotel hallway before he stepped to the door connecting the two rooms he'd rented, and knocked.

"It's unlocked," Lindsay called from the other side. "And yes, I'm decent."

With a smile, he turned the glass knob and pushed open the door. Lindsay sat at the small dressing table to the right of the door, brushing her hair. She wore a pale blue silk dressing gown, the color accentuating the fairness of her skin and the dark circles under her eyes.

"You look like you feel better," she said, laying her brush aside and turning on the seat to smile at him.

"I do," he admitted, absolutely certain that he'd made the right decision. "And you look exhausted. Why don't you go to bed and get some sleep?"

"Because it's not even noon yet," she laughed, rising and going to the foot of the bed where her valise sat, "and sleeping in the middle of the day is sinfully decadent."

"Well, if there's anyone who's earned some sinful decadence, it's you, Lindsay," he pointed out. "Taking care of me as you did, you couldn't have had more than a total of ten hours of sleep in the last three days. You've got to be dead on your feet."

"I'm fine, Jackson," she assured him, giving him a smile that, while bright, didn't reach her eyes. "We came to Boston for a purpose and it isn't for me to sleep the day away," she went on, pulling a chemise and petticoat from the large red leather bag. "I see that you're dressing to go out. Give me twenty minutes and I'll be ready to go with you. Mrs. Beechum relayed your suggestion that I bring comfortable clothes and I did. I won't need any help with lacings, so dressing will be an unusually quick affair."

Jack shook his head and tried one more time to make her be reasonable. "All I'm going to do is track down Percival Little's address and see if I can't find someone who'll tell me what time of the day the mail's usually brought by there. After that, I'm just going to wander around and get the lay of the land."

"You're assuming that a carrier will bring it to the address we have for Little, Bates," she said blithely, continuing to pull items from her bag. "It costs two cents—in addition to the regular postage—to have a postal carrier deliver a letter to a specific address. What if it's simply held at the post office until someone comes to pick it up?"

Damn stubborn woman. "With thousands of dollars at stake, Lindsay, what's two cents? It'll be delivered by carrier. You can bet on it."

"I guess we'll see."

"No, *I'll* see," he declared, stepping to the side of the bed and yanking down the coverlet and the top sheet. "And then I'll tell you all about it." He straightened, took one step, caught her hand in his and drew her away from the valise, saying, "C'mon. You're going to bed."

"Jack," she protested, trying to draw back. "I'm fine. Honestly."

He didn't like having to resort to using physical force, but she left him no other choice. Letting go of her hand, he instantly closed the distance between them and swept her up in his arms. She squeaked in surprise and flung her arms around his neck, holding tight.

"I'm hale and hearty again," he remarked, chuckling as he turned and set her down in the center of the bed. Drawing the bedcovers up over her long, bare legs, he added, "You're one helluva tough woman, Lindsay MacPhaull, but you've met your match. You might as well quit resisting."

With a martyred sigh, she rolled her eyes and then flopped backward, her head landing smack dab in the center of the pillow, her arms straight-out from her sides. "There. Are you happy now?"

She was just a tad bit disgusted with him and maybe even a bit peeved, but it only made her that much more stunningly beautiful. Never in his life had he ached so badly with wanting. Happy? That was a matter of degrees. "Reasonably so," he admitted, drawing the covers up to her shoulders and carefully tucking temptation away. He'd been right that first day; her curves didn't owe a damn thing to any corset.

It took effort to make himself step back from the edge of the bed, but he managed it. "I'm going to lock the doors when I leave. I'll slide the key to yours back under the door so you can have it. But please promise me you won't go out and wandering around on your own. All right?"

"All right, Jack," she agreed, stifling a hard yawn with the back of her hand. With a slow, almost feline wiggle, she settled her body into the mattress and her head deeper into the pillow. Her eyelids drifted closed.

Jackson stood there marveling at her strength and beauty as his impulses and his common sense engaged in a pitched battle. In the center of it were his memories of awakening aboard ship and always finding himself wrapped in the comfort of Lindsay's arms. And each time he'd drifted back off to sleep, his last conscious thought had been a promise to himself that he was going to hold her the minute he had the strength to do so.

His impulses urged him to lie down beside her and honor

his promise to himself. His common sense held that he had things to do and that Lindsay would be there when he returned. To his frustration, it also reminded him just how easily holding Lindsay could get out of hand. His pulse warmed and skittered at the prospect.

Jackson clenched his teeth and made yet another decision, this one infinitely more difficult than the one to insist Lindsay get some sleep. It was a compromise that pleased neither side of him all that much, but it was the only hope he had of moving off the spot of carpet where he stood.

"Sweet dreams," he whispered, leaning down and brushing his lips lightly over hers. "I'll be here when you wake up."

A soft smile lifted the corners of her mouth. Her voice came on a dreamy sigh. "I know."

It occurred to him, as he resolutely turned on his heel and walked away, that all he'd managed to accomplish was to delay yet another contest between his desire and his sense of good judgment. The latter had won this particular contest as it ultimately had all the others, but Jackson couldn't help wondering just how much more frustration his impulses were going to be able to take.

THE STREETS WERE OLD and cobbled and crowded with noisy vendors and women with shopping baskets hanging from their arms. He threaded his way among the throngs and eventually threw himself on the mercy of a pretty young woman selling eggs. She'd been kind and given him precise directions. Two blocks west of the central market area, he turned north onto the street where Little, Bates and Company was supposed to be found. One look and he knew it wasn't there. Each side of the narrow cobbled street was lined with three-storied structures, some brick, but the majority clapboard in desperate need of paint. There were small businesses on the first level of some; a dry-goods store, a millinery, a less than prosperous-looking chandler's shop. The vast majority of the businesses had called it quits and boarded their windows. People moved up and down the walkways on either side, most seemingly intent on leaving the area as quickly as possible. Jackson noted the few numbers he could find on the buildings and moved in the direction they indicated he should.

As he neared the place where he knew he wasn't going to find the offices of Percival Little, he met the gaze of a wide-shouldered young man seated on the stone steps beneath a sign that proclaimed the building to be O'Brien's Boardinghouse. The address was there on the sign and it was the same as the one Percy used.

"Hi!" the young man called, waving his hand as he smiled brightly and warmly. "Hi, mister!"

Jackson smiled, recognizing the pure happiness of a simple soul. "Well, hi there, yourself," Jackson offered in greeting as he stopped in front of the large man-child. "I'll bet they call you Tiny, don't they?"

He beamed and his green eyes lit up. "Do you know them?"

"Nah," Jackson admitted. "But people aren't all that much different no matter where you're from."

"I'm different," Tiny said sadly as his gaze dropped to the scuffed toes of his well-worn shoes.

Jackson felt for him and silently railed at the cruelty Tiny had no doubt endured his entire life. "I can see that," Jack offered brightly. "You're one of the *good* guys."

Tiny's head came up and his grin went from ear to ear. "I have a top. Wanna see it?"

"Sure," Jackson said, sitting down beside him on the steps as Tiny leaned to one side and extracted a wooden top and a long dirty piece of string from his pocket. The paint on the top was almost worn away. Jackson nodded appreciatively as Tiny held out the toy for inspection. "Well, hey, that's a mighty fine top, Tiny. Looks like it's had a lot of spins."

"I'm good at making it go a long time." Straightening the string, he asked, "What's your name?"

"I'm Jack, and I'm glad to meet you, Tiny." At the man's wide smile, Jack nodded toward the top and said, "Would you show me how you make it go?"

"You have to wind it just right, you know. The string has to go around like this, see?" he said, showing Jack as he wound the string tightly, neatly. "It can't be on top of itself or it won't go right when you pull it."

"Top spinning's a fine art," Jack observed.

"I'll teach you if you want to learn."

The enthusiasm of the offer was touching and Jack instantly knew the course to take. Lying was sometimes the kindest thing a person could do for another. "Why, Tiny, that's real kind of you. But you gotta be nice to me if I do it wrong. I've never been very good at it."

"If I'm not nice to you, you'll go away, and I don't want that to happen." He went back to winding the string as he added, "It's nice to have someone to talk to while I sit here and wait."

"What are you sitting here waiting for?"

"The mailman."

Jack blinked, hardly believing his incredibly good fortune. "Oh, yeah? Does he bring you letters very often?"

"Every week. He brings me my rent money. I take it straight to Mrs. O'Brien so nothing happens to it. There's extra money, too. Mrs. O'Brien keeps it for me so I can have clothes and other things when I need them."

"That's good," Jack offered, thinking that Mrs. O'Brien was a kind woman. "A fella doesn't want to find himself without shoes and with nowhere to live."

"And I have to live here or I won't be able to do my job."

"You have a job? What do you do?"

"I wait for the mail."

Jack grinned. "That's a pretty good job. How'd you get it?"

"I've had it since I was a little boy. A man came and talked to my mama. She's gone to be with God, you know."

"So's my mother," Jack supplied.

Tiny paused in his meticulous winding to look up at Jack. "Do you think my mama and your mama know each other?"

"I'll bet they do. Bet God really likes them, too."

"Hey, you made a rhyme!"

"Only accidentally."

Tiny laughed and went back to his task. Jack considered

what Tiny had told him and formed his line of questioning carefully. "So tell me about this man who came to see your mama and gave you the job of waiting for the mail. He must have been nice."

"I never met him. Mama said she didn't like the way he wrinkled his nose the whole time he was talking to her, but she said his money was good and came regular like he said it would, so she'd forgive him."

"How long have you been waiting for the mailman?" *Fifteen years, Tiny?*

"Oh, if he's gonna come to see me," Tiny answered, "he's here after he eats lunch."

"That's good," Jack observed, reining in his grin and reminding himself that the questions had to be very specific. "At least you don't have to sit here the *whole* day."

"I don't have anywhere else to go, so I do anyway. I just play with my top and wave to people who walk by."

Which explained why Jack had come upon just the person he needed to find. There really wasn't all that much luck involved in the encounter. "So how many years have you had this job, Tiny?"

"Oh, lots. Too many to count."

"What do you do when you get the mail? Take it to the people in the boardinghouse?"

"It's not their mail. It would be wrong to give it to someone it didn't belong to. Mama showed me how to do it a long time ago so that I'd do it right without her being with me."

"Oh, yeah?" Jack ventured, hoping. "How do you do it?"

"The mailman gives me the letter." Tiny stopped working with the string and met Jack's gaze as he solemnly continued, "It's always a big packet and he waits while I open it up. Inside is two pennies and another letter. I give the mailman the two pennies and the letter and he takes it away. Then I go inside and put the big packet in the stove in the kitchen. That's my job. That's how I earn my rent money."

Jack nodded, seeing how Tiny's task fit into the larger picture. "So who sends you these letters with the pennies inside?"

"I dunno," he said with a huge shrug before turning his attention back to the string and top. "I can't read, Jack. But I am real good making my top go. Watch."

"You sure are," Jack said sincerely as they both watched the top spin furiously two steps down. When it finally wobbled and then fell to its side, Tiny rose from his seat, bent down, and scooped it up.

"May I take a try at it?" Jack asked as Tiny sat down again.

There was a moment of hesitation and then the toy was handed over as Tiny said with great seriousness, "You gotta wind it just right, remember."

Jack nodded and began to wind the string. "Who sends you your rent money, Tiny?" he asked as he worked.

"The man with the wrinkly nose."

"Is he the same man who sends the letters with the pennies inside?"

"I dunno. You're getting the string wrong, Jack. You gotta start all over again now."

"All right," Jack said, pulling the string off and beginning anew. "So, tell me, Tiny . . . Have you gotten any of the letters with the pennies inside lately?"

"I got one when Mrs. O'Brien broke her toe on her sideboard."

"Was that in the last couple of days?"

"Nah, longer than that. She's walking with just a little limp now."

Timing-wise, it sounded as though Mrs. O'Brien had broken her toe around the time the original offer on the St. Louis property had been made. At any rate, the fact that Tiny hadn't gotten one in the last day or so said that the reply to Percival Little's offer hadn't yet arrived. "Do you suppose I could wait here with you and watch you do your job?"

"The mailman doesn't bring the pennies all the time, Jack," Tiny pointed out rather sadly. He brightened, however, to add, "But you could see me get my rent money. It comes every week."

"Well, that would be interesting to see, too," Jack admitted, knowing that whoever was sending Tiny rent money was the same person posing as Little, Bates and Company. "Would you mind if I brought a friend of mine along? She's very nice."

"Is she your *girlfriend*, Jack?"

Tiny clearly thought the possibility of such a relationship was both very special and bordering on forbidden. Which, now that Jack thought about it, pretty accurately summed up his relationship with Billy's youngest daughter. "Well, I guess she is in a way. Her name's Lindsay."

"Does Lindsay know how to play hopscotch?"

"I'm sure she does."

"I can draw the boxes, but I don't know how to put the writing inside them. Do you think she knows how to do that?"

"Yep. And I'll bet she'd be happy to teach you how." Knowing Lindsay, she'd try to teach him letters as well.

Tiny nodded, but his attention was fully on the toy in Jack's hands. "Jack, you're terrible at winding the string," he said, gently taking it all away from him "Maybe you should watch me do it again."

"I think you're right," Jack agreed, settling in and watching Tiny carefully undo all the wrapping he had accomplished.

"Is Lindsay pretty?"

"She's beautiful. She has blonde hair and big blue eyes." Jack paused as he understood that there was a much deeper truth to be shared. "But you know what, Tiny? It isn't how a person looks that matters. It's what's inside them that counts. Lindsay is a good person who cares about people. You'll like her."

"Do you think she'll like me?"

"Oh, yeah. She'll like you a lot, Tiny. She'll probably want to take you home with her."

"I can't go. I have my job. It's important."

"It is indeed," Jack assured him. "And I'm sure she'll understand that." *In a million years.*

"Her feelings won't be hurt, will they? I don't like hurting people's feelings."

"She'll be fine, Tiny." *She'll just worry about you for the rest of her life.*

"Good. Wanna see me throw this again?"

"Fire away," Jack replied, wondering what kind of work Lindsay was going to find in her household for this simple and needy soul. By the time the toy toppled over, he'd decided that the odds were good that Mrs. Beechum was going to end up with a dutiful, devoted, hulking assistant.

The sun was beginning to set when Mrs. O'Brien came to the front door of her house and told Tiny that it was time for him to come in and wash his hands for supper. Tiny had introduced Jack to his landlady as his 'new friend,' and Jack had understood the suspicious look in her eyes. After Tiny had twisted past her and gone to do as he was told, Jack had assured the woman that he had no intentions of harming or using the young man. Mrs. O'Brien hadn't believed him. And he couldn't blame her.

She'd closed the door on him and he'd slowly walked away, knowing that if it all turned out as he thought it would, everyone was going to be hurt. Because everyone had been used—and used for years. Especially Lindsay. She'd only thought her world had been upended the day he'd walked into her life. When the game finally came to an end and all the dust settled, she was going to be not only impoverished, but deeply and forever wounded by the blackness of the betrayal. The way she looked at the world was never going to be the same again.

Something deep inside him twisted painfully. With the sensation came a sudden and desperate need to get back to the hotel room, back to Lindsay. He lengthened his stride, covering ground quickly and knowing that he was acting on pure instinct, that he was about to cross a line and that he should care, but didn't.

A WHISPER ACROSS HER LIPS drew her gently from the edge of sleep. It came again, lingering longer, soft and warm. *Jack*. She smiled, contented, and opened her eyes to find him lying on his side beside her, his head propped in his hand, his eyes bright and his smile roguish. Was there a more handsome man on earth? She must have done something very, very good in her life to have earned his attentions.

"Anyone ever tell you how delicious you look when you're sleeping?" he asked.

"Not that I can recall," she answered, her pulse racing, her heart hammering with hope. She didn't know what had happened to bring him to her bed and she wasn't going to ask. He was there and that was all that mattered. In that instant she knew that she'd been a dithering fool to ever doubt the rightness of courting Jack's advances.

His gaze holding hers, he lifted his free hand and trailed a fingertip over her lower lip. Then, slowly, deliberately, he drew a line downward, over her chin and along the length of her throat, saying softly, "Then I don't suppose they've ever told you how good you taste, either, huh?"

"No, they haven't," Lindsay replied, her breath catching as Jack trailed his finger lower, into the valley between her breasts.

"Let's keep it our secret," he suggested, his voice husky, his finger gently hooking the edge of her dressing gown and slowly drawing it back to bare her breast.

"Selfish man," she managed to say, anticipation surging through her.

His smile quirked and he winked. "Yep," he whispered in agreement, leaning forward and down.

Lindsay gasped as his mouth closed over the peak of her breast. An exquisite bolt of sensation arrowed into the core of her and set her body wondrously afire, delightfully free. Threading her fingers through the hair at his nape, she arched up to meet his tongue's caress and moaned in delight when he deepened his possession. Sensation came upon sensation, each flitting ever so briefly across her awareness—the feel of silk sliding over her other breast, the warmth of Jack's hand as he cupped her and traced his thumb across the nubbed peak, the heat and strength of his body pressed close to hers.

With a long, slow pull, he released his claim to her breast. Lindsay softly sighed in regret and sank back into the mattress. His hands on either side of her shoulders, he gazed down at her, his breathing winded and his expression somber as he studied her face intently.

"What is it?" she asked, her hands slipping to his chest. His heartbeat thundered into her palms.

"I don't want you to get hurt, Lindsay," he answered softly. "I'd rather die of wanting than have you look back and think poorly of me."

"I don't think that's possible," she assured him, knowing to the center of her soul that no other man on earth would have cared as much for her feelings as he did. "I'm always going to remember Jackson Stennett as the best thing that ever happened to me."

"Are you sure? Are you sure you want to do this?"

"Yes," she answered without hesitation. He continued to search her gaze, obviously unconvinced. "Jack?" she said softly, twining her arms around his neck. She waited until he cocked a brow in silent question before saying, "I'm sorry."

His brows knitted. "For what?"

"Nothing," she answered, smiling up at him. "I'm just terribly, *terribly* sorry."

He blinked and then a slow smile spread across his features. His eyes sparkled with devilment. "You've asked for it, Lindsay MacPhaull."

"Oh, indeed I have. Am I going to get it?"

Jackson gave her a quick kiss, then winked and rolled off the bed and onto his feet.

CHAPTER TWENTY

LINDSAY, HER JAW SLACK IN DISBELIEF, watched him go. "But..." she sputtered, as disappointment niggled at her hopes.

"But what? I kissed you," he said blithely, pulling his shirt from the waistband of his trousers, his expression innocent.

Too innocent, she realized in utter and happy relief. "Yes, you did. But not the way I had in mind," she declared, pushing back the bedcoverings and climbing out after him.

"Oh?" He undid a cuff button and then made a production out of inspecting the buttonhole. He tried and failed at containing a smile as he observed, "It seems to me that if a woman has an expectation, she's more likely to have it met if she's willing to share it with a fella."

Her heart racing, Lindsay nodded serenely, took the ends of her wrapper sash in hand, and pulled. Jack froze as the gown fell open, stopping breathing as it puddled on the floor at her feet. He didn't move his head, but slid his gaze up to meet hers.

With a quirked smile and twinkling eyes, he drawled, "A mite too warm, were you?"

She grinned, her spirit light and soaring free as she stepped in front of him, her nearness forcing him to abandon his shirt cuff and straighten his stance. "More a case, I think, of being overdressed for the occasion."

"And what occasion would that be?" he asked.

"Making love to you," she answered, undoing the top button on his shirt, her pulse thrumming in her fingertips, all along the length of her body. It was so different with Jack, she realized. She wasn't consciously thinking of what she had long ago been instructed to do, what she should say and how she should say it. With Jack, it all came so naturally, so instinctively. Her heart raced with anticipation, not dread. She wanted the seduction to last forever because it was so wonderfully heady and ripe and delicious, not because she wanted to avoid lying beneath him. That, she knew in her heart, would be different, too. She'd found only disappointment and humiliation the one and only time she'd traveled this path before. This time, with Jack, she was going to be richly rewarded, luxuriously pleasured. She knew it to the center of her soul. This was right, the way it should be.

Jackson stood in awed silence, his senses feasting on the glorious woman before him. Golden hair tumbled across her shoulders to lie in soft curls on her breasts. The faint scent of roses drifted to him, beckoning him to step closer. Lindsay was luscious curves and white satin skin that begged to be touched and tasted and adored. And she was so much more. The look of bold and daring anticipation in her eyes as she undid his shirt . . .

Sweet Jesus. And Charles Martens had walked away from this? The man was either a goddamn fool or just flat-out unnatural. Jack couldn't have walked away if he'd tried. The hotel would have to be on fire before he'd even consider letting her get away from him. And even then, it would only be for as long as it took him to find them another room in another hotel. How the hell had he resisted the temptation to this point? And why had he tried? He'd wasted a lot of precious time and denied them both a great deal of pleasure; a sin, he decided, for which he needed to start atoning.

"Mind if I touch?" he asked, placing his hands on her waist.

"Not at all," she said, her voice husky, her eyes darkening. "I was rather hoping that you would."

Her hands continued to move down the front of his shirt, her fingers blindly, nimbly slipping the buttons free. Her gaze remained locked with his, and in the depths of her eyes he saw the smoldering embers of desire and that unmistakable spark of daring. He slowly moved his hands back and down, caressing the warm satin curves of her. He gently cupped her, the pads of his thumbs stroking lightly over her heated skin. He felt and heard her breath catch.

Leaning down, he brushed a feathery kiss across her temple, not trusting himself to take a more intimate taste of her just yet. The seduction was hers to manage for the moment, his to savor and enjoy. Her fingers faltered at their task and her eyes drifted closed as her lips parted to emit a soft sigh. Then, with a deep, languid quiver she collected herself and opened the first button on his trousers, her eyes still closed, a smile shadowing the corners of her mouth. Jackson felt the heat in his loins sharpen and knew that he was rapidly approaching the point when he couldn't bear the slow seduction any longer. He wanted Lindsay, wanted to make love to her with an intensity that he'd never wanted any woman before.

The last of his buttons was undone. Even as he contemplated stepping back and divesting himself of his trousers, Lindsay took the task upon herself. Her hands slipped beneath the fabric, and with warm and gentle certainty, she smoothed them down his hips and over his thighs. There was only the vaguest awareness of them landing around his bare ankles; Lindsay's touch obliterated everything beyond her. Her hands slid back and down, to hold him as he was holding her, to intoxicate his senses and unravel his sense of control.

Conscious thought staggered through the swirl of sensations. His shirt. He had to be rid of it. He wanted to feel her breasts against his chest, the heat of skin against skin.

As much as he didn't want to, he was going to have to release her for just a moment, for just as long as it took to shed the damn thing.

"My shirt," he managed to get past the lump in his throat as he eased his arms from around her and took a half-step back. His movement drew her hands forward onto his hips, the friction so exquisite that he couldn't help but shudder in pleasure.

Lindsay waited, deliberately biding her time until he had the shirt worked down to his elbows. When he had effectively pinned himself, she slipped her hands down the sides of his thighs, and then slowly brought them up the fronts, her fingertips stroking the corded muscles beneath his heated skin. He stopped moving, stopped breathing as his eyes widened and filled with unspoken hope. She paused and waited until he forced himself to swallow and resume the effort to both breathe and remove his shirt.

With smooth and confident certainty, she trailed her fingers higher. The light in his eyes flared with barely bridled passion; his smile dared her to continue. Reaching his hipbones, she traced the angle of them downward and this time when he froze, she didn't give him a respite. She traced the hardened length of him with all of her fingertips; once, twice, three times. He swayed on his feet, his shirt forgotten as he closed his eyes and softly moaned. Only then did she take him fully into her hands.

The throbbing heat and the velvet strength of his arousal flooded over her in a molten, undeniable hunger she had never felt before. Her mind reeled and she abandoned the effort to think, surrendering herself to the heady waves of feeling and the primal desire dancing deep inside her. She leaned forward and pressed a kiss into the center of his chest. His heart hammered against her lips and his manhood surged against her palms, inviting her closer.

He was dying. Dying by magnificently torturous degrees of the most exquisite pleasure he'd ever known. He groaned in acceptance of his wondrous fate, submitting, his senses thrilling wildly as Lindsay slowly, boldly laid a path of searing kisses down his chest, to his abdomen, and then lower still. His heart stopped and his knees went weak.

He reached for her shoulders to steady himself, desperately needing to touch her, to thread his fingers through her hair, to thank her for the incredible wonder of her gift. He gasped in realization that his shirt pinned his arms to his sides and suddenly his patience, his willingness to passively endure was gone. With a snarl, he tore free of his bonds and when he'd flung them away, he reached down, took Lindsay's upper arms firmly, gently in his hands, and drew her up the length of him.

"Sweet siren," he whispered, lowering his mouth to hers. He devoured her, his hunger so urgent that it defied control. She melted into him, heated satin, soft curves, and wild abandon, the passion of her kisses every bit the equal of his own, their demand beyond his power to resist.

He had to have her, and have her *now*. No more waiting, no more slow seduction. He couldn't endure another second of it. Kissing her deeply and hard, he slipped his hands lower behind her, cupped her, and lifted her up. She moaned in breathless sanction, brought her legs around his hips, and twined her arms tightly around his shoulders.

Guided by ageless instincts, they found each other, both gasping and shuddering at the heated perfection of their union, each clinging to the other, their kisses suddenly quick and breathless, a staccato accompaniment to the pulsing rhythm of their timeless dance.

Sheathed in her haven, Jackson nibbled a course down the slim column of her throat, his hunger building, his need for release tightening with every beat of her heart. He turned and leaned down, laying her on the bed with all the care he could, the depth of his possession easing as he did. She whimpered in protest and arched up, drawing him back, deeper than he'd yet touched her. God help him, there was no holding back, no slowing to love her sweetly and gently.

Lindsay arched into his embrace, threading the silken strands of his hair through her fingers as he suckled her breast and filled her body with his own, sending her senses on a dizzyingly swift upward spiral. She strained to ride the crest, softly crying in wonder as he took her higher still and the anticipation deep within her belly gathered tightly into itself. And then, just as she feared she couldn't reach any higher, Jack whispered her name and filled her completely, shattering the tension within her. She was cast, gasping and astonished, into the oblivion of heavenly stars even as her bones melted in a deep pool of fiery sweet satisfaction.

The fading shudders of her completion drew his senses back from the sated realm of his own attainment. He reveled in them, in the incredible sense of happiness that settled over him in their wake. She lay beneath him, her hair a golden fan around her head, her eyes closed, a small smile touching the corners of her parted lips. Her breasts, passion-hued, hard-budded, and taut, rose and fell in a cadence that was as winded as his own.

"Lindsay?" he murmured softly, brushing the back of his hand over her cheek. "Are you all right, sweetheart? Did I hurt you?"

"No, Jack," she answered dreamily, turning her head and kissing the back of his hand. "Nothing hurts. All I can feel is warm and wonderful." Her legs slipped slowly down the length of his as she sighed long and with apparently deep contentment.

"We'll go at it more slowly next time," he vowed, lying down beside her and gathering her into his arms. "I'll love you gently. I promise."

Her head pillowed on his shoulder, she snuggled close to his side and laid an arm across him. "Any way you want to love me is fine, Jack. It doesn't have to be gentle."

Jackson closed his eyes and breathed deep the faint scent of roses and their loving. He did want to love her gently. And hard and quick, too, like they'd just made love. And he wanted to give her all the variations of tempo and passion that fell between those two. He wanted to make love to her all day, all night, for as long as he could be with her. He pressed a kiss to the top of her head and trailed his hand down the sweep of her side, stopping to caress the swell of her perfectly rounded hip. Everything about Lindsay was perfect. They fit together as though they'd been made for each other, only each other. It was going to be hell leaving her behind when he went home. *Maybe . . .* He resolutely closed away the budding thought. She wouldn't go and he couldn't stay. Some things were meant to be and some weren't. He'd learned enough in life to know the difference, to know that trying to make the impossible possible always ended in failure.

Lindsay stirred in his arms and turned her head up to smile at him. She threaded her fingers through the mat of curls on his chest.

"Do I want to know what's going on it that pretty little head of yours?" he asked.

Her smile slowly widened and her eyes sparkled with mischief. "I'm thinking that I may have some difficulty in maintaining celibacy after all. It would seem that there's a great deal to recommend bedding a man that I didn't know about."

The thought of her taking a lover other than him clenched his gut. But it would be her prerogative to do so once he left her, he quickly reminded himself. The admonishment assuaged his feelings only slightly. "Would it help to know that it wouldn't be as good with anyone else?" he offered, only half teasingly.

"My," she said, laughing as she pushed herself up to rest her weight on her elbow and smile down at him, "don't we have a high opinion of ourselves."

"I figure there's no point in false modesty," he drawled. "You know the truth."

"Well, thank you for being willing to share your *greatness* with me."

"You're welcome," he said, slipping his arms around her and hugging her close. "And I'd be happy to share my greatness with you again, any time you want."

Arching a brow, she kissed him lingeringly, then drew back to ask, "How about now?"

The spirit was sure willing, but . . . "I'm not eighteen anymore, sweetheart," he admitted ruefully. "Could you give me just a few more minutes?"

"If I must," she agreed, chuckling as she eased down to rest her head on his shoulder again.

"I promise that you won't feel neglected in the meantime." To prove that he was a man of his word, he cupped her breast in his hand and gently massaged her nipple with the pad of his thumb. It hardened instantly and she made a purring sound deep in her throat.

"Like that, do you?" he asked, grinning and doing it again.

"Well enough," she replied, "that if you expect a few minutes before I demand another performance from you, you should probably stop."

He did, but reluctantly. He held her close, pressing kisses into her hair and listening, feeling, the steady beat of her heart.

"So, are you going to tell me what you did today while I was sleeping?" she asked after a long moment.

"I met a young man," Jack supplied, nuzzling his cheek into her hair. "His name is Tiny and he's simple. I told him that you'd be glad to teach him how to make the numbers inside the hopscotch squares."

"Oh," she whispered, her voice filled with understanding and compassion. "Of course I will."

Jackson smiled at her response, pleased that he'd so accurately predicted it. "Tiny's the Boston end of the game, Lindsay," he went on. "His job is to sit on the steps of his boarding house—which happens, by the way, to be at the address of Little, Bates and Company—and wait for the mail. Every day, all day. He gets rent money weekly and every once in a while he gets a special piece of correspondence. Two pennies and an outgoing letter are inside. He hands both right back to the carrier, and Tiny's job is done."

Lindsay clearly saw the thread and the pattern it made. But there was something about lying in Jack's arms that made it all seem so inconsequential, so beyond her real concern. "The outgoing letter was written in New York and sent here so that it could be postmarked Boston and look genuine."

"Yep. And with it actually moving between the two cities, the timing is always right. No too-quick replies that might lead to suspicions and questions. You've got to admit that it's a good plan."

She shifted her position, turning and half rising. Placing her hands one atop the other on Jackson's chest, she propped her chin on them and met his gaze to ask, "Do you suppose there's a simple soul in each of the four cities?"

"It would be my guess," he replied, slipping his arms around her. "Tiny can't read and he isn't complicated enough to even think of asking questions about what he's doing. He's the perfect accomplice. Whoever set it up did so years ago and through his mother. Tiny doesn't know anything about his employer beyond the fact that he wrinkled his nose the whole time he was talking to Tiny's mother."

"I don't see that there's any point in trying to get our hands on the return piece of mail," she mused aloud, acutely aware that Jack's hands were beginning to wander down the curves of her hips. Her heartbeat quickened in response and it took considerable concentration to hold the thought she'd formed before he'd set about distracting her. "It'll be delivered to us in New York anyway. We know what Percival Little's handwriting looks like already and it's not one I've recognized as anyone else's. It hasn't changed one bit in all the years I've been involved with the business, Jack. And it doesn't bear any resemblance to the correspondence from the other three companies, either. Each is distinctly different."

"Which means," he drawled, his hands moving up her back, "there are probably four people in New York who are paid to write those letters for whoever's behind the scheme."

"But who are they?"

He threaded his fingers through her hair and drawled, "Well, we know that the packet containing the two cents and the return mail was probably sent by Otis Vanderhagen."

"I forgot to tell you," Lindsay said, trying to keep her wits about her as his fingers sent ripples of pleasure down the length of her body. "He stopped by the house to visit Richard the morning I was leaving. He asked me to tell you that he'd seen nothing amiss in your letter."

"Then we wait with Tiny and see if it goes as it always has." He let strands of hair slip through his fingers, his gaze riveted on the falling curtain of gold. "If it does, then we go back and ask ol' Otis some tough questions. One of which will be who's actually writing the letters."

"But it's clearly not Richard who's involved in this."

His gaze came to hers, somber and considering. "I'm not ready to apologize just yet, sweetheart. I haven't heard Vanderhagen's explanation and I can't quite believe that Richard Patterson didn't know what was going on."

"If I didn't, how could you expect Richard to have known?" she pressed gently.

"I just think he did. I can feel it in my gut." He put his hands on her waist, lifted his head to give her a consoling kiss, and then dropped his head back into the bedding to add, "Speaking of which, mine's real empty. Let's go downstairs and see if they know anything about beef in Boston. I'll shave and find a fresh shirt while you get dressed. What do you say?"

She didn't say anything. Instead, she slid her leg across his and pushed herself up so that she straddled his hips. His smile quirked and his hands came up to cup her breasts.

"Then again, maybe the food can wait for a while," he suggested, his eyes bright, his thumbs teasing her as she leaned down to kiss him.

LINDSAY KNEW IT WAS ONLY A DREAM. *She serenely watched herself cross the foyer of MacPhaull House and enter the study. Everyone was there, waiting for her. Proctor had torn out the hearthstones and was planting peonies in the hole in the flooring, muttering all the while about the poor condition of the soil. Primrose and Emile were plucking squawking chickens over by the sideboard, while heatedly arguing over whether there should be apricots or chestnuts in the stuffing. A huge tabby cat perched atop the bookshelves, his tail flicking furiously, his attention fixed on the chickens. Mrs. Kowalski stood below him waving a fish and shouting at him in Polish. Or maybe it was German. Lindsay couldn't tell. Havers sat in a corner wearing a paisley turban, selecting chocolates from a box and pushing his finger into the bottoms of them before either putting them back or popping them into his mouth. John, his arm in a sling and useless, was trying to put a horse into its harness, but the animal kept ducking its head away and trying to back out the door that led into the dining room. Abigail Beechum was, with her one arm, trying to come through the same doorway while carrying a giant tray laden with a dozen teapots and cups and saucers stacked fifteen high.*

Lindsay started forward to help her, but suddenly Agatha stepped into her path. She held out an open jewelry box, stamped her foot, and demanded that Lindsay fill it. Henry pushed their sister aside to wave a set of drawings in her face, yelling that she was going to see that he wasn't embarrassed to entertain in his own home. She stared at them, knowing that she should tell them to go away, but unable to make any words come out of her mouth.

And then, from out of nowhere, Jeb and Lucy walked between her and her siblings, clearly oblivious to all that was going on around them. They were speaking softly, alternately cooing down at their baby in Lucy's arms and looking at each other adoringly. The baby was wrapped in the blanket Lindsay had made for it; the shawl covered Lucy's shoulders. Lindsay watched them leave the room and started after them, wanting to ask them how she could be happy and oblivious, too.

It was Richard who stepped into her path this time. His body whole and sound, he thrust a packet of papers into her hands and told her that she had more important things to do than help a crippled woman with a tea tray or yearn for the mind-dulling slavery of wifery and motherhood. She had responsibilities to fulfill, a business to learn and ably run. There was correspondence that needed to be answered, decisions that had to be made right that minute. Ben stood at his elbow, clutching a ledger and an inkwell. A half-dozen quill pens were tucked behind his ears and he told her that he needed to go over the monthly summaries with her before he went home for the night. She nodded and looked around, searching the chaos for Otis Vanderhagen, knowing that he had to be there. She found him, finally, sitting on the floor under the desk and counting coins into big cloth sacks labeled TINY, LITTLE, BATES. *His lips moved, but he made no sound. Neither did the coins as they fell from his fingers and into the bags. She watched him, puzzled as* to how that could be. Richard's voice droned on, his litany of tasks unending.

And then the sound of her mother's derisive laughter came from a far corner, startling her into dropping the papers Richard had given her. She whirled around amidst the swirling sheets of white to find her mother standing beside a huge potted fern, a sherry glass in her hand, and dressed in a wedding gown of ivory lace. Her mother laughed again and told Richard that Lindsay couldn't do anything right and that he was wasting his time with trying to make something even halfway competent out of her. Lindsay was hopeless, she announced before tossing the sherry down her throat. Someone who knew what they were doing would have to marry Charles Martens and, since Lindsay had failed so miserably at seducing him, she'd have to sacrifice herself to see that the MacPhaull fortune was secured for their children.

At the edge of her vision, Lindsay saw a shadowy figure move in the doorway leading to the foyer. Dread filled her even as she turned to face the next assault on her mind and feelings. But it wasn't Charles Martens who stood there. It was Jackson Stennett, dressed as he'd been the day he'd walked into her life.

Relief washed over and she ran to him, throwing herself into his arms and thanking him for coming to save her from the insanity. He kissed her and then set her from him, his smile soft and sad.

"I have to go now, Lindsay."

"Take me with you."

"I can't. You know why."

"But I love you, Jack."

He shook his head and backed away. "You know you shouldn't have done that. Good-bye, Lindsay."

And then he was gone.

LINDSAY AWAKENED WITH A START, her heart pounding furiously and tears pooling in her eyes. Afraid that her panic would awaken Jack and lead to questions she couldn't and didn't want to answer, she eased from his embrace and slipped out of bed. With trembling hands she snatched her wrapper from the floor and pulled it on, cinching the sash tightly about her waist. Only then did she stop to consider where she was going to go. Her knees weak, she managed to make her way to the upholstered chair in the corner of the room before the images of her dream returned and battered her anew.

She buried her face in her hands and struggled to shut away her emotions, to look at the dream logically and understand why it had so deeply disturbed her. Her life was chaotic, yes; it always had been. That part of her dream hadn't contained any insights that were especially novel or meaningful. And just as common to her existence were the expectations everyone had of her—those of Agatha, Henry, Richard, Ben, and those she had routinely failed to meet of her mother.

But Jeb and Lucy . . . Her heart twisted as she remembered going after them in her dream, wanting so badly to know their secret of being happy. Did it come from being married? Lindsay wondered now. Did it come from having a family of your own creation? Was she dreaming of things she couldn't have and for which she only thought she'd abandoned hope?

Lindsay sighed and shook her head. There wasn't any chance of marriage for her. There wasn't ever going to be any family of her own creation. She looked over at the bed, at Jack sleeping so soundly in it, and knew that if ever there was a man whose children she would want to bear, it would be his. Lindsay shook her head again. Jack had suffered too much loss in his life already and she wasn't willing to put his heart at risk again. She'd taken the precautions necessary to protect the freedom of them both. There would be no child from making love with Jackson Stennett.

Not now, not ever. Because there was no "ever" with Jack. He'd walled away his heart and she understood why he had. Any sane man would have done the same thing. She couldn't ask him to let her in; it would be cruel to make him so vulnerable. She'd known all along that he wasn't going to stay, that he would go home to Texas as soon as he could. Just as she'd always known that her place was here and her responsibilities inescapable.

So why, in her dream, had she asked to go with him? It was an impossibility for both of them and she knew it. She had, at one point in her life, harbored the hope of someday marrying and having a family, but she had never held any such romantic illusions about her relationship with Jackson Stennett.

As for her dreamy declaration of loving him . . . Lindsay quietly scoffed. He was handsome and strong and honorable and protective. She enjoyed his company and his intellect. And there was no denying that making love with him made her heart race and her soul sing. But that was all there was between them. She certainly didn't love him. As he'd reminded her in the dream just before he'd walked away, she knew better.

No, she'd been upset by his leaving her in the dream because it meant that she was going to have to face the disaster and chaos of her life and sort it out on her own. She wasn't going to be able to run away from it. Jackson wasn't her knight in shining armor. He hadn't come to save her from being Lindsay MacPhaull. Her fate was her fate and the only choice she had was to accept it.

"Lindsay?"

She looked over at him and saw that he was sitting up and searching the darkness of the room for her. "I'm over here," she answered, rising from the chair and moving toward him.

"Are you all right?"

"Yes," she assured them both as she undid her sash. "I'm fine, Jack."

"What are you doing up?"

She let the wrapper slide away as she climbed back into the bed, saying, "I had a bad dream. It didn't mean anything and I'm all right now."

"Are you sure?" he asked, gathering her into his arms and easing them down into the softness of the mattress.

Her head cradled in the curve of his shoulder, her shoulders wrapped in the safe circle of his embrace, Lindsay draped her arm over his chest and nodded.

CHAPTER TWENTY-ONE

$\mathcal{L}$INDSAY STOOD BESIDE TINY and watched Jack start down the hopscotch pattern. The last two days had been the best of her entire life. The daylight hours had been filled with laughter and children's games—spinning tops and hopscotch and Cat's Cradle, the nights with making love with Jack. She almost hoped that the mail would never come and that she and Jack could exist forever in the simple world they'd found for themselves.

She watched Jack balance on one foot as he prepared to lean down to scoop up the pebble. He was the most phenomenal man; intelligent and strong, kind and gentle, passionate and daring. Lindsay smiled. It was amazing to think of how deeply she'd resented him at first. Now . . . Her smile faltered. She was going to miss him terribly when he went back to Texas.

"You put your foot down! I saw it!" Tiny declared happily, hopping up and down and pointing.

Lindsay put away her sad thoughts and smiled. "You have to start over again." Jack gave her a grin and a wink as he threw his arms up in the air and huffed as though greatly frustrated. Lindsay laughed and handed Tiny a bit of chalk, saying, "I think the numbers are getting blurry, don't you?"

"I'll make them again!" the young man announced, starting forward. "I can do that!"

Jack came to stand behind her, slipping his arms around her waist and drawing her close against him. "You're a wonder, you know that?" he whispered as, together, they watched Tiny carefully trace the numbers.

"He wants to learn. It makes all the difference in the world," she answered softly. "What's going to happen to him when the game ends, Jack?"

"We'll think of something," he promised, kissing the top of her head. "He won't go without a roof or food or clothes."

Such a good man. "Thank you."

Tiny looked up from his task and his eyes twinkled with merriment. In a singsong, he said, "Jack has a girl-friend."

"Yep. I'm a lucky man, Tiny."

"Is Lindsay going to have your babies?"

She felt Jack's heart lurch, felt him check the impulse to let go of her and step away. Tears swelled her throat. Before they could overwhelm her, she hastily forced a chuckle and answered, "No, Tiny. I'm not. Jack and I aren't married."

The young man tilted his head to study them. "Are you going to get married?"

"No," she replied as Jack slowly released her. *Tell the truth, Linds,* she silently admonished. *For Jack as well as Tiny.* "Jack has to go back to Texas and I can't go with him."

"That's sad."

"Are you going to finish with those numbers, Tiny?" Jack asked, walking—ever so casually—away.

"Yes." Tiny didn't move. "Why can't you go with him?"

So many reasons, Tiny. The roads we've both traveled to become who we are. "I have a job," she answered, fighting to smile serenely as she gave him the simplest of the truths. "It's important, just like yours is. I can't leave it."

"Oh." He nodded and stared down at his feet for a

moment. Looking up at her again, he added, "But it's still sad."

Jack inserted himself into the conversation, saying with flinty coolness, "Sad things happen to people, Tiny. We survive and go on."

Tiny's gaze went to him, puzzled. And then his attention shifted to the walkway and his face instantly brightened. "Look! It's Zachary!" He waved and called, "Hi, Zachary! Hi! Did you bring me my mail?"

Her knees suddenly weak and her heart heavy with dread, Lindsay eased down on the step and watched the letter carrier make his way down the walk.

"Who are your friends, Tiny?" the man asked, looking past the bouncing bulk of Tiny to eye the two of them suspiciously.

"This is Jack," Tiny announced proudly, pointing. "And this is Lindsay. She's my friend, too. But not my girlfriend. She's Jack's girlfriend. She taught me to make hopscotch numbers." With a flourish he indicated the game scratched on the walk. "See?"

To his everlasting credit, the carrier stepped closer and made an interested inspection of the game grid. "Very nicely done, Tiny. Maybe someday you can work at the post office."

Tiny sucked a deep gasp of awed consideration. "Really? I would like that."

Nodding, Zachary handed him two packets.

"Look, Jack! Look, Lindsay!" Tiny exclaimed, whirling around, the packets tightly gripped in both hands. "I got *two* mails!" He quickly dropped down beside Lindsay on the steps, saying with sudden solemnity, "Watch how I do this. It's important."

"We're watching," Jack drawled from his spot on the walk.

"No," Tiny protested, looking up at him and shaking his head. "You got to sit down on the steps with me so you can see."

With a shrug and a good-humored smile, Jack obeyed the command.

"Here, Jack. Hold this for me," Tiny said, thrusting the

smaller of the two packets into his hands. "And don't let anything happen to it, either. It's my rent money."

"I'll guard it with my life."

"Now, I open this letter and see," Tiny said, leaning close to Lindsay so she could see him tearing the seal. "Inside there's another one." He pulled it out and handed it to her as he looked and reached inside, adding, "And the two pennies."

Lindsay looked at the packet he'd given her. It was addressed to herself at the MacPhaull Company offices.

Tiny took if from her hands, quickly showed it to Jack, and then rose to his feet saying, "Then I get up and I give the letter to Zachary. See?"

Jack nodded slowly. "Yep, we see."

"Well done as always, Tiny," Zachary said, giving him a sharp salute. He turned away, adding, "See you next week."

"Wait, Zachary!" Tiny called after him, clearly panicked. "I have to give you the two pennies from the other letter."

The carrier turned and walking backward, said, "Keep them for yourself. Go buy some peppermints or licorice."

Again Tiny gasped in awe. Then he waved and yelled, "Thank you! 'Bye, Zachary! 'Bye!"

Lindsay smiled, finding comfort in the kindness Zachary displayed toward Tiny, and in the knowledge that the young man wasn't all alone in world, that there were people who would watch out for him. The touch on the shoulder came lightly and quick. She turned to find Jack holding out the packet Tiny claimed held his rent money. She didn't note the address; she couldn't see anything beyond the elegant and very familiar penmanship. Her heart twisted and her eyes filled with tears.

Jack watched the color drain out of her face and felt his stomach knot. As tears gathered in her eyes, Tiny turned and said, "Zachary's nice to me. He's my friend, too."

"He is indeed," Jack numbly agreed, his gaze never leaving Lindsay's grief-stricken face. "Here's your rent money," he said, handing over the packet. "Better take it straight in to Mrs. O'Brien."

"See, Lindsay?" he said, flashing the packet in her direction before dashing up the steps. "My rent money came just like I said it would. I'll be right back."

The front door was slamming closed behind him when Jack softly asked, "Who's handwriting is it, Lindsay?"

She wrapped her arms tightly around her midsection. Tears spilled over her lashes as she rocked forward and back and sobbed out, "Abigail's."

His chest tightened. "Oh, Jesus." The one person in the world that Lindsay relied on, the one person she'd trusted all her life. Aching for her, he slid across the step and wrapped his arms around her shoulders. Drawing her to him, he whispered, "Cry all you want, sweetheart. I understand."

She fisted his lapels, burying her face in his chest, and in that instant he understood far more than the pain she felt at discovering Abigail Beechum's involvement. He'd chosen to be alone, had found his comfort in the isolation of his heart and his daily existence. Lindsay was alone, not because she wanted to be, but because everyone in the course of her life had either used, abused, or abandoned her. She deserved better. The unfairness of it made his throat burn and swell.

For Tiny's two cents, he'd pack her up and take her to Texas with him. She could live at Billy's place, and while their passion was likely to fade over time, at least she'd still have a friend she could trust, a friend she could talk to. It wasn't ideal, but it was a helluva lot better than what she had here. There'd be money for her, too. Half the ranch he owned had been her father's; it was only right that she take some of the profits. Besides, he wouldn't have any of it without her help in getting the money to pay the debts and clear the title.

But, now that he thought about it, it wasn't likely that she'd be a spinster living in her daddy's house for long. Just because he didn't want to complicate his life and risk his heart again didn't mean that there weren't men who were willing to do that. Hell, Texas was full of men who could appreciate an intelligent and beautiful woman. There'd be a line ten miles long to court her and it'd start forming the minute she put her dainty foot on the dock at Galveston. She could have her pick of the bunch and he'd make sure only the best got into the line. Lindsay could have a family of her own and she'd get the life she deserved. She'd be happy. He'd be happy. And her husband would be over the moon ecstatic with his good fortune and live every moment of his life only to see that Lindsay never wanted for anything. If he didn't, then he'd have to face Jackson Stennett's two-fisted wrath.

Of course, he had to figure out how to get Lindsay to leave New York in the first place. Just explaining his plan wouldn't do it. She'd claim that she needed to stay to take care of Henry and Agatha. She'd explain how she couldn't leave the business and how she couldn't just dismiss her household staff and—

"Why is Lindsay crying?"

Jack started and hugged her hard before he looked up at Tiny. "She's sad because we have to go home now."

"Will you come back and play with me tomorrow?"

God, he wished he could say "yes." He wished it with all his heart. The last two days had been wonderfully simple and pure and easy.

"No, Tiny," Lindsay said, taking a shuddering breath and gently extracting herself from his embrace. Wiping away her tears with the palms of her hands, she explained, "I wish we could, but we can't. We can't come back again. Our home is a long way away." She smiled up at the simple soul. "But we'll write you letters all the time."

"And I'll send you a new top, too," Jack added.

Again, Tiny gasped in awe and appreciation. "Thank you, Jack!"

"Thank you for letting us watch you do your job," Lindsay managed to say, before she choked on a fresh wave of tears.

Dear, sweet, mothering Lindsay. Jack put his arm around her shoulders and gently drew her down the walk, determined for her sake to end the parting as quickly as he could. " 'Bye, Tiny," he called. "Be good!"

" 'Bye, Jack! 'Bye, Lindsay!" Tiny merrily called after them. "Thank you for showing me how to make hopscotch numbers!"

SHE'D STOPPED CRYING about halfway back to the hotel, but Jackson couldn't help thinking that he'd rather face her tears than the deep silence into which she'd fallen. He stood just inside her room, studying her as she stared blankly out the window.

"He'll be all right, Lindsay," he ventured softly, trying yet again to comfort her. "He has Mrs. O'Brien to make sure he has a roof and food and clothing. Zachary seems the sort to watch out for him, too."

"I know. You're right."

"And I'm sure there's some logical explanation for why Mrs. Beechum's the one sending him the rent money every week," he offered, grasping at the only other straw he could think of. "All we'll have to do is ask and she'll tell us and it will make perfect sense. We'll discover that she doesn't know anything about the second packet with the return letter inside."

"That would be nice."

She clearly didn't believe in the possibility any more than he did. Damnation. He hated seeing her so despondent. God knew she had reason enough to wallow in misery for the next month, but he just couldn't bear to see her unhappy. He needed to distract her somehow, give her something to think about other than leaving Tiny behind and Mrs. Beechum's apparent betrayal.

He could nibble his way down her neck and lead her to bed. Maybe. Then again, maybe not. It rankled to think that she might go just to appease him. Better to thoroughly distract her first, and *then* take her to bed. Icing on the cake. And Lindsay was, without a doubt and bar none, the best cake he'd ever tasted.

Jackson smiled weakly, knowing that she'd have his gizzard if he ever had the sorry misjudgment to tell her that he considered her as something to be served up on a plate. He wanted to distract her, yes, but making her blazing mad didn't seem the way to go about it. There had to be a safer, more productive course.

He considered telling her about his idea of her going to live in Billy's house in Texas and finding herself a husband. Somehow, though, he suspected that she was so miserable that she wouldn't be willing to look at happier possibilities. Given that, she'd likely dismiss the idea out of hand and he'd get nowhere with it. It would be smarter to save it for another time so it'd have a better chance of being seriously considered.

He raked his fingers through his hair. What could they talk about or do that would draw her out of the dark shadows? Business was always a good bet with Lindsay. It was nice and safe and the puzzles of it always fascinated her. Was there anything they needed to talk about? The division of the remaining MacPhaull properties came to mind. Another possibility bolted into his awareness and he instantly saw both the need and potential in it.

"I'll be back in just a minute," he said, turning on his heel. "I need to get something from my bag."

Lindsay watched his reflection in the glass and when he'd gone, she blinked back another wave of tears. He was trying so hard to cheer her and she felt awful for being so inconsolable. And that was just one more brick on the load weighting her shoulders. Jack had accepted the possibility of thievery days ago, but while she'd been willing to entertain the idea on an intellectual level, she hadn't really believed it was possible. She'd held out hope. That hope had been mortally wounded the moment Tiny had produced the packet addressed to her. There *was* a plot to strip the company of assets and she couldn't deny it. Someone had betrayed her trust.

And then to recognize Abigail Beechum's handwriting on the packet containing Tiny's rent money, and to know that the woman who had been like a mother to her for as long as she could remember . . . Lindsay blinked back tears and squared her shoulders. She'd cried enough. Tears didn't accomplish anything. She needed to think, needed to understand the workings of the whole mess. Unless she could, there was no hope of finding a way out of it.

Ben and Otis Vanderhagen had been involved in the correspondence. Jack already suspected the attorney's involvement in the scheme. But Ben . . . Lindsay's stomach grew leaden. He was loyal to a fault. Or so she had always thought. She'd believed the same thing about Abigail and been proven wrong. It was entirely possible she'd misjudged Ben as well. Was she truly that blind and trusting? Was she truly that alone and friendless in the world? Was everyone laughing behind her back?

Everyone except Jackson Stennett, she told herself. But the hope in that thought was tempered by the memory of how he'd flinched and walked away from her when Tiny had asked his questions about babies and marriage. What she had with Jack went no deeper than a mutual respect and the physical pleasure they found in each other. And it would come to an end the day Jackson went back to Texas. She'd known that from the very beginning. Despite that, Jack's distancing had hurt. It had reminded her that she wasn't worth the risk of his heart. She wasn't worth the risk to anyone's heart. Her only value rested in the properties that could be stolen from her.

Tears welled in her eyes again, but she wasn't capable of banishing them this time. They spilled over her lashes and rolled down her cheeks as she saw the years ahead unfolding—friendless and loveless, cold and dark. Her days would be filled only with dreary obligations and joyless responsibilities, her nights lying alone in her bed remembering Jack and the exquisite pleasure she'd known with him.

Enough! she silently railed at herself, scrubbing away her tears. *Enough of the self-pity, Linds. Life is what you make it. You can always run away.* She sucked in a deep breath and forced herself to see the ageless images that had always been her refuge in times of crisis. But this time she deliberately changed them; the oxen didn't die on parched prairie. They survived and so did she. A saloon, she decided impetuously. She'd own a saloon and wear outrageously colorful clothes. She'd drink whiskey and smoke cigars. In public. She'd play cards and win. And she'd never be alone. Her world would be filled with people who laughed and appreciated the haven she provided them. Yes, they'd all be strangers to her, but at least she'd know them for what they were. Never again would she be caught trusting and believing in loyalty and friendship and love.

"Lindsay?"

Her tears dried, she turned from the window. Jack stood just inside the door to her room, his hands in his pockets and an uncertain look in his eyes.

"There's something I've been needing to tell you."

"And you haven't wanted to," she guessed.

"Nope."

She gave him what she hoped was a reassuring smile as she crossed the room. "How bad could it be, Jack?" she asked, stopping in front of him. "It certainly couldn't be any worse than any of the other discoveries I've had today."

"I suppose it can't," he agreed with slight shrug. Pulling his hand from his pocket, he handed her a folded piece of paper while he asked, "Do you recognize the handwriting?"

She opened it and the words leapt up at her. LEAVE OR DIE.

"Oh God, Jack," she whispered, staring at the note, her heart racing, her thoughts scattered. She couldn't bear it if something horrible happened to him.

"Not that I want to add to your obvious distress," he said, stepping around her to sit down on the edge of her bed, "but I reckon I probably ought to mention that it came to the office in a box containing a dismembered rat. It was left in the seat of the desk chair. Ben didn't know anything about it, which means either he's lying or someone besides you, Richard, and Ben have a key to the office."

"When did you find it?" she asked, handing the note back to him. "And, by the way, I don't recognize the handwriting."

"I figured you wouldn't. The package was waiting for me the morning we sailed out."

She nodded and pursed her lips in the way she always did when considering how to approach a problem. "Which was the morning after the terrible scene with Henry and Agatha," she observed after a moment.

Lord, he loved to watch her mind work. It was a

wonderful thing to behold. Jack reined in his smile before Lindsay could catch a glimpse of it. The matter of someone threatening to kill him was serious, but not so much so that he couldn't appreciate how effectively it was diverting her thoughts from the day's other calamities. He leaned back on his elbows, settling in for the show, and willing to play his usual part in it. "Think either one of them could have done something like that? And could either one of them have a key to the office?"

"I just don't know, Jack," she answered, beginning to pace the length of the bed. "But if we look at all that's happened since you've arrived, we know that you had several brushes with near disaster before either of them ever knew about the second Will and the changes in their circumstances. There was the fire, the explosion of the apartment, the beam falling on your head, and then the carriage accident."

"The fire had to have been set," he offered. "The explosion was probably a natural consequence of the heat building up inside a closed room. And it wasn't a beam that took me down on those stairs. A man ran past me and when I called him back to help me drag O'Malley out, he hit me with something. As for the carriage wheel . . . It might have been an accident. Or it might have been deliberate sabotage. And it happened the afternoon of the day the story came out in the *Herald*. They knew by then."

She stopped her pacing to meet his gaze squarely. "You didn't tell me someone had deliberately hit you."

Jack shrugged. "It didn't seem important at the time. I figured it was someone who wanted to get some belongings out before it was too late and didn't have the patience to be waylaid."

"But what if your assumption is wrong, Jack? What if he went up those stairs for the express purpose of finding you?"

"I would have died a hero's death," he drawled. "There'd have been a great newspaper story about me. Pretty good way to go, all in all." He gave her a chagrined smile and added, "Not that I was thinking so at the time."

"Please don't make light of it," she admonished, gathering her skirts in hand and climbing up on the bed beside him. "This is very serious business."

"All right," he agreed, thinking that he was going to get around to the serious business of making love to her in a few minutes and it was nice to have her within such easy reach. "If you hadn't come in after me, it would have looked like I'd died in a tragic accident. No suspicions would have been aroused and no questions would have been asked."

Kneeling, she settled back on her heels and pursed her lips again as she studied him for a long moment. "Who knew we were going to Jeb and Lucy's?"

"Ben. Remember? As we were leaving the office, you told him he could find us there if he needed us."

"I don't think he was behind it, Jack. In the first place, he wouldn't have had time to arrange for someone to try to kill you in the fire. In the second place, and most importantly I think, is the fact that he has absolutely no reason to want you dead." She slowly shook her head. "Frankly, I can't see any reason why anyone would want to kill you. It wouldn't accomplish anything."

"It would complicate the hell out of the transfer of Billy's estate," he pointed out. "And in the end, when all the lawyers and all the judges were through with it, everything I own would go to you, Henry, and Agatha."

She shook her head. "You mean my father's estate would come back to us."

"No. Everything I own, Lindsay. Elmer—you remember, the lawyer in Texas—believes that every man who owns so much as a saddle ought to have a Will and he's damn persistent about doing things right. I finally gave in and let him make me one. Since Billy was the closest I had to family, I figured that he was the one who ought to get my worldly possessions if I happened to go to the great pasture in the sky. I didn't remake it after he died. Didn't even cross my mind."

She stared at him, her eyes wide, and he went on, adding, "Of course, I didn't know Billy had three children. Didn't know he'd ever even been married, for that matter. But you know how lawyers are, Lindsay. They gotta stick in all the right words to cover every possibility no matter how unlikely. Elmer stuck them in because they're supposed to be in a Will, and so, if for some reason Billy couldn't inherit from me, what I own would go to any legitimate heirs he might have."

"Women can't own property in their own names," she said quietly, slowly. "All of it would go to Henry. Unless the Will specifies that he's to set up trusts for Agatha and me, he wouldn't legally have to share the windfall."

He hadn't thought about that. The idea of Henry getting everything and Lindsay nothing was galling. He'd get a codicil written to protect her as soon as he could. "The MacPhaull Company assets combined with what I own would make him a very rich man. As motives to kill someone go, it'd be a good one."

"But how would Henry know about your Will? He couldn't have assumed that you had one or what its provisions might be. And he didn't know about his being disinherited until after the fire."

"It's a helluva complicated web, isn't it?"

"Who *does* know about your Will, Jack? Aside from Elmer. Who in New York?"

"Otis Vanderhagen," he answered, remembering and mentally kicking himself for not seeing the connection before then. God, he needed to keep Lindsay around just to help him think straight. "He came into the office the morning of the fire. Said he had a responsibility as the family attorney to see that the company was legally covered if something should happen to me. I told him about my Will. He offered to write up a codicil for me so that the lawyer wrangling wouldn't go on as long as it would without one." The rest of that morning played out in his mind and he winced with a realization. "But he left before you got there and so he couldn't have heard us tell Ben we were going to Jeb and Lucy's."

"He didn't have to be there," Lindsay instantly countered, her tone calm and certain. "He was at MacPhaull House that morning when the note came from Jeb about the baby being born. He was there when Abigail and I discussed me taking the gifts over once it became a suitable hour for calling."

"Mrs. Beechum knew we were going to Jeb and Lucy's?" Even as the question was spoken, he regretted it. The last thing Lindsay needed was to be reminded of her housekeeper's involvement in the scheme.

"Not *we*, Jack," she replied, clearly not the least bit disturbed by the possibility he'd suggested. "Abigail had no idea you would go with me. She's obviously involved insofar as she's the one sending the rent money, but she hasn't tried to have you killed."

"All right. I'll buy that one," he agreed, utterly relieved to see that she wasn't going to slide back into the gloomy shadows. "Henry was waiting for you out on the walk. He might have overheard you telling Ben that we were going to Jeb and Lucy's."

"The requirements of intelligence and long-term dedication aside, I rather doubt that Henry has any idea of who Jeb and Lucy are, much less where they lived. And I also doubt that the possibility of a Will and its provisions would have crossed his mind. Besides, Jack, at that point, he didn't know anything had happened to upset his expectations. He didn't know you'd inherited until he read the story about the fire in the paper the next morning."

"That's assuming that Otis Vanderhagen didn't actually waddle to the boathouse, find your brother, and tell him everything the first day."

"Oh God, Jack," she whispered, shaking her head. "Henry? Hiring someone to kill you would be such a deliberate and concerted act. And it had be done quickly. Henry's just not capable of such a thing."

He thought it would be just the sort of thing Henry would do. Hell, hiring a murderer might be the one and only thing Henry would be good at. But Lindsay wasn't ready to consider her brother in such a light and Jack was willing to take his time and work his way around to the possibility. "We'll focus on Vanderhagen," he said. "Why would he want me dead? He isn't going to inherit anything except a monumental legal mess to sort out."

"For equally monumental fees. And when he's done sorting, he'll have a very large estate to control, through Henry."

"Yeah, there is that. And then, too, if he's been the one stripping the company assets all along, he'd be able to keep right on doing it when Henry owned it all."

"And it would be easier than it ever has been. He could make an even bigger fortune than he has already. My God, Jack. It is Otis Vanderhagen, isn't it?"

"My money's on him for the correspondence part anyway. But how would he have known that I was going with you to Jeb and Lucy's? He left the office as you were arriving."

"We didn't stay long. He knew where I was going. Maybe he saw us leaving together and made a logical assumption. How long would it take to find a stranger on the street and then arrange for a fire and an assault?"

Jack contemplated the possibility. Not long at all, and for the right price a hungry man would be willing to act quickly. But if Otis Vanderhagen had had the time to arrange the fire and the assault, then so had Ben. And so had Henry. Lindsay's reasons for eliminating both men from consideration were good ones, but he wasn't willing to exclude the secretary or her brother on her assumptions alone. She'd had enough betrayal for one day, though, and he wasn't willing to hammer away at more no matter how likely they looked. "Vanderhagen's hands sure look dirty to me," he said, and then added diplomatically, "but I'm thinking his aren't the only ones."

"You're back to Richard Patterson being involved, aren't you?"

Another likely betrayal. He didn't want to talk about Richard Patterson's possible role any more than he did Ben's or Henry's. "I just don't see how he couldn't have known, Lindsay. Tell me how you think he could have been oblivious for fifteen long years of company decline."

"Why would he want to steal the company assets, Jack?"

She was so certain, so steadfastly faithful, that it made his chest ache. "Maybe he thought he wasn't being paid well enough for managing them," he guessed halfheartedly.

"He could have had whatever salary he wanted."

"Maybe it wasn't the money that mattered to him. Maybe it was the sense of ownership."

"Then he could have offered to buy them outright. I would have agreed—without hesitation—to sell them to him. He had to have known that. Richard had no reason to steal them, Jack. Admit it."

He silently groaned and then resolved to ease her into acceptance as best he could. "All right, so maybe it wasn't the money. Maybe it wasn't a sense of needing to own that drove him. Maybe it was something personal. You've said he had a low opinion of Henry. Could it be that he didn't want there to be anything left for him to inherit?"

"Perhaps," she agreed, nodding. "But in leaving Henry nothing, he would be leaving all of us nothing. I can't believe that Richard would do that to me. I just can't."

"Vanderhagen said that morning when we were discussing Wills that Richard's includes bequeaths to those who meant something to him during the course of his life. I took that to mean that he's leaving you some of his money or property."

"It would have to be in a trust."

"So it's in a trust," he pressed gently. "It'd still be yours and not Henry's. And Richard's conscience would be eased by throwing you a bone in the end."

She considered the idea for a moment and then quietly said, "If the thefts have been going on as long as they apparently have and in the magnitude you think, Jack, then there's several hundred thousand dollars to be accounted for."

Jack heard the softening of her faith, and while he found absolutely no satisfaction in it, he knew it was necessary. "It's cost him hundreds of thousands of dollars to live over the years. I'm thinking Emile wasn't the only cook and that Havers wouldn't deign to clean a house. There was a big household staff, wasn't there?"

She nodded and he went on, saying, "It all costs money, Lindsay. And when the Panic hit and there wasn't a salary to be had from the MacPhaull Company, Richard didn't change one little thing about the way he lived, did he?"

"No."

"To keep on paying for it all he just dipped into the piggy bank he'd stuffed full over the years. There isn't going to be much left in it to give away to others, Lindsay."

Lindsay closed her eyes as a bone-deep weariness settled over her. She didn't care anymore about the business, about property or money or any of it. Thinking about all the possibilities, all the causes and consequences, was exhausting. It would be a blessing to have it all over with, to have nothing, to be free of all the responsibility and worry. "We need to go back to New York," she said, hoping in her heart that they'd get there to discover the end in sight.

"Yes, we do," Jack agreed. She felt him shift his position on the bed as he added, "And that brings me full circle. The reason I started this whole conversation is that I'm worried you might get caught in the cross fire and I want you to be able to protect yourself in case something happens to me and I'm not able to step between you and danger."

Lindsay nodded, hearing his words, but not really hearing them.

"Please open your eyes, sweetheart."

She reluctantly complied with the gentle request and started at the sight of a small silver-plated, pearl-handled pistol lying in the palm of Jack's open hand.

"I bought you this and I want you to carry it with you all the time," he explained. "So you can protect yourself."

"I've never in my life shot a weapon of any sort," she countered, shaking her head emphatically. "This is a very bad idea, Jack. I appreciate the concern and confidence behind it, but I'm more likely to shoot you or myself than I am someone who might be menacing us."

He grinned and rolled his eyes as he slipped off the bed. Putting the pistol on the night table, he said, "You'd be surprised what you can do when you have no other choice, Lindsay. We'll see that you get some practice with it before we head back to New York. You'll do just fine if you ever need to use it."

No, she wouldn't, but she wasn't going to argue with him. He'd see for himself when he tried to teach her how to kill and maim. She simply didn't have it in her and no amount of instruction was going to make any difference. "We'll go overland, right? No more sailing?"

"I'd think you'd want to get back to New York as quickly as possible. Going overland is going to take at least a day and a half longer."

Lindsay knew that. She also knew that the time with Jack was growing short and that she wanted to draw it out for as long as she could. "As Mrs. Beechum pointed out before I left, my being there or not isn't going to change how matters go with Richard. I'd rather take the extra time going back by coach than to sail and have you be so deathly sick. You truly frightened me a time or two on the way here."

He gave her a chagrined smile and raked his fingers through his hair. "I can't say that I'm looking forward to the possibility of climbing aboard a boat with any sense of glad anticipation." He stared at the floor for a moment and then lifted his gaze to hers with sigh of resignation. "All right. We'll go by coach. But only if you promise me you'll carry the gun and practice every evening when we stop."

"It isn't necessary. It truly isn't. No one is the least bit interested in harming me, either deliberately or accidentally."

He studied her for a long moment and she saw his eyes darken with resolve. "So," he finally drawled, "you'd rather have me stand over your grave knowing I'm going to regret for the rest of my life that I didn't listen to my instincts."

Her heart ached and she accepted that she couldn't add to the regrets of his life. "You don't fight fair, Jack."

His smile was rueful as he softly said, "No, sweetheart, I don't. I fight to win." Then, slowly, a warmth sparked deep in his dark eyes. He leaned forward and began to unbutton her shirtfront. "But I try to be a gracious winner," he whispered across her lips.

Lindsay smiled and silently set about ridding him of his clothing, her heart and soul thrilling at the sweet prospect of making love to him. He knew how to touch her, how to make her feel alive and free. And when he filled her, the cares of her world melted away and there was only Jack and the pureness of the pleasure they gave one another. She always felt warm and safe in his arms, protected from the uncertainty and storms of her life.

She kissed him, softly, reverently, knowing that loving him was a gift she was giving to herself, a gift of peace and contentment, precious and worth the price of its inevitable passing. No matter what the future held, the shadows of the past had been banished. The shame that had been the legacy of Charles Martens was gone. That was Jack's greatest gift to her—and she would cherish it forever.

CHAPTER TWENTY-TWO

*I*T WAS HARD for her to hold her eyes open as the rented hack bore them through the city streets toward MacPhaull House. Of one thing she was absolutely certain; as fondly as she'd remember the days she'd spent with Jack in Boston, she'd forever cringe when remembering the journey back to New York. Who would have thought that simply keeping your seat in a coach would be such an exhausting physical endeavor? She'd barely had the strength to stand when they'd stopped each night.

And then there had been the pistol-shooting practice Jack had insisted upon after dinner. Invariably it had drawn a crowd of fellow passengers and led to spirited contests at which Jack had confidently excelled and she'd failed miserably. She'd fallen into bed every night too mentally and physically tired to care that the food had been awful and that the mattress was lumpy. No exhaustion was too deep, though, to have kept her from missing the comfort of falling asleep and waking in the circle of Jack's embrace. The extra time she'd thought to have with him hadn't been enough and her chest ached with the loss.

Deep inside, she knew that it was a harbinger of the pain she was going to feel when he returned to Texas. For the last two nights, in the unguarded moments just before she fell asleep, her last thought had been a whispered prayer that he would decide to stay with her. In the light of day, though, she set aside those hopes for another, more practical and necessary one—that she would be able to keep her composure when she had to tell him good-bye.

"Are you awake?" Jack asked quietly, reaching across the carriage to lay his hand gently over hers. When she managed a nod, he added, "You're home."

Lindsay realized only then that the carriage had stopped. She nodded again, thinking that her return should spark some sense of happiness or comfort within her. It didn't. In MacPhaull House were all the memories, obligations, and turmoil of all the years of her life. She didn't want to be here anymore. It wasn't a home. It was a two-story brick box stuffed full of dark furniture and even darker failure. She was going to sell it just as soon as she could. She'd move to Mrs. Theorosa's house and begin her life all over again.

"Damn."

It took some effort, but Lindsay focused her vision and her awareness on the present. Jack stood just outside the carriage door, his back to her, his shoulders tense and his chin raised. Slowly he turned and offered her his hand. His eyes were dark and soft with regret and sadness.

"Bad news awaits you, sweetheart," he said softly. "Lean on me if you need to. I'll be right beside you."

She knew even before she stepped out that Richard had died. The front door of the house was draped in black crepe and she stood looking at it, holding Jack's hand tightly and swaying slightly on her feet. For a brief instant she felt a stab of grief and denial, and then a blessed numbness mercifully dropped over her. Feeling nothing, her mind incapable of coherent thought, she allowed him to guide her up the front walk. She vaguely heard Jack speak to the hack driver before he sent him on his way, and just as vaguely heard him call out to Mrs. Beechum when they reached the front door.

Jack was gently untying her bonnet ribbons when Mrs. Beechum came from the dining room into the foyer. Lindsay blinked at her, trying to focus on the familiar face, a face that was thinner than she remembered and hollowed by grief.

"Miss Lindsay, I'm so sorry that you've had to come home to crepe," the housekeeper said, coming to a stop, her skirts swirling for a second around her ankles. "Richard passed the day after you left and we tried to delay the services for as long as we could in the hope that you'd return in time to attend them. We didn't know where you'd gone and so we couldn't send a message to bring you home."

"We were in Boston," Lindsay heard herself say. Why? she wondered. It didn't matter where she'd gone. She hadn't been here to pay her last public respects to the man who had been like a father to her.

"It was a lovely service, Miss Lindsay. Truly lovely," Abigail went on consolingly. "Richard had all of the details of it specified in his Will. So many people were in attendance. You would have been pleased. I've saved the obituary for you. It's on the desk in the study, along with all the mail that's arrived in your absence. Ben has been bringing it to the house each evening."

She nodded, wondering if the letter from the imaginary Percival Little had arrived yet. *Better now than later,* Lindsay thought. *Better to know, than not. And I'm too tired for it to hurt.* "Thank you, Mrs. Beechum," she heard herself say. She cleared her throat softly and then found the wherewithal to add, "When we were in Boston we met Tiny."

The housekeeper knitted her brows. "Who is Tiny?"

Lindsay straightened her shoulders, but suddenly it was all that she could do beyond hoping that Jack would pick up the thread and do the unraveling. She was too emotionally battered to do anything more than remain upright and watch her housekeeper in dazed silence.

"Joseph Mallory," Jack clarified. "His friends call him Tiny."

Lindsay recognized first puzzlement and then shock in her housekeeper's eyes. And then the woman sighed and said, "I understand that he's a simple child. Although I suppose that he's really no longer a child. It's been so many years. I do so hope that Richard made provisions in his Will for him and the other three young men."

Three? Oh, yes, Lindsay remembered. The other companies in other cities.

"We need to know," Jack pressed, slipping his arm around Lindsay's waist, "how you became involved in sending them money every week."

"With Richard gone, I suppose that keeping it a secret doesn't matter anymore." She stood taller and took a deep breath before she began. "It was what brought us together for the first time. It seems so very long ago. It was a Christmas fund-raising event sponsored by the Ladies Charitable Association. I was a member in those days. Otis Vanderhagen brought Richard with him that evening and, in the course of it, Richard and I found ourselves in conversation. He told me about the letters he frequently received asking for donations. He said that four had caught his attention as being especially deserving, but he felt that responding to them would open the floodgates of requests. He asked me if I'd be willing to help him secretly help these poor souls. How could I refuse?"

It sounded logical to Lindsay. An act of kindness. So Richard. So Abigail. And Otis Vanderhagen had probably written the requests for charity, duping them both. It was all explained and there was nothing sinister about Abigail's involvement. If she'd have been capable of it, Lindsay would have smiled in relief.

"How long ago was this?" Jack inquired.

"It will be twenty-one years ago this next Christmas, Mr. Stennett."

"So what exactly did you do?"

"I sent them money every week with which to pay their rents and provide for their other needs."

"Richard's money?" Jack asked.

"Yes, of course," Abigail answered, looking at him like it was the most ridiculous question she'd ever heard. "But Richard's involvement was never disclosed. It was the way he wanted it."

"And how did you get the money to send?"

"When we first began, Richard would bring it to me himself and then take me to the post office to send the packets on their way. It was those weekly meetings and carriage rides that led to the development of our more personal relationship." She blushed slightly, cleared her throat, and then took another deep breath. "After the accident, after my convalescence, arrangements were made so that I would find the money every Monday morning here at MacPhaull House, tucked inside four packets and stuck between the jamb and the outside kitchen door. All I had to do was address the packets and take them to the post office while I was out running other errands."

"Who and where are the other three recipients of Richard's charity?"

"There's Waldo Jones in Philadelphia, George Slater in Richmond, and Israel Boniface in Charleston," Abigail supplied crisply. "I do so hope Richard provided for them. I can't bear to think what might happen to them if he didn't."

"I gather his Will hasn't been publically read yet?"

"No, of course not. Except for the provisions regarding his funeral preferences. Mr. Vanderhagen insisted that Miss Lindsay be present before he made Richard's other wishes known. He's asked me to request that you notify him of your return."

Lindsay closed her eyes. God, the reading of the Will. There was something about the division of property that always made death so undeniable. Until then you could believe that it was just a bad dream and that everything would be all right when the sun rose and you could wake up.

"Tomorrow morning will be soon enough," Jack said, drawing Lindsay closer to his side. "Have you sent the rent money this week?"

"Yes. Whoever brings it to the house on Richard's behalf must have the same sense of concern I do, because despite Richard's passing, the money was there this past Monday morning."

"Who do you think brings it?"

"I've always assumed that it's Havers. He would be the most logical person, don't you think?"

"If it's not there next Monday morning, let me know and I'll see that you have it."

Again, Lindsay wished that she was capable of the effort it took to smile.

"You're a very good man, Mr. Stennett. Thank you." Abigail paused and then said tentatively, "May I ask a question?"

"Certainly."

"How did you find out about all this? Was I clumsy in handling the transaction?"

"No, not at all," Jack assured her. "We were following another trail and stumbled across Richard's charitable efforts quite by accident."

Yes, a good man. He wasn't going to taint Abigail's illusions of Richard with his suspicions. She'd have to remember to thank him later for the kindness.

"I assume that you haven't yet had your evening meal," Abigail said. "I'll see that Primrose and Emile prepare something immediately."

"Emile is still here?"

"Yes, sir. As is Havers. I didn't know precisely how to handle the situation of Richard's employees after his passing, so I discussed it with Mr. Vanderhagen. He suggested that they remain here until after the reading of Richard's Will and that Miss Lindsay could make decisions regarding them after that. I formed the impression that while Richard made them bequeaths, he was hopeful that Miss Lindsay would bring them into her household staff."

"And how would you feel about that, Mrs. Beechum?" Jack asked.

"I think that if Miss Lindsay were to let Emile go, Primrose would follow him. Aside from that, he's a very good cook. I wouldn't be opposed to having him around."

"And Havers?"

She hesitated before arching a brow and saying, "He's a bit difficult to tolerate. He thinks very highly of himself and the value of his service."

"Did he ever get his list of demands written?"

"If he has, I haven't seen it." The housekeeper looked between them and then moistened her lower lip before venturing, "Would you care for a household report, Miss Lindsay? Or would you prefer to wait until later?"

"Is there anything of special importance?" Lindsay asked, hoping there were no decisions to be made.

"I've enlisted the assistance of Lucy Rutherford with the household duties. The dust in the dining-room curtains—the ones Mr. Stennet pulled down for you—was such an embarrassment and I thought that you wouldn't mind employing her for a short while to help me with some very necessary deep-cleaning chores. She's quite competent and very willing to work."

If that was the only matter needing her attention, Lindsay would count herself fortunate and grateful. "It's a good idea, Abigail. Perhaps you'd like to have her assistance permanently. I'm sure Lucy would appreciate the wages."

Abigail beamed. "I knew you'd suggest it and Lucy's agreeable. Now, I'm truly off to see to your dinner. Might I suggest that you take a good long nap while it's being prepared? You look exhausted."

"I am," Lindsay admitted.

"And I'll see that she does," Jack declared, gently sweeping her up into his arms. Lindsay twined her arms around his neck and laid her cheek on his shoulder. She was home now, she thought as he started up the stairs with her. Finally. Her eyes drifted closed and she surrendered to the warmth and comfort of the welcome.

JACKSON LAID HER IN HER BED, carefully tucking a feather comforter around her, and then stood there, watching her sleep and marveling at the woman she was. Exhausted from traveling, she'd come home to bad news. Most women would have taken to their beds for a week to recuperate. But not Lindsay. Instead, she'd immediately stepped up to the matter of Abigail's involvement in the shell game. Thank God the woman's explanation had been both reasonable and clearing. If it had been an admission of betrayal, Lindsay would have collapsed on the spot. She was strong, but Jack wasn't sure how much more she could take.

Unfortunately, she wasn't going to have much of a respite. Tomorrow morning they were going to have to confront Otis Vanderhagen. If the attorney wanted to discuss what Patterson had left her in the will, then fine. But one way or the other, Vanderhagen was going to answer some tough questions about the sham businesses and the stripping of the MacPhaull Company assets.

Jack sighed and raked his fingers through his hair. Lindsay's illusions had taken a hard blow on the steps of the O'Brien boardinghouse. But it was going to be nothing compared to the bludgeoning she was going to get in Otis Vanderhagen's office tomorrow. God, if there was any way he could spare her the pain, he would. All he could do, though, was hold her up as best he could and promise her that she wasn't going to be penniless when he left. *When he left . . .*

Time was running down on him, he realized with a start. The auction was two days out, and when it was done, he'd have to head back to Texas so he could meet the deadlines for repaying Billy's loans on the ranch. And he wasn't ready to leave Lindsay. Just thinking about it made his chest ache and his throat tight. She needed a shoulder to lean on, someone who could see her through the rebuilding of her fortunes. It should be him, dammit. No one else in her world cared enough to ease her worries or make her smile.

But since he couldn't stay, maybe the thing to do was what Billy should have done all those years ago. Maybe Lindsay should pack her bags and come to Texas. He could get her there, he could help her adjust to the changes in her circumstances. And then there was the very real chance that she'd find herself a husband and be happy.

He needed to talk to her about it all. And before they headed off to Otis Vanderhagen's in the morning. Lindsay needed to know before she went into that beating that he was committed to doing whatever it took to see that she survived it. Tonight, he decided. He'd broach the subject at dinner after she'd rested some. And he'd lay it out carefully so that she wouldn't be able to turn down his offer. He wouldn't have to leave her behind went he went home. He'd take her with him and everything would be all right.

With a confident smile, he leaned down and brushed a kiss across her lips. Lindsay smiled sweetly in her sleep, and he left the room certain that he was on the correct course.

. . .

LINDSAY SLID A GLANCE across the table, wondering why Jack seemed so tense and preoccupied this evening. Had something of concern arrived in the mail while they were gone? She was about to ask him when he cleared his throat and said softly, "I'm sorry you weren't here for Richard's funeral."

It wasn't what he wanted to say; she could sense it still coiling upon itself under the surface of things. But knowing Jack, she suspected that he was working his way toward it. All she had to do was be patient. "I'm sure Richard understood why I wasn't there."

"Do you think that the dead are aware of what they leave behind?" he mused, studying his plate. "What the living are doing?"

"I don't know. Sometimes, as with Richard, I like to think that they do because it gives me solace." She smiled ruefully as she added, "And sometimes, as with my mother, the greatest comfort comes from hoping that they don't. Why are you asking?"

He looked up and gave her a mischievous smile. "I was thinking about Billy and wondering whether he'd twist himself into a knot if I asked you to sleep with me in his bed."

"Well, I suppose he couldn't be too upset if all we did was sleep."

He laughed and shook his head. "I've spent five long days having my bones beaten to dust on the worst roads mankind has ever seen fit to lay down. And I've spent four even longer nights in roadhouses, sleeping in rooms full of snoring, drooling men, knowing you were on the other side of the wall and that I couldn't get to you. It isn't just sleeping with you that I have in mind."

"Do you ever wonder if my father wanted—" Lindsay bit off the rest of the words, knowing the notion to be on the far side of foolish. When Jack cocked a brow in silent question, she laughingly replied, "Nevermind. It was a silly idea."

"Do I ever wonder if he gave everything to me because he thought maybe there was a chance you and I might find something in each other?"

How had he known what she'd been thinking? It was both a little disconcerting and oddly, deeply comforting. "That's what I was thinking," she admitted. "But for circumstances to allow us to be together, even briefly, is really quite unusual. Most women my age are married and have families. I don't see how my father could have known that I'm not. And he had to have expected Henry to be involved in the business, not me."

Jack nodded, but the light in his eyes darkened and she knew that his thoughts had gone in another direction. "I met Billy when I was ten years old," he said softly, meeting her gaze. "It was when we all went into Texas together with Stephen Austin. I've spent practically all my life thinking that he was the smartest, kindest, most honorable man I'd ever know. But I've discovered that he wasn't what I thought, Lindsay. If he had been all those things, he would have taken you with him when he left. He wouldn't have left you here to grow up alone."

She knew how much it hurt to realize that the reality of people wasn't as bright and shiny as your illusions of them. Jack hadn't gloated over the tarnishing of hers; she couldn't do any less than comfort him in the loss of his own. "You've told me yourself that Texas is a dangerous place. Maybe my father thought that he was doing the best he could for me in leaving me behind."

"He could have come back to see you. He could have written you a letter or two over the years. He could have asked you to come visit him."

"But if he had done those things," she pointed out, "then he would have had to deal with my mother again. Their relationship was horrible, Jack. I remember lying awake in my bed at night and thinking that I wouldn't be at all surprised to wake up in the morning to find that one of them had killed the other." She gave Jack what she hoped passed for a brave and accepting smile. "It was undoubtedly a very intelligent decision on his part to stay away. He built a new life for himself and, from what you've said, it seems that he was happy with it. That's something that can't be said about his life here."

"You're a lot like him, you know," he said softly.

"Same eyes, same intelligence, same taste for risk and high-stakes games."

Lindsay chuckled. "You've forgotten to mention the other character traits we had in common; the penchant for ignoring the opinions of others, the lack of concern for social convention, and the determination to do things our own way. I've heard all about them." She took a sip of wine before adding, "Those are just the most obvious, of course. There are many, many other faults only slightly less grievous."

"You're different from him, too." Jack grinned and cocked a brow. "Billy was a good shot."

Lindsay laughed outright and then protested, "I'm getting better."

"Oh, yeah," he agreed, chuckling. "If whoever comes at you is as big as a barn, you'll do just fine. I need to get you a shotgun."

"I think we'd both be safer if I just stayed very close to you and let you shoot the gun."

He sobered instantly, causing Lindsay's stomach to clench. "Speaking of staying close to me . . ." he said.

They were at whatever it was that was bothering him; she knew it. And it was something he clearly didn't want to talk about, but felt compelled to. Deciding it was best to get it out in the open and over with, she prompted, "What, Jack?"

He took a sip of his wine and exhaled long and hard before saying, "I have an idea and I want you to hear it all the way out and give it some serious thought before you make any decisions about it. All right?"

"All right," she agreed warily, noting that his gaze was fastened on the tablecloth. *Not a good sign, Linds.*

"I was thinking while we were in Boston. . . ."

A long silence stretched between them, and her heart began to race. "Yes, Jack?"

"Well . . ."

She couldn't take much more of his hesitation. "Jack," she ventured, mustering all the patience she had left, "will you please just say whatever it is that you want to say? It doesn't have to be perfectly presented."

He nodded once, crisply, and then all but blurted, "I

was thinking that maybe you should come to Texas with me."

Lindsay vaguely heard herself gasp. Go to Texas with Jack? He was asking her to go with him? Her heart swelled, her pulse skittered, and if she'd been less stunned, she'd have vaulted from her chair and thrown herself into his arms.

"Now, don't say it's impossible, Lindsay," he said hurriedly, his gaze finally coming up to meet hers. "Hear me out. There isn't going to be much property left once the auction's done. What's left when split three ways—which is only fair since there are three of you—means you're going to be strapped until you can make some decent investments and rebuild. I don't care what happens to Henry and Agatha. But I do care about what happens to you. You've earned a better life than the one you've been dealt.

"I wouldn't be able to save the ranch like Billy wanted me to if you hadn't been willing to meet me halfway. It seems only right to me that you should get something out of it. So I'm thinking that you could come to Texas with me. You could live in Billy's house and I'd see to it that you had whatever money you needed to live on. It would come out of the ranch accounts. There's plenty of money for us to do this."

She could live in Billy's house? Lindsay's throat tightened with a sickening realization. Jack wasn't asking her to go to Texas to be with him, to live with him. He was suggesting only that they travel together. God, what a fool she'd almost made of herself. He was looking at her so expectantly, so hopefully, and she knew she had to say something. She summoned a smile and quipped, "Going to Texas isn't at all necessary, Jack. If you're worried about me having enough money, you could just arrange to send me some every week when Tiny is sent his."

"But that wouldn't solve the other problems," he instantly, earnestly rejoined. "You'd still be here, having to face Henry's and Agatha's expectations day in and day out. And you'd be all alone, too. I know you, Lindsay. You'll bury yourself in rebuilding not only your own fortunes but Henry's and Agatha's, too. If you came to Texas with me, you'd be far enough away that they couldn't ask you to take care of them anymore."

And what would she have in exchange? A life alone in the house of the father she had never known. And Jack thought that was an improvement? "Henry and Agatha are my brother and sister," she countered, wishing she could offer a better reason, but not being able to think past how stupidly giddy she'd been at thinking Jack was proposing a long-term relationship. She should have known better than to assume he'd ever suggest such a thing.

"And they're full-grown adults and it's time they took care of themselves."

She shrugged and snatched up her wineglass, desperate to not only distract herself, but to conceal the acute embarrassment she felt. Lord, her cheeks had to be bright red. She could feel the heat fanning over them.

"There's more, Lindsay," Jack went on, apparently—and thankfully—unaware of her discomposure. "See, I figure that the minute you cross over the border, the word's going to go out that there's a beautiful and intelligent woman available and—"

"Available?" she echoed, stunned anew.

He nodded, his smile bright. "Every eligible bachelor in the Republic of Texas will make a beeline for Billy's front door. I'll sort 'em out for you, but you'll have the final say on which one of 'em you want to marry."

"Marry?" she squeaked out. He was planning to marry her off? He was asking her to go to Texas so he could marry her to someone else?

"Well, yes," he admitted, blinking and looking as though he'd finally noticed that she was slightly less than ecstatic over the idea. "You've told me, I don't know how many times, that getting married and having a family of your own isn't something that's in the cards for you. But I know it's something that you'd really like and you're just saying all that to buck yourself up. Sweetheart, pasts don't matter in Texas. You could have any man you want. You can get married and have your family. You could be happy. That isn't going to happen if you stay here."

And it wasn't going to happen in Texas either. Her

stomach roiling, her pulse pounding with barely contained anger and pain, Lindsay said—with what seemed to her to be a surprising degree of calm—"Let me see if I'm understanding this correctly. You want me to go with you when you return to Texas. I'll move into my father's house and you'll financially support me while you arrange to have every man in Texas parade past me for inspection. When I find one that suits my fancy, I'll marry him and live happily ever after. Is that the basic idea, Jack?"

He winced. "It sounded better the way I said it."

"No, Jack," she countered, draining her wineglass. "Trust me; it didn't."

"What's wrong with it?"

Nothing, if I didn't love you. Nothing, if you'd asked me to go with you because you loved me. Her entire body trembling with the effort to hold tears at bay, Lindsay blindly laid her napkin beside her plate.

"Billy walked away and left you behind," Jack said, leaning across the table to cover her hand with his. "He shouldn't have and I don't want to make the same mistake he did. I couldn't live with myself knowing you were here and miserable and that I could have done something simple and easy to see that your life turned out better than it did."

Her heart was breaking. She tried to smile, tried to hide her pain behind a facade of confidence and nonchalance. "I'm not your responsibility, Jack."

"I know that, Lindsay. I just want you to be happy."

But all you're willing to do is pass the responsibility off to another man. She pulled her hand from beneath his. "My road to happiness doesn't lie in marrying a stranger in Texas. But thank you for suggesting the idea, Jack. I understand that there are good intentions behind it."

"Lindsay . . ."

So earnest. So soft. So blindly unaware. Her throat was closing with tears and she knew that she wasn't going to be able to keep them at bay much longer. Desperate to escape before he discovered how deeply she was hurt, just how big a fool she was, Lindsay rose to her feet, saying, "If you'll excuse me, please. Suddenly, I don't feel at all well. It must be from having too much wine. I think I'd best retire for the evening. Good night, Jack."

She fled with what remained of her dignity, keeping her pace sedate and even all the way out of the dining room, across the foyer, and up the stairs. Not once did she look back. And while the tears were streaming over her lashes and down her cheeks by the time she reached the top of the stairs, she managed to close herself away in her room before the sobs tore up her throat and shredded her composure. She fell onto her bed, curling into a ball and knowing that she had never hurt this deeply. Because she had never loved anyone as much as she did Jackson Stennett. And he was willing to let her go.

CHAPTER TWENTY-THREE

*H*E'D SUSPECTED LAST NIGHT that he'd blundered in laying out his offer, but he'd had no inkling of just how badly he'd erred until breakfast. Lindsay had come down with her eyes puffy and her cheeks scraped raw. A blind man would have known that she'd spent the night crying instead of sleeping. And even Tiny wouldn't have believed her repeated assertions that nothing was wrong, that everything was just as fine as it always was. It wasn't and he knew it to the center of his bones. Lindsay might be smiling and telling him he was imagining things, but she was offering the gesture and words from an emotional distance he'd never felt with her before. It was almost as though she'd walked across a bridge without him and then burnt it before he even knew it was there.

She sat on the opposite seat of the rented hack now, her gaze fixed on the world passing outside the window on their way to Otis Vanderhagen's office. Knowing there was no point in asking her yet again what he'd done, he studied her instead and played the memory of last night through his head. He was fairly good at judging people's reactions to things, and he would have sworn that she was initially receptive to his suggestion that she move to Texas. Her breath had caught and her eyes had gotten big and bright. A little smile had been flirting around the corners of her mouth when he'd explained how he thought it could all work.

The first sign he'd had that she might say "no" had been when she'd suggested that he send her money as he intended to send Tiny. What had he said between then and the start that had changed the way she saw the offer? Damned if he could remember anything that might have been off-putting. Billy's house. Making sure she had money to live on. That there was enough to see to her needs. Was she seeing his offer as an act of pity and charity? Surely not. He'd explained why he wanted to do it. Yes, he'd explained that very clearly; not wanting to make the same mistake her father had in leaving her behind alone and lonely. There was no way she could have misunderstood his motives.

She'd become more animated when he'd talked about the possibility of her finding a husband. Maybe, Jack admitted, frowning, he could have put that part better. Judging from the way she'd summed it up for him, it seemed that she thought he might auction her off or something. But she should know him better that. She should know that he wouldn't let anyone around her but the best and brightest and most capable of taking care of her and making her happy. He wouldn't let her marry anyone except someone who really and truly loved her and was worth her. Jesus, didn't she know that he cared about her? That he'd rather die than see her hurt and unhappy? That's why he'd made the offer in the first place. And he'd been real clear about that, too.

Maybe, Jack decided as the carriage pulled to a stop, he needed to take another run at the whole idea after they completed their business with Vanderhagen. He didn't like the distance he was feeling between him and Lindsay, and the longer it went on, the more he worried that they might not be able to get back the closeness they'd had. He missed it, and he missed it badly. It felt more wrong than anything he'd ever felt in his life.

"Ready?" she asked as he assisted her out of the carriage.

Jack nodded, but decided against suggesting that she let him do the majority of the talking, the bulk of the question-asking. He didn't know exactly where he stood with her and the last thing he wanted to risk was inadvertently putting any more distance between them. He'd just have to roll with the punches when they got inside and make the best of it. As god-awful as it was to wish horrible news on anyone, as they entered the office he found himself wishing that the news would be so devastating that it would drive Lindsay into his arms. If he could just hold her, everything would come right again.

"Good morning, Lindsay," the attorney boomed, standing behind his desk. "Good morning, Mr. Stennett. I'm glad to see that you've returned from your trip. As I'm sure you're aware, Richard passed in your absence."

"Yes," Lindsay replied quietly. "Mrs. Beechum said that you needed to speak with me immediately about Richard's Will."

"Yes, yes," the attorney said, motioning to the chairs placed on the other side of his desk.

"The Will aside," Jack ventured, "I have some questions for you."

"I'm sure you do, Mr. Stennett," Vanderhagen acknowledged with a quick nod. "And I've been waiting for them. However, I think that perhaps the reading of Richard's Last Will and Testament will answer most of them. What isn't addressed by that document, I'll answer to the best of my ability."

"When do you plan to disclose the contents?" Lindsay asked.

"If you and Mr. Stennett will have a seat, I can do so right now. There are matters pertaining to others, of course, but they can be informed at another time and privately."

Lindsay dutifully sat, but Jackson felt inclined to refuse just for the sake of refusing. "I'll stand, if you don't mind."

"As you like, Mr. Stennett," the lawyer said while gathering up a stack of documents. He handed one across the desk to Lindsay, saying, "A copy was made for you, Lindsay. And since you're capable of reading it for yourself, I'll dispense with actually reading it for you. Instead, and if you have no objections, I'll summarize for your and Mr. Stennett's benefit."

"Please proceed," Jack instructed, wanting it over just as quickly and cleanly as possible.

With a deep breath that pulled his waistcoat up over his paunch, Vanderhagen said, "Richard begins by acknowledging Henry and Agatha MacPhaull and Benjamin Tipton as his children."

Lindsay instantly gasped and leaned forward. "I beg your pardon?"

Jack sucked in a hard breath. It was one helluva unexpected wrinkle. He would never have guessed something like that.

"Richard, as they say, had quite a bit of swash in his buckle in his younger years," Otis Vanderhagen explained, smiling weakly. "As indelicate as it may be, I'm afraid there's no way around the truth of the matter. Seducing married women was his expertise. Lydia MacPhaull certainly wasn't the first. Abigail Beechum, due to unfortunate circumstances, was his last. But as far as Richard knew, Henry and Agatha and Ben were the only offspring to result from his various liaisons. He legally acknowledges his parentage and provides Henry and Agatha with a reasonable trust from which they may draw specific amounts over the course of the next ten years. After that time, the funds remaining, along with the accrued interest, are to be donated to charities Richard selected.

"Ben will receive a token bequest; largely so that he doesn't have legal grounds on which to contest the Will. If you don't mind, I'll come back to the other reasons a little later in our conversation. It will all make much more sense at that point and in the larger context."

Lindsay nodded her assent. Jackson chewed the inside of his lip and wondered how a man could work day in and day out with his son and never publicly acknowledge the relationship. What a strange man Richard Patterson had been.

"Richard also made similar trusts for Havers and Emile, in recognition of their years of service to him," Vanderhagen went on, pulling Jack from his musing. "Again, the trusts are to exist for ten years and then be dissolved, with the balances going to charity. Richard also established a trust on behalf of Mrs. Abigail Beechum. It will provide her with an income and remain in effect for the rest of her life. At her passing, the remaining monies will go to charities of her own choosing."

The lawyer paused to take a deep breath before continuing. "And he made provisions for you, of course, Lindsay. There are personal remarks for you in the Will itself and I will allow you to read those at your leisure and in the privacy of your own home. But—"

"Does he happen to tell her," Jack asked bluntly, "why he'd spent the last fifteen years stripping the MacPhaull Company of assets?"

Vanderhagen nodded. Even though Jack had expected to find the truth in the end, the gesture, the easy admission of Richard Patterson's theft, struck like a physical blow. He sensed Lindsay start and he instantly put his hands on her shoulders, wordlessly assuring her that she wasn't alone in dealing with the news.

"While Richard was kind enough to say nothing that might compromise my legal integrity," Vanderhagen said, after letting their initial shock pass, "I will admit freely to both of you that I have not only been aware of what he was doing from the beginning, but that I have also been deeply involved in the process. I approved of his motives and I supported his efforts at every opportunity. I could be disbarred and brought up on criminal charges for what I've done, but in considering the situation, I had to do what I believed to be in the long-range best interests of the MacPhaull Company."

Lindsay's voice quavered as she asked, "And just what have you and Richard done?"

A deep breath, a yank on his waistcoat, and then Vanderhagen smoothly replied, "There were two primary concerns underlying our actions. The first is that you, Lindsay, are the one and only known legitimate heir of William Lindsay MacPhaull. The second is that, under the terms of the only Last Will and Testament of William MacPhaull we knew to exist, Henry would inherit all the property. We both knew that it would lead to financial disaster. In the end, you would not only be denied what was yours by birthright, but you would be impoverished by, if not your brother's certain mismanagement, then his selfishness and greed.

"Since William's whereabouts were unknown—even whether he was alive or dead—Richard thought to make things right as best he could and enlisted my aid in establishing a series of companies that exist only on paper."

"We know about them, Mr. Vanderhagen," Jack said. "They're the Little, Bates and Company of Boston, the Michaels, Katz, and Osborne firm in Charleston, the firm of Hooper, Preston, and Roberts, Limited in Philadelphia, and the MacWillman Company in Richmond."

Vanderhagen nodded and, meeting his gaze over Lindsay's head, replied, "Ben said he thought you would soon unravel the puzzle. As usual, he was right. Benjamin Tipton is a very perceptive young man."

"Ben knows?" Lindsay gasped. "He's involved?"

"Very much so. And we come to the matter of Richard's bequeath to him. Ben arrived in the city at his mother's death, determined to claim his birthright regardless of the scandal it might create. Richard was equally determined to keep him from doing so. I suppose, in the crudest analysis, Benjamin has been blackmailing Richard for years. Richard, thinking that it was best to have Benjamin where he could be controlled as much as possible, brought him into the company with a private stipend to supplement his bookkeeper's salary, and with a commitment to recognize him as a legitimate heir at Richard's passing."

Vanderhagen looked down at the document as he added, "Richard, as you might well imagine, resented being placed in such a position. The amount of Ben's bequeath reflects the monies Richard paid to him over the years."

"Does Ben know?" Jack asked, trying to see how the ripples played out.

Vanderhagen shrugged. "I've said nothing to him. Nor have I discussed the terms of the Will with any of the other parties involved. My primary concern has been with informing Lindsay of the circumstances. Informing the others can be seen to in the days ahead. There's no particular hurry."

Jack, sensing that the ripples were turning into waves, asked, "Does Ben know about the shell game?"

Vanderhagen nodded. "Being an intelligent and perceptive man, he caught the pattern of our activities soon after his employment, and it was necessary to bring him into the project." The lawyer smiled wryly. "And while Richard and I did it against our wills and better judgment at the time, we've had to admit that he's proven himself to be an extremely valuable asset over the years. He's very good at devising ways to debilitate businesses without doing harm to any individual life or limb. It has never been our objective to hurt anyone physically."

"Just businesses," Jack felt compelled to add.

"Yes, Mr. Stennett. They were made unprofitable, sold to the phantom companies, rehabilitated, sold again, and the final profits invested in various other business enterprises. All of them—and there are twenty-five—along with a dozen accounts in American and foreign banks make up the trust Richard established for Lindsay. She may draw from the trust as she wishes and can assign it to her heirs as she deems appropriate. As of the last quarterly accounting, the trust was worth in excess of seven hundred and fifty thousand dollars."

Jack clenched his teeth as realization after realization hammered his brain. He'd been as wrong as wrong could be about Richard Patterson. Otis Vanderhagen, too. And Ben Tipton. He hadn't read a single person in this mess right. He'd been wrong about every goddamn thing all along. Lindsay wasn't going to be left poor. She was rich beyond even the wildest of any man's dreams. She didn't need him for anything. There wasn't any reason for her to go to Texas with him. In fact, she'd be a damn fool if she did. He had nothing to offer her that she couldn't buy for herself ten times over.

"You are a very, very wealthy young woman, Lindsay," he heard Vanderhagen say. "And you have Richard to thank."

"And you," she whispered. "And Ben."

"Our parts were small and only in support of an objective that was born of Richard's basic decency and good conscience."

Anger, raw and white-hot, shot through Jack's veins. "Well, if I might intrude on the glorification of Richard Patterson for a moment," he growled, "I still have some questions I need answers for."

Vanderhagen nodded and smiled. "I'll do my best to provide them."

The man's easy manner only added to Jack's ire. "Let's start with who writes the letters for the phantom companies."

"It occurred to Richard and myself early on that Lindsay needed to become involved in the daily operations of the MacPhaull Company in order to learn the skills necessary for her to ably oversee the trust she would eventually inherit. We took every precaution to see that she had no reason to wonder about the legitimacy of the paper companies we'd established. To that end, we looked for and found a person skilled in the art of forgery. Havers is the one and only author of the correspondence for all four companies."

"And who went to the various cities, found the simpleminded children, and set up the correspondence shams?" Jack demanded.

"How do you know about that?"

"We've seen it play out in Boston," Lindsay explained quietly, serenely. "The weekly rent money sent by Abigail Beechum; the return letter sent inside the packet and put right back into the postal carrier's hands."

He looked back and forth between them, his brow cocked. "You two have been very busy people, haven't you?" he asked in a manner that reminded Jack of a schoolteacher who'd caught little boys being naughty.

"Yep," Jack all but snarled. "Who set it up?"

"Richard," the attorney supplied. "And then he came back and enlisted Abigail Beechum's assistance so that if the project was discovered, there was less of a chance of his being immediately implicated in the whole thing. It was theft, you know, and he could have been imprisoned for his actions."

"He used Abigail and didn't tell her that she was being involved in a criminal activity," Lindsay observed, a bit of censure in her voice, but not nearly enough, to Jack's way of thinking.

"Essentially," Vanderhagen agreed, managing to look chagrined on a dead man's behalf. "If it helps any to know, he felt great remorse for that in the years afterward. In part, the structure and amount of her trust fund is something of Richard's atonement. That and his regret for not marrying her. By the time he came to realize that was the course he should have taken, it was too late to pursue it. He regretted the decision the rest of his life. He made amends as best he could and in other ways."

"Blessed be Richard Patterson," Jack groused, not knowing whether he was madder at Lindsay for being so accepting or Vanderhagen for being so damn smooth at making theft and irresponsibility sound honorable. "Who arranged for me to get the chopped-up rat and the note?"

"You posed something of an initial problem, Mr. Stennett," the lawyer said, his chagrined smile still in place. "As you might well imagine, the first consideration was that in examining the books of the company you inherited, you might discover what Richard and I had been doing all these years and file criminal charges against us. I knew that we had some time to both cover our tracks and ascertain your abilities and intentions. I'm sure Richard also understood the ramifications of your unexpected ownership, but he clearly didn't react well to the development."

"No kidding," Jackson commented dryly.

"With Richard's collapse, the project was left in my hands to manage with Ben's assistance. It was his opinion, as a result of having several private exchanges with you, that you were suspicious of the books and that it would be in ours—and Lindsay's—best interests to drive you away. I reluctantly agreed and left the matter in his hands.

"By the time it became obvious that he'd misjudged both your resiliency and your tenacity, it had become equally apparent that you were interested in Lindsay in a romantic sense." He paused to give Lindsay a condescending smile. Jack clenched his teeth and fisted his hands at his sides, trying to decide whether he ought to punch out the bastard's teeth now or later.

"We concluded," the attorney went on, "that even if you did unravel the conspiracy, you wouldn't take any actions that would jeopardize her future financial health. Given that, we decided that eliminating you was no longer a necessity."

"Did it ever occur to you that in trying to 'eliminate' me, you might have inadvertently hurt or killed Lindsay?"

"We were very careful to see that that didn't happen. Your carriage accident was just that, an accident. Neither Ben nor I had any part in it. Lindsay was never endangered by actions we took. What danger she was ever in was the result of her own actions in the situation."

Calmly, quietly, apparently oblivious to Jack's turmoil and anger, Lindsay said, "I have a question or two, if you don't mind, Mr. Vanderhagen."

"Certainly, Lindsay. Ask me anything."

"Can Henry challenge, in any way, Jackson's inheritance of what remains of the MacPhaull Company?"

"No," the attorney answered firmly. "With Richard having formally and legally acknowledged Henry—and Agatha—as his offspring, neither of them meets the legitimacy requirements of your father's initial Will. Which was made immaterial by his second Will leaving everything to Mr. Stennett. You, as a legitimate heir, could challenge it, but Henry doesn't—as we say—have a legal leg to stand on. The estate is Mr. Stennett's to do with as he pleases." He looked up to meet Jack's gaze and smiled. "And I understand that it pleases him to put a great many properties up for auction. Everyone in town is talking about it. Interest in acquiring seems to be running high."

"A very personal question, Mr. Vanderhagen," Lindsay went on. "If you're uncomfortable with it, please don't feel as though you have to answer it. Do you have any idea of whether or not my father knew that Henry and Agatha where Richard's children and not his?"

Vanderhagen sighed, pursed his lips for a moment, and then replied, "Richard confided in me that your father did eventually discover the truth. It apparently led to a significant confrontation between your father and your mother. Your . . . ahem, creation . . . was a consequence of emotions that got out of control. The business relationship between Richard and your father continued—albeit extremely strained—until William left for Texas. But as you might surmise, the personal one ended at the point when William discovered that he'd been cuckolded."

"Thank you. It explains a great deal about my family that I've always wondered about."

And, Jackson silently added, it explained why Billy had left for Texas and never looked back. How could he have been sure Lindsay was any more his child than Henry and Agatha were? Jesus. Now he understood why Billy had left the MacPhaull Company to him. It was vengeance, pure and simple. It all made perfect sense. Sick, twisted sense.

"When am I free to begin drawing from my trust?" he heard Lindsay ask.

"You've had access since the first day Richard and I established it. While, as usual, there are a number of bank officials officially serving as your board of trustees, your single vote outweighs theirs combined. The books are in a safety deposit box. I'll get them and bring them to you whenever you want to have them. Today, if you'd like."

"Tomorrow or the day after will be soon enough, Mr. Vanderhagen." She turned in her chair to look up at Jack. Her eyes were bright with happiness as she asked, "Do you have any further questions?"

Could you be this happy loving me? "Not at the moment," he managed to say, fighting the urge to take her into his arms and demand that she try.

"Mr. Stennett?" the lawyer said. He waited until Jack met his gaze before continuing. "Given the circumstances, I can understand how you might wish to secure the services of another attorney, but I want you to know that I am willing to supervise the transfer of title for those properties sold at tomorrow's auction. Ben, despite whatever feelings you may have about him, should be the one on hand to provide the new owners with any relevant and necessary bookkeeping information."

"Doesn't matter to me which lawyer or which bookkeeper

handles the details," Jack declared, turning on his heel and heading for the door. "All I'm interested in at this point is getting the money I need and going home. The quicker and cleaner, the better."

It's too damn late to save my heart.
Could you be this happy loving me?

The words reverberated through his mind and sent waves of realization crashing through his body. He couldn't breathe and his knees were suddenly so weak that he grabbed the doorjamb to keep himself upright. Desperate, he dragged air into his lungs and willed steel back into his legs. But there was nothing he could do to stem the torrent of his thoughts.

He loved Lindsay. He'd spent the last couple of weeks trying to solve a business puzzle, never realizing that with every minute of every day and night he was falling in love with her. Despite his determination, despite knowing better, despite his certain, rational declarations otherwise, he'd fallen in love with her.

Jesus. Sweet Jesus. He'd asked her to go to Texas with him so that he could help her find a husband. He was the biggest, blindest idiot God had ever turned loose.

Jackson scraped a trembling hand over his face and tried to marshal his thoughts. What was he going to do? If he told her he loved her now . . . if he asked her to marry him now . . . now that she was wealthy beyond even the wildest dreams . . . how could she believe him? Why would she think he was any different from all the others who saw her only for what she could give them? If only he'd had the sense to understand yesterday. Or the day before.

"Jack?"

He blinked and looked down into Lindsay's bright blue eyes. As he watched, the brightness faded, dulled by the shadows of troubled questions. She'd look at him just like that if he was stupid enough to tell her he loved her. She'd always look at him like that. She'd always wonder whether his love had been bought with MacPhaull Company money.

Tears swelled his throat, choking off words and all conscious thought. Instinct surged into the void and he obeyed, desperate to escape it all, desperate to find a hole in which to hide, to find a way to pretend this hadn't happened. He heard her call his name as he walked away, heard the confusion in her voice. He couldn't help her. Not now. Not anymore. He hurt too hard and too deep to help anyone. He couldn't see past it. If he was lucky just once in his life, the pain would kill him.

God, he hated Billy Weathers. He'd been set up, thrown into the lion's den. A naive lamb who only thought he knew something about lying and cheating and who thought honesty and right could triumph over greed and treachery. Billy had known exactly what he was sending him into. He'd been set up and made a fool of. And Lindsay had had a front row seat for the whole show. He'd never forgive Billy for that humiliation.

LINDSAY, HER HEART RACING, watched Jack vault down the front steps of Vanderhagen's office and stride down the walkway. Something was wrong. Terribly wrong. She'd never seen that look in his eyes before. Anger and hurt and something she thought might be fear. Panicking, she darted after him, pushing her way through the throng of pedestrians to reach him. Breathless, she caught his arm and pulled him to a stop as she asked, "Jack, what's wrong?"

"Nothing," he mumbled, avoiding her eyes. "Everything's worked out to be righter than rain, hasn't it?"

"Are you angry because you were wrong about Richard?"

"Yeah," he drawled sardonically, "I'm not nearly as noble as I've pretended to be. Having to apologize—even to a dead man—rubs me wrong."

"Actually, you were right, Jack," she offered. "He *was* stealing the company assets. Just not for the reason you thought."

"All hail Saint Richard," he said flatly, pulling away from her grasp and starting away again.

"Jack!" she cried, planting herself squarely in his path. "Why are you being so hateful? Richard left me a fortune; a fortune out of which I can easily write you a bank draft to cover all the debts on the land my father left you in Texas."

Write him a bank draft to cover the debts her daddy had left him? Jesus. She was a little rich girl turned into a even richer woman. He'd fulfilled his purpose, serving as her daily distraction for as long as it took for Richard Patterson to get on with dying. Now it was done and she could pay Jack Stennett and pack him off to Texas where he belonged. Neat and tidy. Never to be heard from again. His blood shot white-hot through his veins.

He leaned down and Lindsay's heart raced.

"You write me a draft," he said, his voice hard and low, "and I'll tear it to goddamn shreds. Do you understand me?"

She blinked in shock and he stepped around her, saying, "Don't wait supper for me. I'm not going to be there."

Again she blocked his path. "Jack," she gasped, light-headed from the exertion and the constraints of her corset. "I won't let you walk off angry. What's wrong? Why are you so furious?"

He glowered and then tried to go around and past her. Lindsay quickly stepped into his way. "Jack, please."

"All right. You want a load of buckshot, Lindsay, I'll give you one," he ground out, his eyes blazing. "I've had enough and I want to be done with it. I want to go home, climb back into a saddle, ride out over the hills, and sit and look at the land and my cattle. I want to be back where things are simple and straightforward, where people are just what they appear to be, and a man doesn't have to guess what they want and what they're willing to do to get it.

"I'm tired of thinking; tired of trying to find my way in a place I don't know and among people I will never understand. I'm tired of feeling responsible and trying to figure out what's the right thing to do. No one else worries about what's right. Why the hell should I?"

"That's not true, Jack," she whispered.

"Oh, yeah?" he countered instantly. "Patterson fathered three children and didn't acknowledge them as his until he was dead and six feet under. He's stolen another man's property and everyone thinks it's all right because in the end he's given it to the man's daughter in the name of birthright and decency. He's flung his own children a fistful of money for them to play with for a while, but he couldn't be bothered to raise them up into decent and honorable human beings."

He gestured toward the office door behind them. "And Otis Vanderhagen has gone along with the whole scheme because it was the right thing to do for the company? The right thing to do for Lindsay MacPhaull?" Jackson snorted. "Right didn't have a goddamn thing to do with it and you know it. Vanderhagen went along with it because he got paid for his services and because once he was in, there was no way Patterson could get rid of him. Vanderhagen knew enough to blackmail Patterson to hell and back six times. Vanderhagen was guaranteed a slice out of every pie just because he'd been smart enough to jab his fingers into the first one.

"And let's not forget Ben, your lying little two-faced bookkeeper. No, that isn't right," Jackson quickly corrected. "Ben was right up-front in telling me that everything he'd confide about the business would be with your best interests in mind. I was just stupid enough to believe that Ben was saying he'd be honest in what he did say. I've been the fool and Ben isn't to blame for that."

"Oh, Jack," she cried, knowing he was wrong about himself and reaching out to touch him.

"Christ Almighty," he swore, pushing her hand away. "No wonder Billy took off for Texas and didn't look back. I can't wait to do the same. The day after the auction's done, I'm going to climb aboard the first goddamn ship I can find leaving the harbor and sailing south. And being seasick doesn't matter one bit because I intend to be so damn drunk I won't notice whether I'm on land or sea or hanging by my belt loops from a tree limb forty feet in the air."

"Will you listen to me?" she asked, wanting to tell him how much she needed him to help her find her way through the new maze that had sprung up around her.

"No," he said hotly. "I'm not ever going to come back to this place and I'm not ever going to have to deal with these people again, even if I live to be a hundred and fifty.

Otis Vanderhagen can strip a thousand companies blind and it isn't going to be of any concern to me. And Ben can talk out both sides of his mouth until his tongue actually forks and it isn't going to make any difference to my world. Henry and Agatha can bankrupt themselves and each other's sanity and it isn't my problem.

"I couldn't save you people from yourselves even if I tried. And you know what, Lindsay? I don't *have* to try. I was handed a mess to clean up by virtue of being the only man Billy Weathers knew who was stupid enough to walk into it thinking he could. Well, I've come to my senses and I'm getting the hell out. Whatever mess there's left to clean up can just keep on being a mess. Either that or you can clean it up. Dealing with chaos and disaster is your greatest strength. You sure don't need me to do it for you. You don't need me for one goddamn thing."

"That's not true!" she cried. "Not true at all!"

"Maybe I won't wait for the day after the auction," he went on, ignoring her. "Maybe I'll sail out the same day. Why waste time? There's no reason to stay. And come to think of it, there isn't any reason to wait until I climb aboard any damn ship to get roaring drunk, either.

"And I'll stay drunk until I have to stagger to the auction tomorrow morning and get the money I need to keep the ranch intact." He started to turn away, then stopped and turned back to add, "And, by God, I'm not going to take one cent more than what I need. I don't care what the hell happens to the rest of the MacPhaull Company holdings. Primrose and Emile can stuff them and bake them, for all I care."

Lindsay stood in stunned silence as he turned and strode away. He hated her more than she had ever known was humanly possible. Fool that she was, it didn't make any difference. She loved him with all her heart, all her soul. And always would.

Slowly, she turned and walked up the street, heading back toward MacPhaull House, vaguely aware that there was a crowd, that it parted to permit her passage through, and that she had once again made herself the subject of scandalized public comment. This time, though, she was simply too battered to even care what anyone thought, what anyone said.

JACK WATCHED THE SUNRISE through the amber whiskey in his glass. Tossing it down his throat, he surveyed the main room of Mrs. Theorosa's house. He'd been falling in love with Lindsay when they'd come here that afternoon. He'd watched her dust and thought how sweetly domestic and contented she seemed. He'd wanted to stay, to make love to her in the room with the bright purple walls and the brilliant pansies. But he'd been dutiful and responsible and they'd gone back to town like they were expected to. If only he'd known then that it would be the only chance they would ever have to be together in this house that Lindsay liked so much.

If only he'd known. There wasn't enough whiskey in New York to ease the ache deep inside him. If only things had turned out differently. If only Patterson had left her impoverished. But he hadn't and Lindsay was never going to come to Texas and let Jackson Lee Stennett court her. Jack smiled ruefully. No other man would have been allowed within a mile of her. He'd have kept her for himself.

The money didn't really make any difference, though, he admitted. Rich or poor, Lindsay was the kind of woman who wouldn't walk away from obligations and responsibilities. There was no changing her. She was bound to Henry and Agatha as surely as if someone had tied a single rope around all their ankles. There was no point in asking her to cut the ties, because her conscience wouldn't let her.

If only Lindsay didn't need so badly to be needed. If only he could present her with some need of his own that would draw her to him and bind them together. But the only need was his own to be with her, to love her, to make a family with her and grow old with her at his side. It wasn't enough to outweigh all that kept her here and he knew it.

And he couldn't stay here with her. He regretted with all his heart the words he'd flung at her on the sidewalk that afternoon; they'd hurt her. But that didn't change the fact that they'd been the truest ones he'd ever spoken. He hated this place, hated the way it made a man come at the world and live his life. He didn't belong here, didn't want to become like Otis Vanderhagen, Richard Patterson, and Benjamin Tipton. And he sure as hell didn't want to become yet another person depending on Lindsay for his sustenance. He loved her too much to be a burden for her.

No, he couldn't stay here. He wanted his simple life. He wanted to share that with Lindsay. He wanted the impossible.

He wanted roses to bloom in Texas.

He wanted Lindsay's love to twine around his memories of Maria Arabella and all the other losses of his life. He wanted to be whole, happy, at peace with himself and with his past.

Through his tears, Jackson looked out the front window and watched the sun peek over the tops of the distant trees. It was time to head back into the city and do what had to be done. God give him the strength he'd need to face Lindsay and then walk away without proving—yet again—just how big a fool he was.

CHAPTER TWENTY-FOUR

*L*INDSAY HELD HER BREATH, listening to the sound of footsteps coming down the hall. They paused at the door of the adjoining room and then came again after the door opened and closed. Jack had returned. She stared at her reflection in the vanity mirror, searching for some glimmer of the fortitude she needed to face him. All she saw were haunted eyes and and an aching heart. Jack was wrong about her, she realized. Yes, she liked the challenge of triumphing over risk, but there were some games whose stakes were so high that even she didn't dare play. The chances of losing were just too great, too certain. Telling him that she loved him was one of them.

She couldn't hide from him, though. As much as she wanted to, she couldn't. There were business matters they had to discuss. It had always been business with Jack. He'd told her time and time again that that was all there was between them. That and a purely physical desire. She'd been the one who'd violated the rules he'd laid down. She'd agreed to abide by them and then ignored it all and let herself fall in love. Her heartache wasn't Jack's fault. It was hers and only hers.

"Business, Linds," she whispered, forcing a smile. "It's business, not personal. Remember that and you'll do just fine."

Rising from the bench, she smoothed her skirts and then stepped to the door. Taking a deep breath and squaring her shoulders, she knocked, almost hoping he'd tell her to go away.

"It's open unless you've locked it."

Lindsay smiled wryly. What did it say about her that she'd never even looked for the key? She turned the knob, pulled the door open, and then pushed back the tapestry. He stood beside the bed, a clean shirt in his hands, the one he'd removed lying on the floor at his feet. As always, her pulse raced at the sight of him and her heart yearned to be wrapped in his arms, to taste his lips and feel the wonder of his heartbeat against her breast. His gaze met hers for a fraction of a heartbeat before sliding away, and she wanted to cry for what she'd had and lost.

"You're back," she said tightly, tears tickling her throat. "I've been worried about you. Are you all right?"

"Righter than rain," he quipped, pulling on his clean shirt.

"I've never understood that expression," she admitted, noticing the open valise on the end of the bed. Her stomach turned to lead. "It doesn't mean anything."

"It means a lot of your life's a simple one," he replied, his attention fixed on buttoning the shirt. "It's rain that keeps the grass green, the streams flowing, and water in the well. It's what keeps men and cattle alive. Nothing on earth is more important or more right than rain."

Love was more important, but she knew better than to tell him that. It would be too close to a confession of her folly. Neither of them needed that complication. "We come from very different worlds, don't we, Jack?"

He paused for a long moment and then shrugged ever so slightly before saying, "That we do, and I'm heading back to where I belong."

"When?" she asked, hoping the question sounded far more casual than it was.

"Well, as my luck goes, I can't get a berth on a ship out of here until tomorrow morning. I figure it's best if I clear my stuff out of here now and get a room for tonight at a hotel down by the docks."

And so this was to be their farewell to each other. Lindsay caught her lower lip between her teeth. She wouldn't make it difficult for him. She wouldn't embarrass herself by telling him how much she loved him or pleading with him to stay with her. She wouldn't tell him that she'd gladly go to Texas with him if he thought there was any chance he might be the one she could marry. "Before you go," she said, forcing herself to speak before she couldn't, "I think we should discuss what you intend to do with the balance of the MacPhaull holdings."

"It doesn't matter," he said, stuffing his shirttail into the waistband of his trousers. "I can divide it a hundred ways and in the end you're going to hold the reins for everyone. That's your purpose in life; to take care of undeserving idiots. Far be it for me to interfere."

The words cut deeply and freed a surge of anger. Before she could think better of it, she retorted, "I never realized before yesterday that you had such a low opinion of me."

He started, her ire clearly surprising him. His breathing came hard and fast and for a second she thought that he would finally look her in the eyes. She didn't care if she saw anger in them, or even disdain. All she wanted was to look into their dark, soulful depths one more time before he left her.

But he didn't look up. Instead, he sighed, picked his suit coat up from the bed, and pulled it on, saying, "I'll see Otis Vanderhagen before the auction begins and have him draw up whatever paper there needs to be to transfer the remaining properties back into your hands. He'll see that you get it."

It was done between them. Not even business remained to connect them. Grief doused the spark of anger and left her shaking. "Good luck at the auction," Lindsay offered, turning to retreat into the sanctuary of her room. "I hope you get all the money you need."

"You're not going?"

She paused, but didn't dare look back to answer. "No. There's no need for me to be there. It's not my property being sold."

"Lindsay . . ."

She wouldn't let him see her cry. The illusion of pride and dignity was all she had left. "Good-bye, Jack. Have a safe journey home." She blindly closed the door behind her, wondering if there would ever come a day when she thought about Jack without wishing she could just lay down and die.

HE'D HEARD THE WHISPERED COMMENTS all morning. They thought he was calm and collected and coolly aloof, a paragon of business poise and keen acumen. If the bastards knew the truth, they'd have died laughing—after they'd stripped his moony-eyed, distracted carcass clean. But somehow he'd gone through the motions and they hadn't guessed. He'd shaken hands and signed papers, offered thanks and accepted congratulations. And he couldn't have recalled a single name or face out the bunch if he'd had to. They were all a mindless blur behind the memories of Lindsay.

He hadn't known until she'd gone back into her room that he wasn't going to see her again, that the painfully taut conversation was to be their last. He hadn't wanted it to end that way and yet he didn't think he could survive going back to MacPhaull House and making a formal show of their parting. It had damn near killed him to stand beside the bed and get dressed. Every fiber of his being had wanted to go to her, to take her in his arms, to tell her that he loved her, and then lay her down on the bed and make sweet love to her until she agreed to go with him to Texas, to marry him and have their babies.

Jackson shook his head and expelled a hard breath. It was done, over, and going back for another dose of pain was just plain stupid. It hadn't ended the way he'd wanted, but then that was the way life went sometimes. You accepted it and you moved on. You didn't look back and regret. There wasn't any point in it except to make yourself miserable. And God knew he was miserable enough already.

He missed Billy; acutely and more painfully than he ever had. Billy had known how to heal heartaches. When their father died, Billy had offered him and Daniel odd jobs to support their mother. When their mother passed on, he'd given them full wages, full days, and a place to live. Two days after Daniel had been killed, Billy had thrust a set of ledgers at Jack and told him it was time he learned how bookkeeping was done. And soon after laying Maria Arabella and Matthew to rest, Billy had announced that he wanted a business partner and Jackson Stennett was his pick. Billy had filled his life after every tragedy, leaving no room or time for grief to consume him. Jack smiled wryly, suddenly realizing that Billy had done it one last time from the grave. That's really what coming to New York for the money had been all about.

Unfortunately, Billy hadn't known that there would be yet another heartache to come of it. Jack sighed. At least a certainty of course came with seeing the pattern. The only way to heal the hurt of loving Lindsay was to go home and focus on the needs of the ranch and making it all that Billy and he had envisioned.

Jack looked around, noting the few stragglers visiting amongst themselves as auction company employees gathered up the chairs and tables. Ben sat at the makeshift desk he'd occupied throughout the auction, a black metal money box, an open ledger, and a stack of papers in front of him. Jackson strode toward the bookkeeper, determined to deal with the last of the business that needed to be done before he could go home.

"How much cash is in the till, Ben?"

The man didn't look up. "After paying Mr. Gregory for his services," he said, consulting the neatly aligned figures in his ledger, "there's forty-eight thousand seven hundred sixty-six dollars and twenty-one cents."

"A few thousand shy of what I need," Jackson observed. "Is there a letter of credit in the stack for somewhere around four thousand?"

"Yes, sir."

"Pull it and let's go to see the banker."

Ben finally looked up. "You don't need me to go along, Mr. Stennett. The amount has been signed over to you. You need only present it and ask for the payment to be rendered."

The conniving little pipsqueak probably thought he'd end up in an alley with his teeth lying on the pavers around him. It was a tempting thought, but Jack wasn't willing to expend even the slight effort it would take to exact the justice. He was tired of thinking, tired of fighting. Benjamin Tipton wasn't worth it. "Getting the money isn't why you're going," he said. "I need someone to haul the change to Lindsay."

"You could do that yourself, sir."

"Could," Jack agreed. "But I'm not going to. You are. Any others in the stack there that have been signed over?"

"Yes, sir."

"Then bring them along and we'll get them cashed while we're at it. You can take that money to Lindsay, too. I don't want to leave any loose ends behind when I head out of here in the morning."

Coming to his feet, Ben said with a tight smile, "I'm afraid that I can't attend you, Mr. Stennett. Mr. Vanderhagen has asked me to retrieve the trust ledgers from the safety deposit box and to take them to Miss Lindsay. She's expecting me and I wouldn't want to keep her waiting. She is my employer. My allegiance lies with her."

His allegiance? Through clenched teeth Jack asked sardonically, "Didn't it occur to you when you were setting fire to the apartment house that you could have killed not only me, but your employer, too? Not to mention a score of innocent people?"

Ben cocked a brow. "I didn't set that fire."

"All right," Jackson snapped. "Didn't it occur to you when you were *arranging* to have the fire set that—"

"I didn't make any such arrangements," the bookkeeper protested.

"That's not what Otis Vanderhagen says."

"Then he's lying."

"What about the man on the stairs?" Jack pressed,

watching Ben Tipton's eyes for the slightest sign of subterfuge.

"What man? What *are* you talking about, Mr. Stennett?"

Either Ben didn't know or he'd missed his calling for a life on the stage. "How about the rat in the box in the seat of the chair? Know anything about that, Ben?"

"All right," Ben said on a heavy sigh. "I did lie about that. Although," he hastily added, "I didn't know what was in the box or even that there was a box until you showed it to me. As I was coming down the walk that morning to open the office, I saw Otis Vanderhagen leaving. I thought he'd been there to see me and I wasn't all that disappointed to have missed him. I may have assisted in his and Mr. Patterson's scheming, but it was only to help Miss Lindsay. I don't care for the man and I don't trust him. I didn't even suspect that he had a key to the office until you brought out the box and asked about it."

"The thing about lies is that once you get caught in one," Jackson drawled, "your word on anything else is worthless."

"I made no attempts to harm you or Miss Lindsay. I abhor violence of any sort. In all the sabotaging I did for the sake of Miss Lindsay, no one was ever hurt in any way."

"Why would Vanderhagen lie about it?" Jackson pressed. "Tell me that."

Ben gave him a look that suggested that Jack might be the most naive man to ever breathe east of the Mississippi River. "Perhaps he made the attempts on your life and doesn't want to admit his responsibility for them. In case you haven't noticed, he doesn't have many scruples and those he does possess aren't particularly strong."

Otis Vanderhagen might have a great deal of respect for Ben Tipton, but the sentiment sure didn't seem to be mutual. "There wouldn't be any point in his lying about it now," Jack posed, still watching Ben closely. "He's laid all the cards on the table and explained why he saw me as a threat at the beginning."

Ben rolled his eyes and snorted. "Frankly, I never thought there was much of a chance of you marrying Miss Lindsay."

Jack chuckled darkly, the pain in his chest hard and deep. "Where did you get a crazy notion like that in the first place?"

"Mr. Vanderhagen; the first day you came here," Ben said readily, shaking his head and rolling his eyes again. "He returned to the office for the copy of Mr. MacPhaull's will after you, Dr. Bernard, and Miss Lindsay had left with Mr. Patterson. He was afraid that you would marry Miss Lindsay for her money. He thought there was a possibility of her changing her will to make you her sole heir. He went on and on about how unfair it would be and how he just couldn't let that happen."

Jack considered the explanation. Of course Lindsay had a Will. Richard and Vanderhagen would have understood the necessity of it, even if Lindsay hadn't fully understood the size of the estate she'd be leaving behind. She'd provide for Abigail and Primrose, Proctor, and John, but, knowing Lindsay, Henry and Agatha probably got the lion's share. If she were to marry, it would be logical to name her husband and their children as the heirs. He could see why Henry and Agatha would be upset and determined to keep that from happening, but why would it matter to Vanderhagen?

Ben slammed closed his ledger, nodded crisply, and then handed Jackson a short stack of thrice-folded letters of credit while saying, "If you'll excuse me, Mr. Stennett, Miss Lindsay is waiting for me to bring her the trust ledgers."

Jackson watched him walk away, turning the man's words over and over in his brain. Otis Vanderhagen had claimed that Ben was the one who'd tried to kill him. Ben claimed to know nothing about the efforts. Obviously, one of them was lying. Which? And why were they bothering to cast stones at this point in the game? It didn't matter anymore. And there was something about the concern over Lindsay's will that bothered him; something he couldn't see clearly. It just didn't make sense.

"Ah, there you are, Stennett."

At the sound of Otis Vanderhagen's voice, Jackson set aside his mental puzzle and turned, amazed that the man actually knew how to speak in something less than a bellowing roar and wondering why the lawyer had suddenly changed his manner. One look at the man was explanation enough. Vanderhagen was ashen-faced and perspiring even more heavily than usual. There was a decided quiver around his lips and his eyes seemed to be slightly protruding from their sockets.

"I have both the codicil you requested that I draw up and the papers transferring the remaining MacPhaull properties into Lindsay's trust," the man said. He fisted his hand, raised it to his lips, and coughed into it, wincing at the effort, before saying tightly, "Both are ready for your signature, Mr. Stennett."

He laid the documents down on the table beside the cash box, adding, "There are two identical sets of the documents. One for my files and one for you to take back to your attorney in Texas." He turned to a small knot of men standing nearby and with a thin smile managed to raise his voice to say, "Perhaps we can prevail on two of these gentlemen to witness your signature."

Jack laid aside the letters of credit and picked up Ben's pen, dipping it in the inkwell as two men separated themselves from their companions and came to stand behind him. While they silently watched over his shoulder, Jack signed his full name in the places Vanderhagen indicated with a tap of his finger. Straightening, he handed the pen to the stranger on his right, and then stepped back to allow the man to sign his own name.

As the process of witness signatures went on, Jack glanced over at the attorney. His color was even more pasty than it had been only a few moments before.

"You're not looking at all well, Vanderhagen."

He coughed into his hand again and swallowed with great difficulty before answering, "Ben shared with me some poppy-seed muffins he bought from a vendor on the way to the auction this morning. I'm afraid that I ate more than my fair allotment and, in revenge for gluttony, they haven't set well on my stomach."

Jack had seen people suffer the effects of tainted food before, but muffins had never been the culprit. Rancid butter, yes, but most people knew it had gone had at the first taste and didn't eat pounds of it. "Maybe you ought to see Doc Bernard."

"I'm sure it will pass," the lawyer said with a dismissive wave of his hand and a hard swallow. "I presume that you're going back to the Republic of Texas?"

"Yep. First thing tomorrow morning," Jackson replied, nodding his thanks to the two witnesses as they stepped away. Jack picked up the stack of credit letters and perused the names of the financial institutions on which they were drafted. "Which bank is the closest? First National or Merchants?"

"First National." He pointed with a trembling hand, adding, "You can see it right over there."

"Look, Vanderhagen," Jack said, his brows knitted. "I think you really need to see a doctor. If it is food poisoning, you've got it bad."

"I'll be fine," he said with a painful smile as he pocketed the signed documents. "I'm more concerned about Lindsay. She'll be sad to see you go."

"She'll get over it," he coolly assured the lawyer.

"It may take quite some time," the other man observed, his breathing labored. "She's not as resilient as she would like people to believe."

"I've noticed, Vanderhagen, that no one in this town is quite what they want people to believe."

"You're angry that I wasn't straightforward with you," he replied, wiping his jacket sleeve across his forehead. "Would it help to know that I won't oppose Lindsay's plan to rewrite her Will to make you her primary heir?"

He stared at the attorney, dumbstruck. Why in hell's name was Lindsay thinking about giving it all to him? Guilt? If Henry or Agatha had any inkling of what they stood to lose . . .

Vanderhagen's eyes suddenly widened and a breath gurgled and caught deep in his throat. He swayed on his feet as he face turned blue, and Jack instantly grabbed him by the lapels of his coat. Lowering him to the grass, he called out, "Someone send for a doctor! Hurry!"

A bubble of bright red blood glistened between the

lawyer's parted lips as one man ran off and the others gathered around. Jack knew well the signs of death, knew that no matter how fast anyone ran, the outcome would be the same. Otis Vanderhagen was dying. From the inside out. There was nothing that anyone could do to alter the course.

"Has Lindsay actually changed her Will yet?" Jack demanded, desperate to put all the pieces together before it was too late. "Who knows about her decision? It's important, Otis. You've got to answer me."

"Note . . . this morning . . . with Ben . . . asking . . ."

Ben. The bastard son whose father had used him to amass a fortune for another man's child. Ben, who knew how the shell game worked and could continue to work it for his own gain if . . . if Henry and Agatha inherited . . . if Ben, the loyal servant, was the only one alive who knew how to play the game. . . .

Panic struck Jackson like a fist, knocking the air from his lungs and clenching his gut. Breathless, his heart racing, he tightened his grip on Vanderhagen's lapels and roughly demanded, "Did you send Ben to get the trust ledgers for Lindsay just now?"

Vanderhagen's eyes were bulging and his adam's apple bobbed furiously. A bloody froth trickled from the corner of his mouth, but he managed to answer, "No. Only key . . . my desk."

The muffins. The muffins had been poisoned. He'd bet on it. Sweet Jesus. If he was right about Ben, Lindsay would be the next to die. And Ben couldn't afford to waste any time. Ben was the liar. The actor on the stage of greed.

"Stay with him," Jack commanded the others as he rose to his feet. "I've got to get to MacPhaull House."

He ran, not looking back. *God, let me be wrong. Please let me be wrong.*

A MOVEMENT IN THE STUDY DOORWAY caught her attention. Lindsay looked up from the correspondence she was sorting to find Ben Tipton standing there, his hands in his pockets, his gaze fixed on the carpet in front of the desk.

"Hello, Ben," she said. "I didn't hear you come in. Was it a successful auction?"

His lips moved, but she didn't hear a thing. Perplexed, she came around the desk, saying, "You'll have to speak up, Ben. I can't hear a word you're saying."

He lifted his gaze, slowly focused it on her, and then drew a long, deep breath. "I said that I'm going to kill you," he said softly as he removed his hands from his pockets. In his right one, he held a pistol.

Her blood went cold. Ben? Ben wanted to kill her? "Why?" she asked, her mind racing.

"You really are the stupidest woman God ever thought to put on the face of the earth."

Her own pistol was in her reticule. Her reticule was on her vanity upstairs. It was of no use to her up there. Was Ben any better a shot than she was? Primrose and Emile were at the market. But Abigail was somewhere in the house. So was Lucy. Did she want them involved in this?

No. No, she didn't want them hurt. But if they were to hear and go for help . . . God, her mind was going in too many directions at once. She needed time, she needed to focus on something so that she could think straight. "Since I am so stupid," she said with all the calm she could muster, "would you mind explaining why you're doing this? It seems to me that if I'm going to die, I ought to a least know why you think it's necessary."

"You're a wealthy woman because of all that I've done for you over the years. I deserve to be wealthy too."

"Richard acknowledged you as his son and left you a considerable sum of money. Haven't you seen his Will?" she asked, trying desperately to find a way out of the nightmare.

"No, Otis Vanderhagen hasn't deigned to share the details yet. But he doesn't have to. My *father* was ever so honest about what he intended to do. There'll be a bone tossed my way, what's left, I'm sure he'll say, of the ineritance I've already spent. But I want more than a bone. I deserve more."

"Then I'll write you a bank draft," she offered. If she

could put the huge desk between her and Ben's apparent madness . . . "How much do you want?"

"I want it all and I'm going to get it."

"Fine," she agreed, edging backward and gesturing to the books lying open on the desk. "Tell me what to write and it's yours."

"Stop right where you are," he commanded, lifting the pistol to shoulder height and aiming the muzzle at the center of her forehead.

Lindsay froze, suddenly and absolutely certain that he was indeed capable of shooting—and with great accuracy.

"It's not that simple," he went on. "Thanks to Mr. Stennett's tenacity and Otis Vanderhagen's mouth, you now know how the game is played. You could write me a draft and then go to the authorities and tell them everything. I'd be arrested and imprisoned and you could have it all back." He shook his head slightly. "No, the only way is for me to kill you. Henry and Agatha will inherit and then I can go on with the scheme my father and Otis Vanderhagen so kindly put into place for me. I can have it all, and without either of them ever knowing that I'm stripping the assets."

"For yourself."

"Absolutely. Why share if you don't have to?"

"I can see the logic," she offered, her heart pounding furiously. "Very sound, actually. But why have you picked today to carry out your brilliant plan? Wouldn't tomorrow or some day next week work just as well? I'd prefer to wait, if it's all the same to you."

"I understand why you would. Unfortunately, if we waited, you'd have time to change your Will and leave all your pretty money to Stennett. He wouldn't be as easy to lead as Henry and Agatha will be. And then there's the fact that Stennett will be gone tomorrow. No, I think it's best and easiest if you die today."

He stomach slid down, leaden and cold, to rest on the soles of her feet. "You're going to say that Jack killed me?"

"Of course not. God, you're so stupid," he sneered. "I'd have to arrange for him to have no alibi, and it's such an unnecessary amount of effort. As for why today. . . It's a perfect opportunity. I might have to wait years for another one as perfect. Now kindly gather your skirts and get up the stairs to your room."

Relieved to know that Jack wasn't going to be blamed for whatever Ben planned, Lindsay exhaled and marshaled her thoughts. "Why upstairs?" she asked, knowing instinctively that she shouldn't go.

"A spurned lover doesn't normally kill herself in a study. She does it in her bedroom, the place of her humiliation and shame."

No one who knew her would believe she would commit suicide. "Wouldn't it be more believable for me to wait to kill myself after Jack's gone?" she proposed, trying to shake his confidence and buy herself some time to think. And perhaps just the tiniest piece of luck. "There is hope until Jack actually sails, you know."

Jack, I need you. Please help me. Please.

Ben snorted. "There is no hope of a reconciliation. I heard about him railing at you outside Vanderhagen's office yesterday. The whole city knows about it, about your failed affair. Given your past, no one will be the least bit surprised to learn that you couldn't bear the thought of being publicly embarrassed a second time. Now be a good little girl and get up the stairs to your room."

Oh, God help her. It made sense. It was entirely believeable. "No," she declared, inching backward again. "You'll have to shoot me right here and figure out how to explain my obvious murder to the authorities. I won't play into your hands."

"You stupid—"

An enraged screech reverberated through the room in the same instant that a flash of movement came from the doorway behind Benjamin Tipton. Lindsay's brain barely had time to recognize her housekeeper before Ben whirled about and swung his arm across Abigail's face.

"Abigail!" Lindsay screamed, darting forward as her friend dropped the closed umbrella and crumpled to the carpet.

"Stay, Lindsay," Ben snapped, stepping into her path and pointing the pistol at her head again.

Abigail moaned and Lindsay froze in her tracks. "Don't

hurt her," Lindsay pleaded. "Please, don't hurt her. She was only trying to protect me."

"Do as you're told and I'll try to think of some way she can keep breathing."

Lindsay nodded and watched as Ben backed toward the weakly struggling woman. His eyes never left Lindsay as he bent down, grabbed a fistful of gray hair, and used it to haul a whimpering Abigail to her feet. "Thank you," he said mockingly, "you're just what I needed."

In one smooth, quick movement he jerked Abigail in front of him, put an arm around her waist, and pulled her back against him. For a split second the pistol shifted away from Lindsay, but before she could blink, the muzzle came to rest against Abigail's temple.

Lindsay clenched her teeth. Never in her life had she hated a human being as much as she did this vicious monster. If she got even half a chance, she'd kill him. Jack had been right; when you were pushed hard enough, you could do things you never imagined that you could. And you could do them with a smile.

"Now, upstairs, little Miss Lindsay," Ben said, "or I'll put a bullet in her brain."

Lindsay went because she had no other choice and because he wanted her to go where her pistol was. Never turning her back on him, she stepped into the foyer, across it to the base of the stairs, and started up. Abigail started to struggle when it came her turn to start up the stairs. Ben growled and pressed the muzzle harder against her head.

"Don't fight him, Abigail," Lindsay cried. "It'll be all right. Don't make him angry. Just do what he wants."

Abigail looked up at her. One eye was swollen closed, the other was awash in tears.

"It'll be all right," Lindsay assured her again, resuming her backward climb up the stairs. "Just come up the stairs without fighting him."

Abigail gathered her skirts in her one hand and obeyed woodenly, tears streaming down her cheeks. Lindsay continued to the top, mentally judging the distance between herself and Ben, herself and the door to her bedroom, the door to the vanity. Her heart thundered with the realization that she wasn't going to be able to dash ahead and grab her own pistol without endangering Abigail. The attempt to save them both would have to wait until they were all in the room together. Meager as it was, it was the only hope they had.

Once Ben had maneuvered his captive to the top of the stairs, he pushed her forward, quickly closing the distance between them and Lindsay. She backed into her bedroom only a few feet ahead of them.

Even as she started for the vanity, Ben snarled, "Wrong way, Lindsay. Step over to the bed and pull off the sheet."

She hesitated, knowing that if she obeyed, their one chance might well be gone forever. There was a slow, metallic click as Ben cocked the pistol. Abigail choked back a sob and Lindsay instantly darted toward the bed. She flung away the comforter and with trembling hands yanked off the linen sheet as she'd been instructed.

"Very good," Ben congratulated her snidely. "Now, tear off a long, fairly wide strip, if you would. Use your teeth to begin the tear if you have to."

"There's a pair of scissors in the drawer of the vanity," she suggested, her voice quavering with fear and desperate hope.

"Women committing suicide in the throes of despondency don't think about getting scissors from the vanity," he countered, smiling thinly. "And an intelligent man staging it all doesn't allow her to have anything that might be used as a weapon against him. Use your teeth and be quick about it."

She accomplished the task slowly, straining to hear beyond the rasping of her own breathing, the shredding of cloth, and the confines of her room. Where was Lucy? Had she gone for help? Please, please let her have gone to get help. Let them come quickly and loudly so that Ben would be thrown into a panic. If he dithered, even for a moment, she could get to her pistol. She could kill him just as surely as he was going to kill her and Abigail.

"Reasonably well done for a stupid woman. Throw the end over the—" Ben frowned up at the area above her bed. "Well, there's a problem. Let me see . . . We need something high and fairly sturdy." He looked around the room and then his face brightened. "Ah, the curtain rod will do. Take the footstool over and put it on the window seat."

"Lindsay, don't do it."

"If you don't, the last thing you'll see are your beloved housekeeper's brains splattered all over your wallpaper," he announced with a cold, tight smile. "Get on with it, Lindsay. I don't have all day."

She retrieved the footstool from in front of the chair and headed toward the window. Could she throw it at him? she wondered. Would he flinch before he thought of pulling the trigger and killing Abigail? She didn't know and she couldn't take the risk with her friend's life. If only she'd asked Jack to pull down her curtains. . . .

Jack. Dear God, she hoped Jack didn't believe she'd actually killed herself. He had regrets enough in his life without adding her death to them. Maybe he'd sail before her body was discovered. Maybe he'd never know. That would be for the best. She loved him so much, she didn't want his heart hurt again.

"That's a good girl," Ben crooned as she placed the footstool on the cushion of the window seat. "Now climb up and tie the end of the sheet around the curtain rod. And tie it right. We wouldn't want it to slip loose at the wrong moment, would we?"

Lindsay hesitated yet again, considering the window itself and wondering if she'd survive the fall. But in leaping, she'd be leaving Abigail at the madman's mercy.

"Get up there and get the strip tied as you were told or she dies right now!"

Lindsay gathered her skirts and scrambled onto the cushion. As she gained her feet and stepped up onto the precariously balanced footstool, she said, "In case this ends badly, Abigail, I want you to know that it's not your fault. You—"

"In case this ends badly?" Ben chortled. "In case? Who do you think is going to come save you? Certainly not the little slip of a thing that opened the door for me."

Lindsay's heart lurched. "What did you do to Lucy?"

"The front step was slightly too public to eliminate her

permanently, but I do believe I hit her hard enough that she's still lying quietly in the front shrubbery. Were you hoping that she went to summon help?"

Lindsay met her housekeeper's gaze and tried to smile bravely. "Jack will be here any minute," she promised. *Please, Jack, please. If ever there was anything at all between us, please know that I need you. That I love you.*

"No, he won't," Ben corrected. "He's busily cashing his letters of credit. And he told me himself that he has absolutely no intention of seeing you again before he sails. I almost fainted with gratitude when he passed along that bit of information. Oh," he added, his smile brightening, "just in case you're wondering, Vanderhagen won't be waddling this way either. If he isn't dead yet, he will be in just another few minutes. The man ate enough poison for breakfast to kill a horse."

Dear God in heaven. How had she never seen Ben's ruthlessness? His obvious greed and insanity. You had to be insane to kill people so callously. Why hadn't she seen that the mask of civility and loyalty hid a monster?

"Get on with tying the end to the rod and be quick about it. I have a luncheon engagement and I don't want to be late."

"Bastard," she snarled, hating him with every fiber of her being. "I hope you choke to death on the first bite."

Ben rammed the muzzle hard against Abigail's head and bellowed, "Do it, Lindsay! Now!"

She obeyed, stretching up to stand on her toes, tying the knot as best she could, and then pulling the makeshift rope to test not the strength of the knot, but how well the rod had been anchored into the wall. Jack had pulled down the dining-room curtains with one single tug. She knew she couldn't equal the strength he had in his arms, but perhaps the weight of her body would be enough to accomplish the same end. She thought she heard what might have been a slight cracking of plaster, and she quickly feigned a whimper in the hope of covering the sound and keeping Ben from hearing it, too.

"Good. Tie the other end of the strip around your neck. And don't leave any slack in the sheet, either. We want it nice and taut so there's no having to stop and do it over again."

Lindsay moistened her lips with the tip of her tongue and slowly draped the strip of linen around her neck. Knotting the linen at her nape, she braced herself, focusing only on the feel of the strip leading up the back of her head. If she could grab it with both hands in time—

"Lindsay, no!" Abigail screamed.

"Oh, shut up!" Ben bellowed, slamming the butt of the pistol and then his fist into her face. Abigail crumpled to the floor like a tattered rag doll, silent and deathly still.

"You son of a bitch!" Lindsay screamed, frantically clawing at the knot behind her head, trying to undo it. "You're going to rot in hell!"

"Would you like to knock the stool out from under yourself?" he asked, sidling toward her and pocketing the pistol. "Or would you prefer that I do it for you?"

"You bastard!" She kicked at him, determined to keep him out of his arm's reach.

Ducking beneath the reach of her leg, he grabbed the seat cushion, crying, "And it's a bastard's revenge I want!" and pulled it all from under her.

The world fell away. She couldn't breathe and a scream strangled low in her throat as the world went gray. At the far distant edge of it, she heard someone call her name. The voice was frightened, but there was nothing she could do to reassure it. Then there came, from a long way away, the rumble of thunder, the brush of a sweeping wind against her body, the crack of splintering lightning. And then there was nothing at all.

CHAPTER TWENTY-FIVE

*T*EARS ROLLED DOWN his cheeks. *Dear God, anything you want. Let her be alive. Let me have gotten here in time. Please.*

"Lindsay!" Jackson called, frantically clawing through the drapery fabric, his pulse thundering, his breathing ragged gasps. She couldn't be dead. She couldn't. He needed her. He loved her with all his heart.

"Lindsay!" Bits of white plaster cascaded down the folds of dark rose velvet, but he was only barely aware of them, heedless of the debris in which he knelt. *Name the price. I'll pay it.*

A bit of blue brocade skirt, a flutter of lace, and his heart hammered wildly as he jerked the heavier fabric aside to uncover her. She lay sprawled on her back on the carpet, silent and still, her golden hair fanning around her head like an angel's halo, the white noose encircling her neck. Choking back a cry, he scrambled to undo the deadly cord, his fingers fumbling and burning as they slipped on the fabric in his frenzied effort to pull the knot apart.

She moved; a feeble, dazed effort to lift her hand. Hope flared in his heart and soul as he ripped the deadly strip of sheet from around her neck and flung it away.

"Breathe for me, sweetheart," he begged, gathering her carefully into his arms. Kneeling in the remnants of curtains and plaster wall, cradling her in his arms, Jack looked down at her face and poured his heart into a sobbing plea. "Breathe for me, Lindsay. Love me or hate me; it doesn't matter. Just don't die. Please."

Her breath shuddered and her chest rose. Jack held his own breath, and tightening his arms around her, willed what remained of his strength into her body. Her eyelids fluttered and then came open. Blue eyes. She had the most beautiful blue eyes he'd ever seen. His heart flooded with relief and he smiled down at her, knowing that he'd remember for the rest of his life the pureness of wonder and hope that he saw in her eyes as she gazed back at him.

"Jack?" she whispered, reaching up to gently touch his cheek. "Jack?"

"I'm here, sweetheart," he crooned, drawing her closer, desperate to hold her, determined never to let her go. "I've got you. You're safe."

She collapsed into him, gathering fistfuls of his jacket into her hands as the memories struck her and her entire body began to tremble. He rocked her back and forth, pressing kisses to the top of her head and reveling in the warmth of her pressed against him, in the miracle of her survival.

Suddenly she started, catching him by surprise. "Abigail!" she cried, frantically trying to push out of his embrace.

He eased his hold on her, but only enough so that he could look into her eyes again. Such fear, such concern. "Emile's taking care of her," he assured her, glancing to the foot of the bed. Gently brushing a tendril of golden silk from her cheek, he softly added, "She's alive and she'll heal."

"Lucy—"

"We found her," Jack interrupted soothingly, drawing her close again. "She's a little scraped up, but she's fine, sweetheart. Primrose has gone to get the constables. They should be here any minute now."

She sighed and relaxed, nestling into him and nuzzling her cheek against his shoulder. Just as suddenly as before, she started in his arms and tried to pull back. He held her tight this time, understanding the new cause of her panic. "He's dead, Lindsay," he said softly, noting with satisfaction the shattered window glass. "Ben can't hurt you. Can't hurt anyone. It's over."

"Oh God, Jack," she said softly, her voice thick and edged with tears as the last of her strength ebbed away. She fell into him and, through her sobs, poured out the horror of her ordeal. "He wanted the money, Jack. All of it. He couldn't let me change the Will. He . . . he . . ."

"I know, sweetheart. I know. I figured it out at the end of the auction."

She shuddered and drew a deep breath. "He wanted everyone to think I'd killed myself. I was so afraid. I couldn't do anything. He had Abigail and he kept saying he'd shoot her. All I could do was hope you'd know how much I needed you. That you'd come save me."

Jack tightened his hold on her as she began to sob again. "I did know, Lindsay. I came as fast as I could."

But God, he'd been so close to too late. So heartbreakingly close. He'd always remember the terror he'd felt as he'd come through the front door to hear Abigail Beechum scream. And even if he lived ten thousand years, he'd never forget the sheer horror of scrambling into the bedroom just in time to see Ben pull the cushion from under Lindsay's feet, to see her dangling, clawing at death. If he'd been one second later . . .

Tears filled his eyes as he realized how very close he'd come to losing her. He'd lost so many of those he loved; he couldn't bear the thought of losing her, too. She had become his life, the best and brightest light of his days and the sweetest comfort of his nights.

From downstairs drifted the sounds of booted footsteps and voices. Emile left Abigail's side and hurried to the door to summon everyone to what Jack knew the papers would refer to as "the scene of the crime." All hell was going to break loose. He was going to have to let go of Lindsay so they could both answer the constables' questions. Dr.

Bernard would have to be summoned and then Abigail and Lucy tended to and comforted. All of it was necessary and couldn't be avoided, but he regretted it just the same.

As footsteps thundered up the stairs, Jackson pressed a kiss into Lindsay's hair and then laid his cheek on the warm pillow of golden threads. "When everyone's gone, sweetheart," he whispered, "we're going to talk."

She nodded and hugged him tight. An image drifted through his mind. Tiny, pale blue morning glories surrounded and supported by a mass of pink roses. And he understood why it felt so right.

LINDSAY PAUSED AT THE DOOR of Abigail's room. Dr. Bernard sat beside her housekeeper's bed, holding her hand and murmuring reassurances. Abigail, her face covered by the wet compresses Primrose had prepared, clung tightly to the physician's hand and waited for the laudanum to work its miracle. Lindsay offered them a tired smile that neither of them saw and then pulled the door closed behind herself.

Upstairs, Jeb was caring for Lucy in much the same way. Emile, on the heels of the constables' arrival, had been dispatched to the courthouse to summon the young bookkeeper. Jeb had come careening through the front door of MacPhaull House breathless and ready to kill. He'd swept Lucy into his arms, kissed her soundly, and then promptly carried her upstairs to their room.

Lindsay leaned back against the wall outside Abigail's room and closed her eyes, remembering awakening amidst the debris and in Jack's embrace, the deep sense of being safe and cherished that had eased the terror from her mind. And then the world had intruded and she'd had to stand alone again. Jack had said they were going to talk when everyone left. She didn't want to talk, though; she wanted to be held, wanted to pretend that Jack was always going to be there when she couldn't be brave or stalwart or resolute.

But talk they must and Lindsay knew there was nothing to be gained in avoiding or delaying it. She needed to thank

Jack properly, formally, for having thrown Ben out the window and pulling down the draperies, to thank him for nothing less than saving her life.

With a deep sigh, she pushed herself off the wall, squared her shoulders, and started toward the main part of the house in search of him. As she went, she recalled reading about some cultures in the world that believed saving a person's life indebted them to you, that required the saved soul to commit their lives to serving their savior until the debt could be repaid in kind. What would Jack do, she wondered, if she insisted on accompanying him to the ends of the earth, living for him until the end of time?

She had no ready answer and in that she saw a glimmer of hope. Was she brave enough to propose it? Did she have anything to lose in taking the chance? Only her pride and dignity. And what were they worth when compared to the possibility of spending forever without Jack?

JACK PACED HIS BEDROOM, trying to organize his thoughts and failing spectacularly. He eyed the whiskey decanter he'd brought up from the study and wondered whether he could keep his hands steady enough to pour himself a glass of courage. Deciding that it wasn't likely, he scrubbed his face with the palms of his hands and then pushed his fingers through his hair.

Jesus. He had rocks for brains. If only he'd realized that he loved her before either one of them had known she was a wealthy woman. If only he'd had the good sense to ask her to marry him the night he'd suggested that she go to Texas with him. And to think that he'd been so stupid as to suggest that he'd help her find a husband. That one had been a masterpiece of sheer blindness.

How the hell was he going to fix the mess he'd made of it all? How was he going to convince Lindsay that he loved her and that her money didn't have a damn thing to do with it?

"I've been looking all over for you."

His heart slammed upward, lodging high in his throat.

He turned to find her standing on his side of the door connecting their rooms, the tapestry sliding back into place behind her. Her eyes were soft and warily searching his and he ached to hold her. *I love you, Lindsay*. He bit his tongue and tried to summon some sort of strategy more sensible than dashing forward and pulling her into his arms.

She took a shaky breath, moistened her lower lip with the tip of her tongue, and then said, "I assume the constables have gone away satisfied?"

"Horatio Wellsbacher, too," he managed to get out around his heart. "How's Abigail?"

"Fine," she answered, nodding. "Dr. Bernard's still with her. I think he's planning to stay the night at her side. And just between us, I don't think his attentions are purely professional." She drew another unsteady breath. "You said we needed to talk and I agree. There are some things I need to say to you, Jack."

"There are some things I need to say to you, too, Lindsay," he blurted, the words rushing past his determination to be calm. "And please forgive the lack of gallantry, but I'm going first. I want to apologize for being an absolute horse's ass yesterday afternoon and an even bigger one this morning."

"Apology accepted," she said softly, her smile tremulous and her breathing suddenly ragged. "May I ask why you were so angry?"

God, let me do this right. I love her so much. "Do you want the long version or the short one?"

"I'm willing to take whatever you're willing give me, Jack."

Calm and certainty washed over him. And he knew in that moment that it didn't matter how the words came out. She trusted him, had never asked anything of him beyond honesty. She gave of herself without condition, and he cherished her for understanding it had been the way he needed to be loved.

"I'll give you the long one, sweetheart. You deserve it," he answered, slowly closing the distance between them. He stopped in front of her and gazed down into her beautiful blue eyes; eyes so full of yearning that it made his heart ache. He took a deep breath and put his hands on her waist to steady himself.

"As Vanderhagen laid everything out," he began, "my grand, charitable plan for your life fell apart right in front of my eyes and there wasn't anything I could do to save it. I stood there in his office and all I could see was the fact that I'd been wrong from the beginning. And that you'd just been handed all the money in the world and that you didn't need me for anything. And knowing that hurt like a son of a bitch. All I could think about was getting away, of hiding and licking my wounds."

He took a deep breath and then gave her the hardest truth, saying, "And even as I tried to run, I realized that Billy had known all along what he was sending me into; that he didn't have enough kindness in him to even warn me so I'd know just what I was facing, so that I wouldn't make a complete jackass of myself. I've spent my life worshiping the ground Billy Weathers walked on, but I hated him in that moment more than I've ever hated anyone. And when you came after me, I poured all that hurt out on you. I'm sorry, Lindsay. From the bottom of my heart, I'm sorry. You've never done anything to earn that kind of poison."

"Oh, Jack," she whispered, her heart breaking for him. She reached up and brushed her fingertips over the chiseled planes of his cheek. So many losses in his life. To have his illusions die, too . . . "I knew you were hurting. And I felt so awful not knowing how to ease it for you. I've never felt so lost or so alone as when you closed yourself away and wouldn't let me in. Promise me you won't ever do that to me or yourself again. Promise that you'll let me help."

She always gave of herself. A promise to let her was such a small thing to give in return. "I promise, sweetheart. Good, bad, coherent, or completely confused—you'll get nothing but honesty from me from now on."

"Thank you." She smiled softly. "But I think you're being too hard on my father. He couldn't have known about the shell game, Jack. He didn't know that he was sending you into a spider's web."

The irony of her words wasn't lost on him. Somewhere

along the way they'd each come to see her father in a different light. How Lindsay had managed to set aside a lifetime of hurt was beyond his understanding. Jack wasn't as willing to forgive. The pain was too new, too raw.

"He knew what kind of man Richard Patterson was, sweetheart. He could have guessed easy enough what was going to happen to the company once he was gone. No, Lindsay. No forgiveness. No excuses. He left you at Patterson's mercy and never looked back. He was a selfish son of a bitch."

She shook her head and her smile was bittersweet. "You once told me he was the one who made you into the man you are. He couldn't have been all bad, Jack. I will never know a better, finer man than Jackson Stennett."

"Billy knew me well enough to know that I'd try to make everything right before I walked away," Jack countered, unable to set aside his anger. "He set me up to play the fool. And I did it beautifully. Right out where you could see every misstep."

"You're no fool, Jack. And there were no missteps, no mistakes."

Such conviction, such groundless faith. He reached up to gently trace the purpling line just under the curve of her jaw. "I wasn't right about a single thing except how the game worked," he said softly. "And taking as long as I did to figure out that it hadn't really ended yet . . ." He met her gaze. "I almost got you killed. Just one heartbeat, Lindsay." His throat swelled and tightened. "Just one heartbeat and I would have been too late."

"But you weren't too late and that's all that matters," she protested. "You knew I was in danger and you set aside everything else and came to me as fast as you could." She stretched up to stand on her toes and feathered a kiss across his lips. "Thank you, Jack," she murmured as she eased away. "Thank you for knowing. For caring. I owe you my life."

He had no right to the gift, but his heart begged him to take it, to accept what she was willing to give and to spend the rest of his days earning the wonder if it. "I love you, Lindsay," he said quietly, earnestly. "Heart and soul."

The words echoed in her heart, joyously rippling through her, filling her with a kind of happiness she'd never known. She wanted to believe it was all she'd ever hoped for, needed to know with absolute certainty that she held all of Jackson's heart. "You weren't going to let yourself love again," she said cautiously. "I distinctly remember you telling me that."

"It's not *again*, Lindsay. I've never loved anyone the way I love you. I'll always remember Maria Arabella and I'll always regret. But life is more than looking back over your shoulder. And while you may not need me in your tomorrows, I sure do need you in mine."

"Oh, Jack," she whispered, her eyes misting with tears as she reached up to touch his cheek with a trembling hand. "My darling Jack."

"I don't want to go back to Texas without you, sweetheart," he went on, pouring his hope into every word. "I don't want to go anywhere without you. Ever. I don't have anything to offer you, Lindsay. You can buy and sell me ten times over. But if there's any way we could be together . . . Could you grow to love me? Could you be happy with me? I'm willing—"

Lindsay pressed her fingertips to his lips and gently silenced him. Her heart overflowing, she met his dark gaze and offered him her own truths. "I already love you, Jackson Stennett. I think I've loved you since the very first day I met you. And I *do* need you. You're my rain, Jack. If you want me to go with you to Texas, I will."

She felt his heartbeat leap and dance, saw the light of joy spark in his eyes. And then he stiffened slightly and eased his lips away from her touch.

"I'll stay here if that's what you'd prefer. I can sell the ranch and—"

"No," she interrupted softly. "You were right yesterday; life here is too complicated, too full of lies and ambitions and greed. You don't belong here, Jack. And neither do I. Not anymore. All I want is to love you and spend the rest of my life with you. In Texas."

He blinked and, as though he didn't dare let himself

believe in the completeness of his good fortune, asked cautiously, "How are you going to manage your trust?"

She wanted to laugh, to assure him that nothing would keep her from his side from this moment on. But she knew Jackson, knew the way his mind worked and how he needed to make his way to conclusions one step at a time. "Jeb and I will write a lot of letters to each other."

"What about Mrs. Theorosa's house? I thought you wanted to live there."

"It's a house, Jack," she said with a shrug. "I wouldn't be happy unless you were there to share it with me. Perhaps we could give it to Jeb and Lucy."

"All right," he agreed. He cocked a brow and she knew what he was going to ask even before he said, "What about Henry and Agatha?"

"I'm sorry," she answered, smiling up at him, "but they can't come along. They'll have to stay here and muddle through on their own."

"What if they make a mess of it?"

"It's not *if*, Jack. It's *when*. We both know that. But you're right; it's time they learned to stand on their own and suffer the consequences of bad decisions. Besides," she added, twining her arms around his neck, "I've spent a lifetime trying to make them happy, and failed. I have noticed, however, that I do seem able to make you smile from time to time."

He wrapped his arms around her and gently drew her fully against him, "That you do, sweetheart," he whispered, smiling and brushing a kiss over her lips. "You make me a very happy man. All the time. And if I ever manage to work my way around to forgiving Billy for what he did, it'll only be because I found you in the middle of it all."

"And I have to be grateful that he went to Texas all those years ago. If he hadn't, you would have never walked into my life and I would have never known how wonderful it is to love and be loved."

The tension eased out of his shoulders. He gazed down at her adoringly. "I have to leave within a week. I don't have any more time than that. Will you go with me, Lindsay? As my wife?"

She answered him with a kiss and his arms tightened around her, drawing her deeper into the circle of his embrace. No words were necessary. The promise was made deep in their hearts, made part of their souls. They would love each other for all time and through all things. There would be roses in Texas. And they would thrive.

ABOUT THE AUTHOR

LESLIE LAFOY grew up loving to read and living to write. A former high-school history teacher and department chair, she made the difficult decision to leave academia in 1996 to follow her dream of writing full-time. When not made utterly oblivious to the real world by her current work in progress, she dabbles at being a domestic goddess, and gives credible performances as a hockey, Little League, and Boy Scout mom. A fourth generation Kansan, she lives on ten windswept acres of prairie with her husband and son, a Shetland sheepdog, and Sammy the cat.

The enchanting wit of *New York Times* bestseller

BETINA KRAHN

"Krahn has a delightful, smart touch."
—*Publishers Weekly*